CLIVILIUS
INTERCONNECTED STORIES. INFINITE POSSIBILITIES

© 2024 Nathan Cowdrey. All rights reserved.
First Edition, 28 April 2024
ISBN 978-1-4457-6491-7
Imprint: Lulu.com

Step into Clivilius, where creation meets infinity, and the essence of reality is yours to redefine. Here, existence weaves into a narrative where every decision has consequences, every action has an impact, and every moment counts. In this realm, shaped by the visionary AI CLIVE, inhabitants are not mere spectators but pivotal characters in an evolving drama where the lines between worlds blur.

Guardians traverse the realms of Clivilius and Earth, their journeys igniting events that challenge the balance between these interconnected universes. The quest for resources and the enigma of unexplained disappearances on Earth mirror the deeper conflicts and intricacies that define Clivilius—a world where reality responds to the collective will and individual choices of its Clivilians, revealing a complex interplay of creation, control, and consequence.

In the grand tapestry of Clivilius, the struggle for harmony and the dance of dichotomies play out across a cosmic stage. Here, every soul's journey contributes to the narrative, where the lines between utopia and dystopia, creator and observer, become increasingly fluid. Clivilius is not just a realm to be explored but a reality to be shaped.

Open your eyes. Expand your mind. Experience your new reality. Welcome to Clivilius, where the journey of discovery is not just about seeing a new world but about seeing your world anew.

Also in the Clivilius Series:

Luke Smith (4338.204.1 - 4338.209.2)

Luke Smith's world transforms with the discovery of a cryptic device, thrusting him into the guardianship of destiny itself. His charismatic charm and unpredictable decisions now carry weight beyond imagination, balancing on the razor's edge between salvation and destruction. Embracing his role as a Guardian, Luke faces the paradox of power: the very force that defends also threatens to annihilate. As shadows gather and the fabric of reality strains, Luke must navigate the consequences of his actions, unaware that a looming challenge will test the very core of his resolve.

Jamie Greyson (4338.204.1 - 4338.209.3)

Haunted by shadows of his past, Jamie Greyson navigates life with a guarded heart, his complex bond with Luke Smith teetering on the brink of collapse. When Jamie is thrust into a strange new world, every moment is a test, pushing him to confront not only the dangers that lurk in the unknown but also the demons of his own making. Jamie's quest for survival becomes a journey of redemption, where the chance for a new beginning is earned through courage, trust, and the willingness to face the truth of his own heart.

Paul Smith (4338.204.1 - 4338.209.3)

In a harsh, new world, Paul Smith grapples with the remnants of a hostile marriage and the future of his two young children. Cast into the heart of an arid wasteland, his survival pushes him to the brink, challenging his every belief.

Amidst the desolation, Paul faces a pivotal choice that will dictate where his true allegiance lies. In this tale of resilience and resolve, Paul's journey is a harrowing exploration of loyalty, family, and the boundless optimism required to forge hope in the bleakest of landscapes.

Glenda De Bruyn (4338.206.1 - 4338.209.4)

Dr. Glenda De Bruyn's life takes a perilous turn when her link to a government conspiracy forces her to flee. Thrust into Clivilius, she confronts medical crises and hints of her father's mysterious past. As danger and discovery entwine, Glenda's relentless quest to uncover her family's secrets propels her into the unknown, where every clue unravels the fabric of reality as she knows it.

Beatrix Cramer (4338.205.1 - 4338.211.6)

Beatrix Cramer's life is a delicate balance of contradictions, her independence and keen intellect shadowed by her penchant for the forbidden. A master of acquisition, her love for antiques and the call of the wild drives her into the heart of danger, making her an indispensable ally yet an unpredictable force. When fate thrusts her into the clandestine world of Guardians, Beatrix must navigate a labyrinth of secrets and moral dilemmas. Caught in the crossfire of legacy and destiny, she faces choices that could redefine the boundaries of her world and her very identity.

4338.207.1 - 4338.211.2

KAIN JEFFRIES

CLIVILIUS
INTERCONNECTED STORIES. INFINITE POSSIBILITIES

"With each nail I drive, I'm not just building structures; I'm crafting the next chapter of the Jeffries legacy—an ode to the past, a foundation for the future."

- Kain Jeffries

4338.207

(26 July 2018)

DISTURBED

4338.207.1

As I lay back, my body melted into the luxurious embrace of the plush double pillows, a heavenly oasis that enveloped me like a cocoon as I languidly stretched my arms above my head, yearning for a fleeting moment of tranquility amidst the frenzy of the upcoming day. The tautness in my legs and the rhythmic clenching of my glutes mirrored the undulating movements of my toes and hips, each purposeful stroke sending shockwaves of electric ecstasy rippling through every fibre of my being. The waves of rapture ebbed and flowed like the ceaseless tides, my throbbing arousal pulsating and dancing to the primal beat of desire.

Her lips, supple and velvety, tantalised me with their cool caress as her deft tongue flicked playfully across the hypersensitive tip, igniting bolts of electrifying bliss that surged through my chest like an unstoppable tsunami. The impending climax loomed on the horizon, a mounting pressure that threatened to shatter me into a million shimmering fragments as the smouldering inferno within me burned ever hotter, consuming me from the inside out.

Suddenly, the intimate reverie was shattered by the abrupt intrusion of my mother bursting into the sanctuary of my bedroom. "Kain. Get up. I need you to do something for me," her voice cut through the haze of passion like a blade, catching me completely off guard. Startled, my legs and waist jerked reflexively, the sudden movement causing a jolt of discomfort that extinguished any lingering hope of reaching that blissful pinnacle.

In a panicked flurry of movement, I hastily yanked the blanket across my exposed side, desperate to preserve some semblance of modesty in the face of my mother's invasion. Brianne, my beloved fiancée, emerged from beneath the tangle of sheets like a radiant nymph, the briefest flash of her delicate beauty seared into my mind's eye.

"Oh god!" Mum, exclaimed, her hand flying up to shield her eyes as she quickly averted her gaze. As she hesitantly turned back, Brianne and I huddled together, the thin cotton blanket a flimsy barrier between us and the mortifying reality of the situation.

I could feel the searing heat of embarrassment flooding my face, painting my cheeks a vivid shade of crimson that betrayed my profound discomfort. Shrugging helplessly at my mother, I silently questioned her unexpected intrusion, my mind reeling with a jumble of emotions.

Without another word, Mum turned on her heel and left the room, the decisive click of the door closing behind her echoing in the awkward silence. There was no time to waste. I leapt out of bed, my eyes scanning the room in a frantic search for my discarded underwear and jeans, carelessly tossing aside the tangled sheets and pillows in my haste.

"Seriously? Again?" Brianne's voice dripped with exasperation, her annoyance palpable as I once again abandoned our intimate encounter to cater to my mother's whims.

"You know how she gets," I replied, my words muffled as I tugged my t-shirt over my head, the fabric clinging to my sweat-dampened skin.

"You give in to her far too easily," Brianne muttered sullenly, a petulant pout tugging at the corners of her lush lips.

"It is her house," I gently reminded her, leaning in to press a tender kiss to her forehead, my lips lingering for a heartbeat. "I'm sure I won't be gone long, and besides, we didn't get to finish!" I added with a mischievous wink, blowing her a playful kiss before reluctantly tearing myself away, leaving Brianne to wallow in her disappointment as I stepped out into the hallway, my mind already bracing for whatever task my mother had in store for me.

❖

As I navigated the kitchen, my hand deftly snatched a slice of buttered toast from the plate perched atop the breakfast bar. I brought it to my mouth, sinking my teeth into the golden, crisp exterior, relishing the satisfying crunch that reverberated through my jaw. The rich, velvety butter melted on my tongue, its creamy essence intermingling with the rustic, crusty texture of the bread in a heavenly symphony of flavours.

"Close your mouth when you chew," my mother's disapproving voice cut through my reverie, her words tinged with a hint of maternal exasperation as she carefully placed two more slices of freshly toasted bread onto the plate before me, the steam rising in lazy tendrils from their golden surfaces.

Undeterred by her admonishment, I deliberately took another generous bite, savouring the audible crunch that filled the room like a defiant crescendo. The crust shattered between my teeth, each morsel a miniature explosion of texture and taste that danced across my palate.

My mother's piercing glare met my gaze, but I countered with a wide, toasty grin, my fingers nonchalantly wiping away a rebellious smudge of butter that had escaped the confines of my mouth and trickled down my chin, leaving a glistening trail in its wake.

Shaking her head in resigned amusement, she muttered, "You're lucky you have such a pretty face." Her attempt at scolding me crumbled as the corners of her mouth twitched, fighting back the smile that threatened to break through her stern façade.

Seizing the opportunity, I grabbed another slice of toast, hastily polishing off the first one by stuffing it unceremoniously into my mouth, the chaotic dance of chewing and swallowing a testament to my voracious appetite.

"You two really need to get your own place," my mother remarked, her words carrying a mixture of concern and gentle reproach.

I met her gaze with a flash of seriousness, my brow furrowing slightly as I silently rebuked her statement. "I know. We're working on it. I promise we'll be out before the baby arrives," I assured her, my voice steady and sincere as I attempted to allay her worries and appease her maternal instincts. "Anyway, what was so urgent that you needed to interrupt us?" I asked, steering the conversation back to the matter at hand, curiosity mingling with a lingering sense of frustration over the untimely disruption.

"Oh, I nearly forgot," my mother began, her tone softening as she shifted gears, the urgency of the previous moment dissipating like a wisp of smoke. "I need you to go and check on Uncle Jamie for me. Make sure he's okay."

"I'm sure he's fine," I insisted, my words tinged with a hint of exasperation as the remnants of my earlier frustration bubbled to the surface. My mother had been persistently trying to reach her brother for days, her calls and messages met with nothing but silence and unanswered rings. After consulting with our grandmother, a woman known for her dramatic flair yet uncanny wisdom, she had now decided to send me as an emissary to Jamie's house, tasking me with the responsibility of ensuring his well-being.

After a final, halfhearted attempt at disagreeing with my mother, I reluctantly acquiesced, grabbing my keys and heading towards the door. As I stepped out into the crisp morning air, a swirling maelstrom of annoyance and curiosity churned within me, propelling me forward on this unexpected errand.

TRICKERY

4338.207.2

The early morning air hung heavy and oppressive as I pulled my car into the driveway of Uncle Jamie's house, the weight of my frustration and interrupted morning with Brianne settling over me like a suffocating blanket. With each step up the three stairs leading to the front porch, my irritation simmered, threatening to boil over. I raised my hand and knocked on the door, a sense of dread pooling in the pit of my stomach when it was Luke, not Jamie, who answered, his eyes still bleary with the remnants of sleep.

"Oh. Hey, Kain," Luke mumbled, his words slurring together as he rubbed his eyes and swung open the front door, the hinges creaking in protest.

"Sorry, I didn't mean to wake you," I apologised, a flicker of surprise darting through me at the sight of Luke. It was unusual for Jamie not to answer the door when I visited, but then again, this was the first time I had shown up unannounced, a fact that only served to fuel my growing unease.

"Nah, I was already awake. It's about time I got myself out of bed," Luke responded, his voice thick and groggy, as though he were wading through a fog of exhaustion.

An awkward silence descended upon us, the air heavy with unspoken questions and a palpable tension. I shifted my weight from foot to foot, struggling to find the right words, my mind a jumbled mess of thoughts. I had come here to speak with my uncle, not engage in meaningless small talk with Luke.

"So, what can I do for you?" Luke inquired, his words cutting through the stillness and snapping me back to the present.

"I'm looking for Uncle Jamie," I stated, my tone matter-of-fact, masking the turmoil that churned within me. "Well, not really, but my mom has been trying to reach him for days, and he's not answering his phone. So, she got worried and told Nan, who had a bit of a freak-out and convinced Mum that something might have happened to him. And now, here I am," I explained in a single breath, the words tumbling out of my mouth in a rush.

Luke's gaze drifted, his attention seemingly caught by something in the distance, his expression distant and distracted.

"So, is Uncle Jamie here?" I interjected, my words sharp and insistent, cutting through Luke's momentary reverie.

Luke closed his eyes briefly, his face contorting with discomfort and uncertainty, as though he were grappling with some internal struggle. "Right," he finally muttered, his voice strained and hesitant. "Umm... Well... Umm..." His words trailed off, leaving me hanging in a state of frustration and growing annoyance.

Irritation pulsed through me, hot and insistent, my patience wearing thin. It was a simple question, and Luke's evasiveness was testing the limits of my composure.

"He just popped out for a little bit," Luke blurted out, the words spilling from his lips in a rushed and unconvincing manner.

I narrowed my eyes, skepticism etched across my face, suspicion gnawing at the edges of my mind. The excuse seemed too convenient, too rehearsed, and I couldn't help but question why Luke was the one answering the door instead of Jamie. Something felt off, a nagging sensation that refused to be ignored.

"But isn't that his car in the driveway?" I pointed out, gesturing towards the vehicle parked outside, its presence a glaring contradiction to Luke's words. *Perhaps my grandmother's concern was justified after all*, I thought to myself, a sinking feeling settling in the pit of my stomach.

Luke's demeanour remained calm, but a flicker of unease flashed in his eyes, a brief crack in his façade. "Ah, yes, it is," he admitted, his tone feigning nonchalance, a forced lightness that did little to dispel my doubts. "Gladys picked him up."

Skepticism washed over me in waves, but I decided to let it go, at least for the moment, choosing to pick my battles. "Okay," I said, a hint of resignation lacing my voice. I turned to leave, ready to report back to my mother and put an end to this wild goose chase, but Luke's next words caught me off guard, stopping me in my tracks.

"But you're welcome to stay and wait for him to return. He shouldn't be too long," Luke offered, his words hanging in the air between us, an invitation that felt more like a trap.

I hesitated, my mind scrambling to find an excuse, a way out of the awkwardness that awaited me if I agreed to stay. But I came up empty-handed, unable to decline his offer without seeming rude. "I guess," I conceded, a heavy sigh escaping my lips.

Luke stepped aside, allowing me to pass and enter the lounge room, the silence that greeted me oppressive and unsettling, a stark contrast to the usual lively atmosphere that permeated Uncle Jamie's house. "Where are Duke and Henri?" I inquired, my words echoing in the stillness, a nagging sense of wrongness creeping up my spine at the absence of Jamie's beloved Shih Tzus, who typically bounded towards me with unbridled enthusiasm upon my arrival.

"They must be outside," Luke responded, his voice barely above a whisper, a feeble attempt at reassurance that did little to quell the growing unease that gnawed at the edges of my mind.

I sank into the black leather couch, my gaze drifting towards the window, seeking solace in the world beyond, a momentary escape from the uncomfortable atmosphere that hung heavy in the room.

"Would you like a coffee?" Luke offered, gesturing towards the countertop where the kettle sat, its metal form gleaming in the muted light, beckoning to be filled with the liquid melody of the sink's flowing water.

"Yeah, thanks," I replied, grasping at the offered distraction, desperate for something to occupy my mind, to divert my attention from the nagging sense that something was amiss, a feeling that refused to be ignored, no matter how hard I tried to push it aside. The house felt too quiet, too still, devoid of the usual playful energy that infused every corner.

As Luke busied himself with preparing the coffee, the rich aroma of freshly ground beans wafting through the air, I seized the opportunity to excuse myself, seeking a moment of solitude to gather my thoughts and compose myself. "Can I use your loo?" I asked.

"Sure, you know where it is," Luke replied.

I walked down the hallway, my footsteps echoing eerily in the stillness, each step a reminder of the unnatural quiet that pervaded the house. I reached the small bathroom on the left, a sigh of relief escaping my lips as I closed the door behind me, the click of the latch a temporary respite from the growing sense of unease.

As I finished my business and washed my hands, the cold water a shock to my senses, the feeling of unease intensified rather than dissipated, a heaviness settling in my chest. The house remained eerily silent, devoid of the usual sounds of life that accompanied Uncle Jamie's presence. *And where were*

Duke and Henri, the ever-present canine companions? Duke had a knack for sensing people's presence, his keen nose always attuned to the comings and goings of everybody. It was unusual for him not to have come inside by now, his absence a glaring red flag that I couldn't ignore. I contemplated stealing a quick glance at the backyard through the bedroom window, a fleeting thought that was quickly overshadowed by the tightening knot of apprehension in my chest. Instead, I made my way back to the kitchen, my mind a tangled web of uncertainty and unsettledness.

As I entered the kitchen, the sight that greeted me only served to heighten my concern. Coffee beans were scattered across the floor, a haphazard mess that spoke of carelessness or distraction. And there was Luke, looking flustered and perspiring, his brow furrowed in concentration as he attempted to clean up the spill.

"Everything okay in here?" I inquired, my voice tinged with worry for Luke's well-being.

"Yeah, the stupid coffee lid came off as I was taking it out of the cupboard," Luke explained, his words rushed and agitated, his frustration palpable in the tense set of his shoulders.

"Do you need some help with that?" I offered, taking a step towards the mess, a gesture of support in the face of his obvious distress.

"Nah, it's all good," Luke insisted, his voice strained, a forced lightness that did little to mask the underlying tension. "But, um, I actually remembered something. I wanted to move the TV cabinet downstairs. Jamie keeps saying he'll help me, but he never seems to get around to it. Don't suppose you can lend a hand? It'll only take a couple of minutes," he added, his tone verging on desperation, a plea that I couldn't ignore.

I hesitated, glancing at my watch, the hands ticking away the precious seconds of my morning, before my gaze drifted back to Luke, his eyes wide and imploring. *Is he serious?* I thought to myself, a wave of resignation washing over me as I realised that declining his request would only prolong the awkwardness of the situation, drawing out the discomfort. "I guess I can," I conceded with a sigh of acceptance.

"That'd be awesome! Thanks heaps," Luke exclaimed, relief flooding his features, a brief respite from the tension that had gripped him moments before. He motioned towards the closed sliding door that led to the stairs, gesturing for me to lead the way.

As we walked, Luke rambled on about something he had witnessed across the road the previous night, his words a jumbled mess of incoherent thoughts and half-formed sentences. It was as though he were speaking in a foreign language, his words lost in translation, their meaning obscured by the fog of my own preoccupation. But I paid little attention, my focus consumed by the impending task, the weight of uncertainty pressing down upon me.

Luke slid open the door, the sound harsh and grating in the stillness of the house. And in that moment, a sharp jab struck my back, a sudden and unexpected intrusion that sent a jolt of surprise through my body. "What the—" I began, the words caught in my throat, cut off by the force of my own surprise as I stumbled forward, my arms flailing out to grip the doorframe, desperate to regain my balance, to prevent myself from falling into the swirling, technicolour abyss that materialised on the wall before me.

"Fuck!" Luke exclaimed, his voice filled with alarm.

Clive sees you, Kain Jeffries, a haunting, whispering voice emanated from the depths of the vivid display, the words echoing in my mind, sending a chill down my spine, their meaning lost in the maelstrom of confusion and fear that gripped me.

"What?" I gasped, my eyes darting back to Luke, my thoughts spiralling out of control, a dangerous cocktail of adrenaline and terror coursing through my veins.

Before I could comprehend the situation, before I could make sense of the madness unfolding around me, my right hand slipped, my grip on the doorframe faltering. And then I felt it, a sudden nudge behind my knee, a force that sent me tumbling forward, surprise twisting my features as I fell headlong into the swirling colours, the world around me dissolving into a blur of motion and light.

As the brightness of daylight enveloped me, the gentle caress of a warm breeze tousling my blonde hair, a voice, the same haunting voice that had whispered to me moments before, penetrated my consciousness. It wasn't audible, not in the traditional sense, but its words reverberated through my very being, echoing in the depths of my soul, sending shivers down my spine.

Welcome to Clivilius, Kain Jeffries, the voice intoned, its words heavy with foreboding, casting a shadow of uncertainty over my fate, a dark promise of the unknown that lay ahead.

And as I stood there, surrounded by the unfamiliar, the weight of the voice's words pressing down upon me, I couldn't help but wonder what lay in store, what twisted game of fate had brought me to this strange and terrifying place. But one thing was certain: my life would never be the same again.

NIGHTMARE

4338.207.3

In the vast expanse of Clivilius, I stood awestruck, my voice barely a whisper as I tried to comprehend the barren dust stretching endlessly before me. The question lingered on my lips, "What the heck is Clivilius?" My gaze drifted upward, captivated by the warm sunbeams piercing through the cloudless, brilliant blue sky, their radiance a stark contrast to the desolate landscape. "Where the hell am I?" I muttered, bewilderment flooding through me as I spun around, my eyes drinking in the unfamiliar surroundings that seemed to mock my very existence.

A mesmerising array of vibrant, pulsing colours danced before my eyes, their ethereal presence commanding my attention. They collided and intertwined, creating new bursts of hues that filled the air with an otherworldly energy. As I attempted to process the spectacle before me, to make sense of the surreal beauty that defied all logic, a woman's voice called out from behind, shattering my trance-like state and yanking me back to the harsh reality of my predicament.

With a quick turn, I found myself face-to-face with a tall, slender woman, her golden hair cascading gracefully around her shoulders, caught in the gentle caress of the breeze. A surge of accusatory frustration swelled within me, a bitter cocktail of anger and confusion, as I blurted out, "Did Luke push you too?" My tone dripped with suspicion and annoyance, a reflection of the tumultuous emotions that raged beneath the surface.

Shaking her head, the woman replied, her accent thick and foreign, yet difficult to place, adding an air of mystery to her presence. "No," she said, concern lacing her voice, a genuine worry that resonated in her words and tugged at something deep within me. "I'm guessing he pushed you, though?" Her question hung in the air, a reminder of the betrayal that had led me to this godforsaken place.

"Yes," I replied curtly. "At least, I think he did." The words tasted sour on my tongue, a bitter admission of the uncertainty that plagued my mind.

Before I could process the situation further, before I could even begin to unravel the tangled web of confusion that ensnared me, "I see you've met Glenda already," Luke's voice echoed from behind me, causing me to whirl around once again, my heart pounding in my chest.

Anger surged through me, a searing heat that consumed every fibre of my being. My face flushed crimson, a physical manifestation of the rage that boiled within me as I confronted Luke, our faces mere inches apart, the tension between us palpable. "You're a fucking arsehole, Luke!" I shouted, my voice raw with fury as I shoved him forcefully in the chest, watching with a twisted sense of satisfaction as he stumbled backward, a flicker of fear crossing his features.

Stammering, Luke struggled to regain his balance, his voice barely audible. "I'm sorry, Kain. But Jamie needs you," he managed to utter, his words a feeble attempt at justification.

Confusion enveloped me, my mind racing to make sense of the situation, to reconcile the pieces of the puzzle that refused to fit together. "What? Uncle Jamie is here?" I inquired, my thoughts colliding with the realisation that Uncle Jamie was supposed to be with Gladys, a fact that now seemed like a distant memory, a fleeting glimpse of a life that had been ripped away from me. The unspoken question hung in the air, a heavy weight that pressed down upon us, fuelling my internal turmoil and the resentment that simmered just beneath the surface.

"Yeah," Luke replied, uncertainty creeping into his voice.

My face hardened, determination taking hold, a steely resolve that coursed through my veins. "Take me home, Luke," I commanded firmly. "And I'll be taking Uncle Jamie with me." The words were a promise, a vow that I would not rest until I had returned to the life I knew, to the woman I loved, and the child we had created together.

Swallowing hard, Luke's gaze dropped, avoiding my piercing stare, a coward's retreat from the intensity of my anger. "I can't," he whispered softly, his words a crushing blow that shattered any remaining hope I had clung to.

"What do you mean you can't?" I exclaimed, frustration surging through my veins, a potent mix of desperation and disbelief. Images of Brianne and our unborn child flooded my mind, their faces a haunting reminder of all that I stood to lose. The love that we shared, the future we had dreamed of, the life we had built together—all of it hung in the balance, threatened by the cruel twist of fate that had brought me to this desolate place.

Head hung low, Luke murmured his reply, barely audible amidst the tension that crackled in the air between us. "I'm sorry, Kain," he whispered, his words a hollow apology that did little to soothe the ache in my chest or the fury that burned within me.

"Sorry?" I sneered, my voice dripping with sarcasm, a bitter mockery of the remorse he claimed to feel. "You're sorry! Sorry for what?" The question was a challenge, a demand for answers that I knew he could not provide, for explanations that would never be enough to justify the hell he had thrust upon me.

At that moment, Glenda, the tall woman, stepped forward, her hand finding its way to my shoulder in a comforting gesture, a gentle touch that offered a moment of respite amidst the mounting conflict. "It's impossible for us to return," she explained, her voice gentle yet resolute, a truth that I did not want to accept, a reality that I could not bear to face.

Fuelled by a potent mix of anger and desperation, I lunged at Luke, our bodies colliding in a whirlwind of dust and fury, a tangle of limbs and raw emotion as we sprawled to the ground. Glenda's piercing shriek of "Kain, stop!" reverberated in my ears, a distant echo that was drowned out by the pounding of my own heart and the roar of blood in my veins. My rage consumed me, a blinding force that propelled me forward, my fist pulled back, ready to strike, to inflict the pain that I felt, to make Luke suffer as I suffered.

But Luke was quick, rolling out of harm's way, a desperate bid for self-preservation that left my fist colliding with the unforgiving ground. Pain jolted through my hand, a searing agony that radiated from my knuckles as they cracked and began to bleed, a physical mirror of the emotional wounds that tore at my soul.

Adrenaline coursed through my veins, blurring my vision, a red haze that obscured all else as I reached for Luke's foot, desperate to pull him closer, to make him feel the wrath of my frustration, the depth of my despair. But Glenda's authoritative voice sliced through the chaos, commanding us to halt, to cease the madness that had taken hold. "Both of you. Stop it, now!" she yelled, her tone brimming with a power that demanded obedience, a strength that could not be denied.

I hovered on the edge, poised for another strike, my body coiled like a spring, ready to unleash the fury that burned within me. But a movement caught my eye, diverting my attention, a split-second distraction that changed everything. I turned my head, my gaze falling upon the unintended consequences of my rage, the collateral damage that I had never meant to inflict. Glenda cradled her jaw, wincing in pain, a silent accusation that pierced my heart like a dagger, a reminder of the monster I had become in my blind pursuit of vengeance.

Guilt and remorse surged within me, a tidal wave of shame that crashed over me, threatening to drown me in its depths. I had never meant to hurt her, never intended to cause harm to an innocent bystander caught in the crossfire of my own personal hell. But before I could apologise, before I could even begin to make amends, Luke took advantage of my momentary distraction, launching himself at me with a force that sent me hurtling backward, the air forcefully expelled from my lungs.

Gasping for breath, I lay sprawled on the ground, my chest heaving as I struggled to regain my composure, to find my footing in a world that had been turned upside down. Luke rose to his feet, his expression morphing into one of menace and dominance, a dark triumph that glinted in his eyes as he towered over me, a victor in a battle I had never asked to fight.

But Glenda's voice cut through the tense atmosphere once more, her palm outstretched in a halting gesture as she massaged her bruised jaw, a silent plea for peace, for reason to prevail. "Luke, don't," she commanded, her authority permeating the air.

Lying there, struggling to regain my breath, I watched as Luke's features softened, the menace fading from his eyes, replaced by a flicker of remorse, a glimmer of the man I had once known. He extended a hand, offering assistance, a gesture of truce that hung in the space between us, a lifeline that I was not sure I could trust.

Doubt gnawed at my mind, a persistent whisper that warned me of the dangers of forgiveness, of the folly of letting my guard down. *Could I trust him now, after all that had transpired, after the betrayal that had brought me to this place?* I hesitated, wavering between uncertainty and the realisation that we were both in the same unimaginable situation, two lost souls trapped in a nightmare from which there seemed to be no escape.

Eventually, I reached up, my hand grasping his, allowing him to help me to my feet, a tentative truce forged in the crucible of our shared misery. A sigh of relief escaped Glenda, her shoulders sagging under the weight of the recent turmoil.

"I suppose we don't have any ice either," she lamented, her resignation evident in her voice, a wry observation that spoke to the bleak reality of our predicament.

Luke's head shook slightly, his voice barely a whisper as he confirmed her suspicions. "No, we don't," he replied.

My gaze fixated on the swelling lump forming on Glenda's jaw. Shame washed over me, a wave of regret that threatened to drown me in its depths. I knew that violence wasn't in my nature, that I was not a man prone to fits of rage or acts of aggression. But the fear of losing Brianne and our unborn child had consumed me, leaving me overwhelmed by a sense of hopelessness, a desperation that had driven me to the brink of madness.

I'm only twenty-three, I thought to myself, my mind reeling with the injustice of it all. *Our lives together are far from over. They can't be.* The words were a silent prayer, a desperate plea to the universe, to whatever cruel twist of fate had brought me to this place, to spare me the agony of losing all that I held dear.

"I'm sorry, Glenda. I didn't mean to hit you," I spoke, my voice filled with genuine remorse, a heartfelt apology that poured from my lips, a feeble attempt to make amends for the harm I had caused, the pain I had inflicted.

Glenda attempted a smile, though it twisted into more of a wince, a valiant effort to mask the discomfort that radiated from her injured jaw. Nonetheless, she extended her hand, offering it to me, a gesture of forgiveness, of understanding in the face of the unimaginable.

I grasped it firmly, a tangible connection formed in that moment.

"I'm the camp's doctor," she introduced herself, releasing my hand, a flicker of pride shining through the pain that clouded her features.

"And I'm—" I started, before pausing, lost in thought.

Before I could utter another word, Luke interjected with a grin, a feeble attempt to diffuse the remaining tension, to inject a note of levity into a situation that defied all reason. "And you're our new construction expert," he declared, his words a mockery of the life I had left behind, the career I had built, the dreams I had nurtured.

I closed my eyes, a mix of frustration and disbelief clouding my mind, a silent scream that echoed through the chambers of my soul. *Is any of this even real?* I wondered, my thoughts spiralling out of control, a dizzying whirlpool of doubt and desperation. *Did I merely hit my head in the fall, a cruel trick of the mind that had conjured this nightmare, this hellish landscape that stretched out before me?*

In that moment, a small, familiar bark reverberated across the desolate landscape, a sound that pierced the silence, a beacon of recognition that cut through the haze of my confusion. *Duke or Henri?* I pondered, my thoughts racing, my heart pounding in my chest. *No, it's definitely Henri,* I realised with a start, the certainty of that knowledge a fleeting comfort amidst the turmoil that surrounded me.

I exhaled deeply, closing my eyes in temporary relief, clinging to the hope that this was all just a dream, a figment of my imagination, a twisted fantasy that would fade away with the light of dawn. But as my eyes fluttered open, my heart sank, a leaden weight that settled in the pit of my stomach, a crushing realisation that shattered any remaining illusions of escape.

The glaring sunlight pierced my vision, a harsh reminder of the reality that surrounded me, the barren landscape that stretched out before me in an endless expanse of dusty browns, yellows, and reds. Horror engulfed me as I realised with a sinking feeling that I was still trapped in the unfamiliar place called Clivilius, a prisoner of a fate I could not comprehend, a captive of a world that defied all logic and reason.

"Something's wrong!" Luke's panicked voice broke through the silence, jolting him into action. He sprinted away, his figure disappearing into the distance, a blur of motion that was quickly followed by Glenda, her own urgency propelling her forward, a desperate bid to reach the source of the disturbance.

My mind raced to catch up, struggling to comprehend the gravity of the situation, the urgency that had seized them both. For a moment, I turned my gaze to the strange colours that had brought me to this new world, the swirling vortex of hues that had captivated me, entranced me with their otherworldly beauty.

A sense of foreboding settled deep within my chest, a dark premonition that whispered of the dangers that lay ahead, the perils that awaited us all in this uncharted realm. The pulsing colours that had initially captivated me now seemed ominous, their vibrant dance taking on an eerie quality, a sinister undercurrent that sent shivers down my spine.

They swirled and intertwined, their movements hypnotic, a seductive siren song that threatened to lure me into their depths, to ensnare me in their ethereal embrace. It was as if the very essence of Clivilius possessed a life of its own, a volatile force that pulsed with an ancient power, a primal energy that defied all comprehension.

And then, as suddenly as they had appeared, the colours evaporated entirely, vanishing into the ether like wisps of smoke on the wind. In their wake what appeared to be a large, translucent screen, a shimmering barrier that separated me from the world I had once known, a cruel reminder of the fate that had befallen me.

❖

A surge of determination welled up within me, propelling my legs forward as I chased after Luke and Glenda, my heart pounding in rhythm with each desperate stride. The barren landscape stretched out endlessly before me, a vast expanse of nothingness that seemed to mock my very existence. Each step kicked up a cloud of dust behind me, a ghostly trail that marked my passage through this desolate realm.

Questions swirled in my mind, demanding answers, yet evading me at every turn. *What is this place?* The thought echoed through my consciousness, a haunting refrain that refused to be silenced. *How did I get here?* The mystery of my arrival gnawed at the edges of my sanity, a puzzle with missing pieces that left me grasping for understanding. And most importantly, *how do I find my way back?* The desperate need to return home, to the life I had known, consumed me, driving me forward with a fierce intensity.

The landscape offered no solace, no clue as to the answers I sought. It stretched out before me, a vast expanse of emptiness that seemed to swallow me whole, its silence oppressive and unnerving. My senses heightened, attuned to the slightest sound or movement, yet there was nothing, only the deafening silence broken by the ragged sound of my own rapid breaths. The air carried a subtle hint of something unfamiliar, a scent I couldn't quite place, as if Clivilius itself held its secrets close, refusing to divulge them to mere mortals like myself.

I pushed my legs to their limits, muscles straining with each step, desperate to catch up with Luke and Glenda, who seemed to be vanishing into the distance, their forms growing smaller and more indistinct with each passing moment. My mind buzzed with a heady mix of fear and determination, a potent cocktail that coursed through my veins, urging me onward. My heart pounded in my chest, a frantic drumbeat that echoed the uncertainty and panic that gripped me, threatening to overwhelm me at any moment.

With each stride, the landscape shifted around me, revealing new contours and hidden crevices, a kaleidoscope of desolation that seemed to change with every blink of my eyes. The ground beneath my feet felt uneven and treacherous, littered with loose rocks and hidden pitfalls that threatened to send me sprawling. Yet, I pressed on, fuelled by a fierce determination to unravel the mysteries of this bewildering place, to find the answers that eluded me, to claw my way back to the world I had known.

Suddenly, a sharp pain shot through my leg, a searing bolt of agony that caused me to stumble, nearly losing my footing on the unforgiving terrain. I gritted my teeth, biting back a cry of pain, refusing to let it deter me from my mission. The pain seemed distant, insignificant compared to the urgency of the situation, the desperate need to catch up with Luke and Glenda, to find some semblance of familiarity in this alien world. I forced myself to keep moving, to push past the limitations of my body and the gnawing doubts that threatened to consume me, to focus with single-minded determination.

Several large tents came into view, their canvas walls fluttering in the gentle breeze, a jarring contrast to the lifeless landscape that surrounded them. I skidded to a halt, my eyes scanning the area, searching for any sign of Luke and Glenda, my heart sinking as I realised they were nowhere to be seen.

"Where did they go?" I muttered aloud, my voice hoarse and strained, barely recognisable to my own ears. My gaze swept over the empty space before me, searching for any clue, any hint of their passage, but there was nothing, only the eerie stillness of the abandoned campsite.

A sudden piercing scream shattered the eerie silence, echoing through the air like a gunshot, causing my heart to leap into my throat. Without a second thought, I followed the sound, my instincts guiding me behind the tents, my mind racing with a thousand horrible possibilities. Fear tightened its icy grip on me as I beheld a horrifying sight—my uncle Jamie lying face down in the water, his feet ensnared by the rocks at the riverbank, his body still and lifeless. Helplessness consumed me, mingling with shock and disbelief as I whispered hoarsely, "Uncle Jamie?"

"Help me roll him," a man's voice instructed, snapping me back to reality, pulling me out of the haze of shock that had enveloped me.

Standing a few feet behind Glenda, I watched, my heart racing, as Luke joined the other man, sliding into the water with a splash. "Go," he directed, his voice resolute, tinged with a hint of urgency. "I've got him."

Following Glenda's lead, the group worked in unison, their coordinated efforts guided by her urgent commands. "Three. Two. One. Roll!" she shouted. Their synchronised movement turned Jamie's body over, freeing his feet from the treacherous rocks that had trapped him, revealing the full extent of the horror that had befallen him.

The sight before me left me in awe and confusion, my mind reeling as it struggled to process the nightmarish scene that unfolded before my eyes. My eyes widened as they fell upon the unknown man, his presence unnerving, a stark reminder of the unfamiliar world I had stumbled into. "Who the fuck is that?" I cried out, my voice trembling with fear and uncertainty. The shock of encountering another stranger in this desolate camp was overwhelming, compounded by the eerie realisation that he was clearly lifeless, his body still and unmoving in the shallow water. *But at least it isn't Uncle Jamie*, a small voice whispered in the back of my mind, a fleeting moment of relief amidst the horror.

The unknown man stared solemnly at the lifeless body, his voice tinged with sadness as he replied softly, "No idea."

Disbelief washed over me, leaving me speechless, my mind struggling to comprehend the implications of his words. "Shit," I muttered under my breath, grappling with the unsettling revelation that not only was he unknown to me, but it seemed that he was unknown to everyone else in the camp, a stranger in a world already filled with unfamiliarity and danger.

Anxiety gripped me tighter, its icy fingers closing around my throat, intensifying as Glenda's urgent question filled the air. "Is he breathing?" she demanded, her voice sharp and insistent.

Luke's calm voice cut through the tension, his reply tinged with an eerie calmness that sent shivers down my spine. "I don't think so," he said, his words hanging heavy in the air, a confirmation of the worst.

The urgency escalated as Glenda's hands waved frantically, directing the group to bring the lifeless body to shore, her movements sharp and purposeful. But the unknown man's voice shattered their hopes, sharp and resolute, cutting through the chaos like a blade. "No," he stated firmly, his words a death knell that echoed through the stillness.

"What?" Glenda exclaimed, shock etched on her face, her eyes wide with disbelief.

"I don't think it will help," the unknown man explained softly, his voice heavy with a quiet resignation. "His throat has been slit."

The horror of the situation crashed over me like a tsunami, a tidal wave of terror and revulsion that threatened to sweep me away. "Fuck!" I exclaimed, my body shaking uncontrollably, my mind reeling with the implications of his words. I clasped my hands tightly at the back of my head, my fingers digging into my scalp, and began to pace, my mind racing as the grim reality took hold, the full extent of the nightmare I had stumbled into sinking in with sickening clarity. *His throat has been slit?* The thought echoed through my mind, a horrifying refrain that refused to be silenced. *What kind of twisted, fucked-up world have I stumbled into?*

Amidst the turmoil, Glenda persisted, her determination unwavering, a beacon of strength in the face of unimaginable horror. "We should bring the body in anyway," she insisted, her voice firm and resolute.

Luke countered, his skepticism evident, his words sharp and biting. "What good will that do? If he's been murdered and someone comes looking for him, perhaps we shouldn't be the ones caught with his body."

My mind screamed in disbelief, the implications of his words sending a shockwave of terror throughout my body. *Murdered? This is fucking insane!* The thought echoed through my consciousness. Luke has dragged me into an empty world where survival seems impossible, where death and violence lurk around every corner. "I'm with Luke," I called out, desperation seeping into my trembling voice, my words a plea for sanity in a world gone mad. "Yes, get rid of the body."

The unknown man nodded in Glenda's direction, his gaze fixed on her, his expression unreadable. "Regardless, he deserves a proper burial," he said, his voice heavy with a quiet solemnity.

"Proper burial!" Luke scoffed, his disbelief evident, his words dripping with scorn. "You don't even know the guy."

I silently cheered Luke's practicality in this dire situation, my mind latching onto his words. Get rid of the body. Dispose of the evidence. That's our best chance at survival, the only way to avoid being caught up in a nightmare that seemed to have no end.

Glenda, however, held firm, her determination unyielding. "If we can bring him in, I can perform a rough autopsy," she insisted, her voice laced with a quiet intensity.

Luke's skepticism remained. "Is that really necessary? I think it's pretty obvious what happened to him."

Glenda's tone grew resolute, her voice laced with a mix of curiosity and duty, a determination to uncover the truth no matter the cost. "A rough autopsy might provide us with more information, a glimpse into the story of how he met his fate," she said.

My body trembled with an overwhelming sense of terror. My face burned with a flush of fear, my skin hot and prickly, making it hard to catch my breath. I closed my eyes, bowing my head, attempting to steady myself and suppress the bile that rose in my throat, threatening to choke me.

"Calm down," I whispered to myself, my voice a hoarse rasp, barely audible over the pounding of my heart. I fought to find some semblance of composure, to cling to the tattered shreds of my sanity. But the reality of the situation threatened to engulf me, making my whole body ache as if it were being torn apart from the inside out.

Gritting my teeth, I clutched my fists tightly, my knuckles turning white with the force of my grip. I forced my eyes open, locking my gaze on the scene unfolding before me, determined to face the nightmare head-on. The unknown man's question pierced the air, his voice filled with panic, his words a desperate plea for answers. "Where's the body?" he demanded, his eyes wide with fear.

Confusion swirled within me as I scanned the area, my eyes widening in shock, my mind struggling to comprehend what I was seeing. The body was nowhere to be seen, vanished as if it had never existed at all. "Shit," I muttered, my mind racing to comprehend what I had missed, to piece together the fragments of the nightmare that had unfolded before me. The panic attack had only lasted a few moments, but now the unknown man and Luke were drenched, their clothes clinging to their bodies, and the body had vanished without a trace.

"Where's Jamie?" Luke's voice trembled with panic, his face still speckled with water droplets from the river, his eyes wide with fear.

What the fuck did I miss? The thought echoed through my mind, a desperate plea for understanding in a world that made no sense. My mind whirled, struggling to grasp the sequence of events, to make sense of the madness. The panic attack had clouded my perception, leaving me disoriented and confused, a stranger in my own skin.

"He went to the lagoon," answered Glenda, her voice carrying a sense of urgency, a hint of fear that sent shivers down my spine.

"Lagoon?" Luke queried, his voice tinged with worry, his brow furrowed in confusion.

"Downstream," replied the first man.

"Shit," Luke muttered, his eyes widening in alarm, his face pale with fear. He turned to the unknown man, his expression intense, his words a desperate plea for action. "We need to retrieve that body. Now!"

"But... but you just said..." The unknown man's words faltered, confusion etched across his face, his eyes wide with disbelief.

"Forget what I said. You were right. We are better off keeping the body," Luke declared, his words a sharp contrast to his earlier skepticism. He scrambled onto the riverbank, his movements frantic and desperate. Without hesitation, he sprinted off, chasing after the body as it floated downstream, his figure quickly disappearing into the distance.

"Go!" Glenda instructed, shoving me in the direction of Luke, her voice sharp and insistent.

"Fuck off," I replied, avoiding Glenda's second attempt.

The unknown man wiped a smudge of vomit from his mouth, his features a mix of shock and determination, his eyes glinting with a fierce intensity. "I'll go," he announced, his voice steady and resolute as he walked up to me, his gaze locked on mine.

"Introductions can wait," Glenda interjected, her words a sharp reminder of the urgency of the situation. She urged the unknown man to depart without delay, her voice tinged with a hint of desperation.

He brushed past me and bolted away, disappearing into the distance, his figure quickly swallowed up by the vast expanse of the desolate landscape.

My wide eyes stared after them, my mind reeling from the chaotic events that had unfolded before me, the horror and confusion that had engulfed my world. The realisation sunk in with sickening clarity—I'm trapped in a nightmare, a world filled with death and uncertainty, a hellish landscape that seemed to have no end.

"Are you okay?" Glenda's hand rested heavily on my shoulder, her voice filled with genuine concern, her eyes searching mine for some sign of sanity.

I struggled to find the words to answer her question, my mind a chaotic whirlwind of emotions and half-formed thoughts. Far from okay, I felt shattered, as if the ground beneath me had crumbled away, leaving me adrift in a sea of horror and despair. Tears streamed down my face, hot and bitter, mixing with the dust that clung to my cheeks. "What the fuck is going on?" I managed to choke out, my voice trembling with a mix of fear, confusion, and despair, the words a desperate plea for answers.

"Come," Glenda said, her voice gentle and reassuring. "I think you're in shock. Let's get you inside the tent."

Numbly, I nodded, feeling too drained to protest, too shattered to do anything but follow her lead. With Glenda's support, I stumbled towards the tent, my steps unsteady, my legs threatening to give out beneath me at any moment. My vision blurred as dizziness overcame me, the world spinning wildly around me, but I forced myself to keep moving, my legs carrying me forward, guided by some primal instinct for survival.

The tent's entrance beckoned, offering a momentary respite from the harsh reality outside, a fleeting illusion of safety. I collapsed onto the ground beneath the tent's canopy, the soft dust providing a modest cushion, a small comfort. My body sank into the earth, fatigue washing over me in waves, threatening to drag me down into the depths of unconsciousness.

Glenda handed me an unopened bottle of cool spring water, the condensation beading on its surface, a small mercy in the oppressive heat. "Here, drink this," she said, her voice laced with concern, her eyes soft with sympathy. "You probably need all of it."

Grateful for the offering, I managed a weak smile, my lips cracking with the effort, and took a few deep gulps, the water soothing my parched throat, washing away the bitter taste of fear and despair.

Closing my eyes, I rested my head in my hands, seeking solace in the darkness, in the momentary respite from the horrors that surrounded me. The silence enveloped me, a heavy blanket that muffled the chaos of the outside world, a fragile bubble of peace. For a brief moment, I felt a semblance of tranquility, the quietude seeping into my bones, offering a fleeting glimpse of the life I had left behind. But the tranquility was short-lived, shattered by a blood-curdling scream that tore through the air, piercing my soul, ripping away the illusion of safety and plunging me back into the heart of the nightmare.

My eyes snapped open, filled with terror and confusion, my mind reeling with the implications of the sound. "Did you hear that?" I asked in a trembling voice, my words a hoarse whisper that hung heavy in the air. I searched for Glenda's presence, desperate for some sign of reassurance, some confirmation that I wasn't alone in this hell. But she was already gone, running towards the source of the scream, her figure quickly swallowed up by the vast expanse of the camp.

Desolation settled over me like a heavy shroud, loneliness weighing heavily on my shoulders, a crushing burden that threatened to drag me down into the depths of despair. I rolled onto my side, curling into a tight ball, my knees drawn up to my chest, seeking comfort in the familiar position, in the illusion of safety it provided. Salty tears continued to stream down my face, tracing a path through the layers of dust that clung to my skin.

Lost and adrift in Clivilius, my mind echoed with unanswered questions, with the desperate need for understanding in a world that defied all reason. *How did I end up here?* The thought haunted me, a persistent spectre that refused to be silenced. *Will I ever find my way back?* The question hung heavy in the air, a suffocating weight that pressed down on my chest, stealing the breath from my lungs. The desolate landscape offered no solace, its barrenness a reflection of the emptiness that consumed me, the void that had opened up within my soul.

As the tears soaked into the dust beneath me, I lay there for what seemed like an eternity, lost in the labyrinth of my own thoughts, trapped in the endless cycle of fear and torment. The minutes stretched until time itself seemed to become a meaningless construct in a world where nothing made sense.

ALIVE OR DEAD

4338.207.4

I lay curled up on the barren ground, my body convulsing with tremors, each shudder echoing the desperation that clawed at my mind. The gritty texture of the dust beneath me pressed into my skin, a harsh reminder of the unforgiving nature of this desolate place. I squeezed my eyes shut, as if by doing so I could will away the nightmare that had become my reality, could somehow find an alternative explanation for the horrors that had befallen me.

Slowly, painfully, I forced my eyes open, blinking away the tears that blurred my vision. But to my dismay, nothing had changed. The stark landscape stretched out before me, a mocking reminder of the emptiness that had seeped into my soul. Glenda's figure still receded in the distance, growing smaller with each passing moment as she ran farther away from me, a cruel abandonment that left me feeling more alone than ever before.

In the periphery of my blurred sight, a familiar mix of white and tan fur caught my attention, a flash of movement that sent a jolt of recognition through my battered body. The constant panting sound that accompanied the sight was a balm to my frayed nerves. "Duke," I whispered hoarsely, my voice barely more than a croak, the name a desperate plea for some semblance of recognition in this twisted world.

The small Shih Tzu barked in reply, his tail wagging with excitement, a joyous greeting that stood in stark contrast to the bleakness that surrounded us. The sight of him, so familiar and yet so out of place, sent a surge of emotion through me, a bittersweet mix of relief and despair.

Summoning my last reserves of strength, I unfurled my legs and pressed my palms into the gritty dust, pushing myself upright with a herculean effort that left me trembling with exhaustion. Every muscle in my body screamed in protest, a silent rebellion against the demands I placed upon them. But I refused to give in, refused to let the darkness claim me once more.

I reached out and gently patted Duke's head, my fingers sinking into his soft fur, the sensation confirming his reality, a tangible anchor in a world that seemed determined to slip away from me at every turn. The warmth of his body, the steady beat of his heart, was a reassuring presence, a reminder that I was not alone, that there was still some small measure of hope to cling to.

Duke barked again, his eyes flickering towards Glenda's disappearing form, a silent urging for me to follow, to not let her slip away into the vast expanse of this unforgiving landscape. The urgency in his gaze, the insistence in his bark, was a call to action that I could not ignore.

Despite my trembling legs, despite the weariness that threatened to drag me back down, I managed to rise to my feet, swaying slightly as the world tilted and spun around me. I peered down at Duke, who sat faithfully at the front flap of the tent. "What in the hell is this place, Duke?" I murmured.

Duke tilted his head, his eyes meeting mine with a look of canine curiosity, as if attempting to comprehend the depth of my question, the enormity of the situation we found ourselves in. But there were no answers to be found in his gaze, no explanations for the madness that had engulfed us.

A surge of renewed energy coursed through my veins, propelling me forward with a sudden burst of determination, a fierce need to find my uncle, to unravel the mysteries of this godforsaken place. "Uncle Jamie," I whispered to myself, the name a talisman against the darkness.

I caught up with Glenda as she approached the top of the third small, rolling hill, my lungs burning with the effort, my heart pounding in my chest. Together, we stood at the crest, and my jaw dropped in awe at the sight that greeted us. Before us stretched an incredible panorama of yellow, brown, and red shades, scattered across the vast expanse of the landscape, a kaleidoscope of desolation that took my breath away.

The clear, blue waters of the lagoon stood out as a striking contrast, a shimmering oasis amidst the barren wasteland that surrounded it. The sight was at once beautiful and eerie, a reminder of the beauty that could be found even in the midst of the most unforgiving environments. "It's so empty," I murmured to myself, marvelling at the sheer vastness of the landscape, the absence of any sign of human life or civilisation.

The urgent voices of uncle Jamie and Luke drew our attention to where they stood, engrossed in studying the dead body lodged on a sandbar at the point where the river branched, flowing into the serene lagoon. On the opposite side of the lagoon, a few metres away, the unidentified man cowered, his form hunched and trembling, a picture of abject terror.

A sigh of relief escaped my lips as I saw Uncle Jamie, alive and apparently unharmed. The familiar sight of him sent a surge of emotion through me, a fierce love and loyalty that burned bright even in the face of the unimaginable.

Glenda swiftly broke into a brisk jog along the perimeter of the lagoon, heading towards uncle Jamie and Luke with a determined stride, her movements graceful and purposeful, a dancer's poise even in the midst of the absurd.

"Uncle Jamie!" I called out, my voice laced with concern, the words a desperate plea for reassurance, for some sign that he was truly alright, that the nightmare that had engulfed us had not claimed him as well.

He cast a brief glance in my direction, his eyes meeting mine for the briefest of moments, but didn't respond further, his attention quickly returning to the grim body in the water. A furrow formed on my forehead, a pang of worry gripping my heart, a silent fear that something was deeply wrong, that my uncle had been irrevocably changed by the horrors he had witnessed.

The chaos and drama overwhelmed me. I yearned to return home, to resume the life Brianne and I had planned before my mother's interruption. Salty tears welled up in my eyes. *Will I ever see her again?* The thought was a bitter one, a cruel reminder of all that I stood to lose, all that had been ripped away from me by the twisted machinations of fate.

Turning my attention back to the lagoon, I uttered, "What the—" in surprise, my words trailing off as I struggled to comprehend the sight that greeted me. Jamie, Luke, and Glenda were slowly carrying the body along the lagoon's perimeter, directly toward me, their movements solemn and purposeful, a grim procession that sent a shiver down my spine.

Eager to assist my uncle, to offer what little comfort and support I could in the face of such unimaginable horror, I joined their procession, sliding into position to relieve Glenda, who had been supporting the man's legs, her slender frame straining under the weight of the lifeless body.

"Thank you," Glenda whispered softly, her voice filled with gratitude, a gentle acknowledgement of the small kindness I had offered, the tiny gesture of humanity.

I managed a strained smile in response, though my facial muscles involuntarily contorted into more of a grimace.

Quickly averting my gaze, I felt my cheeks flush with embarrassment, a hot rush of blood that only served to deepen my discomfort.

"You coming, Paul?" Glenda called across the lagoon to the cowering man, her voice carrying across the still waters, a lifeline thrown to a drowning soul.

Paul looked up, his eyes wide and haunted. "I'll meet you there soon," he replied, his voice wavering with hesitation.

With that, I focused what little remained of my attention on the grim task at hand, the weight of the lifeless body a reminder of the fragility of life, the evanescence of our mortal existence. The stillness of the corpse, the pungent scent of death that clung to it like a shroud, filled my senses, a macabre assault that left me reeling.

My heart pounded with a heavy beat, a mournful dirge that echoed the despair that consumed me. An eerie sensation of an unknown malevolence lingered just beyond my understanding, a sinister presence that seemed to hover at the edges of my consciousness, a dark spectre that threatened to engulf me at any moment.

As I gazed upon the motionless figure, a shiver of unease crawled up my spine, a prickling sensation that set my nerves on edge. The sight of his wide, vacant blue eyes staring upward, unseeing and yet somehow accusatory, sent a chill through my entire being, a bone-deep fear that left me trembling. It felt as if, somehow, he was still alive, despite the lifelessness that enveloped him, a mute testament to the cruelty of the world we now inhabited.

❖

As we approached the camp, a bitter-sweet wave of relief washed over me. The inadequacies of our meagre surroundings seemed to mock us, highlighting the severity of the man's condition and the desperate nature of our situation. It seemed unlikely that he could survive the journey back, let alone endure the prolonged suffering that may await him in this desolate place.

"Put him on the mattress," my uncle Jamie instructed as we neared the campfire, his voice steady and resolute, a beacon of authority.

But Glenda hesitated, her voice tense with concern, a quiver of apprehension running through her words. "I don't think that's a good idea. We only have one mattress, and he could be infected."

The weight of her words was a crushing blow that sent a shiver of terror down my spine. *Infected?* The mere thought was enough to make my blood run cold, to send a wave of panic crashing over me.

"Bit late for that now," my uncle snapped. "If Joel is infected, then it's likely we are too," he spat in Luke's direction, his words a venomous accusation that hung heavy in the air.

Glenda's features tightened, a flicker of resistance crossing her face, but she didn't argue further. Instead, she hastened to hold the tent flap open for us as we carried the man inside, her movements swift and purposeful.

Once within the confines of the tent, I gently released Joel's legs, my muscles aching with the strain of the journey. With careful precision, uncle Jamie and Luke laid Joel down on the mattress, the blankets hastily removed to accommodate his still form.

Luke and I stood back, observing silently, our gazes fixed on the motionless figure before us. I could faintly perceive the subtle rise and fall of Joel's chest as he breathed, a whisper of life amidst the stillness, his lips sealed in a deathly silence. His piercing blue eyes remained fixed on the tent's roof, unblinking and unseeing, and I studied them intently, searching for a trace of familiarity that danced just beyond my grasp, a flicker of recognition that never came.

Glenda knelt beside the mattress, leaning over Joel's body, her gaze and fingers probing gently, a healer's touch that sought to unravel the mysteries that lay before us.

My eyes fixed on Joel's pale, clammy flesh, a sickly hue that spoke of death and decay, and a sense of his lifelessness overwhelmed me, a suffocating weight that pressed down upon my chest. He appeared thoroughly deceased, a husk of a man, devoid of the spark of life that once animated his being.

Finally, Glenda spoke, her voice tinged with uncertainty, a hesitance that betrayed the depth of her confusion. "All the major arteries seem to have healed, assuming they were ever severed. Aside from the obvious slit across his throat and the bumps and bruises from his time in the river, he doesn't appear to have any other major physical wounds. I'm not sure how he could have lost all his blood if not through major arterial damage," she explained, her words a jumble of medical jargon that only served to deepen the mystery.

Lost all his blood? I echoed silently, my mind reeling with the implications. *What does she mean? Could Joel truly be devoid of blood, a walking corpse that defied all logic and reason? Is that why he appears so lifeless, so utterly devoid of the warmth and vitality of the living? But why are his eyes open, staring sightlessly into the void? Why does he still appear to breathe, a mockery of life in the face of such overwhelming death?*

"Shit," I muttered under my breath, the curse a feeble attempt to express the horror that gripped me. *I'm trapped in a tent with a bloody zombie, a creature that should not be, an abomination that defied all the laws of nature.* Panic seized my senses, a primal fear that sent my heart racing and my palms sweating, and I took several hurried steps toward the tent's entrance, desperate to escape the suffocating confines of this macabre scene.

"His throat was definitely slit. There was a lot of blood," Luke confirmed, his voice steady and matter-of-fact.

My mind raced, a frenzied whirlwind of thoughts and emotions. *I have to get out of here, to escape this nightmare before it consumes me whole, before the horror of it all drives me to the brink of madness.*

Glenda shrugged in response, her shoulders sagging with the weight of her own confusion. "It's not making much sense," she concluded, her words a feeble understatement that did little to capture the sheer absurdity of the situation.

No kidding, I thought, my eyes darting nervously toward the sole exit, the flimsy barrier that separated me from the relative safety of the outside world.

Uncle Jamie's voice brimmed with anger as he demanded answers, his words a snarling accusation that cut through the tension like a blade. "What do you mean you know his throat was slit? And how the fuck would you know how much blood there was?" he spat at Luke, his eyes blazing with a fury that seemed to radiate from every pore.

My eyes widened in shock, a sickening realisation dawning upon me with the force of a thunderbolt. *Oh my God! Luke did it!* The accusation surged through my mind, a tidal wave of horror and disbelief that threatened to sweep me away. Accusations swirled within me as I fixated on Luke's back, my gaze drilling into him, a silent condemnation that burned with the intensity of a thousand suns. *He's the one responsible, the monster who unleashed this nightmare upon us all!*

"No signs of defensive wounds?" Luke questioned, his voice steady and calm, a jarring contrast to the bewilderment and anger that raged around him.

Glenda shook her head, her brow furrowed with confusion. "No, none. Were you expecting there to be?" she asked, her words a tentative probe, a search for answers in a sea of uncertainty.

Luke shook his head slowly, his expression pensive and thoughtful. "Not necessarily. I guess that means whatever happened to him, it happened quickly and likely took him by surprise," he said, his words a chilling assessment that sent a shiver down my spine.

Caught him off guard? My mind echoed, the accusation a searing brand that burned itself into my consciousness. *Caught off guard because of you, because of the treachery and deceit that you wrought upon us all!*

"Well? You still haven't answered my question," uncle Jamie's voice seethed with anger, a barely contained rage that threatened to boil over, demanding an explanation that seemed forever out of reach.

My eyes shifted downward, avoiding direct eye contact with anyone, a feeble attempt to shield myself from the horror that surrounded me. I need to be prepared, to have something to defend myself with in case Luke loses control again, in case the monster within him rears its ugly head once more. Or in case the zombie attacks, a mindless creature driven by an insatiable hunger for flesh and blood!

Luke took a deep breath, his voice steadying, a forced calm that did little to dispel the tension that hung heavy in the air. "Joel was the driver that delivered the tents back home," he began, his words a shocking revelation.

A collective gasp reverberated through the air. Luke pressed on, undeterred, his voice a steady drone that seemed to come from a great distance. "I was surprised to see him. I didn't recognise him at first. Not until I saw his name sewn into his shirt."

Luke knows him? I questioned silently, my mind reeling with the implications, searching my uncle's face for a reaction, for some sign of the turmoil that surely raged within him. Jamie's eyes held pain, a deep and abiding anguish that spoke of a wound that would never heal, but not fear. *Should I be afraid?* I wondered, my own fear a palpable thing that seemed to fill the tent, a suffocating presence that threatened to choke the very life from me. *Or am I overreacting, letting my imagination run wild?* I shook my head lightly, a feeble attempt to clear the cobwebs of confusion that clung to my mind. *You're standing next to a bloody zombie, and the potential killer is right here, in this very tent. Of course you're not overreacting!*

Glenda examined a small rip in Joel's polo shirt, her fingers probing gently, slowly unravelling a hidden word that had been sewn into the fabric. "Joel," she read aloud, her voice a hushed whisper that seemed to echo in the stillness.

"Henri and Duke's coming here was all an accident," Luke continued, his words a rushing torrent that spilled forth like a dam bursting its banks. "Joel accidentally let Henri outside and he ran through the Portal when we tried to catch him. I forgot I was still carrying Duke when I followed after Henri."

"And Joel saw all this?" asked Glenda cautiously, her voice trembling with apprehension, a quiet dread that seemed to seep into every corner of the tent.

Luke nodded, his guilt-laden voice barely above a whisper, a confession that seemed to tear itself from his very soul. "Yes. And when I returned I found him lying in a pool of blood in the back of the truck."

The words hung in the air, heavy with the weight of a terrible truth, a revelation that seemed to suck the very air from the tent. A soft exclamation escaped my lips, barely audible, as a cold shiver coursed through my body. It was difficult to comprehend the magnitude of the horrors that had unfolded, the sheer scale of the tragedy that had befallen Joel.

Uncle Jamie's voice rose, anger seeping through every syllable. "But that was yesterday!" he accused, his eyes blazing with a mix of fury and hurt, a betrayal that cut deeper than any knife. "Why didn't you tell me?"

Luke swallowed hard, his throat visibly constricted, a physical struggle to force the words past the lump that had formed there. "I thought... I thought you would blame me for it," he admitted, his voice choked with regret, a confession that seemed to tear him apart from the inside out.

"I do fucking blame you for it!" cried Uncle Jamie, his face contorting with rage, a mask of fury that twisted his features into something almost unrecognisable.

The tent crackled with tension, each word hanging in the air like a jagged shard of glass, a cutting accusation that seemed to slice through the very fabric of reality. Glenda's voice cut through the mounting storm, her tone firm and commanding, a lifeline thrown into the churning waters of our collective despair. "Boys!" she interjected, her voice rising in urgency, a desperate plea for sanity. "Enough!"

But the echoes of Uncle Jamie's anger lingered, reverberating within the confines of the tent, a ghostly presence that refused to be silenced. He exploded with bitter accusations, the force of his words shaking the very foundation of our fragile reality. "And then you brought him here and dumped his body in the fucking river! That's some seriously fucked up shit!" his voice echoed, each syllable laced with a mix of disbelief and rage, a condemnation that seemed to hang in the air like a physical thing.

A surge of nausea churned in the pit of my stomach, a sickening wave of revulsion that threatened to overpower me. It was unfathomable to imagine that Luke, my uncle's partner, the man he had chosen to share his life with, could be implicated in such a heinous act, a crime that defied all comprehension. The walls of the tent seemed to close in around me, suffocating me in a web of deceit and horror, a nightmare from which there seemed to be no escape.

The frantic desperation in Luke's voice pierced through the turmoil, his words a desperate plea for understanding, for some shred of mercy in the face of such overwhelming condemnation. "It wasn't me! I would never do something so terrible!"

Glenda's voice rose again, her urgency cutting through the mounting tension. "Stop it!" she yelled, her words a commanding presence that demanded obedience.

The tent fell into an eerie silence. We were left grappling with the enormity of the situation, the unsettling truth that Joel's life had been brutally extinguished, snuffed out like a candle in the wind.

"Well, what did you do with the body?" asked Uncle Jamie, his voice heavy with anger and accusation.

"We buried him," replied Luke, his words a feeble admission that seemed to hang in the air like a condemned man's last words.

"We?" queried Glenda, her eyebrow raised in a silent question, a probing inquiry that sought to unravel the tangled web of deceit.

Luke hesitated for a moment, his eyes darting nervously around the tent, before reluctantly admitting, "Beatrix, Gladys and I."

The pain in my stomach intensified, a searing agony that threatened to double me over, to bring me to my knees in a moment of abject despair. "This is insane!" I cried out, the words tearing themselves from my throat, a primal scream of anguish that echoed through the tent, the agony of the moment twisting my body in torment.

But the conversation continued around me, oblivious to my distress, a relentless tide of accusations and recriminations that swept me away in its wake. The world spun, my head throbbing with a dizzying intensity, a pounding ache that threatened to split my skull in two. I stumbled out of the tent, my vision blurred with tears, each step an eternity of pain and suffering, my legs giving way beneath me as I collapsed onto the ground outside, the impact jarring my already shattered spirit.

I sat there, on my knees, my hands instinctively clutching my aching stomach, a feeble attempt to hold myself together, to keep the pieces of my shattered psyche from flying apart. The ground beneath me was hard and unforgiving, a cold and unyielding presence that mirrored the turmoil within, the chaos that raged in my heart and mind. The rustling of the tent flap signified another person leaving, but I couldn't bring myself to care, couldn't summon the energy to even lift my head, to acknowledge the presence of another living soul. I remained in that moment, a broken figure on the edge of despair, lost in the maelstrom of my own anguish.

Through the haze of tears that blurred my vision, I heard Paul's voice call out, reaching me like a distant echo, a faint and muffled sound that seemed to come from a world away. "Luke! Wait!" he shouted, his words a desperate plea. The voices faded into the distance, swallowed by the overwhelming tumult that consumed my senses, a cacophony of pain and despair that drowned out all else.

Gingerly, I reached up, my fingers trembling with the effort, and wiped away the tear stains that streaked my cheeks, a feeble attempt to erase the evidence of my emotional unravelling, to hide the depths of my torment from the world. The taste of bile lingered in my mouth, a bitter reminder of the visceral response that had overtaken me, the physical manifestation of the revulsion that churned within my gut.

Duke, ever loyal, sensed my distress and approached, his tiny form a welcome presence in the midst of the unimaginable, nuzzling his cold nose against my hand in a gesture of comfort and solidarity. I pushed him away gently, unable to bear the weight of his comforting presence in that moment, too lost in the depths of my own misery to accept the solace he offered. In a hasty attempt to hide my vulnerability, to conceal the evidence of my weakness from prying eyes, I scooped handfuls of fine dust, covering the remnants of my sickness until it was no longer visible, a feeble attempt to bury the evidence of my own frailty.

"Duke," I murmured, my voice wavering, a hoarse whisper that seemed to hang in the air, commanding him to return to the safety of the tent, to the relative comfort of the only home we had in this strange and terrifying place. With a quick lick against my palm, a fleeting gesture of affection and loyalty, he darted back inside, leaving me alone with the overwhelming weight of my overwhelming thoughts.

A small, wistful smile tugged at the corner of my mouth, a fleeting moment of solace, a brief respite from the storm that raged within me. Duke's unwavering spirit, his boundless energy and enthusiasm, undimmed by the terror around him, offered a glimmer of hope in the darkest of times, a reminder that even in the midst of such unimaginable horror, there was still some small measure of goodness in the world. *But where was his brother, Henri?* I pondered, my gaze instinctively searching for his familiar presence, for the comforting sight of his furry form bounding across the barren landscape. *Had he sought refuge within the confines of the tent, hiding from the horrors that lurked outside?* I couldn't recall seeing him earlier, lost in the maelstrom of the revelations that had turned my world upside down.

Curiosity mingled with unease, a nagging sensation that tugged at the edges of my consciousness, urging me to rise from my vulnerable position, to seek out the answers that eluded me. My stomach, still unsettled, emitted a disconcerting growl. I took a deep breath, steadying myself, determined not to repeat the earlier episode, to maintain some semblance of control over my own faculties. With cautious steps, I approached the front flap of the tent, my heart pounding in anticipation, a sense of trepidation washing over me as I prepared to face whatever lay within.

BREATH OF A ZOMBIE

4338.207.5

As I pushed the fabric aside, a hush settled over me, the world within the tent shifting into focus, a tableau of quiet intensity that seemed to hang in the air. Glenda and Uncle Jamie remained huddled near Joel's motionless form, their faces etched with a mixture of determination and trepidation, a silent struggle playing out across their features. The scent of antiseptic lingered in the air, a sharp and clinical odour that mingled with the earthy musk of the surroundings, a jarring contrast that set my nerves on edge.

Duke sat on the edge of the mattress, his gaze fixated on the scene before him, a silent sentinel keeping watch over the unfolding drama. His ears perked up, attuned to the rhythm of their voices, the subtle inflections and unspoken tensions, as if he sensed the significance of the situation. But one question remained unanswered—*where is Henri?*

As my eyes swept the dimness of the tent for the third time, searching every shadowed corner and hidden recess, they finally settled on the familiar mass of white and tan fur, a sight that sent a flicker of relief coursing through my veins. There, on the far right of his small bed, curled up in a tight ball, was Henri, his tiny form a picture of contentment and ease, just as I should have expected. A small chuckle escaped my lips at his predictable behaviour.

Slowly, reluctantly, I backed away from the entrance of the tent, my gaze lingering on Henri for a moment longer, a silent farewell to the comfort and familiarity he represented, before turning my attention elsewhere, steeling myself for the challenges that lay beyond the tent.

Almost immediately after stepping outside, the cool caress of the breeze against my skin a welcome relief from the stifling confines of the tent, Paul's voice broke the silence, his tone filled with curiosity. "What's going on in there?" he asked.

I turned to face him, my own eyes still adjusting to the change in light, the harsh glare of the sun a blinding contrast to the muted shadows of the tent. "Glenda is doing some surgery," I replied, my voice carrying a tinge of unease.

"Surgery?" Paul repeated, his eyes widening in surprise.

I swallowed hard, my throat dry. "Yeah," I replied, my voice wavering. "She's going to stitch his throat back together."

Paul's expression reflected a mix of disbelief and skepticism, a warring of emotions that played out across his features like a silent battle, a struggle between hope and despair. "So, Glenda really thinks he might be alive?" he asked, his tone laced with uncertainty.

I shrugged. "Yeah, I guess so," I replied, my voice barely above a whisper, a fragile thread of hope.

"Shit," Paul muttered, his hand rubbing anxiously against his face. "This isn't making any sense."

"That's a bit of an understatement," I scoffed, the frustration seeping into my voice, a sharp reminder of the absurdity of our situation.

Paul closed his eyes, taking a deep breath as if attempting to gather his thoughts. I watched him intently, my gaze fixed upon his face, searching for any trace of emotion, any hint of the thoughts that swirled within his mind, the secrets that lay buried beneath the surface. It was clear to me now that he was Luke's brother, the resemblance unmistakable, his presence marked by a rugged and athletic build, a physique that spoke of strength and vitality, his gaze holding an intensity that hinted at hidden depths, a complexity that belied his outward appearance. The lines of worry that etched his brow, the furrows that creased his forehead, betrayed the weight of his own concerns.

With a gesture of camaraderie, a silent offering of support and understanding, Paul extended his right hand toward me. "Paul," he announced, his voice steady. "I'm Luke's brother."

I hesitated for a moment, the uncertainty of our circumstances pressing down upon me. But ultimately, I reached out and gripped his hand firmly, my fingers closing around his in a gesture of solidarity.

"Kain," I replied, my voice filled with a mixture of weariness and determination, a steely resolve that burned bright within me, a stubborn refusal to surrender to the darkness that threatened to consume me.

Paul's eyes studied me intently, his gaze lingering, a searching look that seemed to pierce the very depths of my soul, to lay bare the secrets that lay hidden within. "You know Jamie?" he asked, his voice laced with curiosity, a probing inquiry that sought to unravel the tangled web of our connections, to make sense of the unfortunate events that had brought us together.

"Yeah," I replied, my voice carrying a hint of sadness. "He's my uncle."

"I see," Paul murmured, his gaze shifting, a flicker of understanding crossing his face, as if reevaluating his perception of me, seeing me in a new light, a different context. "So how did you end up here?" he asked, his tone gentle yet inquisitive.

I sighed. "My mother sent me to check on Uncle Jamie," I explained, my voice tinged with regret, a bitter admission that tasted like ashes on my tongue. "She hadn't been able to contact him for a few days. So I went over, and Uncle Jamie wasn't there. Luke told me he was out and would be back soon. And that's when it got weird," I continued, my voice trailing off uncertainly, a hesitance that betrayed the depth of my own confusion.

"Weird?" Paul prodded, his brow furrowed.

I ran a hand through my hair, frustration evident in my voice. "Well," I began, struggling to find the right words, to give voice to the unexplainable, the twisted game of fate that had brought me to this place. "I was about to leave, but then Luke suggested I hang around and wait for Uncle Jamie to get home. He insisted that he wouldn't be much longer."

Paul's eyes narrowed with curiosity, a flicker of suspicion crossing his face. "That doesn't seem too weird," he remarked, his tone skeptical.

I shook my head, feeling a flush of embarrassment creeping up my cheeks, a hot rush of blood that spoke of my own naivety, the foolishness of my actions. "I guess not," I conceded. "But then I had to go to the bathroom. When I came out, Luke asked if I minded helping him with something downstairs. I can't even remember what he wanted now. It all happened so quickly. As we approached the top of the stairs, there was a bright flash of colours when Luke slid the door open, and then I felt something shove me in the back. I'm pretty certain it was Luke."

Paul's face contorted with concern. "So, Luke had no idea you were coming?" he asked, his voice tinged with disbelief.

I nodded, a heavy sigh escaping my lips. "I don't think so," I admitted.

A grimace passed over Paul's face, a flicker of anger that mirrored the turmoil within my own mind. "I'm sorry for what my brother has done," he said, his voice tinged with genuine regret. "I really am."

I shrugged again. "It's not your fault," I replied softly, my words a feeble attempt at reassurance, a hollow comfort that did little to ease the ache that burned within me.

"So, if your mother sent you, does that mean you still live with her?" Paul inquired carefully, his eyes searching mine for answers.

A wave of sadness washed over me. As I thought of Brianne, my beloved fiancée, and the tiny life that grew within her, a fierce love and longing surged through me, a desperate need to be with them, to hold them close and never let go. "Both me and my fiancée live with my parents," I confessed.

"What's her name?" Paul asked.

"Brianne," I replied, my voice filled with a mixture of pride and concern, a fierce love that burned bright within me, a stubborn refusal to let go of the life we had built together. "She's six months pregnant," I added.

Paul's expression softened with empathy, a flicker of understanding crossing his face. "Shit," he muttered under his breath.

I looked at Paul longingly, my eyes pleading for him to tell me that Glenda had been mistaken, to offer some glimmer of hope in the darkness that surrounded us, some promise of a way back to the life I had known. "Is there really no way to go back home?" I asked, my voice a desperate whisper, a fragile plea.

Paul shook his head, a gesture of defeat that spoke volumes about the hopelessness of our situation, the inescapable reality that had become our new normal. "Not that we know of," he said, his words a crushing blow, a final nail in the coffin of my own dreams, my own desperate hopes for a future that seemed forever out of reach.

I glanced down at the ground, my emotions swirling within me.

"I know this is an unfortunate situation," Paul began, his voice gentle yet resolute. "But the truth is, Jamie and I could really use your help right now."

I looked up, meeting Paul's gaze with a mix of uncertainty and determination, a fierce resolve that burned bright within me. "What can I do to help?" I asked, my voice a quiet strength of my own conviction, the unshakable hope that together, we could weather any storm.

The start of a small smile tugged at the corners of Paul's mouth. "Follow me," he said, his voice filled with quiet resolve.

And so, with a deep breath, I fell into step beside him, ready to fight for our survival with every ounce of strength and courage I possessed. For in this strange and terrifying place, there could be no turning back, no retreat from the horrors that surrounded us. There was only the desperate struggle for survival, the fierce and unyielding fight to hold onto our humanity in the face of the unimaginable.

❖

Together, we navigated the dusty terrain, Paul leading the way with a sense of purpose, his strides confident and assured as he guided me through the unfamiliar landscape. The earth beneath our feet was a tapestry of muted browns and reds. With each step, the dust billowed up around us, clinging to our clothes and skin.

As we walked, Paul showed me the Drop Zone, a designated area where Luke would deliver supplies, his voice tinged with a mix of gratitude and frustration as he explained the need for constant monitoring. "Luke has a habit of dropping items without informing us," he said, his words suggesting a strained relationship between the brothers. "We have to keep a close eye on this area, to make sure we don't miss anything important."

I absorbed the information, my mind racing with possibilities, a flicker of hope igniting within me. *You never know what information might help you find a way out of here*, I repeated to myself, the words a mantra, a desperate plea for some glimmer of salvation. The piles of supplies at the Drop Zone caught my attention, a tangible reminder of the outside world.

"You haven't started constructing any of the sheds yet?" I asked as Paul showed me the boxes and materials, an unexpected hint of excitement creeping into my voice, a tentative hope that perhaps, in this small act of creation, I might find some semblance of purpose.

Paul grimaced. "Well, I'm pretty sure we've screwed up the first slab of concrete we tried to lay," he admitted, his voice tinged with frustration.

I chuckled, a flicker of amusement breaking through the tension. "You better show me then," I said, my voice carrying a hint of determination.

❖

Paul and I trudged through the brown and red Clivilius dust, our feet sinking into the soft earth with each step, the heat of the sun beating down upon us like a merciless tyrant. We stopped when we reached the base for the first shed, a jumble of concrete and debris that seemed to mock their efforts, a cruel reminder of the futility of Paul and uncle Jamie's endeavours.

I stared at it with earnest, my eyes taking in every detail, every flaw and imperfection that marred its surface. It barely resembled anything but a mess. "Yeah. That's pretty fucked," I said, matter-of-factly, my voice devoid of emotion, a blunt assessment of the situation.

Then I continued, a flicker of pride welling up within me as I recalled the memories of building with my father, the hours we had spent together, working side by side. "I helped my father put our garage together," I said, a wide grin spreading across my face, a momentary burst of confidence.

Paul's eyebrows shot up in surprise, a flicker of admiration in his eyes. "Straightforward?" he laughed, his skepticism evident. "And just how big was this garage?"

"Oh, it was ten meters by ten meters," I replied, my voice filled with a quiet confidence, a certainty that spoke of the depth of my own knowledge, the breadth of my own experience.

Paul's eyebrows shot up even further, a look of genuine surprise and admiration crossing his face. "Impressive," he remarked, a flicker of hope igniting within him.

Together, we moved toward the second slab, crouching down to assess its quality, our eyes scanning every inch of its surface, searching for any sign of imperfection or flaw. I ran my palm across the rough concrete, feeling the unevenness beneath my fingers, the tiny ridges and bumps that spoke of the hurried nature of its creation. It wasn't perfect, far from it, but there was potential there, a glimmer of promise that shone through the cracks and imperfections.

"We followed instructions for that one," Paul called out from behind me, his voice tinged with a mixture of hope and uncertainty, a desperate plea for validation, for some sign that their efforts had not been in vain.

"It shows," I said, rising to my feet and dusting off my hands, a flicker of satisfaction crossing my face as I surveyed their handiwork. "It's a little rough, but I think this one will actually be okay for what you need," I offered, my voice carrying a glimmer of optimism, a tentative hope that perhaps we might be able to salvage something from this mess.

Relief washed over Paul's face, the tension in his shoulders visibly easing. "Really? That's the best news I've heard today," he said, optimism lacing his voice.

I surveyed the area, taking in the piles of supplies, the half-poured concrete slabs, and the vast expanse of barren land that stretched out before us. "It looks like you've already got so much work to do. The less rework, the better," I remarked.

Paul smiled, a flicker of hope reigniting within him. "Well, let's get to it," he said, gesturing for us to begin our work.

With renewed eagerness, I headed in the direction of the Drop Zone, Paul hurrying to catch up and match my stride. As we approached the two piles of small stones marking the site's entry, Paul spoke up, his voice filled with a mix of curiosity and trepidation.

"So, what do we do first?" he asked. "Dig up that first one?"

I stared at him, momentarily taken aback by his suggestion, a flicker of disbelief crossing my face as I realised the depth of his ignorance. "Shit, no," I replied, shaking my head, a rueful chuckle escaping my lips as I contemplated the absurdity of the suggestion. "There's no point touching that for now. We'll get the slabs done for a few more sheds first. We have to let them cure for seven days."

Paul's brow furrowed deeply, confusion etched across his face. "Cure for seven days?" he repeated slowly, each word a heavy weight upon his tongue. "What the hell does that mean?"

A chuckle escaped my lips, the sound mingling with a mix of amusement and understanding. "It means that once we have poured the concrete, we have to leave the slabs for seven days before we can build the sheds on them," I explained, trying to simplify the concept, to break it down into terms that even a novice could understand.

"Shit," Paul muttered under his breath, his eyes widening with realisation, a dawning comprehension of the sheer magnitude of the task that lay before us. "I've never heard of that before."

"I'm not surprised," I replied with a slight grin, a flicker of amusement crossing my face as I realised the steep learning curve that lay ahead of him.

❖

Under my guidance, Paul and I worked together, finding a rhythm as we set the next slab of concrete, our bodies moving in unison, a silent dance of sweat and toil. Surprisingly, we made quick progress, our combined efforts making the work feel almost effortless.

As I witnessed Paul's ability to follow instructions and adapt, I couldn't help but feel a growing sense of camaraderie, a tentative bond forged in the fires of our shared struggle. We were two lost souls, adrift in a sea of uncertainty, but in that moment, as we worked side by side, our hands calloused and our brows damp with sweat, I felt a flicker of something else stirring within me, a faint glimmer of hope that refused to be extinguished.

Amidst the labour, we engaged in occasional non-work-related conversations, our words a desperate attempt to find solace in each other's company.

"So, you've been separated from your family too?" I ventured, my voice tentative, a probing inquiry that sought to unravel the tangled web of Paul's own life.

Paul's gaze softened, a hint of sorrow flickering in his eyes, a silent acknowledgement of the depth of his own loss. "Yeah," he replied solemnly, his voice heavy with emotion, a quiet ache that seemed to emanate from the very depths of his soul. "I have two kids. Mack is ten, and Rose is six."

My heart ached with empathy, a fierce pang of understanding that tore through me like a knife, a reminder of the precious lives that had been ripped away from us, the families that we had been forced to leave behind. "I can only imagine how much you miss them," I said softly, my voice filled with understanding.

Paul's voice trembled with emotion. "I miss them terribly," he admitted, his words a broken whisper.

The thought of my own family crossed my mind, a fleeting image of Brianne's face, of the child that I might never have the chance to meet. The longing to be reunited with her, to hold her close and never let go, was overwhelming at times, a physical ache that seemed to consume me whole.

I bit down on my inner cheek, fighting back the wave of emotions, the tears that pricked at the corners of my eyes, hot and bitter. "Have you considered bringing them here?" I asked, my voice barely above a whisper, a tentative inquiry that sought to probe the depths of Paul's own desperation.

A pause hung in the air. "I have," he finally replied, his voice resolute, a quiet determination that spoke volumes about the depth of his own conviction.

"And?" I probed gently, my voice soft and encouraging, a plea for him to continue.

"I've already made up my mind that I want to bring them here. That's why I'm so determined to get this small settlement functioning as soon as possible," Paul declared, his words a solemn vow, a promise that he would not rest until he had created a safe haven for his loved ones, a place where they could be together once more.

A mix of emotions washed over me, hope intertwining with the fear of staying trapped in this unfamiliar world, a tangled web of conflicting desires. I couldn't help but envision the possibility of bringing my own family here, of creating a new life, of building something beautiful and meaningful in the face of such overwhelming adversity.

But even as the thought crossed my mind, I quickly pushed it aside, a feeble attempt to shield myself from the pain that lay in wait, the crushing disappointment that would surely follow. My priority was finding a way back home, back to the life I had known, the love that awaited me on the other side of this nightmare.

"I don't want them to forget me," Paul confessed, his voice heavy with longing, a quiet desperation that spoke volumes about the depth of his own fears.

My heart clenched in sympathy, a fierce pang of understanding that ripped through me like an unforgiving tornado.

The fear of being absent from my child's life, of them growing up without a father, without the love and guidance that I so desperately wanted to provide, weighed heavily upon me.

"How long have you been trapped here?" I asked, my voice barely audible.

"This is our third day," Paul revealed, his words laden with a mix of resignation and disbelief.

"Really? Is that all?" I exclaimed, my mind reeling with the implications of his words, the brevity of time that had passed since he had been torn away from his home and loved ones.

Paul's expression turned distant, his gaze fixed upon some unseen point in the distance. The silence stretched between us, heavy with unspoken burdens and shared uncertainties.

I held Paul's gaze for a moment longer, a flicker of unease settling in the pit of my stomach, a quiet dread that whispered of the horrors yet to come. But even as the fear threatened to encroach upon me, I forced myself to focus on the task at hand, on the tangible work that lay in front of us, the small victories that we could claim.

❖

"Paul! Kain!" Glenda's urgent call pierced the air, drawing my attention back to the tent where she and Uncle Jamie struggled to carry Joel's lifeless form. In a moment of misstep, Jamie lost his footing, causing Joel's limp body to collapse onto the unforgiving ground, a heap of tangled limbs and sightless eyes. Glenda, too, lost her balance, her knees meeting the rough terrain with a sickening crunch.

Without hesitation, I sprang to my feet, a surge of adrenaline coursing through my veins as I rushed over to assist Glenda, my hand outstretched in a gesture of support and solidarity. She brushed off the dirt from her knees with a grimace, her determined gaze fixed.

"I'll take him," Paul offered, his voice steady as he stepped forward to lift Joel's shoulder.

I positioned myself on the other side, my hands gently grasping Joel's limp form, a tentative touch that sought to offer some small measure of comfort, of dignity in the face of such overwhelming tragedy. Questions swirled in my mind, a maelstrom of confusion and uncertainty, but I pushed them aside, focusing instead on the immediate urgency of the situation.

"Where are we taking him?" I asked, my voice low and steady, a forced calm that belied the turmoil that raged within me.

"To the lagoon," Glenda instructed.

With an unspoken understanding, our small group worked in unison, taking turns supporting Joel's lifeless body as we made our way toward the nearby lagoon, a shimmering oasis amidst the barren wasteland. Uncle Jamie rushed ahead to prepare for our arrival, his figure quickly swallowed up by the vast expanse of the landscape.

As we reached the edge of the lagoon, the cool, clear waters lapping at our feet, Paul and I carefully lowered Joel into the shallows, our arms trembling under the weight of his lifeless form. Glenda's voice cut through the tension, a sharp cry that demanded our attention, our obedience.

"Make sure he is on his back!" she shouted, her words a clear directive amidst the flurry of activity.

Without hesitation, I waded into the lagoon, the cool water caressing my skin like a lover's touch, a momentary respite from the heat and the dust that clung to my body like a second skin. A strange sensation surged through my legs, an inexplicable tingling that set my nerves on edge, a feeling that I couldn't quite place, couldn't quite understand. Confusion swept over me, my mind grappling with the unexpected response, a silent struggle to make sense of the sensations that had engulfed me. *What the hell was that?* I questioned myself.

Paul bent down, his fingers reaching for the laces of his shoes, but before he could begin, Jamie's voice cut through the stillness, a sharp interruption that halted his movement.

"No, Kain and I have got him covered," Jamie insisted, his voice firm.

Another wave of pleasure coursed through my body, my groin responding with an unwelcome surge of arousal. I glanced around, my eyes darting anxiously, scanning the faces of those around me, searching for signs that anybody had noticed.

Following uncle Jamie's lead, we began to wade deeper into the lagoon, the water rising up to our chests, enveloping us in its cool embrace.

Paul paused, uncertainty etched across his face. "Are you sure?" he asked, seeking confirmation.

"Certain," uncle Jamie replied, his voice resolute.

I felt the growing bulge in my jeans press uncomfortably against my boxers, a mix of embarrassment and frustration filling me. "Just ignore it," uncle Jamie whispered quickly, sensing my unease. "It'll pass."

"Can you see?" Glenda's voice called out from the shore, her concern evident in every syllable, a desperate plea for answers.

"No," Paul's voice carried across the water, a faint echo that seemed to hang in the air like a ghostly presence. "It would be nice if they didn't keep their backs to us. I can't see much at all."

I glanced at my uncle, a silent question passing between us, a flicker of uncertainty that danced in the depths of his eyes. He shook his head almost imperceptibly.

My heart pounded in my chest, a frantic drumbeat that seemed to fill my ears, drowning out all other sounds. A speckle of faint glow emerged before us, a shimmering light that danced upon the surface of the water, a ghostly apparition that seemed to beckon us forward, to draw us deeper into the heart of the mystery that lay before us. I squinted, attempting to discern its source, my mind racing with possibilities, with half-formed theories that seemed to dissolve like mist in the face of such inexplicable beauty. *Could it be some kind of bioluminescent algae?* I wondered, my thoughts a jumble of scientific curiosity and primal fear.

A surge of anticipation quickened my breath, a palpable sense of something momentous unfolding before our very eyes. The glow approached, a shimmering veil of light that seemed to envelop Joel's exposed flesh, seeping into his pores like a living thing, a force of nature that defied all explanation.

Suddenly, Joel gasped for air, his bright blue eyes springing open with renewed vitality, a spark of life that burned bright within him, a fierce and unyielding flame that refused to be extinguished. Confusion mingled with awe as I stood witness to the inexplicable, my mind reeling with the implications of what I had just seen, the sheer magnitude of the miracle that had unfolded before us. *What in God's name is this place?* I thought, my mind a whirlwind of questions and half-formed answers.

"What's happening?" Glenda's voice cut through the charged atmosphere, a sharp cry that echoed the collective bewilderment.

Uncle Jamie turned toward Glenda, a wide smile stretching across his face. "He's breathing again!" he exclaimed, his voice filled with a fierce and unyielding hope.

I stood rooted in awe, my senses overwhelmed by the unfathomable events unfolding before me, a silent witness to the miraculous, the impossible made flesh. It felt as if the world had shifted on its axis, a seismic upheaval that left me suspended in a surreal reality, a waking dream from which there seemed to be no escape.

Joel's arms began to twitch involuntarily, a flicker of movement that belied the life coursing through his veins, the vital force that animated his once-lifeless form. Acting on my uncle's instructions, I pressed Joel's left arm against my belly, providing support and stability.

"Just breathe gently. It's okay. You're okay," uncle Jamie murmured soothingly, his voice a calm and steady presence that seemed to fill the air around us, a balm to the raw and jagged edges of our shattered psyches.

In that moment, time seemed to stand still, a fragile bubble of peace. My breathing steadied, aligning with the rhythmic rise and fall of Joel's chest, a silent symphony of life and vitality that filled the air around us. I pressed my fingers against his wrist, feeling the flutter of his pulse beneath my fingertips, a tangible reminder of the miracle that had unfolded.

"He has blood flow now?" I looked up at uncle Jamie, surprise mingling with disbelief in my voice.

"Of course he does," uncle Jamie responded matter-of-factly, a steadfast belief in the extraordinary, an unshakable faith in the power of the unknowable, the ineffable forces that moved in the shadows, just beyond the reach of our understanding.

As the twitching subsided, I gently released Joel's arm, watching in amazement as a renewed spark of life flickered in his eyes, a fierce intelligence that seemed to follow uncle Jamie's every move in the water.

"What's going on out there?" Glenda's voice broke through the momentary trance, her concern pulling us back to the present.

"It's okay," uncle Jamie called out reassuringly, his voice steady and strong. "We've got it under control."

Glenda seemed reluctant to leave, her professional instincts tugging at her, a silent struggle between duty and desire, between the need to stay and the inexorable pull of the unknown that lay beyond the confines of the lagoon. Paul, on the other hand, grew increasingly impatient, a restless energy that seemed to crackle in the air around him, a barely contained need to be elsewhere, to be doing something, anything.

Within moments, he was coaxing Glenda to her feet, his words a gentle persuasion, a silent plea for her to follow him back to the relative safety of the camp. Their figures retreated into the distance, fading into the shimmering heat haze that hung heavy in the air.

"I should probably leave too," I murmured, my voice low and uncertain, a tentative suggestion that belied the depth of my own conflicted emotions, the tangled web of fear and fascination that held me in its thrall.

"Kain, wait," uncle Jamie rushed, desperation lacing his voice.

I glanced back at my uncle, his eyes pleading for my presence, a silent supplication that tugged at my heartstrings, that called to some deep and primal part of me that I didn't quite understand.

"Please stay with me. Just for a while," uncle Jamie implored, his voice filled with vulnerability.

Against my better judgment, I nodded.

A softness settled over my uncle's features, a flicker of gratitude that danced in the depths of his eyes. "Thank you," he whispered.

And as I stood there, grappling with the unexplainable, my mind reeling with the implications of all that had transpired, a sudden wave of intoxicating sensual emotion crashed over me, a tidal wave of intense pleasure, leaving me gasping for breath, my senses heightened and bewildered.

"Get out of the fucking water!" Uncle Jamie's voice shattered the silence, a thunderous command that jolted me from my stupor.

My eyes snapped open, instantly wide with shock, and my heart hammered against my ribcage, a frantic drumbeat of fear and confusion. Panic surged through me as I lurched forward, my limbs betraying me with their clumsiness. I stumbled onto the shore of the lagoon, each step a battle as my knees buckled and sank into the soft, yielding dust that lined the water's edge. It felt as though the earth itself was pulling me down, anchoring me to this moment of vulnerability.

I dug my fists deep into the ground as a loud, pleasurable moan escaped my lips. My entire body shuddered. A large load exploded into my underwear, and I collapsed on my back. The new shuddering that began in my legs moved up my body quickly, and I let out another soft moan.

In that moment, lying on the shore of the lagoon, the intensity of my experience melded into a surreal sense of peace. Uncle Jamie's urgent shouts, the sound of the water lapping against the shore, even the sensation of the warm dust beneath me—all of it faded into a background noise, a distant clamour that couldn't reach me in the depths of my elated darkness.

FACING DESPAIR

4338.207.6

Raising my hand to shield my eyes as they squinted against the bright sun, slowly, I sat upright. Uncle Jamie was still moving Joel about as he floated on his back.
"What the hell just happened?" I asked in a groggy voice.
"I'd say you've just had your first true orgasm," replied Uncle Jamie with a loud chuckle.
"Holy fuck," I muttered under my breath. I looked back up at my uncle.
"You passed out," said Uncle Jamie. "But don't worry. It wasn't for long."
My face turned hot with embarrassment. I looked away. The sticky mess in my underpants made me feel nauseatingly uncomfortable.
The water splashed gently as Uncle Jamie sat himself on the bank of the lagoon, his feet underneath Joel's back, balancing him delicately in the water. "Consider yourself lucky the others had left already," he said with a smile.
"Is..." I stammered. "Is this why you didn't let them come in?" I asked.
"Mostly," replied Jamie.
"Only mostly?" I asked, curious to what other secrets my uncle held, the glowing algae that he seemed unperturbed by, springing to the forefront of my mind.
"I think it happens to all of us," said Uncle Jamie. "But perhaps a little differently," he mused.
"How differently?" I asked.

"Well sure, I've felt aroused in the lagoon. But nothing like you experienced."

My eyebrow raised in thoughtful surprise. I didn't expect my uncle to be so upfront. But then I remembered that my uncle was known for speaking his mind. It wasn't often he sugarcoated anything at all. It was one of the traits I admired most about him. I, on the other hand, wasn't as good at sharing my true thoughts at all.

Uncle Jamie continued, "Parts of the river seem to have a similar effect. Although very minor."

I grew confused, giving Uncle Jamie a quizzical look. "So," I began hesitantly, "How do you think this affects Joel?"

"Hmm," he said. "I uh..." he started but stopped.

"It's okay," I said, jumping in quickly. "You don't have to explain, really."

"You saw that glow in the water, didn't you?" asked Uncle Jamie.

"Yeah," I replied. "What was that? Looked like some sort of algae or something."

"It was sperm," said my uncle, chuckling lightly. "My sperm."

My mouth dropped. "What the fuck," I said softly, my body giving an impromptu shiver as I tried to shake the image from my mind. I looked back at my uncle. "But I saw it enter Joel's body. Through his skin!" I exasperated.

"Yeah," said Uncle Jamie. "I don't really understand it. But I think the water might have healing properties. See this scab on my chest?" he asked, lifting up his shirt.

I gasped loudly, staring at the large, crusty scab near his left pec.

"Just yesterday this was a life-threatening welt. I probably would have died if not for this lagoon," he said. "And Glenda," he added.

"Oh," I said. I hadn't realised it was so serious. And so recent. It didn't look much more than a healing scab now.

"And what you saw today wasn't the first time," said Uncle Jamie.

"It wasn't?" I asked in surprise.

"No," said Uncle Jamie. "I uh... I had a wank in the lagoon yesterday. As soon as I ejaculated, I noticed the glow immediately, so I assumed that's what it was."

I felt my stomach churn, unsure if my curiosity could hold back the growing nausea much longer. But I pressed on. I had to know now. "So, that glow was still from yesterday?" I asked delicately.

"I think so," said Uncle Jamie quickly, before his face screwed up in odd reflection.

"What?" I prodded, unsure if I really wanted to know.

"Unless it was from someone else," said Uncle Jamie, scrunching his nose once more.

My instincts had been right. I didn't want to know. My body shivered again and I caught myself gagging on some distasteful mucous.

"But I'm pretty sure it was mine," said Uncle Jamie confidently.

I closed my eyes. At this point, there wasn't anything Uncle Jamie could tell me that would make any of it feel alright.

"I should probably clean myself up," I said, and I pushed myself to my feet.

"Make sure you take the river," Uncle Jamie told me. "But stay close to the edge. It gets deep quickly and has a strong current."

"Sure thing," I responded with an acknowledging nod.

"Hey Kain," Uncle Jamie called out before I had covered more than a few metres.

I swivelled on my heels, sending short bursts of dust clouds into the air.

"I'm sorry you ended up here," he said. "But I'm also glad we've got your help."

My mouth opened to reply, but I answered with a simple shrug of my shoulders instead. Turning once more, I headed for the river, around the bend and away from Uncle Jamie and the creepy zombie kid.

❖

The desolate wasteland stretched out before me, an endless expanse of lifeless earth and merciless sun. Each weary step kicked up puffs of dust that clung to my sweat-drenched skin and clogged my throat. The air hung heavy with a suffocating stillness, broken only by the distant flapping of tent fabric and my own laboured breaths.

Thoughts churned in my mind, a relentless maelstrom of confusion and dread. The lagoon, the eerie glow, Uncle Jamie's haunting words - none of it made sense. It felt like reality itself was unravelling at the seams.

"Am I losing my mind?" The words slipped from my cracked lips, barely a whisper, as if I feared voicing the question aloud would make it true. I could feel my sanity fraying at the edges, unravelling thread by thread with each inexplicable event that I encountered. A tremor ran through my weary body and I shook my head, trying in vain to dislodge the heavy shroud of confusion that clung to me like cobwebs. "I don't understand any of this," I muttered, my words fading into the vast emptiness that surrounded me.

Glenda looked up from where she wrestled with an uncooperative tent, her hands wrapped in the stubborn fabric. Perspiration glistened on her brow and strands of hair clung damply to her face, but she still managed a small smile meant to be reassuring. "Just give yourself a few days to adjust," she said, swiping at a bead of sweat trickling down her cheek. "It'll all start to make sense in a few weeks." Her words rang hollow in my ears, but I could see she wanted to believe them.

Paul's voice drifted out from beneath the collapsed tent he was working to resurrect, thick with unmistakable skepticism. "It will?"

"Sure," Glenda responded, infusing the single word with a confidence I wished I could feel. She ducked back out of sight, turning her attention once more to her Sisyphean task.

I wanted nothing more than to cling to their fragile optimism, to wrap myself in the threadbare comfort of believing that things would somehow sort themselves out. But I couldn't shake the searing images that seemed permanently etched into my mind - the eerie, lifeless landscape coated in a thick layer of dust, the haunting spectre of a young man with glassy, lifeless eyes, the mesmerising allure of that unearthly lagoon that pulsed with an unnatural glow. It all defied explanation, a tangled Gordian knot of mysteries that left me floundering.

"So, how is Joel doing anyway?" Paul's question pierced through the thick haze of my spiralling thoughts like a beam of light, offering a momentary respite from the suffocating weight pressing down on me.

I stared unseeing at the cold ashes of last night's campfire, still swirling in faint eddies of wind, my mind's eye filled with the shimmer of unnatural water and the limp form of a man floating in its mesmerising depths. "He's... umm... he's alive, I guess," I finally managed to force out, the words catching in my parched throat, scraping like sandpaper. *How could I even begin to explain the impossible scene I had witnessed out there by the lagoon?*

Relief flickered briefly across Paul's sun-weathered face at my halting answer, but before he could respond, Glenda's authoritative voice rang out across the makeshift camp. "Hey,

Kain! It looks as though we've left the tent pegs for the next tent back at the Drop Zone. Can you go have a look, please?"

"Sure," I replied dully, welcoming any chance to escape, even briefly, from their probing gazes and unspoken questions. I desperately needed to be alone with the tempest of my tortured thoughts, to try to make some sense of the turmoil raging inside my pounding skull.

"Thanks. It's probably in a small, rectangular box," Glenda called after me as I turned to leave, her words nearly lost to the gentle wind.

❖

The merciless sun beat down on my aching shoulders as I walked, its blistering heat seeping through my already sweat-dampened clothes and seeming to penetrate deep into my very bones. My lengthening shadow stretched out before me, an ebony stain upon the dusty earth. Each heavy step carried me closer to the looming Drop Zone and deeper into the morass of my own troubled mind. Fragments of disjointed thoughts and half-formed fears collided and spun sickeningly, slowly coalescing into one inescapable truth - I was trapped in a never-ending waking nightmare, and I couldn't see any way out.

Despair rose up to choke me, wrapping its icy fingers around my throat, and I felt a primal scream building in my constricted chest, clawing to get out. The sheer unfairness of it all threatened to crush me beneath its massive weight, driving me to my knees. I should be home right now, eagerly awaiting the imminent birth of my beloved daughter, surrounded by the loving embrace of my family. Instead, I found myself ripped away from everything I knew and loved, and thrust mercilessly into this twisted mockery of reality.

Uncle Jamie's presence here should have been a glimmer of light in the all-consuming darkness. But even that small comfort was tainted by a creeping sense of unease that prickled along my spine. His unsettling fixation on Joel, a seemingly perfect stranger, made absolutely no sense to me. *Was the same insidious insanity that sought to claim me now reaching out with grasping tendrils for Uncle Jamie as well?* The thought made me shudder involuntarily despite the oppressive heat.

Lost in the dizzying labyrinth of my own frenzied mind, I almost didn't notice the towering Portal looming ahead of me until I was nearly upon it. The immense transparent screen rose from the dusty earth like an ancient monolith, dominating the desolate landscape. I had to crane my neck to take in its full imposing height, easily five metres tall and at least three metres across. Its sleek surface seemed to mock me, an impenetrable high-tech barrier separating me from the life I so desperately longed for. In just a few short months, I should be celebrating my twenty-fourth birthday surrounded by my loved ones, holding my precious newborn baby in my arms. Instead, I stood before the very thing that had callously ripped me away from them, trembling with a volatile mix of impotent fury and soul-crushing sorrow.

"I want to go home!" The anguished words violently tore themselves from my raw throat in a howl of pure despair, echoing endlessly across the barren expanse. Dust exploded around my foot as I drove my boot into the unyielding ground with all my strength, a futile attempt to vent the raging maelstrom inside me.

You are home, Kain Jeffries, the familiar, cold voice suddenly resonated within my mind, its robotic cadence slicing through the thick air like a keen blade.

My legs buckled beneath me and I sank heavily to my knees, all the blazing anger draining out of me in a dizzying rush. "Fuck you, Clivilius," I whispered brokenly, the muttered curse emerging as little more than a choked sob. Scalding tears burned my eyes as I crouched there amidst the swirling eddies of dust. Hopelessness wrapped around me like a heavy shroud and I let my head fall forward into my trembling hands, my shoulders shaking with silent, wracking sobs.

In that bleak moment, I felt more lost and alone than I ever had before in my entire life, adrift in a fathomless sea of unanswered questions with no hope of rescue in sight. The vast expanse of the hostile landscape stretched out around me, mirroring the yawning emptiness in my heart as I knelt there in the dust, the unforgiving sun beating down on my bowed head. Thoughts of my family, my home, my entire world - all lost to me now - swirled through my mind as grief threatened to pull me under. I squeezed my burning eyes shut against the tears, but it did nothing to block out the pain. In this strange place, surrounded by unfamiliar faces, I had never felt more utterly, hopelessly alone.

❖

A sudden burst of joy lit up my face and I hastily brushed away the remnants of tears from my cheeks, the rough fabric of my sleeve scratching against my skin. "Sleeping bags," I exclaimed, the words tumbling out with a startling surge of enthusiasm that caught me off guard, piercing through the heavy shroud of despair that had settled over me. "Luke must have left them here," I murmured, bending down to grasp the sturdy carry string of the first bag, the coarse fibres digging into my palm.

Glancing up, I squinted against the warm glow of the sun as it slowly sank towards the distant mountains, painting the sky in a breathtaking array of oranges and pinks. The vast expanse of unblemished blue stretched out above me, a cruel reminder of the beauty that still existed in this harsh, unforgiving world. The dwindling daylight suggested that only a precious few hours remained before darkness would blanket us, wrapping us in its chilling embrace. The serendipitous discovery of these sleeping bags couldn't have been more perfectly timed, a small mercy.

The string dug into the tender flesh of my palm as I hefted the bag over my left shoulder, the weight of it strangely comforting, a tangible connection to the world I had left behind. I followed suit with the second bag, draping it across my right shoulder, the rough fabric scratching against my neck. Positioning the third strap behind my neck, I allowed the bag to rest against my chest, the solid mass of it pressing reassuringly against my racing heart. It jostled softly with each movement, a minor nuisance easily overshadowed by the precious time it would save me from making another arduous trip across the unforgiving terrain.

In my haste to adjust the bags, I twisted too quickly, my muscles protesting the sudden movement. The bag on my left slammed into a small, rectangular box teetering precariously on the edge of a larger container, sending it clattering to the ground with a sharp, metallic clang that echoed across the barren landscape.

"Ah, the tent pegs," I muttered, the realisation of Glenda's forgotten request flooding my thoughts, momentarily pushing aside the whirlwind of emotions that had consumed me.

Luke's voice broke through my reverie, his words carried on the hot, dusty breeze. "Hey Kain," he greeted, his voice laced with a warmth and camaraderie that felt jarringly out of place.

I quickly retrieved the small box, my fingers trembling slightly as I stood upright with a wobble, the sleeping bags bouncing against my body in rhythm with my unsteady movements.

"Come join us for a drink," Luke invited, a bottle clutched casually in his hand, the amber liquid inside sloshing gently. My gut instinct told me it held something of the alcoholic variety, a tantalising promise of temporary oblivion.

"Shit, yeah," I muttered under my breath, my curiosity piqued, a desperate yearning for any escape from the relentless torment of my thoughts. Without a moment's hesitation, I made the final adjustments to the sleeping bags and hastened to catch up with Luke, my boots kicking up small clouds of dust with each hurried step. The bags bounced uncomfortably against my body as I attempted a gentle jog, my anticipation growing with each laboured breath.

"What have you got?" I inquired, my words punctuated by lightly panted breaths.

Luke paused, holding the bottle towards me with a mischievous grin, his eyes glinting in the fading light. I eagerly reached out, securing the small box of tent pegs under my armpit to free up my hand. With a swift motion, I grabbed the bottle, the cool glass a shocking contrast to my sun-warmed skin. Bringing it to my lips, I indulged in a long, satisfying swig, the liquid fire cascading down my parched throat. My eyes clenched shut as the potent whiskey ignited a fiery heat within, spreading its tendrils through my chest and limbs.

"Fuck, that's some strong shit," I remarked, wiping away a small dribble of saliva that had escaped from the corner of my mouth with the back of my hand, the rough skin scraping against my chapped lips.

"Of course," Luke agreed with a knowing smile, a flicker of amusement dancing in his eyes. "It's the only way."

As we trudged our way towards the camp, the weight of the bags seeming to increase with each step, Luke and I engaged in light conversation. I suspected Luke intentionally matched his pace to mine, a gesture of consideration that I silently appreciated, even as a small part of me bristled at the implied pity. It would have been even more welcome if he had offered to relieve me of one of the bags, to share the burden that pressed down on my aching shoulders.

Nevertheless, the whiskey was already working its insidious magic, soothing the jagged edges of my frayed mind, blurring the sharp contours of reality. A fleeting smile flickered across my face, momentarily illuminating my eyes, but I was well aware that this respite was only temporary, a fragile illusion that would shatter all too soon.

As we walked, Luke ventured into more delicate territory, his words cutting through the haze of the alcohol. "Forgive me yet?" he asked in a coy manner, his voice laced with a knowing undertone that set my teeth on edge.

Distraught wrinkles etched their way across my forehead as I processed his question, my mind reeling. *How the hell could Luke ask such a thing, as if forgiveness was a trivial matter to be tossed around lightly?* I ripped the whiskey bottle from Luke's hands, my face falling into a serious expression, my eyes hardening. "I'm doing this for Uncle Jamie. Not for you," I said harshly, my words hanging heavily in the air between us. And with that, I took another long swig from the bottle, the burning liquid dulling the sharp edges of my anger.

Without another word, I shoved the bottle against Luke's chest, the force of it causing him to stumble back slightly. *Forgiveness isn't an option, not now, not ever.* The wounds were too raw, the betrayal too deep. I turned away from him, my jaw clenched tight, and continued my solitary march towards the camp, the weight of the bags bearing down on my shoulders like the burdens of the past.

"Let me take one of those bags from you," Luke called out, his voice laced with genuine concern, a feeble attempt to bridge the chasm that yawned between us.

But my rage clouded my ability to respond, the pounding in my head drowning out his words. Silently letting a single sleeping bag drop to the ground, I forged ahead, my steps fuelled by a simmering fury that threatened to boil over at any moment.

As I approached the campfire, the flickering flames casting dancing shadows across the ground, I called out, "Luke's here," alerting Glenda to his presence. She was diligently working on one of the tents, her face etched with concentration. Despite the absence of tent pegs, I couldn't help but notice the progress she and Paul had made on the fourth tent.

"Luke!" Glenda's voice rang out in a welcoming tone, her eyes lighting up with a warmth that made my chest ache. "Haven't seen much of you since this morning."

"I know," replied Luke, his voice tinged with a hint of guilt.

Glenda continued quickly, her words tumbling out in a rush, "But I've noticed new supplies at the Drop Zone so I figured you hadn't forgotten us."

"Of course not," agreed Luke, a small smile tugging at the corners of his mouth.

Dropping the package of tent pegs under the protective canopy of one of the tents, I paused briefly, my chest heaving with exertion. Sucking in a deep breath, I pushed my way into the third tent, the cool shade a welcome respite from the relentless heat. With a sigh of relief, I released the burden of the sleeping bags from my shoulders, the muscles screaming in protest as I tossed one into each wing of the tent. I silently concluded that this is where Paul and I would be spending the night, the thought of sharing close quarters with him sending a flicker of unease through me. Undoubtedly, Uncle

Jamie would remain by the side of the peculiar Joel, his obsession with the man bordering on the unsettling. And Glenda, ever the caretaker, would find solace among her medical supplies, ready to tend to any needs that might arise.

The tents themselves were expansive, capable of housing ten individuals each, featuring two spacious wings, a generous central living area, and a canopy extension at the front. *At least Luke made a few sensible choices,* I thought to myself, although I refused to let any hint of sentimentality seep further into my mind, my defences still firmly in place.

Emerging from the tent, I caught sight of Luke offering Glenda the whiskey bottle, a peace offering of sorts. "More?" Luke inquired, holding the bottle towards her, the amber liquid sloshing gently.

"No thanks," Glenda politely declined, her hand raised in a gentle gesture of refusal.

"Bag," I called out, motioning for Luke to toss it over.

Luke complied, a smile spreading across his face as he lobbed the bag in my direction. I deftly caught it, the weight of it solid in my hands, and made my way inside the medical tent. The pungent smell of antiseptic assaulted my nostrils as I stepped into the dimly lit space, the supplies casting eerie shadows on the fabric walls. Contemplating the idea of spreading the sleeping bag across the floor for Glenda's comfort, a small gesture of kindness in this harsh reality, I ultimately decided against it. Instead, I placed it gently in the unoccupied wing of the tent.

"Glenda!" Paul's voice broke through urgently from outside, the note of alarm in his tone sending a jolt of adrenaline surging through my veins.

Poking my head through the flaps of the tent, my eyes widened in bewilderment at the scene unfolding before me. *The freak is walking—or at least attempting to,* his movements jerky and uncoordinated. Joel was propped up between Paul and Uncle Jamie's arms, their faces etched with concern as they supported his weight.

Glenda and Luke rushed over as the trio neared the camp, their footsteps kicking up small clouds of dust in their wake. Choosing to remain at a safe distance, I observed the scene unfold from the front of the tent, my heart pounding in my chest.

"He's bleeding!" Glenda exclaimed, her voice filled with alarm, her eyes wide with shock. "Luke, get me some tissue from the medical tent," she directed.

Unable to ignore the call to help, the instinct to offer assistance overriding my reservations, I left the comfort of my position and began rummaging through the bags of supplies. My hands shook slightly as I searched for anything that might serve the purpose, my mind racing with the implications of this new development.

"I got it!" I called out triumphantly as I emerged from the tent, clutching a wad of tissues in my hand. I noticed that Luke had remained stationary, frozen in place by the shock of the moment. Hastening over, I handed the tissues to Glenda, our fingers brushing briefly in the exchange.

"Ta," Glenda replied simply, accepting the tissues and pressing them against Joel's dripping nose, the stark contrast of the white fabric against his pallid skin making my stomach churn. "Let's get him sitting," she instructed, her voice steady despite the tremor of unease that ran through it.

Paul and Uncle Jamie guided Joel to sit on a large log by the campfire, their movements careful and deliberate. I trailed several steps behind, maintaining a cautious distance, my eyes never leaving the hunched form of the man who had become the centre of this twisted mystery.

"Not too close," Glenda insisted, stepping between the men and the warmth of the campfire, her hands raised in a warning gesture. "Is it just his nose?" she inquired, her brow furrowed with concern.

"I think so," Uncle Jamie responded, his voice thick with worry.

"I didn't even notice it was bleeding," Paul admitted, his face etched with a mixture of confusion and disbelief.

Glenda knelt before the weakened Joel, still supported on either side by Paul and Uncle Jamie, their faces cast in flickering shadows by the dancing flames. "I don't understand how he can be bleeding. I was certain there was no blood in him earlier," Glenda pondered aloud, her voice filled with a perplexed fascination.

Uncle Jamie shook his head, his expression mirroring Glenda's bewilderment. "I didn't give him any blood. But he seems to have plenty of it now," he stated.

A wave of discomfort washed over me as the memory of my earlier conversation with Uncle Jamie resurfaced, the unease settling like a lead weight in the pit of my stomach. *Oh, you gave him plenty,* my mind whispered sarcastically, the irony of the situation not lost on me.

Glenda continued her examination, her deft fingers poking gently at various points on Joel's arms and legs, her touch clinical and detached. "There is definitely blood in his veins now," she confirmed, her voice carrying a sense of disbelief, as if she couldn't quite trust the evidence of her own senses.

I stood there, rooted to the spot, unable to comprehend the situation unfolding before my eyes. The thought of it all sent a chill down my spine, a creeping sense of wrongness that I couldn't shake.

"It's a medical anomaly!" Glenda declared, her voice tinged with a mix of professional curiosity and morbid fascination. Rising to her feet, she reached for the whiskey bottle in Luke's hand, her fingers trembling slightly. "You better lie him down again once the bleeding stops," she directed, taking a swig from the bottle.

Luke let out a loud chuckle, finding a dark humour in the midst of the perplexing circumstances. But I couldn't find anything remotely amusing in the situation, my mind reeling with the implications of what we were witnessing.

Observing the darkening sky, Paul remarked, "Nightfall can't be too far away. I'll prepare some food." His words were a welcome reminder of the practical realities we faced, a tether to the world we had left behind.

Quickly seizing the opportunity to divert my thoughts, to distance myself from the unsettling scene before me, I chimed in, "I'll help you." I needed a distraction, something to keep me occupied and away from Uncle Jamie and his strange obsession with the zombie-like Joel, the man who defied all logical explanation.

Paul acknowledged my offer with a nod, a flicker of understanding passing between us. Together we ventured towards the cooking area. As we busied ourselves with the mundane tasks of survival, the comforting routine of preparing a meal, I couldn't shake the feeling that we were merely going through the motions, playing at normality in a world that had long since ceased to make sense.

EMBRACING TRADITION

4338.207.7

As the darkness deepened, the campfire's flickering light danced across our tired faces. The crackle and pop of the burning logs filled the night air, accompanied by the occasional burst of our laughter as we passed a bottle of whiskey around, the warm amber liquid bringing temporary solace from our burdens.

Amidst our mirth, Glenda's attempts to stifle her grin only intensified her infectious giggles. She pressed her fingers to her lips, a futile effort to suppress the laughter that erupted from her. "Shh," she hushed, her voice barely a whisper, her eyes sparkling with mischief. "The zombie is sleeping."

Her infectious joy spread through our small group huddled around the fire. I found myself chuckling despite the persistent ache in my heart, the liquor pleasantly dulling my senses for a precious moment. "I didn't know how else to describe him," I said with a wry smile.

Paul leaned forward, brow furrowed with concern even amidst our temporary levity. "Are we sure it's safe in there? We don't really know what's going on."

Luke let out a weary sigh as he stood, swaying slightly and using Glenda's shoulder to steady himself. "Don't be so stupid, Paul," he muttered, though there was no real bite to his words. He moved unsteadily toward the dark, silent tent.

Paul feigned hurt feelings, his face twisting into a comical expression of wounded pride. "Ah," he gasped dramatically, placing a hand over his heart.

Watching Luke's retreating form, I turned to Paul, lowering my voice. "Is he alright?" Shadows from the crackling flames played across Paul's face as he waved off my concern. "Oh, he's fine."

Silence descended upon us, and the crackling fire became the focal point of our attention. I stared into the fiery glow, its radiant warmth lulling me into a sense of temporary tranquility. The flames danced, casting their mesmerising light upon my weary face.

Glenda's voice broke the calm, her words resonating with finality as she tossed her paper plate into the fire. "Well, dinner was tasty," she declared, her eyes fixed on the disappearing plate as it was consumed by the hungry flames.

My gaze remained fixed on the fire's relentless devouring, a metaphor for the transient nature of our existence. The plate vanished, transforming into smoke and ash, lost to the ephemeral dance of the flames.

"Thank you both," Glenda expressed her gratitude, her voice carrying a weight that belied the simple words. "I wonder whether now might—" she began, her words trailing off.

Paul's sharp interruption silenced her, a warning gesture in the dim light of the campfire. "Shh," he hushed, his eyes darting towards the tent.

We listened intently, our senses heightened, as voices rose from the tent. The pitch and tension in their tones carried a haunting cadence, unsettling the previously serene atmosphere.

Paul rose from his seat on the log, his movements deliberate, filling the air with a palpable sense of unease. The darkness seemed to close in around us as he pushed himself up. With a sudden burst of energy, a dark figure stormed out of the tent, breaking the peaceful stillness. A chill ran down my spine, the hairs on my arms standing on end, as a foreboding shadow cast its cloak upon me.

"Luke!" Paul's voice filled with concern, calling out into the night. But Luke paid no heed, his feet propelling him forward in a frantic dash, leaving behind a trail of disturbed dust.

A surge of apprehension washed over me, dispelling the fleeting calmness that had settled within. The disbelief etched on Paul's face mirrored my own bewildered thoughts, a flurry of questions swirling in my mind about what could have transpired inside the tent.

Paul, his body tensed with a readiness to intervene, made a move to follow Luke's hasty retreat. However, Glenda, her eyes widening with caution, swiftly intervened, restraining him with a firm wave of her hand. The unspoken understanding passed between them, urging Paul to stay put.

In the distance, the ethereal glow of bright Portal colours danced across the uneven landscape, momentarily illuminating the darkness before vanishing just as quickly. Its fleeting presence further added to the mystique and uncertainty of our surroundings.

"Yep. Looks like it's definitely you and me tonight, Paul," I murmured, my voice tinged with resignation.

Paul nodded in agreement, his weary eyes scanning the surroundings. "I might get used to this dust yet," he mused, his voice laced with a touch of dry humour, a feeble attempt to lighten the weight of the situation.

A sudden realisation struck Glenda, her eyes widening in concern. "Oh no," she interjected, a flicker of worry evident in her voice. "There's a sleeping bag for you in the other tent."

Paul's surprise was palpable as he looked at Glenda. "Really?" he exclaimed, a glimmer of gratitude in his eyes. "That should make a nice change." He shifted his gaze toward me. "But the tent's all yours," he stated nonchalantly. "I'll sleep out here again tonight. I don't want to let the fire completely burn out."

I raised an eyebrow in surprise, puzzled by Paul's aversion to the dark. "Don't like the dark?" I inquired, my tone casual yet curious.

Paul's response carried a hint of unease as his eyes met Glenda's briefly. "Hmph," he grumbled, the corners of his lips twitching with a conflicted expression. "Something like that."

A pang of unease coursed through me, tightening the knot in my stomach. The persistent twist within me urged me to seek a more satisfactory explanation. I bit my lower lip gently, contemplating whether to press further. "Is there something out there?" I asked cautiously, my voice laced with a mix of curiosity and concern. "Other people, maybe?"

Paul's response was guarded, his voice dropping to a low and cautious tone. "Not that we know of," he replied, the weight of uncertainty colouring his words.

The knot in my stomach tightened, its grip constricting further. Placing a hand across my belly, I sought to quell the rising unease, though the effort proved futile. There was an underlying tension in Paul's words that unsettled me, heightening my sense of vulnerability. "But," I blurted out, the words tumbling forth, "if Luke is telling the truth about not bringing—" I hesitated, my thoughts briefly entangled, "about not bringing Joel here, then who did? And how did they get him here without any of us seeing something? There isn't exactly any cover here. And he looked like he had spent a fair amount of time in the water."

Glenda shifted uncomfortably on her log, her movements betraying her unease. Her eyes darted around, scanning the enveloping darkness that surrounded our camp. The flickering light of the campfire played on her face, revealing the worry etched in her features.

Paul's gaze shifted to Glenda, suspicion creeping into his voice. "Do you know something that you're not telling us?" he questioned, his tone laced with caution.

Glenda hesitated, her eyes meeting Paul's for a fleeting moment before dropping to the ground. Her voice barely rose above a whisper as she finally responded, "I'm just as confused as the two of you are."

A wave of dread washed over me, intensifying the unease that had settled within me. The words slipped out before I could restrain them, blunt and unfiltered. "I don't think we're safe here," I declared, the gravity of the situation outweighing any concern for diplomacy.

Paul's response was a soft sigh, a tinge of resignation colouring his voice. "Right now, we don't really have any other option. I'm sure Luke would have warned us if it wasn't safe," he tried to reassure, yet the uncertainty in his tone betrayed his own doubts.

I scoffed loudly, my skepticism lingering from the revelations of Uncle Jamie's secrets. "Luke doesn't know everything," I retorted, my voice laden with doubt.

Paul's raised eyebrow signalled his suspicion, his penetrating gaze fixed on me. I bit down on my lip, a nervous habit. Secrets weighed heavily on my conscience, and I feared that revealing one might unravel the fragile trust between us. *Or perhaps it won't be the only secret I'll expose.*

Fortunately, Paul either failed to notice or chose to let it slide. "We'll just have to watch out for each other," he asserted firmly, his tone resolute. "We're all we've got right now," he added, glancing pointedly at Glenda.

Glenda shifted uncomfortably once again, the weight of uncertainty pressing upon her. "I think it's time for bed," she announced, slapping her thighs lightly. Without waiting for a response, she rose from her log and retreated into her tent, her footsteps fading into the night.

Surprised by the abruptness of her departure, I watched her vanish into the darkness, a sense of unease settling deeper within me.

"I'll go grab a sleeping bag then," Paul said, breaking the silence as he rose to his feet once more. His eyes met mine, seeking confirmation. "Does it matter which one?" he asked.

I shook my head, still grappling with the sudden turn of events and Glenda's swift exit. "Nah," I replied, my voice barely audible.

❖

As the campfire dwindled, an eerie silence descended upon the air, broken only by the occasional pop and crackle of the dying embers. I closed my eyes, attempting to push away the tendrils of unease that coiled within me like insidious serpents. The fading warmth of the fire served as the sole remaining comfort, a rhythmic reminder of our solitude in the vast and uncertain expanse that stretched out beyond the flickering light. Taking several deep, shuddering breaths, I tried to steady my frayed nerves, clinging desperately to the flicker of hope that whispered of a new day, a tomorrow when this endless nightmare might finally come to an end.

My momentary trance was shattered by a sudden movement on the log beside me, the rough bark digging into my skin through the thin fabric of my clothes. Caught off guard, my body teetered backward, and I found myself unceremoniously sliding onto the dusty ground with a muffled thump, the impact sending a jolt through my already aching muscles.

"Glenda!" I exclaimed sharply, frustration lacing my words like venom, my voice rough and raw in the oppressive stillness. "What the hell!"

Glenda's lips formed a silent apology, her hand extending towards me in an attempt to pull me back onto the log, her slender fingers grasping at the air between us.

"Glenda!" Paul hissed in a hushed whisper, catching us by surprise.

Startled, Glenda visibly jumped, her eyes wide and darting towards Paul, a flicker of fear dancing in their depths. I held onto her outstretched hand, my grip tight and unyielding, helping her regain her balance on the uneven ground.

Paul's chuckle broke the tension, a sly grin playing on his lips, the shadows cast by the dying fire making his features appear almost sinister. "Sorry," he whispered mischievously, dropping his sleeping bag onto the dusty ground beside his log with a soft rustle.

"No, you're not," Glenda retorted, a smile gracing her face despite herself, softening the moment and easing the tightness in my chest ever so slightly.

Curiosity piqued, I interjected, nodding towards the medical tent from which Glenda had emerged, its white canvas walls glowing faintly in the darkness. "You don't like the tent?" I inquired, gesturing towards its entrance with a tilt of my head.

Glenda's voice took on a more serious tone as she replied, her words heavy with unspoken meaning. "Actually, there's something I think we should do as a group first."

My eyebrows arched with intrigue, a flicker of interest sparking within me despite the weariness that seemed to seep into my very bones. "What is it?" I asked, curiosity lacing my voice, the words feeling thick and clumsy on my tongue.

"Gratitude," Glenda stated simply, her eyes glimmering in the gentle glow of the campfire, the flames reflected in their depths like tiny stars.

"Gratitude?" I scoffed, not quite comprehending her intentions, the concept seeming almost absurd in the face of the horrors we had endured.

"Hear me out," Glenda insisted, cutting off any further remarks before they could be made.

Reluctantly, I fell into silence.

"It's something my father taught me. I've done it every day since..." Glenda's voice trailed off abruptly, her words catching in her throat, a visible struggle evident in the way her lips trembled and her eyes glistened with unshed tears. She swallowed hard, the sound loud in the stillness, before continuing softly, "It's become a nightly tradition for me."

Glenda gracefully knelt down in the dust, near the gentle embers of the campfire, the heat emanating from the glowing coals warming her skin. She extended an invitation, her voice filled with a quiet strength that I couldn't help but admire. "Come join me," she encouraged, her eyes meeting mine, a silent plea in their depths.

Glancing at Paul, unsure of his response, I was surprised when he merely shrugged and joined Glenda, settling onto the ground beside her with a soft grunt, his long legs folding beneath him.

Still uncertain, I hesitated, my mind whirling with conflicting thoughts and emotions, the urge to flee warring with the desire to find some small measure of peace in this godforsaken place.

"It's okay," Glenda assured, turning her gaze towards me once more, her voice gentle and soothing. "We're not praying or anything."

Relenting, I knelt in the soft dust on Glenda's other side, feeling the gritty texture beneath my knees.

With our positions settled, Glenda spoke once more, her voice calm and composed. "I'll go first," she declared, her words hanging in the air before fading into silence, swallowed by the vast emptiness that surrounded us. "I'm grateful for life," she stated simply.

I knelt uncomfortably, gazing into the darkness that pressed in on all sides, as a heavy silence draped over our small group. Uncertainty filled the space between us, and I couldn't shake off the awkwardness that settled within me, twisting my gut into knots. *Should I say something?* I wondered, feeling the weight of expectations pressing down on me.

The campfire continued its mesmerising dance, casting flickering shadows across our faces, the light playing over our features and making us look almost otherworldly in the darkness. The minutes stretched on, each one feeling like an eternity, and just as the silence threatened to consume us entirely, Paul finally broke it, his voice rough and low. "I'm grateful for the river," he stated, the words carrying a touch of solemnity, as if he were imparting some great wisdom.

Glenda's elbow prodded me in the side, urging me to speak, the contact startling me out of my thoughts. But I remained silent, my mind racing and my heart pounding, the blood rushing in my ears like a roaring river. *It's not that I don't want to participate, I just don't know what to say,* I reassured myself, feeling a mix of frustration and self-doubt churning within me.

Glenda's elbow nudged me once again, more insistent this time, the pressure of her touch sending a jolt through my body. I shifted uncomfortably on the hard ground, my knees aching from the prolonged kneeling, the dust and grit digging into my skin. My thoughts swirled in a jumbled mess, fragments of memories and half-formed fears colliding and spinning out of control. *Come on, think of something, anything,* I urged myself, desperate to break the oppressive silence.

The quiet stretched on, broken only by the soft crackling of the dying fire, and when Glenda's elbow jabbed me a third time, I finally gave in, the words tumbling from my lips before I could stop them. "I'm grateful for Uncle Jamie," I blurted out, my voice sounding harsh to my own ears, the words hanging in the air like a confession.

Paul's hand flew to his mouth, but it was too late to stifle the light chuckle that escaped, the sound grating on my nerves like sandpaper. Annoyance surged through me, hot and fierce, and I quickly got to my feet, frustration bubbling to the surface like magma rising from the depths of the earth.

"Kain, I'm sorry," Paul called out, genuine remorse in his voice, but I ignored him, my feet carrying me past the fading glow of the campfire and into the enveloping darkness beyond, the cool night air brushing against my exposed skin.

I hardly registered the freshness of the air as I ventured further away from the dwindling light, my mind consumed with thoughts of betrayal and frustration. Squinting into the darkness, I muttered an expletive under my breath, my foot catching on an unexpected shift in the ground, sending me stumbling forward. I slid down a steep embankment of loose dust, my heart pounding in panic, the blood roaring in my ears. "What the fuck!" I exclaimed, my voice echoing in the vast emptiness, disoriented and desperately searching for any source of light to guide me back to the safety of the camp.

"Oh, shit," I repeated, my hands blindly clawing at the ground, my fingers digging into the loose earth as I strained to climb back up the treacherous slope, my muscles burning with the effort. Fear consumed me, cold and clammy, as I gasped for air, each breath ragged and frantic, tearing at my lungs like shards of glass. Finally, through the veil of darkness, I caught a faint glimmer of the campfire's glow in the distance, a beacon of hope in the overwhelming blackness. *How have I strayed so far?* I wondered, my mind reeling with confusion and disbelief.

With renewed determination, I pushed through the exhaustion, my muscles screaming in protest as I retraced my steps, stumbling and sliding on the uneven ground. Soon, I reached the faint light of the campfire, its wavering flames providing a sense of relief and familiarity.

Paul sat alone on his log, his figure outlined by the dying embers, the shadows playing across his face and making him look almost ghostly in the flickering light. *Have they finished without me?* I wondered, a mix of regret and resentment churning within me, twisting my gut into knots. Silently, I settled back onto the dusty ground, near the remnants of the fire's warmth, the heat radiating from the glowing coals providing a small measure of comfort in the face of the overwhelming darkness.

I gazed upward, my eyes fixating on the dark expanse above, devoid of moon or stars, an endless void that seemed to stretch on forever. My body shivered involuntarily, whether from the chill of the night air or the weight of my own emotions, I couldn't discern, the two blending together until they were indistinguishable.

As the fire flickered and gradually waned, Paul placed his sleeping bag near my prone form, the rustling of the fabric breaking the stillness of the night. Without a word, he retreated, leaving me alone with my thoughts, the silence pressing in on me from all sides.

I stared at the dark green material, its fabric beckoning me, promising warmth and comfort in the face of the cold, dusty ground. Knowing it would be wise to use it, I reached for the sleeping bag with trembling hands, pulling it from its protective case, the zipper rasping loudly in the quiet. Stripping down to my underwear, I crawled inside, cocooning myself within its comforting embrace, the soft fabric enveloping me like a second skin. The edges were tucked tightly under my chin as I lay on my back, staring up into the void above, my mind whirling with thoughts of home and family, of the life I had left behind.

Loneliness and isolation washed over me, amplified by the presence of Paul just a few feet away, his steady breathing a reminder of the gulf that stretched between us. I fought against the onslaught of negative thoughts, focusing instead on the gratitude that Glenda had encouraged, a small flicker of light in the overwhelming darkness. Lying there, gazing at the starless sky, I couldn't help but feel a sliver of gratitude for the small remnants of light that still pierced the darkest of times, a reminder that hope was not entirely lost.

"I'm sorry, Kain," Paul's voice finally broke the silence, laden with sincerity and remorse.

I let out a soft sigh, the tension within me gradually dissipating, like a knot slowly unravelling. "I'm grateful for the light," I responded, my voice carrying a mix of acceptance and forgiveness. With that, I closed my eyes, allowing the gentle sound of the fire's dying embers to lull me into a fitful sleep, my mind drifting off into a world of dreams and nightmares, where the lines between reality and illusion blurred.

4338.208

(27 July 2018)

UNSETTLING REALISATIONS

4338.208.1

As I slowly emerged from the depths of sleep, my bleary eyes adjusting to the harsh glare of the morning light, I surveyed the camp that was already abuzz with activity. The crisp air carried the lively conversation of Glenda and Paul, their words intermingling with the gentle rustling of the wind as it stirred up small plumes of soft dust, creating a hazy veil that hung over the campsite.

Paul's voice drifted towards me as he disappeared into Jamie's tent, his words slightly muffled by the flapping fabric. "I'll just grab my suitcase first," he called out to Glenda, his tone casual and untroubled.

Still feeling the remnants of sleep clinging to my mind like cobwebs, I approached Glenda with a croaky voice and a groggy demeanour, my limbs heavy and uncooperative. I longed for the comforting embrace of a steaming mug of coffee before attempting to make sense of their conversation, the bitter liquid a necessary fuel to jumpstart my sluggish brain.

"Have you seen Uncle Jamie this morning?" I inquired, my voice thick with the remnants of slumber as I slowly made my way toward Glenda, my feet dragging slightly in the dust.

"I have," she replied, turning to face me, her gaze meeting mine with a hint of concern. "You should go and visit with him." Her words carried a weight that settled heavily in the pit of my stomach, a sense of unease that I couldn't quite shake.

Nodding in acknowledgment, I continued to rub the back of my neck and stretch my arms above my head, trying to ease the stiffness that had settled into my muscles during the night. The grogginess still clung to me, and I could feel the beginnings of a headache throbbing behind my temples, a dull ache that pulsed in time with my heartbeat.

Paul's voice interrupted our conversation as he emerged from Uncle Jamie's tent, suitcase trailing behind him, the wheels leaving faint tracks in the dust. "Do you have a preference to side?" he called out, his words laced with an air of ambiguity that left me puzzled.

My brow furrowed in confusion, struggling to decipher Paul's cryptic question. *Preference to side? What the hell is he on about?* I thought to myself, my foggy mind failing to comprehend the meaning behind his words. I could feel the beginnings of frustration stirring within me, a prickle of irritation that threatened to ignite into something more volatile.

Glenda responded matter-of-factly, her voice cutting through the haze of my confusion. "You and Paul are moving to the third tent," she informed me.

Ah, now it makes a little sense. "They're both the same, really," I called back, stretching my arms above my head once more and giving my sides a much-needed stretch, feeling the satisfying pop of my joints as they realigned themselves.

"I'm going for a walk to the Drop Zone," Paul declared, reappearing from his brief visit inside the new tent, his face etched with determination. "Take stock of what Luke's left us."

Glenda's expression twisted into a frown, her concern evident in the furrow of her brow. "I doubt you'll find anything new," she stated, her voice tinged with a hint of resignation. "I haven't seen him yet this morning. But I'm sure there might be useful things we didn't notice before." Her words carried a glimmer of hope, a faint spark of optimism that struggled to stay alight in the face of our dire predicament.

As their conversation delved into practical matters, a restlessness began to gnaw at me, an itch that I couldn't scratch. The effects of last night's drinking still lingered in my head, a dull throb that refused to dissipate, and the practicalities of survival failed to engage my interest. Seeking a moment of solitude, a chance to gather my thoughts and centre myself, I quietly retreated into the tent, my mind yearning for respite from the constant chatter and activity.

"Hey, Uncle Jamie," I greeted as I stepped into the tent, my voice laced with a mix of anticipation and caution.

Uncle Jamie's response was sharp and filled with frustration. "Anyone else want to interrupt us this morning!?" he snapped, his eyes rolling with exasperation, the lines of his face deepening with annoyance.

Embarrassment flushed my cheeks, a hot rush of blood that spread across my face like wildfire. "Sorry. I didn't mean to interrupt," I stammered, hastily attempting to make my exit, my feet tangling together in my haste to escape the suffocating tension that hung heavy in the air.

"Kain, wait," Uncle Jamie called out, his tone softening, a hint of regret creeping into his voice as he urged me to pause, to stay.

Reluctantly, I turned back to face him, my heart hammering in my chest, unsure of what he was about to say, of what fresh hell awaited me.

"It's... It's okay if you stay," he said, his voice gentle and understanding, a welcome contrast to the harsh words that had spilled from his lips just moments before.

Relief washed over me like a cool wave, and I released a breath I hadn't realised I was holding, the tension slowly seeping from my muscles. "I... I just wanted to see how Joel was doing," I stammered my explanation, my body shifting nervously under the weight of the moment, my hands twisting together in a futile attempt to still their trembling. Conflict and tension were familiar territories, an inevitable companion in a household of sisters, but I had always strived to avoid them whenever possible, to keep my head down and my mouth shut.

In the dim light of the tent, Uncle Jamie's face came into focus, his features etched with a mix of weariness and concern, the lines around his eyes and mouth more pronounced than I remembered. I took a few cautious steps toward the mattress where Joel lay, his presence a source of both comfort and uncertainty, a reminder of the fragility of life in this twisted reality.

"I'm fine," whispered Joel, his voice barely audible, a faint whisper that carried the weight of a thousand unsaid words.

"Oh, you can talk now?" I asked, surprise colouring my words, my eyebrows shooting up in disbelief. I had grown accustomed to Joel's silence, to the vacant stare that had haunted his eyes since the moment we had pulled him from the water.

"Getting there," Joel croaked, his voice faint and raspy, a hint of pain lingering in his expression, a grimace that twisted his features into a mask of suffering.

Uncle Jamie interjected, his voice firm but gentle, urging caution and care. "You'd better give your voice a rest and have more water. Keep your throat hydrated," he advised, gently pressing a cup of water against Joel's cracked lips before assisting him in reclining back onto the mattress.

Just as a sigh of relief threatened to escape my lips, a momentary reprieve from the constant tension that hung heavy in the air, Glenda's abrupt entrance disrupted the fragile peace. "You ready?" she asked, her tone brisk and businesslike.

My gaze shifted to the bag she carried, a sharp instrument visibly pressing against its side, the outline of the tool clear even through the thick fabric. A wave of dread washed over me, my mind conjuring images of the worst possible scenarios, of blood and pain and endless suffering.

"You don't need me, do you?" I blurted out, my voice tinged with anxiety as I glanced between Glenda and Uncle Jamie, silently pleading with the universe to spare me from whatever torment lay within the confines of that ominous bag.

"No, Jamie and I can handle it," Glenda replied, her response devoid of reassurance, her words falling flat and lifeless in the stifling air of the tent. "He's getting good practice."

"I'm not your fucking lap-dog," Uncle Jamie snapped, his eyes flashing with barely contained anger.

Heat rushed to my cheeks, mingling with the embarrassment and discomfort that swirled within me, a volatile cocktail of emotions that threatened to spill over at any moment. I stumbled over my words, desperately seeking an exit. "I'm going to give myself a quick wash," I muttered, hastily retreating from the tent, my feet carrying me away from the uncomfortable scene that was unfolding, the tension that crackled in the air like static electricity.

The cool morning air greeted me as I stepped outside, offering a respite from the suffocating atmosphere that had hung heavy in the tent. I gulped in deep breaths, filling my lungs with the crisp, clean air, trying to clear my mind of the dark thoughts that encroached within. The sun beat down on my face, its warmth a welcome contrast to the chill that had settled deep in my bones.

❖

Making my way towards the river, the weight of the previous day's events clung to my thoughts like a suffocating shroud, refusing to loosen its grip on my troubled mind. Each step felt heavy, as if the very earth beneath my feet was conspiring to hold me back, to keep me tethered to the camp and the horrors that had unfolded within its confines. The image of my uncle's bewildering experience replayed in my mind's eye, a haunting loop that left me unsettled and hesitant, a constant reminder of the strange and terrifying world I now found myself in.

As I approached the riverbank, the sound of rushing water filled my ears, gently drowning out the tumultuous thoughts that raced through my mind. I stood there for a moment, my gaze fixed on the swirling currents, the water's surface glinting in the early morning light like a thousand shattered diamonds. The temptation to fully undress and immerse myself in the water's cool embrace was strong, a longing to wash away the grime and sweat that clung to my skin, to feel the rush of the current against my body and let it carry away the burdens that weighed heavily upon my soul.

But the memory of my experience with the lagoon held me back, a nagging fear that whispered in the back of my mind, warning me of the mysteries that lurked beneath the surface. With a heavy sigh, I settled for removing my sweat-stained shirt, the fabric peeling away from my skin like a second layer, exposing my torso to the crisp morning air. The chill sent goosebumps racing across my flesh, a shiver running down my spine as I knelt along the riverbank, my knees sinking into the soft, damp earth.

I took a moment to steel myself, to gather the courage to face the icy waters that beckoned me forward. With a deep breath, I plunged my hands into the rushing stream, the cold shocking my system. The water's touch was like a thousand needles pricking my skin, a sensation that was both invigorating and painful all at once.

My fingers worked methodically, scrubbing at the dirt and grime that clung to my skin, the water washing away the evidence of the previous day's trials. I cupped my hands, bringing the cool liquid to my face, feeling it trickle down my neck and chest, a momentary reprieve from the warmth that seemed to radiate from my very core. Despite the water's chill, the experience left me feeling somewhat refreshed, the droplets clinging to my tousled blonde hair and trickling down my bare skin, leaving behind a lingering sense of coolness that seeped into my weary bones.

I lost myself in the task, my mind wandering as I worked, the repetitive motions of scrubbing and rinsing becoming a sort of meditation, a way to quiet my thoughts. Time seemed to slip away, the minutes bleeding into each other as I focused on the sensation of the water against my skin, the rush of the current filling my ears and drowning out the rest of the world.

With a shuddering breath, I pulled myself to my feet, my muscles aching from the prolonged kneeling.

Gathering my shirt, the damp fabric heavy in my hands, I began the trudge back to camp, my bare feet sinking into the soft dust with each step. I yearned for the luxury of a soft, fluffy towel to dry off the remnants of the water, to wrap myself in its comforting warmth and block out the harsh realities of the world, if only for a moment.

❖

Approaching the camp, the sound of Glenda's frustrated curses filled the morning air, her voice rising above the crackling of the campfire, the intensity of her expletives revealing the depth of her exasperation. I glanced over her shoulder, my eyes surveying the scorched bacon sizzling in the pan, its charred appearance signalling its imminent demise, a culinary catastrophe in the making.

"Everything alright, Glenda?" I asked, concern lacing my words, my brow furrowed as I fixed my gaze on the bacon that seemed to be teetering on the edge of inedibility, a blackened mess that bore little resemblance to the crispy, golden strips I craved.

"How the hell am I supposed to control the heat on this thing?" Glenda vented, her annoyance palpable as she tossed the ruined strips of bacon into the glowing coals with a huff, the burnt offering disappearing into the flames with a sizzle. "Bacon should be fuck-easy to cook!" she exclaimed, her voice tinged with frustration and disbelief.

Sympathy washed over me, a flicker of amusement tugging at the corners of my lips, but I managed to suppress the smile that threatened to escape, knowing that it would only fuel Glenda's ire.

"Would you like me to take over?" I offered, squatting beside Glenda and reaching out to take hold of the frying pan, my fingers brushing against the warm metal, ready to relieve her of the burden of breakfast duty.

"No!" she replied curtly, yanking the pan out of my reach, her grip tightening on the handle. She took a few deep breaths, her chest rising and falling as she struggled to regain her composure, the frustration slowly dissipating from her features. "I need to be able to get this right," she said, her voice softer now, tinged with a hint of determination.

"Well, perhaps the easiest way to control the heat is to move to a cooler or hotter part of the fire," I suggested, pointing towards a spot that seemed to offer a lower, more manageable heat, the flames flickering gently in the morning breeze. "It should give you better control over the cooking process," I added, hoping that my advice would prove helpful.

"Thanks," Glenda responded, adjusting her position around the edge of the fire, following my guidance, her movements more deliberate now, a newfound focus in her eyes.

"And normally, it's better to cook on a grill plate to keep the pan level, but unfortunately, we don't have one," I added, silently lamenting the lack of proper cooking equipment. *Especially with you as their supervisor, it seems*, I thought to myself, the words remaining unspoken, a flicker of humour in the midst of the drama.

Glenda gazed into the crackling fire, her eyes narrowing in deep concentration, the flickering flames casting a warm glow on her face, illuminating the determination etched into her features. "Can I rest the pan on the coals?" she asked, her voice tinged with a hint of uncertainty.

"I wouldn't. Not with bacon and eggs, anyway. They'd end up like charcoal very quickly," I replied, suppressing a shudder at the thought of the culinary disaster that would ensue. "You'll just have to try and keep your arm as steady as you can, and remember to raise or lower the pan from the heat if it gets too hot," I advised, silently hoping that if the bacon remained in Glenda's capable hands at all times, it might have a better chance of survival, of emerging from the fire as something edible.

"Of course," Glenda replied, nodding her head in understanding, a flicker of confidence returning to her eyes as she absorbed my words, her grip on the pan loosening slightly.

"I'll talk to Paul and see if he can convince Luke to bring us some more camping equipment," I said, a glimmer of optimism surprising even myself. *I'm supposed to be finding a way out of this place, not settling*, I silently reminded myself, a pang of guilt twisting in my gut.

"Thank you," Glenda acknowledged, placing several more rashers of bacon into the sizzling pan, the sound of the meat hitting the hot metal filling the air, mingling with the aroma of cooking breakfast.

The immediate mouth-watering scent filled the air, triggering a hungry rumble in my belly, my stomach clenching with anticipation. *Please don't screw this up*, I silently pleaded, my taste buds tingling at the thought of crispy bacon.

Before I could head towards the tent, my mind already drifting to the tasks that lay ahead, Glenda's voice called out to me, her tone firm yet not unkind, catching my attention. "Oh, Kain?"

I turned to face her, curiosity piqued.

"Yeah?" I replied, shifting my focus towards her, my brow furrowed slightly in anticipation.

"Paul went to the Drop Zone. Can you please find him and let him know that breakfast is mandatory for everyone this morning?" Glenda requested.

"Sure," I responded, nodding in affirmation, a flicker of understanding passing between us. Without another word, I turned and disappeared into the tent.

❖

"Glenda's cooking breakfast," I called out as soon as I spotted Paul wandering around the Drop Zone. I had hurried over to find him almost immediately after realising that heading back to my tent for fresh clothes would be a futile endeavour—I had no fresh clothes to begin with, the harsh reality of our situation hitting me once again.

Paul looked up, surprise etched on his face, his eyebrows raising slightly. "You came all this way just to tell me that?" he asked, a hint of amusement colouring his voice, a small smile tugging at the corners of his mouth.

I chuckled nervously, rubbing the back of my neck, the skin still damp from my impromptu wash in the river. "She insists that we all have a hearty meal. We need to keep our strength up for the busy day ahead of us," I explained, hoping that Glenda's cooking would be palatable at the very least, my stomach grumbling in anticipation at the thought of a warm, filling breakfast.

"Sounds like she's got plans," Paul replied, a hint of laughter in his tone, his eyes crinkling at the edges.

"I believe so," I said, standing beside him, my gaze sweeping over the Drop Zone, taking in the seemingly endless expanse of dusty ground and scattered supplies. "So, what's your assessment?" I asked, curious to hear his thoughts on our current situation.

Paul seemed momentarily caught off guard by the question, his brow furrowing slightly as he considered his response. "Well, I'd really like us to get some more concrete poured for the sheds. Nearly everything here has been here for less than twenty-four hours and it's already covered in dust," he said, swiping his finger along the top of a large tent box nearby and showing me his freshly dusted fingertip, the fine particles clinging to his skin.

I gazed at the fine layer of dust that seemed to coat everything in the Drop Zone, my shoulders slumping slightly. "I don't think it matters what we do," I sighed, realising the futility of the situation, the dust an ever-present reminder of the harsh environment. "We're never going to stop that. But the sheds should help," I added, trying to inject a note of optimism into my voice.

"Hmm," Paul mused, lost in his own thoughts, his eyes distant as he considered our options.

"Any more tents?" I inquired absentmindedly, momentarily forgetting about the nearby box.

"Yeah," Paul replied, his gaze shifting to the box in question. "Looks like there's one left. We can take the boxes back to camp when we go for breakfast," he suggested, a note of practicality in his voice.

"Yeah," I agreed with a chuckle, the thought of Glenda's determination bringing a smile to my face. "I'm sure Glenda will have it up quick."

Paul nodded in agreement, a flicker of admiration in his eyes. "She definitely knows what she's doing with them. Far more than I do," he admitted, a self-deprecating laugh escaping his lips.

"And me," I added, a tinge of self-doubt seeping into my words, as I considered my own inadequacies.

Paul glanced at me, a reassuring look in his eyes, his hand reaching out to give my shoulder a gentle squeeze. "Don't doubt yourself, Kain. You've got amazing skills," he said, his voice filled with a quiet conviction that caught me off guard.

I nodded shyly, accepting his words, a flicker of warmth spreading through my chest at the unexpected praise. But before I could dwell on it further, my attention was drawn elsewhere, my eyes catching sight of something wedged between two boxes. "Is that a pillow?" I asked suddenly, my head snapping upwards, my voice rising with excitement.

"Where?" Paul squinted, following the direction of my pointing finger, his gaze scanning the area intently.

"Wedged between those two boxes," I answered, manoeuvring around the tent boxes and carefully navigating between the neatly stacked shed boxes, my heart pounding with anticipation. "It is!" I exclaimed with a cheer, pulling the pillow free, the soft fabric a welcome comfort in my hands.

"Just one?" Paul asked, a hint of disappointment in his voice, his shoulders sagging slightly.

"Looks like it," I confirmed, making my way back to Paul, the pillow clutched tightly to my chest like a precious treasure.

A frown of frustration creased Paul's forehead, his brow furrowing. "Like sharing a single pillow will do us much good," he muttered bitterly, the words tinged with a hint of resentment.

"What are you two creeping around for?" Luke's familiar voice cut through the air as he approached the Drop Zone.

Paul and I spun around, our attention swiftly shifting towards Luke, our faces a mix of surprise and apprehension.

"Hey, Luke!" Paul called out sharply in reply, his voice carrying a note of accusation. "When did you drop off the sleeping bags?" he demanded, his eyes narrowing slightly.

"Umm," Luke paused, pondering the question, his brow furrowing in concentration. "Would have been some time late yesterday afternoon or early evening. Why?" he asked, a hint of confusion in his voice.

"Didn't you think it might be a good idea to let someone know?" Paul retorted, annoyance lacing his words as he thrust the single pillow at Luke, the gesture filled with frustration.

"I... uh..." Luke stumbled, momentarily lost for words, his eyes widening slightly at the unexpected confrontation.

"If Glenda hadn't sent Kain over to collect the box of tent pegs, we wouldn't have had the sleeping bags last night," Paul argued, frustration evident in his voice, his cheeks flushing with anger. He turned to me, silently seeking support, his eyes pleading for me to back him up.

Raising my hands in a gesture of surrender, I backed away slightly, not wanting to get caught in the middle of their argument. I knew better than to get involved unnecessarily in a sibling squabble, the memories of my own sisters' fights fresh in my mind.

"I have a lot planned to bring through the Portal for you, and I don't have time to take it further than the Drop Zone," Luke defended himself, a hint of exasperation in his voice, his hands spread wide in a placating gesture. "Besides, wasn't the Drop Zone your idea? You're the one who told me to leave stuff there," he pointed out, his voice rising slightly.

"Yeah, but you need to at least tell someone," Paul fired back, his voice tinged with annoyance, his fists clenching at his sides.

Stepping back even further, I feigned interest in the items surrounding me, pretending to examine a nearby box with great intensity, trying to distance myself from the escalating argument. However, I couldn't help but overhear their continued exchange, the words drifting over to me on the warm, dry breeze.

"I don't have time for that crap, Paul!" Luke snapped, his face twisting into a scowl. "You, or someone else, will just have to check frequently," he said.

Paul fell silent for a moment, seemingly taken aback by Luke's response, his mouth opening and closing as he struggled to find the right words.

"Hey, Kain!" Luke suddenly called out, redirecting his attention towards me, his voice cutting through the tense silence.

My back stiffened, a sense of unease washing over me, a knot forming in the pit of my stomach. I really didn't want to get involved, the thought of being dragged into their argument filling me with dread. I tried to send Luke a telepathic message, pleading with him to spare me from any further entanglement, my eyes wide and imploring.

"Do you have the keys to your ute on you?" Luke asked, his voice calm, a distinct contrast to the tension that crackled between him and Paul.

Patting my jeans, I reached into the back pocket, my fingers brushing against the cool metal of the keys. "Actually, I do," I replied, raising the keys in the air, a genuine sense of surprise evident in my voice.

"If you give them to me, I'll bring it through," Luke offered, a glimmer of hesitation in his voice, as if he wasn't entirely sure of the wisdom of his own suggestion.

"Really?" I asked, stepping closer to Luke, my excitement growing, the prospect of having a familiar piece of home with me filling me with a sense of comfort and nostalgia.

Luke nodded, a small smile tugging at the corners of his lips, his eyes softening slightly.

"That's mad!" I exclaimed, dropping the keys into Luke's waiting hand, the metal clinking softly against his palm.

Paul's expression suddenly turned sour, his brow furrowing in disapproval. "But what happens when it runs out of fuel?" he interjected, his words cutting through the momentary excitement, bringing me crashing back down to reality.

Shit! I thought, my heart sinking, a cold dread seeping into my veins. I hadn't even considered that possibility, too caught up in the thrill of having my ute to think about the practicalities of the situation.

"I'm working on a solution for that," Luke replied cryptically, his voice low and mysterious, a hint of a smile playing at the corners of his mouth.

"Like what?" Paul pressed, a hint of skepticism in his voice, his arms crossing over his chest.

Luke shrugged, his shoulders rising and falling in a noncommittal gesture. "I'm not one hundred percent sure yet. But I'm getting close," he assured us, his voice filled with a confidence that I couldn't help but envy.

"That's very vague of you," Paul commented dryly, his eyebrows raising in disbelief.

"Have you spoken to my mother?" I interjected, curiosity seeping into my voice.

"Umm... nope," Luke replied nonchalantly, his voice casual and unconcerned.

"So, she has no idea where I am?" I asked, a twinge of disappointment colouring my words, my shoulders slumping slightly at the confirmation of my fears.

Luke shook his head, his expression neutral. "Not that I know of," he said, his voice devoid of any real emotion.

"Don't you think you should tell her?" Paul chimed in, his voice laced with concern, his eyes flickering between me and Luke. "You know that his fiancée is pregnant, right?" he added, his voice rising slightly with indignation.

"Umm," Luke hesitated, clearly agitated by Paul's accusation, his jaw clenching slightly. "Have you asked me to tell Claire and the kids where you are?" he retorted, his voice sharp and cutting.

Paul fell silent, a sheepish expression crossing his face, his cheeks flushing slightly at the realisation of his own hypocrisy.

I took that as a no, a bitter taste filling my mouth at the thought of our loved ones back home, oblivious to our fate.

"That's what I thought," Luke sneered, his frustration seeping into his words, his eyes flashing with anger. He took a deep breath, attempting to regain composure, his shoulders rising and falling with the effort. "The less anyone outside Clivilius knows of its existence, the better. It's safer for all of us that way," Luke explained, his voice firm and unyielding, his gaze intense.

Paul nodded in agreement, accepting Luke's reasoning, a flicker of understanding passing between them. I, however, hesitated, torn between wanting my mother to show concern for my well-being and the realisation that bringing her to a place like this might not be the wisest decision, the thought of exposing her to the horrors I had already faced filling me with a sense of dread.

"But I guess I could try and bring your mother through the Portal if you'd like," Luke offered, a hint of hesitation in his voice, as if he wasn't entirely comfortable with the idea himself.

"No," I replied, shaking my head. "I think we could do without her... for now," I added quickly, not wanting to completely shut the door on the possibility, my heart aching at the thought of being separated from her indefinitely. While I yearned for my mother's concern, the idea of bringing her into this uncertain world seemed foolish, a risk I wasn't willing to take.

"Well, I'd better go get your ute," Luke said, turning to walk away, his footsteps crunching on the dusty ground.

"Oh, hey, Luke!" Paul called out, attempting to regain Luke's attention, his voice carrying a note of urgency. "Can you bring Jamie's car through too?" he asked, a hopeful note in his voice.

"Umm, nope," Luke teased mischievously, a grin spreading across his face.

"Why not?" Paul asked, annoyance evident in his tone, his brow furrowing in frustration.

Luke's expression grew more serious, his smile fading. "I need it to drive to Collinsvale," he explained matter-of-factly.

"Where the hell is Collinsvale?" Paul asked, turning to me with a mixture of confusion and curiosity, his eyebrows raising in question.

"Not far from his house," I replied, unable to stop myself from adding to the conversation, leaving me wondering whether I was about to get dragged into another disagreement.

Paul turned back to Luke, a hint of exasperation in his voice. "Oh, so, you could walk there then," he told him, his tone slightly condescending.

"It's not that close," I chimed in, trying to lighten the mood and defuse the tension that was once again settling between the brothers, a nervous laugh escaping my lips.

"Gotta go now," Luke declared, his voice carrying a finality that brooked no further arguments. With a smile and a wave, he made his way toward the Portal, disappearing into its swirling colours, the shimmering vortex swallowing him whole.

Glenda's distinct yet unintelligible voice carried across the listless air, the sound faint and distant.

"Breakfast must be ready," Paul remarked, redirecting the conversation away from the disagreement, his voice filled with a forced cheer that didn't quite reach his eyes.

"We might as well wait for Luke to bring my ute. Imagine everyone's surprise when we drive it back to camp," I said, hoping to delay our return a little longer.

"Yeah, it will be a surprise," Paul agreed, a sense of excitement returning to his voice, his eyes sparkling with anticipation. "By the way, have you seen Jamie or Joel yet this morning?" he asked, his voice casual.

"Yeah, I went and saw them just after you left," I replied casually, attempting to downplay the encounter, the memories of the uncomfortable tension in the tent still fresh in my mind. "I'm surprised Luke didn't ask about them," I added, a hint of confusion in my voice.

"I think Luke's a bit distracted right now," Paul said, his gaze following Luke's retreat, a flicker of concern crossing his face.

Before I could respond, both of our jaws dropped in unison as my ute came bunny-hopping through the Portal, stalling just inches away from a proper arrival, the engine sputtering and dying. Laughter erupted from deep within us, bubbling up from our chests and spilling out into the air, our bodies bent over with the force of our mirth, tears streaming down our faces.

A sulking Luke emerged from the ute, his frustration palpable, his face twisted into a scowl.

"Luke! Wait!" Paul called out, struggling to stifle his laughter, his voice strained with the effort.

Luke paused, his steps halting, but he didn't turn around. "I said no," he replied dismissively, his tone slightly annoyed, his shoulders stiff with tension.

Curiosity stirred within me, but the excitement of seeing the ute overwhelmed my desire to eavesdrop on the brothers' conversation. I made a beeline for the driver's seat, my hands gripping the leather steering wheel, the familiar sensation sending a thrill of excitement through my veins. Closing my eyes for a moment, I allowed myself to imagine the sensation of my foot pressing down on the accelerator, the engine roaring to life, the wind whipping through my hair as we sped across the barren landscape. A mischievous smile crept across my face, surprised at my own restraint in not actually turning the key, the temptation almost too great to resist.

Glancing back at Paul and Luke, their voices still locked in conversation, their faces tense, I found myself grateful that their disagreement remained verbal, the clashes between my own sisters often taking a more physical turn, leaving me with memories of countless squabbles and bruised egos.

Impatience tugged at my senses as I tapped my foot restlessly on the vehicle's floor, the rhythmic sound echoing in the enclosed space. I stole occasional glances at Paul and Luke, silently urging them to bring their conversation to a swift conclusion, my eagerness to return to camp and show off my newfound prize growing with each passing moment.

Just as Luke disappeared through the Portal, the shimmering vortex swallowing him whole once more, I honked the horn, the loud blast cutting through the stillness of the air. It was a playful signal that Paul's attention was no longer required, a reminder that there was no reason for him to stand idly by any longer. I couldn't help but wear a grin, the thrill of the moment overtaking any lingering unease.

Paul turned to look at me, his eyes widening with surprise, his eyebrows raising in question. With a few brisk strides, he joined me in the passenger seat, his body sinking into the worn fabric, a sigh of contentment escaping his lips.

"Let's go!" I exclaimed, my voice brimming with enthusiasm as I gave Paul a thumbs-up, my eyes sparkling with barely contained excitement.

"No, wait!" Paul cried out, his voice filled with urgency, his hand reaching out to grip my arm, stopping me from turning the key in the ignition.

I glanced at him, a mix of confusion and impatience clouding my features, my brow furrowing in frustration. "What now?" I asked incredulously, my voice tinged with annoyance.

"We may as well pack those tent boxes in the back," Paul suggested, a mischievous twinkle in his eyes, his lips curving into a sly grin.

A frown tugged at my brow, a surge of annoyance rising within me, my fingers tightening on the steering wheel. The idea of delaying our triumphant return to camp, even for a moment, filled me with a sense of irritation, the prospect of manual labour dampening my enthusiasm.

"It'll save us coming back for them," Paul prodded, his voice cajoling, his eyebrows raising in a silent plea.

"Fine," I huffed, my voice laced with irritation, my shoulders slumping in defeat. "But make it quick!" I added.

Paul laughed at my reaction, the sound filled with genuine amusement, his eyes crinkling at the corners. He quickly scrambled out of his seat, his movements filled with a newfound energy, his feet hitting the ground with a soft thud.

"You're helping too," he declared playfully, his voice carrying a note of challenge, his eyebrows raising in expectation.

My eyes rolled, a heavy sigh escaping my lips, the sound filled with resignation. But with a grumble of acquiescence, I opened my door and reluctantly stepped out of the vehicle, my feet dragging slightly on the dusty ground.

The task ahead may have been an inconvenience, a delay in our much-anticipated return, but if it meant saving ourselves a return trip, I begrudgingly accepted the challenge. With a determination born of necessity, I made my way towards the tent boxes, my steps heavy with the weight of my annoyance.

As we worked together to load the boxes into the back of the ute, our muscles straining with the effort, sweat beading on our brows, I couldn't help but feel a flicker of camaraderie, a sense of shared purpose that transcended our individual frustrations. Despite the disagreements and tensions that had marred the morning, there was a certain comfort in the knowledge that we were all in this together, bound by the strange circumstances that had brought us to this weird world.

Having moved the ute closer to the Drop Zone during the process, and now, with the last box securely stowed, I slammed the tailgate shut, the sound echoing across the barren landscape. Dusting off my hands on my jeans, I turned to Paul, a satisfied grin spreading across my face.

"Ready to make a grand entrance?" I asked, my voice filled with a renewed sense of excitement, my earlier annoyance forgotten in the thrill of the moment.

Paul nodded, a matching grin on his own face, his eyes sparkling with anticipation. "Let's do it," he said, his voice filled with a determination that mirrored my own.

With a whoop of joy, I slid back into the driver's seat, my hands gripping the steering wheel with a sense of purpose. As Paul climbed in beside me, the engine roared to life, the sound filling the air with a promise of adventure.

❖

Carefully, I manoeuvred the packed ute through the Drop Zone, its bulky frame navigating between the towering rock piles that stood like stoic sentinels, marking the entrance to the site. The steering wheel felt solid beneath my hands, the vibrations of the engine thrumming through my fingers as I guided the vehicle with a sense of purpose. With a confident turn of the wheels, we embarked on the chosen path, veering left towards our destination, the anticipation building in my chest with each passing moment.

The engine roared with power, the sound filling the air with a primal growl that sent a thrill down my spine. The tires churned through the thick layer of dust that blanketed the ground, the coarse particles flying up in our wake, creating a hazy cloud that obscured our view. The impact sent vibrant plumes of red and orange swirling into the air around us, painting the landscape in a surreal hue that seemed to pulse with an otherworldly energy. The ute's tires kicked up a swirling storm of dust, enveloping us in a cocoon of colour and motion, the world beyond reduced to a blur of muted shapes and shadows.

"What are you doing?" Paul asked, his voice tinged with both excitement and apprehension, the words barely audible over the roar of the engine. He clutched the sides of his seat tightly, his knuckles turning white with tension, his body bracing against the jolts and bumps of the uneven terrain.

"Just a short detour," I replied, unable to contain the wide grin that spread across my face, the exhilaration of the moment overtaking any sense of caution or restraint. The ute took a sharp turn to the left, veering around the roughly-marked perimeter of the Drop Zone, bouncing along the uneven ground with a jarring motion that sent shockwaves through our bodies.

Laughter erupted from us, the sound mingling with the growl of the engine in a raucous symphony of joy and abandon. The ute roared through varying depths of dust, surmounting small hills and dips with a reckless abandon that sent our hearts racing, the adrenaline pumping through our veins in a dizzying rush. The landscape unfolded before us, a captivating display of reds, browns, and oranges stretching out for kilometres, the colours shifting and blending in a mesmerising dance that seemed to pulse with a life of its own. The vista abruptly ended at the base of majestic mountains that pierced the blue sky, their jagged peaks reaching towards the heavens in a silent challenge to the forces of nature.

"How much petrol?" Paul yelled out as the ute neared the top of another hill, his voice strained with a mix of excitement and trepidation.

"Still three-quarters," I replied, grinning widely as the ute peaked once more, the engine revving with a triumphant roar as we crested the summit, the world stretching out before us in a breathtaking panorama of colour and light.

"Floor it!" Paul yelled, his excitement contagious, his eyes sparkling with a wild abandon that mirrored my own.

I eagerly complied, my foot pressing hard on the accelerator, the pedal sinking to the floor with a satisfying click. The ute surged forward, propelled by a burst of power that sent us hurtling across the flat terrain, the landscape blurring into a kaleidoscope of colours as we tore through the dust, leaving behind a thick cloud in our wake. Our boisterous adventure carried on for a little over a hundred meters, the ute bouncing and jostling with each bump and dip, our bodies slamming against the seats with a jarring force that only added to the thrill of the moment.

Suddenly, without warning, the engine sputtered and died, the ute coasting to a stop with a final, shuddering gasp. The silence that followed was deafening, the absence of the engine's roar leaving us feeling strangely bereft, as if a vital part of ourselves had been ripped away.

Paul turned to me, his eyes wide with confusion, his brow furrowed in disbelief. "What the hell?" he asked, his voice filled with a mixture of surprise and frustration, the words hanging heavy in the sudden stillness.

I attempted to restart the engine, turning the key in the ignition repeatedly, my fingers gripping the metal with a desperate intensity. But the engine stubbornly refused to comply, the silence broken only by the feeble clicks of the starter, each one a mocking reminder of our predicament.

With synchronised frustration, we opened our doors and stepped out of the vehicle, our feet hitting the ground with a dull thud that sent up small puffs of dust. We gathered at the front of the ute, our faces etched with identical expressions of concern and dismay.

I lifted the bonnet, the metal hot to the touch, and a string of expletives slipped past my lips as I stared at the thick layer of dust that coated the engine, the particles clinging to every surface in a suffocating blanket. "How are we going to clean that?" I exclaimed, my voice tinged with exasperation, my hands gesturing helplessly at the clogged machinery.

Paul leaned in, his face set with determination, and blew forcefully into the confined space, his breath sending a large cloud of fine dust billowing into the air, the particles hanging suspended for a moment before slowly settling back down. "Help me blow," he said, looking over his shoulder at me, his eyes glinting with a hint of mischief.

Surprised by the simplicity of his suggestion, I shrugged my shoulders and leaned in beside Paul, our faces mere inches apart as we exhaled with all our might, our breath mingling in a focused stream of air that sent the dust flying in all directions, coating our skin and clothes with a fine layer of grit.

"It's working," Paul exclaimed, stepping back to take a breath of fresh air, his face flushed with exertion, a triumphant grin playing at the corners of his mouth.

Determined, I rushed back to the driver's seat, my fingers fumbling with the key as I turned it in the ignition, my heart pounding with a desperate hope. A plume of dust floated out from under the hood, causing me to momentarily doubt the effectiveness of our impromptu cleaning efforts.

But then, Paul stepped into view, his face illuminated with excitement, his eyes wide with disbelief. He gave me two enthusiastic thumbs up, signalling that the engine had started and we were good to go, his grin stretching from ear to ear. With a satisfying thud, he closed the bonnet and settled back into his seat, his body sinking into the worn fabric with a contented sigh.

The journey back to camp proved challenging, as we narrowly avoided getting stuck several times in areas where the dust was exceptionally thick, the ute's tires spinning helplessly in the loose soil. The engine struggled in certain spots, the sound of its laboured breathing filling the air with a sense of impending doom, forcing us to stop intermittently and clear away the dust from the air filter and radiator to prevent overheating, our hands growing black with grime as we worked.

"We need some roads," I sighed, glancing over at Paul as we approached our small settlement, the makeshift tents and shelters coming into view, a welcome sight after our harrowing journey. "We need to contain this bloody dust!" I exclaimed, my voice tinged with frustration, my hands gesturing at the swirling clouds that seemed to follow us wherever we went.

Paul furrowed his brow, deep in thought, his expression one of concentration as he pondered the problem, seemingly unconvinced by the feasibility of my suggestion.

"Even if we just clear a few trails down to the hard crust beneath, it should be good enough to drive on," I encouraged, my voice filled with a newfound enthusiasm, eager to find a solution to our dusty dilemma.

Paul's eyes brightened momentarily, a flicker of interest sparking in their depths, before dimming again. "There's so much to do," he muttered softly, his voice barely audible over the rumble of the engine, his gaze distant and unfocused.

"We need a bulldozer," I chuckled, attempting to inject some optimism into the conversation, my voice filled with a forced levity.

Paul looked at me, his expression serious, his eyes filled with a sudden intensity that caught me off guard. "That's actually not a bad idea," he said, his voice filled with a quiet determination.

"More people?" I squinted ahead as we crested a hill, my eyes scanning the landscape, searching for any signs of life beyond our small group, a flicker of hope stirring in my chest at the thought of reinforcements.

"Huh?" Paul turned his attention back to the front, his brow furrowed in confusion, his mind still lost in thoughts of bulldozers and roads.

As I slowly brought the ute to a stop in the camp, the engine sputtering and dying with a final, shuddering gasp, my gaze fell upon two unfamiliar figures standing near Glenda, their silhouettes stark against the dusty backdrop.

"Shit!" Paul exclaimed, his voice filled with realisation, his eyes widening with a sudden understanding. "I forgot about Karen!" he said, his tone filled with a mixture of guilt and apprehension.

Who the hell is Karen? I wondered, my curiosity piqued, as I peered through the front windscreen at the tall, lanky woman and her short, frumpy companion standing beside Glenda, their faces unfamiliar. Questions swirled in my mind, a growing sense of unease settling in the pit of my stomach as I contemplated the implications of their presence, the delicate balance of our small group suddenly thrown into disarray by the arrival of these mysterious strangers.

Yet, the adrenaline still coursing through my veins from the thrill and excitement of our ute adventure quickly trumped any further thoughts of concern.

EMERGING HOPES

4338.208.2

"That was bloody awesome," I exclaimed, slapping Paul a high-five as we met at the front of the dust-covered ute. The exhilaration of our impromptu joyride lingered in the air, a momentary escape from the harsh realities of our new world. The ute stood before us, a testament to our reckless abandon, its once-shiny exterior now caked in a thick layer of red dust, a badge of honour from our thrilling adventure.

"Apart from clogging the engine!" Paul laughed, his face beaming with excitement, his eyes sparkling with the thrill of our shared adventure.

I grinned back at him, the rush of adrenaline still pumping through my body, my heart pounding with the residual excitement. "Come on," I said, giving Paul an encouraging glance, my hand resting on his shoulder, the fabric of his shirt rough beneath my fingertips. "You gotta admit, even that was fun." The words tumbled out, laced with a childlike enthusiasm that felt foreign in this unforgiving landscape.

Before our playful banter could continue, Glenda's voice cut through the air, interrupting our camaraderie, her tone holding a hint of reservation that immediately set me on edge. "We have two new guests," she announced.

My head swivelled in Glenda's direction, curiosity piqued, my gaze landing on the unfamiliar figures standing before us. The tall, lanky woman and the short, frumpy man stood there, their faces etched with a mix of uncertainty and determination, their eyes scanning the surroundings with a keen intensity that made my skin prickle.

"I wouldn't call them guests," said Uncle Jamie from where he stood at the edge of the tent's canopy, his voice carrying a note of skepticism that echoed my own thoughts. "They're not going anywhere." The words settled like a lead weight in the pit of my stomach, a stark reminder of our own entrapment in this world.

My uncle's words sent my stomach lurching, a wave of nausea washing over me. I didn't need to be reminded about my fiancée and unborn child, the thought of them waiting for me back home, unaware of my fate, tearing at my heart with a fresh raw intensity. The likelihood that I was never going to be going home to them, never going to hold my baby in my arms or see Brianne's smiling face again, was a bitter pill to swallow, a reality that I couldn't quite bring myself to face.

"I'm Paul," said Paul, walking toward the couple with a welcoming smile, his hand outstretched in a gesture of friendship. He extended his hand to the man, who firmly shook it.

"Chris Owen," the thin-haired man replied, his voice calm and steady, his eyes meeting Paul's with a quiet intensity. "And this is my wife, Karen." He gestured to the woman beside him, who nodded in acknowledgment, her gaze sweeping over us with a calculating air.

"Kain," I said, following Paul's lead, and offering my hand, the skin rough and calloused from the hard work of survival. "Jamie's nephew." As I approached, I couldn't shake the uneasiness that crept up within me, a sense of foreboding that settled in the pit of my stomach like a coiled snake.

"I see you've met Jamie," Paul said, motioning towards my uncle, who stood stoically at the edge of the tent's canopy, his face an unreadable mask. Henri was by his side, looking both wary and intrigued by the newcomers, his ears perked up in alert.

Karen nodded, her expression guarded. "We've only just met him," she replied, her voice smooth and measured. "But Luke has told us a lot about him over the years." The mention of Luke's name sent a jolt of surprise through me, the realisation that these strangers had a connection to him adding another layer of intrigue to the situation.

My mind churned with questions, the gears turning as I tried to make sense of this new development, but the weight of my own internal turmoil kept me at a distance, a barrier between myself and the others. Slowly, I began inching towards my ute, finding solace in its familiar presence amidst the uncertainty, the cool metal of the door handle a comforting anchor.

"Us?" Chris interjected, his forehead wrinkling with confusion, his brow furrowed in thought. "I've never heard his name before.".

Karen turned to her husband, correcting him gently, her voice soft and patient. "Not you, darling. Jane," she clarified, the name falling from her lips like a secret, a piece of the puzzle that I couldn't quite fit into place. *Who was this Jane, and what role did she play in all of this?*

Paul chimed in, breaking the tension, his voice filled with a forced levity that didn't quite reach his eyes. "Ah, Jane. You must be one of Luke's bus friends," he said with a chuckle.

"Bus friends?" I muttered under my breath, my skepticism shining through, my eyebrows raised in disbelief. I couldn't help but scoff at the notion of Luke having bus friends, the idea seeming absurd. *What kind of person had bus friends?*

Karen shared my perplexity, her brow furrowed in thought. "Yes," she replied simply, the word hanging in the air, a confirmation that only raised more questions than it answered.

Turning to Chris, I couldn't suppress my curiosity any longer, the need for answers burning within me like a flame.

"But where is Luke?" I asked, realising that their presence was likely due to him, yet he was conspicuously absent, a ghost in the machine of our new existence. I looked to Chris, hoping for some clue, some hint of the truth that seemed to be elusive.

"He's not here," Karen responded on behalf of her husband, her words cryptic and unsatisfying, only serving to deepen the mystery that surrounded their arrival at our camp.

Glenda's voice broke the silence, her disappointment evident in the slump of her shoulders and the weariness in her eyes. "Appears this was another accident," she said, the words heavy with the weight of past experiences, of the seemingly endless string of misfortunes that had brought us all to this place.

A bitter taste filled my mouth as I muttered, "Figures." After my own chaotic arrival in this place, another 'accident' seemed to be the norm, a twisted sort of fate that seemed to govern our lives now.

Paul seized the opportunity to redirect the conversation, his eyes alight with a newfound interest. "Not to be rude, but what do you actually do?" he asked, addressing the couple, his gaze flickering between them with barely contained eagerness.

Karen's face beamed with pride as she responded, her voice filled with a quiet confidence that seemed to radiate from her very being. "I'm an entomologist," she declared, the word rolling off her tongue with a practiced ease.

Paul's confusion was apparent as he asked, "A what?" his eyebrows raising in a quizzical expression, his head tilting slightly to the side.

"She studies bugs," I interjected, trying to simplify Karen's profession, the words coming to me unbidden, as if from some long-forgotten memory. Although I wasn't sure how I knew that piece of information, it seemed to flow naturally from my lips, a remnant of a past life that still clung to me like a shadow.

Karen shot me a glare, her eyes narrowing in disapproval, her voice sharp and cutting as she corrected me sternly. "Insects. Not bugs." The distinction seemed to hold a great deal of importance to her, a matter of professional pride and integrity.

I could feel my cheeks redden with embarrassment under her scrutiny, a hot flush creeping up my neck and spreading across my face. I felt like a scolded child, a bumbling fool who had dared to speak out of turn. "Insects," I muttered, my gaze shifting downward, avoiding further eye contact.

Unfazed by my reaction, Karen continued, her words flowing effortlessly, her passion for her work evident in every syllable. "Insects need an environment to thrive. I work with the University of Tasmania to understand how they contribute to ecosystems and collaborate with local communities and environmental groups to advocate for greater protections." The words painted a picture of a life dedicated to the study and preservation of the natural world, a calling that seemed to transcend the boundaries of our current predicament.

Paul's enthusiasm broke through the awkwardness, his eyes wide with genuine interest, his voice filled with excitement. "That's great!" he exclaimed, clearly impressed by Karen's work, his admiration shining through in his tone and expression. He then turned to Chris, urging him to share his occupation, his curiosity piqued by the couple's backgrounds.

"I do yard work," Chris replied calmly, his words simple and unassuming, leaving us all puzzled, our minds grasping for some deeper meaning behind his statement.

"Yard work?" I asked, struggling to comprehend his role, my brow furrowing in confusion. *Is he a gardener or involved in general maintenance?* The questions swirled in my mind, a tangled web of possibilities that seemed to lead nowhere.

Chris crouched down and silently scooped a handful of dust, the fine particles sifting through his fingers like sand in an hourglass. The action seemed to hold some deeper significance, a silent commentary on the nature of our existence in this barren wasteland.

"It's everywhere!" exclaimed Paul, a little too excitedly for my liking, as though he was almost happy with it, his eyes wide with a manic sort of glee. The dust seemed to hold a strange fascination for him.

Chris let the dust slip through his fingers, his demeanour composed, his face an inscrutable mask. "Yeah, I've noticed that," he replied, unperturbed, his voice even and measured. Looking up at Karen, he added, "But if this is our home now, we'll find a way."

I stared at the couple, a mix of confusion and admiration brewing within me, a strange sort of respect for their resilience in the face of the unknown. Chris hadn't elaborated on his interpretation of yard work, his words cryptic and enigmatic, leaving us to fill in the blanks with our own assumptions and speculations. And their calm acceptance of this new environment seemed unnaturally serene, a tranquility that bordered on the surreal. *Have they been here before?* The thought lingered in my mind, seeming both impossible and plausible at the same time, a paradox that I couldn't quite wrap my head around.

"Call me crazy," Karen said, a smile illuminating her face as she glanced at her husband, her eyes filled with a fierce love and unwavering loyalty. "But I trust Luke." The words hung in the air, a declaration of faith in the face of overwhelming odds, a testament to the bond that seemed to exist between them and Luke.

Uncle Jamie's scoff pierced the air, his sneer conveying his disbelief, his eyes rolling in a gesture of contempt. My shoulders slumped, a sense of melancholy settling within me, a heaviness that seemed to seep into my very bones. I found myself leaning towards my uncle's skepticism rather than Paul's optimism, a natural inclination born of a lifetime of disappointment and broken promises. In a world of uncertainty, their unwavering acceptance felt foreign to me, a luxury that, given the circumstances, I felt that I couldn't afford to indulge in.

Karen stood her ground, a radiant glow enveloping her face, her eyes shining with an inner light that seemed to come from some deep wellspring of hope and positivity. Her words flowed with an effortless grace, a poetry that seemed to transcend the harshness of our surroundings. "A beautiful masterpiece starts with a single brushstroke. This is our blank canvas. Let's create a masterpiece. Together." The words hung in the air, a challenge and an invitation.

A heavy silence descended upon the camp. I could hear the faint call of my ute, its comforting interior beckoning me, a siren song that promised escape and solitude. But despite the pull, my feet refused to budge, and I remained rooted to the ochre ground, lost in contemplation, my mind whirling with the implications of what had just been said.

"I better check-in with Joel," Uncle Jamie finally broke the silence, his voice cutting through the stillness, his departure casting a fleeting shadow over our gathering. "Nice to meet you both," he said with a light wave before retreating into the tent, his figure disappearing into the darkness within.

Curiosity piqued within me as I heard Karen's questioning voice, her words filled with a genuine interest and concern. "Joel?" she asked, her brow furrowing with curiosity, her head tilting slightly to the side in a gesture of inquiry.

Glenda provided an answer, her voice tinged with concern, her eyes flickering towards the tent where Jamie had disappeared. "Jamie's son," she said simply, the words heavy with unspoken meaning.

"He's not been well," Paul quickly interjected, casting a meaningful glance at Glenda, his eyes conveying a silent message that I couldn't quite decipher. "I'm sure he'll be fine after a few days' rest." The words seemed hollow, a flimsy reassurance that did little to alleviate the tension that had settled over the group.

I couldn't help but chuckle inwardly at the understatement, a bitter sort of amusement that held no real mirth. Joel was grappling with a much deeper battle, one that extended beyond mere physical health, a struggle that seemed to consume him from the inside out. The poor boy was struggling to discern his own existence in this newfound reality, a crisis of identity that threatened to tear him apart at the seams.

"Yes," Glenda agreed, her voice filled with empathy as she returned Paul's sideways glance, a silent communication passing between them. "Perhaps you and Kain would be best moving back into the tent for a short time," she suggested, nodding towards the shelter where Jamie and Joel resided, her words filled with a gentle insistence.

My heart sank at the thought, a leaden weight settling in the pit of my stomach. While I appreciated my uncle's presence, a familiar face in a sea of strangers, I was relieved when Paul informed me that we would be moving out, a respite from the suffocating closeness of the tent. I had embarrassed myself in front of my uncle, exposing a part of me that shattered my youthful innocence, a vulnerability that I couldn't bear to face. *I doubt he will ever see me the same way again*, the thought a bitter pill to swallow.

Paul's eyes lit up with an idea, a spark of inspiration that seemed to chase away the shadows that had settled over his face. "We have another tent," he exclaimed, gesturing towards the ute, his voice filled with a renewed sense of purpose and excitement.

Of course! What an idiot I am! The thought hit me like a bolt of lightning, a moment of clarity amidst the fog of my own self-pity. The solution was right there in front of us, a simple answer to a complex problem.

"Brilliant!" cried Glenda, her voice filled with relief, her eyes shining with gratitude, a weight lifted from her shoulders at the prospect of a resolution.

Eager to keep moving, to push forward and leave the past behind, I lifted the first of the tent boxes from the back of the ute, the weight of it solid and reassuring in my hands. Red dust swirled in the air as I gave the top a rough blow, trying to free it from the clinging particles that seemed to permeate every surface.

Chris, seemingly ready to lend a hand, to pitch in and do his part, took the box from me, his grip strong and sure. "Here, let me take that," he offered, his voice filled with a quiet confidence that I couldn't help but admire.

"Thanks," I replied, grateful for the assistance.

"Looks like they got a little dusty," I commented, a wry smile gracing my lips as I handed Karen another box, the understatement of the century.

"Thanks," she said, her gaze lingering on me for a moment, her eyes searching mine for something that I couldn't quite define, a question that remained unspoken. She took the box from my hands, her fingers brushing against mine for the briefest of moments, a fleeting touch that sent a shiver down my spine, before joining her husband, the two of them moving in sync like a well-oiled machine.

Paul gathered the final box, his movements quick and efficient, a sense of purpose driving him forward, a need to keep moving. I felt a sense of urgency building within me, a restless energy that buzzed beneath my skin like an electrical current, a need to escape the confines of the camp and the weight of my own thoughts.

"I'm going back to the Drop Zone for the concrete," I announced, my voice loud and clear. I finally opened the door of the ute, the metal cool and solid beneath my touch, a lifeline to the world beyond.

"Hold up," Paul interjected, his voice sharp and urgent, almost dropping the box in his haste to grab my arm, his fingers digging into my skin with a desperate intensity.

Confusion washed over me, a frown creasing my brow, my eyes narrowing in annoyance. "What?" I asked, my voice tight with irritation, pulling my arm free from his grip, the sudden contact feeling like an invasion of my personal space.

"If we want these sheds up, we have to get this concrete poured ASAP," I explained, my voice filled with a quiet determination, a need to see this task through to the end, to prove myself capable and competent in the face of our growing community.

Frowning, Paul stared at me for a moment, his eyes searching mine for something that I couldn't quite define, a flicker of doubt crossing his face. "Five to seven days?" he asked, his voice hesitant, seeking confirmation of the timeline that stretched out before us.

"Five to seven days," I confirmed with a nod, my voice firm and unwavering, a statement of fact. "Although, if we keep getting these cloudless skies, we might get away with four," I added, a hint of optimism creeping into my tone.

Glenda looked at us quizzically, her brow furrowed in confusion, leaning against the roof of the ute on the opposite side, her eyes darting between Paul and me. "What's five to seven days?" she inquired, her voice filled with curiosity, a need to understand the intricacies of our plan.

"We have to let the concrete... rest," Paul explained, his voice halting, struggling to find the right words to convey the process, the importance of allowing the material to set and cure before putting it to use.

"Ahh," Glenda nodded, understanding dawning upon her, her face brightening with a sudden clarity, a puzzle piece falling into place. "That makes sense," she added, her voice filled with a quiet respect, an appreciation for the knowledge that Paul and I brought to the table.

A smile tugged at the corners of my lips, a flicker of amusement dancing in my eyes as I witnessed Paul's realisation that even Glenda, with her limited experience in construction, grasped the basics of concrete pouring.

Glenda shifted the conversation, her gaze filled with anticipation, her voice eager and curious. "How many sheds are we talking about?" she asked.

Uncertain, I raked my memory, searching for the details amidst the jumble of supplies at the Drop Zone, the mental inventory that I had taken during our last visit. "Not sure. I'll check how many Luke's left us," I replied, my voice trailing off, hoping that the mention of the Drop Zone would hasten our departure, would give me the excuse I needed to escape the confines of the camp.

Paul chimed in, his enthusiasm evident, his voice filled with a newfound energy. "We may as well do as many slabs for the concrete we have," he suggested, his eyes scanning the dusty landscape, his mind mapping out the potential sites for construction. "I don't think we can have too much storage and protection here," he added, his voice filled with a quiet conviction.

Glenda's words echoed Paul's sentiment, her voice filled with a quiet determination. "And Luke can always bring us more sheds," she added, her eyes shining with a glimmer of hope.

Nodding in agreement, I felt a surge of determination, a renewed sense of purpose that drove me forward. "I'll bring all the concrete supplies we have," I declared, my voice firm and unwavering, a statement of intent that left no room for doubt or hesitation. I quickly climbed into the front seat of the ute, my hands gripping the steering wheel with a fierce intensity, my foot hovering over the accelerator, ready to push forward.

"I'll come with you," Paul offered, his voice filled with a quiet enthusiasm, moving towards the passenger side, his hand reaching for the door handle, ready to join me on this mission.

A desire for solitude welled up within me. "No offence, but maybe you'd be better off helping Glenda with the new tent," I suggested, my voice calm and measured, hoping to savour some moments of introspection during my trip to the Drop Zone.

"Chris and I can help," Karen chimed in, appearing beside us after spending a few moments alone by their new tent site, her voice filled with a quiet confidence, a willingness to lend a hand and contribute. "We're used to camping on our short trips. Shouldn't take too long," she added, her voice filled with a quiet assurance, a sense of competence that belied her unfamiliarity with this new world.

"That'd be great," Glenda agreed, her smile warm and genuine, her eyes shining with gratitude, a silent acknowledgment of the help and support that Karen and Chris were offering.

"Okay," Paul relented, shrugging his shoulders, a flicker of disappointment crossing his face before being replaced by a mask of acceptance, a recognition of the practicality of the plan. "So what am I doing now?" he asked, his voice filled with a quiet resignation, a need for direction in the face of his uncertainty.

My mind screamed, *Not coming with me*, but I held my breath, waiting for someone else to fill the void, to give Paul the direction that he so desperately craved.

"You're helping us put up the tent," Glenda answered, her voice filled with a quiet authority, patting Paul on the shoulder, a gesture of reassurance and encouragement.

I released the breath I had been holding, relief washing over me like a wave, a weight lifted from my shoulders at the prospect of a moment of solitude. The engine roared to life, a primal sound that filled the air with a sense of power and purpose, and a wide smile spread across my face, a flicker of excitement dancing in my eyes.

"Great. Let's get to it!" Paul exclaimed, his voice filled with a renewed sense of energy, moving towards the pile of boxes, his hands already reaching for the first one, ready to tackle the task of erecting the next tent.

As the ute vanished over the crest of the hill, the camp receding into the distance behind me, I revelled in the sense of solitude, the vast expanse of the landscape stretching out before me like a blank canvas, waiting to be filled with the colours of my own thoughts and emotions. The faster I drove, the less the wheels struggled against the endless battle with the dust, the tires gripping the hard-packed earth with a fierce intensity, propelling me forward.

Yet, no matter the speed, fine particles found their way into every corner of the air, forever blurring the boundaries between clean and dusty. The dust was a part of me now, a part of my very essence, a symbol of the challenges that lay ahead and the obstacles that I would have to overcome.

❖

Another bead of sweat trickled into my eyes as Uncle Jamie and I meticulously ran the screed over the freshly poured concrete slab for the sheds, the rough surface biting into my palms as we worked. The sun beat down mercilessly, its heat radiating off the hardening concrete in shimmering waves, making the air thick and heavy with the promise of exhaustion. With Glenda lending her assistance, her brow furrowed in concentration as she followed our lead, our progress was steady, and her growing enthusiasm for learning became infectious, a spark of light amidst the drudgery of the task.

Curiously, I asked Glenda, who squatted beside me, her hands coated in a fine layer of dust and grime, "What do you think of them?" The question hung in the air between us, a momentary reprieve from the monotony of our labour.

Glenda scanned the levelled surface before responding, her eyes narrowed against the glare of the sun, "It looks mostly even. Maybe a bit more over there," she pointed to Uncle Jamie's end, her finger tracing a line in the air, a silent critique of our workmanship.

A soft chuckle escaped my lips, the sound strange and foreign in the stillness of the afternoon. "I meant the new people," I clarified, my voice tinged with amusement at the misunderstanding.

Glenda turned her gaze towards the direction Karen and her husband had disappeared, their figures receding into the distance like mirages on the horizon. They seemed to have followed a trail of newfound fertile soil, leaving camp in their wake.

"They are well-educated, especially Karen. I can understand why Luke brought them here," Glenda shared her thoughts, her voice filled with a mix of admiration and curiosity, a hint of something deeper lurking beneath the surface.

"You really think that..." I began, the words forming on my tongue, a question begging to be asked, before our conversation was interrupted by the sound of an excited dog barking, the high-pitched yips cutting through the stillness. I looked at Glenda in surprise, my eyebrows raised in silent question, but she seemed to recognise the distinct bark that was definitely not Duke or Henri, her face lighting up with recognition.

Rising to her feet, Glenda exclaimed, "Lois!" She jogged towards the gorgeous golden retriever bounding into camp from behind the nearest hill, its coat gleaming in the sunlight like spun gold, its tail wagging furiously with unbridled joy.

I glanced at my uncle, who sat back on his haunches, his hands dirty from the concrete, a look of annoyance etched onto his weathered face. "Not another fucking dog," he muttered, just loud enough for me to hear, his voice dripping with disdain.

"Lois, down!" Glenda instructed, redirecting my attention as Lois energetically jumped up at Joel, who emerged from the tent accompanied by Duke and Henri, their own tails wagging in greeting.

A chuckle escaped my lips as I observed the interaction between the dog trio, their antics a welcome distraction from the weight of our responsibilities. Duke approached cautiously, circling around Lois while sniffing curiously, his nose twitching with interest. Suddenly, Lois jumped backward in surprise, her tail wagging excitedly, a playful dance of canine curiosity. Tail down, Henri quickly sought refuge inside the tent, presumably retreating to his bed, where he spent most of his time, a silent observer of the madness unfolding around him.

Approaching the group, Lois continued her playful antics, her barks filling the air with a sense of joy and exuberance, while Duke maintained a careful assessment of her, his eyes never leaving her form, a silent guardian watching over the newcomer.

"We need a road," Paul announced, his voice cutting through the moment like a blade, trudging down the final slope into camp, his face etched with frustration.

Lois left the company of Duke and Joel and bounded toward Paul, her tail wagging incessantly, a furry missile of enthusiasm and affection.

With deft reflexes, Glenda caught the keys that Paul tossed her way before he crouched down to give Lois a friendly ear scratch, his hands sinking into her soft fur.

"Wait, my car's here?" Glenda asked, holding up the keys, her eyes wide with surprise, a flicker of hope dancing in their depths.

"Yeah," replied Paul, still engrossed in petting Lois, his voice muffled by her fur. "It got bogged just over the hill," he added.

A smile played at the corners of my mouth, a flicker of amusement dancing in my eyes. "We definitely need a road," I remarked, assuming Paul would see the humour in the situation. Two dust-covered cars in such a short time... it was almost comical, a twisted sort of irony that seemed to define our existence in this place.

"I wouldn't be laughing if I were you," Paul retorted sternly, his voice sharp and cutting, his eyes narrowing in disapproval. "You wanna be the one to collect the stuff from the car or dig it out of the dust?" he asked, his words a challenge.

My face tightened, caught off guard by Paul's unexpected seriousness, the smile fading from my lips as quickly as it had appeared.

"Honestly," huffed Glenda, frustration evident in her voice, her hands thrown up in exasperation, "this camp is like living with a bunch of children sometimes." With that, she began walking in the direction Paul had pointed, her strides purposeful and determined, Lois and Duke following obediently behind her, their tails wagging in sync.

Uncle Jamie playfully nudged me, a mischievous glint in his eye. "I don't think she has any children," he jested, his voice low and conspiratorial.

"I heard that!" Glenda's voice carried from a distance as she continued her march, her words sharp and cutting, a reminder that nothing seemed to escape her keen ears.

As the BMW came into view, my spirits lifted, a flicker of hope sparking to life in my chest. The car's once-charcoal colour was barely visible beneath the ochre dust, a ghost of its former self, but the sight brought a comforting familiarity from the world I had been torn away from.

"Fuck! You've done a good job, Paul," Uncle Jamie commented, crouching beside the buried back wheel, his fingers tracing the outline of the tire, a look of impressed disbelief etched onto his face.

"It all happened so quickly," Paul replied, his voice tinged with a mix of embarrassment and frustration, his hands rubbing the back of his neck in a gesture of self-consciousness.

"I bet it did," Uncle Jamie chuckled, his candid nature shining through, a glimmer of amusement dancing in his eyes.

I joined in the laughter, the sound bubbling up from my chest, a moment of shared mirth. Uncle Jamie never minced his words, his blunt honesty a refreshing change from the carefully crafted façades that people often hid behind.

"You're not staying, Paul?" Glenda called out as he began to walk towards the Portal, her voice tinged with a hint of disappointment, a silent plea for him to stay.

Paul paused, his attention still on Lois, his hand resting on her head in a gesture of affection. "I don't think Luke's done yet," he dryly replied, his words heavy with unspoken meaning, before resuming his stride, his figure receding into the distance.

"Think we can dig it out?" I asked, crouching beside Uncle Jamie, running my hands along the rim of the wheel.

"Not with our hands," Uncle Jamie answered, demonstrating the impracticality of such an attempt, his fingers sinking into the soft earth, a futile gesture of defiance against the unyielding dust.

"Shovels, then?" I suggested, my mind racing with possibilities, a desperate need to find a solution.

Uncle Jamie took a deep breath, his chest rising and falling with the effort, a look of contemplation etched onto his weathered face. "A shovel might work. It's probably the best we can do," he conceded, his words tinged with a hint of resignation, a recognition of the limitations of our resources.

"I'll go grab them," I offered, my voice filled with a newfound sense of purpose.

"Hold on," Uncle Jamie said, grabbing my arm as I made an effort to stand, his grip firm and unyielding. "Go check the Drop Zone first. The shovels we've been using are covered in cement. It might make it a little more challenging for us," he explained, his voice filled with a quiet wisdom.

"Sure," I replied, nodding quickly as I rose to my feet.

As I trudged along the increasingly familiar path to the Drop Zone, the sun beating down on my back like a merciless taskmaster, a mirage briefly shimmered before my eyes, conjuring the image of a sprawling civilisation rising from the ochre dust, a tantalising vision of a future that seemed just out of reach. I shrugged off the illusion, attributing it to the heat, the relentless sun playing tricks on my mind.

Uncle Jamie was right—this camp is only temporary. We will find a way back home, a way to reclaim the lives that had been so cruelly ripped away from us, to rebuild the world that we had lost.

HARMONIOUS REVELRY

4338.208.3

The campfire crackled and roared, casting dancing shadows upon the faces gathered around, the flickering light playing across features etched with a mix of exhaustion and camaraderie. I thrust another log into the vibrant flames, the rough bark biting into my palms as I fed the hungry blaze. A flurry of sparks ascended into the night sky, carried away by the gentle breeze, their ephemeral glow a fleeting moment of beauty amidst the darkness. As the smoke billowed, thick and acrid, a fresh gust swept across Paul's face, causing him to shield his eyes from the impending sting of ashes, his hand raised in a futile attempt to ward off the irritation.

"Sorry. Didn't mean to do that," I called out to Paul, my voice carrying over the crackling fire, a note of apology threading through my words, an acknowledgment of the discomfort I had inadvertently caused.

He waved off my apology dismissively, his hand cutting through the air in a gesture of nonchalance. "All good," he replied, his tone laced with good-natured tolerance, a flicker of amusement dancing in his eyes, the incident already forgotten in the face of the evening's festivities.

Luke emerged from the flickering glow, his figure materialising out of the shadows like a spectre, bearing plastic containers brimming with aromatic Indian delicacies. The mouthwatering scent of butter chicken permeated the air, rich and creamy, igniting a primal hunger within me, my stomach growling in anticipation of the feast to come.

"Butter chicken for you?" Luke offered, presenting the container to Paul with a flourish, a grin playing at the corners of his mouth, the promise of a satisfying meal hanging in the air between them.

"Yeah, thanks," Paul replied, a spark of anticipation in his eyes, his hands already reaching for the proffered container, eager to dig into the savoury delights within.

Luke's attention then shifted to Karen, his gaze settling on her expectant face, extending the same offer with a container of Chicken Tikka, the aroma of spices and grilled meat mingling with the smoky scent of the fire. As Paul savoured his meal, his eyes closing in blissful appreciation, I settled onto a log beside Glenda, the rough surface digging into my thighs, a mischievous smile tugging at the corners of my lips. From the corner of my eye, I couldn't help but observe Paul's sauce-coated antics, his tongue darting out to capture every droplet that threatened to escape the container, a comical display of gluttony that brought a flicker of amusement to my face.

Glenda's firm command broke my focus, her voice cutting through the din of conversation and laughter. "Lois, sit!" she instructed the exuberant retriever, who had become Paul's constant companion, shadowing his every move with a wagging tail and a hopeful gaze, her eyes fixed on the tantalising morsels that danced just out of reach.

Uncle Jamie intervened, his gruff voice tinged with a hint of affection, directing Lois's attention towards Duke, the dog's calm demeanour a stark contrast to the retriever's boundless energy. Duke was settled, finding solace between the feet of Uncle Jamie and Joel, his head resting on his paws, a picture of contentment.

Luke passed Uncle Jamie the next container of butter chicken, the exchange brief and efficient, receiving a simple expression of gratitude in return, a nod of appreciation for the much-needed sustenance. Glenda and Lois shared a quiet interaction, the woman's hand resting gently on the dog's head, a moment of connection amidst the bustle of the evening. It was reminiscent of the dynamic between my own dog, Hudson, and visitors to our home, the way he exuded boundless enthusiasm, his tail wagging furiously at the prospect of new friends and potential treats. But when it came to food, Hudson possessed little patience. Observing Duke's composed demeanour, a result of Uncle Jamie's diligent training, I couldn't help but find comfort in the familiar display of manners.

Amidst the tranquil atmosphere, an abrupt outburst pierced the air, jolting me from my reverie, my heart leaping into my throat at the sudden intrusion. "Hey, what about Joel?" It was Uncle Jamie, his voice seething with frustration, his eyes flashing with a mix of anger and concern. Startled, I flinched slightly, momentarily taken aback by the sudden intensity, my body tensing in anticipation of the confrontation to come.

"I'm sorry," replied Luke, his voice filled with genuine contrition, his hands raised in a placating gesture. "I didn't realise he could eat," he added, his words trailing off, a hint of uncertainty creeping into his tone, as if he were grappling with the complexities of Joel's condition.

"Of course he can fucking eat!" Uncle Jamie snapped, his voice rising in volume, his face flushed with indignation, the veins in his neck standing out in sharp relief against his skin.

"What do you want?" Luke inquired, stepping closer to Joel, his voice softening, a note of concern threading through his words, his gaze settling on the young man's face, searching for some sign of preference or desire.

The response came in the form of a nonchalant shrug, Joel's shoulders rising and falling in a gesture of indifference, diffusing the tension that had momentarily gripped the group, a silent acknowledgment that the matter was of little consequence to him.

I allowed my mind to return to the thoughts I had momentarily lost, murmuring to myself about Henri's peculiar behaviour, the way he had evaded Lois and the burgeoning crowd throughout the day, seeking refuge near the fire, his tail tucked between his legs, his eyes filled with a wary apprehension. Uncle Jamie had strategically placed the dog beds outside, near the warmth of the flames, and Henri had unerringly discovered his sanctuary amidst the unfamiliarity, curling up on the soft fabric with a contented sigh. Curiously, he displayed an uncharacteristic calmness around food, resisting the temptation to join the meal despite casting longing glances in its direction, his nose twitching with the tantalising scent of spices and meat.

Luke's words redirected my attention, his voice cutting through my musings, causing my stomach to twist with anticipation. "Looks like butter chicken it is for you, too," he declared, a mischievous glint in his eyes, his lips curving into a sly grin. "Good thing that's what I got the most of," he added, his words tinged with a hint of self-satisfaction, as if he had anticipated the evening's culinary preferences with uncanny accuracy.

"You can't really go wrong with a good butter chicken," I exclaimed eagerly, my eyes practically bulging from their sockets, the words tumbling from my lips in a rush of enthusiasm. The aroma had my senses ablaze, the rich scent of spices and creamy sauce filling my nostrils, making my mouth water with desire. I could almost taste the succulent flavours on my tongue, the tender meat and velvety sauce a promise of gastronomic bliss. My hunger became all-consuming, a gnawing emptiness that demanded to be filled, overriding any concerns for the dogs' hunger pangs, their plaintive whines fading into the background as my own desires took centre stage. My mind raced with fleeting memories of Hudson, his furry face and wagging tail a bittersweet reminder of the life I had left behind, as if he were attempting a comeback, a last-ditch effort to reclaim his place in my affections. But in that moment, my singular focus was on satisfying my insatiable appetite, the primal need to sate the hunger that clawed at my insides.

"You can have the last one then," Luke offered, extending the container of delectable butter chicken toward me, the plastic warm against my eager fingers, the weight of it a comforting presence in my hands.

❖

Caught off guard by Paul's sudden interruption, his voice cutting through the haze of anticipation like a blade, I glanced up, finding him awkwardly clearing his throat, his face a mask of discomfort and uncertainty. He swiftly transitioned into a battle against the cacophony of the group's chatter, his voice rising above the din, attempting to convey a more serious matter, his brow furrowed with concentration.

"I need everyone to check in at the Drop Zone regularly," Paul asserted, his voice cutting through the previously jovial atmosphere. "To see whether Luke has brought any of your belongings. Or perhaps there might be something there that you find you need," he added, his gaze sweeping over the assembled faces, a silent plea for cooperation and understanding.

A heavy silence descended upon the group, each person processing Paul's unexpected request. The air crackled with tension, the easy camaraderie of moments before evaporating like smoke in the wind, replaced by a palpable sense of unease and resistance. Karen was the first to show her dissent, her eyes flashing with a stubborn defiance, her lips pressed into a thin line of disapproval.

"That sounds reasonable enough," Chris chimed in, his voice cutting through the tension like a beacon of rationality, attempting to diffuse any mounting opposition, his hands raised in a placating gesture, a silent appeal for calm and cooperation.

"Reasonable?" Karen retorted, her gaze piercing her husband with a challenging intensity, her voice dripping with sarcasm and disbelief. "It's a long way to walk just to check. I'm too busy to wander over to simply... check," she added, her words tinged with a hint of disdain, as if the very idea of such a mundane task was beneath her, an affront to her sensibilities.

Uncle Jamie swiftly joined in, his voice rising above the din, aligning himself with Karen, a united front against Paul's perceived imposition. "I'm with Karen on this one. Too busy," he declared, his words clipped and final, his eyes flashing with a stubborn determination that I knew all too well.

"Busy!?" Paul exclaimed, incredulity colouring his tone, his eyes widening in disbelief, his hands thrown up in a gesture of frustration. "All you've done is sit in the tent for the past two days!" he added, his voice rising in volume, a note of accusation threading through his words, a challenge to Uncle Jamie's perceived indolence.

My heart sank, a leaden weight settling in the pit of my stomach, and I could feel myself shrinking within, my shoulders hunching forward as if to protect myself from the mounting tension, the crackling energy that threatened to explode at any moment. This was not a conversation I wanted to engage in, caught between the tensions of the group, the warring factions that threatened to tear us apart at the seams, a house divided against itself.

"Fuck off, Paul!" Jamie's outburst reverberated through the clearing, his voice harsh and grating, punctuated by the unfortunate mishap of a saucy chicken piece tumbling into his lap, a comical moment amidst the rising hostilities.

Luke interjected, his voice calm and measured, attempting to steer the discussion back on track, to find some common ground amidst the disunion. "Didn't you want to be responsible for managing the Drop Zone anyway?" he quipped, casting a sideways glance at Paul, his eyebrow raised in a silent challenge, a reminder of past conversations and agreements.

Chris, the self-designated peacemaker of the group, the voice of reason and compromise, offered a solution, his words measured and thoughtful. "I'm happy to wander over. It'll be a nice break, and good to see what's there," he said, his voice filled with a quiet determination, a willingness to shoulder the burden for the sake of the group. Realising the odds were stacked against him, he swiftly redirected his attention to his plate, swiftly swallowing another forkful of food, a silent acknowledgment of defeat, a tactical retreat in the face of overwhelming opposition.

"You make a good Drop Zone Manager, Paul," Glenda interjected, slipping a morsel of rice to Lois, the dog's tail wagging in appreciation. Her sharp glances in my direction brought my attention back to the conversation, a silent reprimand for my momentary lapse in focus. Instant regret washed over me as I muttered under my breath, the words slipping out before I could stop them, "Well, he is shit at building things," a petty jab that I immediately regretted, a moment of weakness that I wished I could take back.

Glenda's gaze met mine, her eyes filled with a mixture of admonishment and understanding, a silent communication that spoke volumes, a reminder of the need for unity and cooperation. I hastily averted my eyes, focusing once again on my food, the butter chicken suddenly losing its appeal, the rich flavours turning to ash in my mouth, a bitter reminder of my own shortcomings. Her voice rang out, capturing my full attention, her words filled with a quiet wisdom that commanded respect.

"I think our settlement has a better chance of thriving if we each focus on our own strengths," Glenda spoke, her words resonating with a quiet authority, a call to set aside our differences and work towards a common goal. Her gaze returned to Paul, her eyes softening, a flicker of empathy dancing in their depths. "With Luke bringing supplies through so quickly now, perhaps it would be best if the Drop Zone had a dedicated manager," she added, her words a gentle nudge, a subtle encouragement for Paul to embrace his new role, to find purpose and meaning in the essential task.

Paul's response came in the form of a hefty shrug, his shoulders rising and falling in a gesture of resignation, conceding defeat in the face of Glenda's persuasive argument.

"Fine. I'll be responsible for notifying people when things arrive for them and for keeping the Drop Zone in some sort of order," he said, his voice filled with a weary acceptance, a recognition of the inevitability of his new position.

"Marvellous," Karen chimed in, her tone laced with an air of finality, eager to move on from the discussion, to put the unpleasantness behind her and return to the more pressing matters at hand, the cultivation of her own interests and pursuits.

"But..." Paul hesitated, his voice trailing off, a note of uncertainty creeping into his tone, as if he were grappling with the implications of his new role. He paused for a moment, gathering his thoughts, before regaining his momentum, his words tumbling out in a rush of determination and resolve. "If I am going to be going back and forth so often, we need to do something about this bloody dust! We need to build a road," he declared, his voice rising in volume, a call to action, a challenge to the group to rise to the occasion, to take control of their own fate.

Glenda nodded in agreement, her face reflecting understanding, a flicker of approval dancing in her eyes, a silent acknowledgment of the wisdom of Paul's words. "That sounds fair enough," she said, her voice filled with a quiet certainty, a recognition of the need for infrastructure and development.

Chris, displaying an eagerness akin to that of a conscientious student, his hand raised as if volunteering for a noble cause, a flicker of excitement dancing in his eyes. "I can help with that," he said, his words a promise of support and collaboration.

"Yeah, I guess we could all pitch in," I chimed in, my voice filled with a newfound enthusiasm, a desire to contribute to the greater good, to make even a small measure of difference. I scanned the circle of faces, searching for signs of validation, for some indication that my words had struck a chord, that my sentiment was shared by those around me. I shared Paul and Chris's sentiment wholeheartedly—this relentless dust was driving us all to the brink of insanity.

"I'll help, too," Joel's raspy voice sounded a touch stronger than before, a flicker of life dancing in his eyes, a spark of determination that had been absent in the days prior. His words raised a few eyebrows within the group, a moment of surprise and uncertainty, a recognition of the progress he had made, the strength that he had regained in the face of overwhelming odds.

As positive reactions spread, conversations resumed their social ambience, weaving a tapestry of laughter and camaraderie. The fluid dynamics of the gathering led to a shift in seating arrangements, and before I knew it, I found myself seated beside Chris, a newfound sense of unity weaving through our interactions.

❖

As the fiery orb sank behind the distant mountains, casting hues of gold and crimson across the sky, the lively chatter around the campfire intensified, the voices of my companions rising and falling in a symphony of camaraderie and shared experience. Amidst the cacophony of sound, a raspy hum rode the gentle breeze, its haunting melody captivating my attention, drawing me in like a moth to a flame.

Joel? The thought flashed through my mind, a flicker of recognition sparking to life as I turned my gaze towards the hunched figure seated across from me, his face illuminated by the dancing flames.

The hum gradually transformed into coherent words, the lyrics seeping into the air like a bittersweet melody, each syllable dripping with a poignant longing that tugged at my heartstrings.

"Let us celebrate our story,
The words we've yet to write."

The song was unfamiliar to my ears, its haunting refrain evoking a pang of longing deep within my chest, a yearning for the life I had left behind. In a moment of reflex, my hand instinctively reached for my trouser pocket, seeking solace in the comforting weight of my phone, the smooth metal and glass a tangible reminder of the connections I had lost. But reality struck like a hammer blow, and my heart sank as I realised the absence of modern technology in this mysterious world, the emptiness of my pocket a stark reminder of the isolation that surrounded us.

A lump formed in my throat, a bitter knot of emotion that threatened to choke me, and I stole a glance at Uncle Jamie, his unwavering gaze fixated on Joel, a flicker of something unreadable dancing in his eyes. *Has he forgotten our purpose, our quest to find a way back?* The thought twisted my stomach into knots, mingling with a tinge of anxiety that settled like a lead weight in the pit of my stomach, a gnawing fear that we would be trapped in this abnormal and unforgiving world forever.

Glenda rose gracefully from her seat, her movements fluid and purposeful, commanding the attention of all those gathered around the fire and silencing Joel's haunting melody. A tinge of embarrassment flushed his pale face, a rosy hue spreading across his cheeks as he ducked his head, avoiding the curious gazes of those around him. But Glenda's gentle words breathed life into his spirits, a soothing balm that eased the sting of self-consciousness.

"Please, don't stop. You have a beautiful voice," Glenda encouraged Joel, her voice a melodic lilt that seemed to dance on the evening breeze, a note of genuine admiration threading through her words.

Baffled, I furrowed my brow in contemplation, my mind struggling to reconcile the discrepancy between Glenda's praise and the rough, scratchy timbre that had emanated from Joel's throat. All I heard was a roughness, a raw quality that seemed at odds with the notion of beauty and grace. *Did Glenda perceive something different, something beyond the surface?*

Joel resumed his raspy hum, the sound filling the air once more, restarting the tune from the beginning with a newfound confidence that seemed to radiate from his very being.

Glenda reemerged from her tent, cradling a violin in her hands, the polished wood gleaming in the firelight like a precious jewel. A smile blossomed on her face, a radiant expression of pure joy, as her bow danced across the strings, weaving a harmonious tapestry with Joel's melody, the two sounds intertwining in a breathtaking display of musical prowess. Though I lacked musical talent myself, the melodic notes that filled the air were a welcome respite from the day's haunting silence, a gentle reminder of the enduring beauty of art, the power of creativity to transcend boundaries.

Karen's curiosity prompted her to inquire, her voice filled with a mix of wonder and confusion, "You know this song?"

"Not until now," Glenda replied, her focus unwavering as she continued to play, her fingers dancing across the strings with a fluid grace.

As Joel's voice effortlessly carried the words, the lyrics seeming to flow from his lips like honey, Luke, the ever-attentive host, circled the gathering, his steps light and purposeful, ensuring that no hand remained empty. I welcomed the refill, the liquid sloshing gently in my glass as he poured, grateful for the comforting embrace of the drink, hoping that it would grant me solace in the forthcoming night's slumber, a temporary respite from the demons that haunted my dreams.

With each repetition of the four lines, a haunting familiarity echoed faintly in my mind, a whisper of recognition that sent an involuntary shiver down my spine, raising goosebumps on my skin despite the warmth of the fire. A voice from another time and place seemed to whisper in my memory, intertwining with the present in a dizzying dance of déjà vu.

"Let us celebrate our story,
The words we've yet to write.
How we all wound up with glory,
In the worlds we fought to right."

My body trembled involuntarily, as if resonating with the weight of the words, the untold stories and uncharted destinies that lay ahead. The lyrics seemed to speak directly to my soul, a message from the universe itself.

"To Joel!" Luke's exclamation pierced the air, his voice ringing out, his glass raised in a toast that rallied the collective spirit of those gathered around the fire, a unifying force that brought us all together in a moment of shared purpose.

I lifted my glass of vodka and coke, my voice joining the chorus of cheering and chanting that reverberated into the silent distance, echoing across the barren landscape like a battle cry. "To Joel," I uttered, the words feeling heavy and significant on my tongue, a tinge of hesitancy underlying my voice, for within them lay an acknowledgment of the unknown, the unwritten chapters that lay ahead, the challenges and obstacles that we would face together as a group.

As I took a sip of the drink, the alcohol burning a fiery path down my throat, I couldn't shake the feeling that we were on the precipice of something momentous, a turning point in our shared story that would shape the course of our lives forever.

4338.209

(28 July 2018)

INTO THE SHADOWS

4338.209.1

Sensing movement in the water from where I lay on my back, resting close by the lagoon's shore, yet being mindful to keep my flesh distant, I opened one eyelid, catching the last of the small wave as it rippled to the shore, the water sending a zing of pleasure through the tips of my toes as it unexpectedly reached them. The sensation was electric, a tantalising promise of the delights that awaited me in the lagoon's crystal-clear depths.

Surprised that I was no longer alone, I opened the other eyelid, my gaze sweeping across the tranquil surface of the water. Glancing toward the lagoon, I could see the top of a head breach the surface of the otherwise still water, sending ripples cascading outward in ever-widening circles. Looking about, there remained not another soul in sight, the surrounding landscape a barren expanse of ochre dust and jagged rock formations.

Curious, I watched as the familiar red hair began to emerge from below the surface, the strands clinging to the young woman's face, framing her delicate features in a halo of fiery colour.

"Brianne?" I asked, surprised, my voice tinged with disbelief as I sat up, leaning back on my elbows for support, my heart pounding in my chest with a mixture of excitement and trepidation.

"What the hell? What are you doing here?" I squeaked, my voice rising in pitch as I struggled to comprehend the sight before me.

"Shh," Brianne hushed me, bringing a finger to her lips, a coy smile playing at the corners of her mouth. More ripples, larger ripples, began to lap at my feet as Brianne took slow, careful steps toward me, her hazel eyes locked seductively on mine, a smouldering intensity in their depths that sent shivers down my spine. Her body rose from the water with each step, the droplets cascading down her sun-kissed skin in a mesmerising display of sensuality.

My gaze moved from her eyes, down her slender neck, and paused at the small, purple bikini top that held her breasts in position, the fabric straining against the lush curves of her body. *They fit so perfectly*, I told myself, grinning broadly, a surge of desire coursing through my veins at the sight of her barely concealed flesh.

The water ran easily down Brianne's soft skin, dripping back into the lagoon in a hypnotic rhythm that seemed to match the pounding of my heart. As she continued her slow, almost rhythmic walk towards me, her hips lightly swaying as she placed one foot in front of the other, her inner thighs touched gently with every step, a tantalising glimpse of the paradise that lay hidden beneath the flimsy fabric of her bikini bottoms.

Not wanting the moment to be spoiled too quickly by the lagoon's enhancing abilities, I slid myself backwards at least a good body length away from the water's edge, my movements hurried and clumsy in my haste to put some distance between myself and the intoxicating allure of the water. Whatever impulses I felt, I wanted it to all be because of her, because of the natural beauty and sensuality that radiated from her every pore. *She is naturally beautiful*, I told myself, my eyes drinking in the sight of her like a man dying of thirst, *I don't need the lagoon to interfere.*

Reaching the edge of the lagoon, her body now in full view, as though reading my intentions, Brianne spoke, her voice low and sultry, a siren's call that threatened to undo me completely. "The lagoon's waters don't simply influence our physical sensualities. It doesn't diminish any part of your being, it enhances what already exists within," she said, placing her hand across her bosom, her fingers trailing lightly over the swell of her breasts, a teasing caress that sent my pulse racing.

A shiver ran down my spine as I thought about her words, the implications of what she was saying, the promise of a pleasure that went beyond the merely physical. "I do love you. Very much," I told her, my voice thick with emotion, my heart swelling with the depth of my feelings for her.

"I know," replied Brianne, her hand caressing herself as it made its way down her body, tracing the curve of her waist, the flare of her hips, before coming to rest on her belly, the slight swell there a reminder of the life that grew within her. "I am carrying your child," she said, her words filled with a fierce pride, a love that transcended the boundaries of time and space.

Brianne stopped short of leaving the water, the lagoon barely covering her bare feet, the droplets clinging to her skin like diamonds in the sun. "Come here, Kain," she beckoned with her left hand, her fingers curling in a come-hither motion that sent a jolt of desire straight to my core.

I squirmed uncomfortably, my body torn between the desire to close the distance between us and the fear of what the lagoon's waters might do to me, the memory of my last encounter still fresh in my mind. "I'm not sure I should go in the water," I said, my voice hoarse with a mixture of longing and trepidation, my dick beginning to surge as I recalled the overwhelming sensations that had flooded through me, the inextricable awkwardness of the conversation with Uncle Jamie that had followed.

Brianne inhaled deeply, her chest rising and falling with the motion, her hand slowly moving from her belly and sliding beneath her bikini pants, disappearing from view. Eyes closing, she moaned softly as she exhaled, the sound a throaty purr of pleasure that sent shivers racing down my spine.

"Shit," I muttered, wiping my brow anxiously as the sexual tension began to form small beads of sweat across my forehead, my body responding to the sight of her with an intensity that threatened to consume me whole.

The long, pleasurable moan coming to an end, Brianne opened her eyes, the hazel depths smouldering with an unspoken desire, a hunger that matched my own. With one hand still hidden beneath her bikini, the other hand beckoned me again, her voice low and commanding. "I'm ready. Come and fuck me, Kain," she said firmly, her tongue running salaciously across her red lips.

Instincts needing no further call, I sprung to my feet, my body moving of its own accord. Within seconds, my hands glided behind Brianne's smooth body, pulling her against me, letting her wet flesh dampen my own, the contact electric, sending jolts of pleasure racing through my nerve endings. The feelings of intense desire that pulsed through the soles of my feet were immediate, a tidal wave of sensation that threatened to sweep me away.

"Embrace it," said Brianne, her voice a husky whisper in my ear, her hand sliding into my shorts, her fingers wrapping around my engorged cock, squeezing it hard, a delicious pressure that sent stars exploding behind my eyelids. "Let the waters enhance what's inside," she said calmly, her words a soothing balm, a promise of ecstasy.

I gasped softly as my dick left the safety of the fabric that had been concealing the swelling passion, the cool air a shock against my heated flesh. I brought my lips closer to Brianne's, my breath mingling with hers, my gaze locked on her glowing eyes, the depths of them pulling me in, drowning me in their intensity.

Allowing my mind to surrender to Brianne's sexual encouragement, her hand pulled me toward her, the silky material of her bikini rubbing against the head of my exposed cock, sending a shudder through my body, a jolt of pure, undiluted pleasure that left me weak in the knees.

Brianne's breath was warm against my neck, her tongue sensitively tickling my ear as it circled several times, a teasing caress that sent shivers racing down my spine. "Enhance yourself inside me," she whispered, grinding her body against mine, the friction delicious, maddening, a promise of the paradise that awaited me.

A hoarse, pleasurable moan fell from my lips as Brianne pulled back the bikini material, her hand guiding the tip of my cock as it gently penetrated her slick folds, the sensation indescribable.

"Deep inside me," she breathed deeply, lowering her body to consume my entire shaft, the tight, wet heat of her enveloping me, driving me to the brink of madness with each thrust of my hips.

"Fuck!" I hissed, my eyes springing open, my legs clenching instinctively as the pleasure reached a crescendo, the intensity of it intoxicating. *Did I stop it in time?* I asked myself, my body shuddering involuntarily, the aftershocks of my release rippling through me like waves on the shore. And as though my body felt entirely in sync, I rolled to the side, my hand reaching into my trousers, pulling my dick out and releasing the unstoppable pressure into the dust surrounding me, the sensation a blissful relief.

Another body shudder, and I took several deep breaths, my heart pounding in my chest, the blood roaring in my ears as I struggled to regain my composure, to ground myself in the reality of the moment.

Lois's deep growl reverberated through the night, filling the air with an unsettling energy, a reminder that I wasn't alone in my wakefulness. The realisation that I wasn't the only one who hadn't made it back to the tents last night struck me like a bolt of lightning, a sobering thought that chased away the lingering tendrils of my dream. "Shit," I muttered, hastily wiping my sticky hand across my abdomen, the darkness engulfing us, making it impossible to discern anything beyond the vague outlines of shapes in the gloom.

My thoughts were abruptly interrupted by Lois's persistent and disconcerting growl, the sound sending a chill down my spine, a sense of unease settling in the pit of my stomach like a lead weight.

"The wind is picking up. Do you think it's another dust storm?" Luke's voice sliced through the heavy darkness, its direction unclear in the obscurity, a disembodied sound that seemed to come from everywhere and nowhere at once.

"I hope not," Paul's whispered response barely reached my ears, the words carried away on the rising wind.

I recognised that type of growl, a chilling reminder of Hudson. Grateful that it wasn't directed at me or my unsettling dream, I couldn't shake the eerie tingle that crawled down my spine, a sense of foreboding that settled over me like a shroud.

"I think something's out there," I whispered, my voice hoarse with fear, cautiously shifting through the dust to position myself between Luke and Paul, seeking safety in numbers, in the comfort of familiar presences in the darkness.

The tension in the air mounted rapidly, pricking uncomfortably at the back of my neck as the three of us, likely wearing equally wide-eyed expressions, stared into the pitch-black void, waiting, our hearts pounding in our chests, our breath coming in short, shallow gasps.

Lois let out a sharp bark, followed by a low snarl, the sound sending a jolt of fear through me, my muscles tensing in anticipation of some unseen danger.

"What's going on?" Glenda called out, her voice filled with concern as she swiftly approached from behind. "Why is Lois barking?"

"We don't know," Paul responded, his voice tight with fear.

"Probably just the wind stirring up the dust," Luke offered, his tone unconvincing, a feeble attempt at reassurance that fell flat in the face of the rising tension.

As Luke's words faded, an unexpected gust of wind whipped through, throwing a cloud of dust directly into my face, the particles stinging my eyes and coating my tongue with a gritty film. I could feel the sting on my cheeks, but my tongue worked feverishly, desperately trying to rid my mouth of the gritty particles, the taste of dirt and sand overwhelming my senses. I closed my eyes, shielding them with my raised hands, a futile attempt to protect them from the onslaught. While I couldn't alleviate the stinging sensation, I could at least prevent further assault, my eyes watering with the effort.

"We should seek shelter in the tents!" Luke's voice rang out, filled with a sense of urgency, a call to action that spurred us into motion.

"Come, Lois," Glenda commanded, her voice firm and unyielding.

Blinking rapidly, tears forming to wash away the dust, I struggled to clear my vision, the world around me a blur of indistinct shapes and shadows, the darkness pressing in on me from all sides.

Ignoring Glenda's instruction, Lois persisted with her relentless growling, the sound a low, menacing rumble that sent shivers down my spine, a warning of some unseen danger lurking in the shadows.

"Duke! Get back here!" Uncle Jamie's voice called out from somewhere behind me, a distant echo that seemed to come from another world entirely.

Finally able to open my eyes, I gasped, certain that I caught sight of a creature lurking in the distance, its silhouette outlined against the fading embers of last night's campfire, a shadow within a shadow that sent a jolt of fear through me, my heart leaping into my throat.

"Shit! We're surrounded!" I cried out, catching a glimpse of another figure darting in the opposite direction, a fleeting impression of movement that vanished as quickly as it had appeared. I inched as close to the fading warmth of the embers as I dared, without risking setting myself ablaze, seeking comfort in the fleeting remnants of light and heat.

A tent rustled, sending a shiver of unease coursing through my shoulders, my muscles tensing in anticipation of some unknown threat. *Was it movement from within or without?* The question twisted my stomach into a painful knot, a sense of dread settling over me like a suffocating blanket. *Stay calm*, I admonished myself, attempting to steady my breathing as another gust of wind showered me with dust, the particles clinging to my skin like a second layer, a gritty film that coated every exposed surface.

"What's happening?" Karen's voice trembled with panic.

The sound of her voice brought a modicum of relief, signalling that she had emerged from her tent, seemingly unharmed.

"Is that Luke?" Karen's voice trembled with uncertainty, a note of hope threading through her words, a desperate plea for reassurance in the face of the unknown.

Confused, I turned my head toward the direction where I thought Luke was, my eyes straining to pierce the gloom, to catch a glimpse of his familiar figure in the darkness. I gasped, catching a faint glimmer of the Portal's vibrant, rainbow hues dancing across the dunes in the distance, the colours a striking contrast against the inky blackness of the night sky. The colours provided a momentary respite from the oppressive darkness, but their radiance was fleeting, disappearing as quickly as it had appeared, leaving us once again at the mercy of the shadows.

"I think it's just a dust..." Paul's voice trailed off, the words dying on his lips, a feeble attempt at reassurance that fell flat in the face of the rising tension.

"I'm right here," Luke's reassurance reached Karen's ears.

I fervently wished for Lois to cease her growling, seeking solace behind my makeshift shield, my body trembling with a mixture of fear and adrenaline, my heart pounding in my chest like a drum.

"Duke, stop barking!" Uncle Jamie's voice pierced the whistling wind once more, a sharp command that carried a note of desperation.

A bone-chilling scream pierced through the gusts of dust, sending a wave of terror rippling across the camp, a sound that seemed to come from the very depths of hell itself, a cry of pure, unadulterated fear that sent shivers racing down my spine.

"Lois!" Glenda's scream echoed, her dog bounding off into the night in an instant, disappearing into the swirling vortex of dust and shadows.

Panic gripped me fully, driving my actions to irrationality, a primal instinct for survival that overrode all other concerns. Without a moment's hesitation, I found myself running through the darkness, following the path set by Paul and Glenda, my feet pounding against the dusty earth, my lungs burning with the effort of each gasping breath. Barefoot, my feet sank into the fine sands, causing me to stumble and fall, my hands and knees scraping against the rough ground, the pain a distant echo compared to the fear that consumed me. The intensified wind lashed against any exposed flesh, leaving a stinging sensation as if I were its personal pin cushion, each gust a thousand tiny needles that pierced my skin, leaving me raw.

Digging my fingers into the shifting sand, fuelled by adrenaline coursing through my veins, I pushed myself back onto my feet, my muscles screaming with the effort, my body protesting every movement. Stumbling forward for several strides, I came to an abrupt halt, my heart pounding in my chest, my breath coming in short, sharp gasps. "Where the fuck am I!?" I hissed, my voice filled with frustration, unable to discern anything in the all-encompassing blackness, the darkness pressing in on me from all sides.

Another shrill scream pierced through the air, sending a shiver down my spine, a sound of pure, unadulterated terror that seemed to come from everywhere and nowhere at once. My gaze turned back to the fleeting brilliance of the Portal's radiant colours illuminating the night, the swirling vortex of light a beacon of hope in the darkness, only to fade quickly, plunging the world into an oppressive darkness that felt suffocating. Undeterred and fuelled by determination, a desperate need to find safety, to escape the horrors that lurked in the shadows, I broke into a steady jog, my feet pounding against the ground in a relentless rhythm, my heart hammering in my chest.

"Good. I'm going in," I heard Luke's voice declare. And once again, the land was bathed in the vivid hues of the Portal, the colours swirling and dancing in a mesmerising display that lit up the night sky like a fireworks display, a momentary respite from the suffocating darkness.

"Whoa!" I yelled as an unknown force collided with my legs, the impact sending me tumbling head over heels, my body spinning out of control as I careened down the dusty slope, the world around me a blur of motion. Panting heavily, I finally came crashing to a halt at the bottom of the dune, my body aching and battered, my lungs burning with the effort of each gasping breath.

Shielding my eyes from the onslaught of dust, I felt a warm breath on the back of my neck, the sensation sending a shiver of fear down my spine. A droplet of saliva landed on the tip of my ear, slowly trickling down the side, followed by a deep, bone-chilling growl that seemed to come from the very depths of hell itself. *Shit!* My heart pounded fiercely in my chest, a frantic drumbeat that echoed in my ears, drowning out all other sounds. *There's something here,* I thought, my mind racing with the possibilities, each one more terrifying than the last.

With no time to consider my options, no chance to weigh the risks and rewards of fight or flight, I let out an agonising scream as razor-sharp teeth sank into my leg, the pain blinding, all-consuming, a white-hot agony that tore through me like a bolt of lightning. Propelled backward, my head slammed into the ground, stars exploding behind my eyelids as the creature in the shadows took off, dragging my helpless body behind it, my flesh tearing and bleeding as I was pulled across the rough ground. The pain surged through me with an intensity that made me wish for unconsciousness, for the blessed relief of oblivion, anything to escape the torment that consumed me.

Flailing my arms and free leg aimlessly, every attempt to fend off the savage beast proved futile, my efforts as useless as trying to stop the wind from blowing. I was moving too swiftly, the ground beneath me a blur of motion, and with no light to guide me, no way to see my attacker or my surroundings, escape seemed impossible.

Suddenly, the sandy ground ceased its movement, and the creature released its grip on my leg, emitting an unexpected yelp, a sound of pain and surprise that cut through the night like a knife. Uncertain of what had transpired, yet terrified of its return, my eyes darted about in search of any opportunity to escape, any chance to flee from the horrors that lurked in the darkness. It was then that I noticed a small, faint light in the distance, a glimmer of hope that pierced the gloom like a beacon, a promise of safety and salvation.

The light drew nearer, a shadow passing in front of its glow, a fleeting impression of movement that sent my heart racing, my muscles tensing in anticipation of some new threat. Every muscle in my body tensed as I grimaced in excruciating pain, attempting to bring myself to my feet, to flee from the approaching figure before it could do me further harm. *It's too late*, I told myself, sinking back into the dust, my body screaming in protest, as a diminutive figure approached, its features obscured by the darkness.

Eyes closed in defeat, I braced myself for further torment, for the inevitable end that seemed to loom before me like a gaping maw, ready to swallow me whole. A rough tongue sloppily licked across my face, the sensation startling me out of my fear-induced stupor, my eyes flying open in surprise.

"Lois found him!" Glenda's voice rang out, filled with a mixture of relief and concern, a promise of safety and protection in the face of the unknown horrors that lurked in the shadows.

"Lois," I whispered, my voice hoarse and trembling, tentatively reaching out to feel for her presence, my fingers brushing against the soft fur of her coat. "Is it really you?"

Though my teeth were clenched tightly, my jaw aching with the effort of holding back the screams that threatened to tear from my throat, a small sense of relief washed over me as my fingers brushed against Lois's soft golden fur, the warmth of her body a comforting presence in the darkness.

"Kain," Glenda said, her voice filled with concern as she pushed Lois away from my face, her hands gentle but firm as she examined me for injuries. "Kain, are you okay?"

"Is he alive?" Paul's voice called out, filled with a mixture of fear and hope.

Wincing as pain seared through my leg, my reply emerged garbled and undecipherable, a string of incoherent sounds that bore little resemblance to human speech. I nodded in the direction of my injured limb, a feeble attempt to communicate the source of my torment, my body shaking with the effort of holding back the screams that threatened to tear me apart.

"Yes. But his leg is wounded. Come help me move him," Glenda yelled, her voice now more composed and reassuring, dispelling the earlier panic.

Suppressing a scream born of relentless pain, I bit down on my tongue, the coppery taste of blood flooding my mouth, a little too hard. "My leg!" I finally managed to scream, the words tearing from my throat in a spray of bloody saliva, the agony of my injury overwhelming my senses, drowning out all other concerns.

The wind continued to strengthen, the gusts of dust and debris whipping around us in a frenzied dance, but Paul, thankfully, managed to locate us.

"I think it's bleeding," I said, my voice choked with tears that I could no longer hold back, the pain and fear and exhaustion of the night's events finally catching up to me.

"It is," Glenda confirmed, her voice filled with a quiet urgency as she shone the phone's light across my leg, the beam illuminating the torn flesh and pooling blood in stark relief against the pale skin.

Glenda turned to Paul, her voice filled with a quiet determination. "We have to get him out of this dust storm," she commanded firmly.

Paul's slight pause sent a dry gulp down my throat, my anxious palms growing sweatier. *Is my leg that bad?* I wondered, consumed by worry, my mind racing with the possibilities, each one more terrifying than the last.

"You hold the light, I'll help him," Paul finally responded, his voice tight with fear, his words clipped and terse as he moved to my side, his hands gentle but firm as he reached behind my shoulders, lifting me up with a strength born of desperation.

"Try not to let him put pressure on the leg," Glenda instructed, her voice filled with a quiet authority, a reminder of her medical training, her expertise in the face of crisis.

"Okay. We can seek shelter at the Drop Zone for now," Paul said, his voice trembling slightly, a quiver that betrayed his own fears and doubts. Turning his attention to me, he continued, his words filled with a forced calm, a reassurance that rang hollow in the face of the pain that consumed me. "We're going to stand," he said, his grip tightening on my shoulders as he lifted me to my feet, my body screaming in protest with every movement.

A torrent of dark thoughts flooded my mind as we struggled toward the Drop Zone, each step an agony, each moment a lifetime of suffering. I couldn't discern whether my body trembled from the damage to my leg or the all-encompassing terror that seized me, a fear that went beyond the physical, beyond the pain and the blood and the sweat. *I must be leaving a trail of blood,* I thought, my mind consumed by a final, nightmarish notion that caused my body to tremble uncontrollably from head to toe, a full-body shudder that wracked me with a fresh wave of agony, until the Portal's giant transparent screen illuminated the dark night.

"Paul!" Luke's familiar voice rang out.

"We're almost at the Drop Zone," Paul shouted in reply, his voice strained with the effort of supporting my weight, his breath coming in short, sharp gasps as we struggled forward.

"I need to check the house. I'll be back soon," Luke's voice continued to carry through the darkness, a distant echo that seemed to fade into the night, swallowed up by the howling wind and the swirling dust.

The glimmer of hope that had briefly sparked inside me was quickly extinguished as we were once again plunged into near pitch-blackness, with Glenda's phone serving as the only remaining source of light, a feeble glow that did little to pierce the suffocating gloom that surrounded us.

"Do you think we're safe here?" I asked, my voice barely above a whisper as we settled among the larger shed boxes, my body screaming in protest as I tried to find a comfortable position, making sure there was enough space to keep my injured leg straight, the pain a constant companion.

"Lois hasn't growled since we found you," Paul responded, his voice filled with a forced optimism, a desperate attempt to find some shred of hope.

"As soon as the wind calms, we need to get back to camp. Kain's leg needs care," Glenda asserted firmly.

"Of course," agreed Paul, his voice heavy with exhaustion as he rested his head against a box, his body sagging with the weight of the night's events.

Although I didn't feel entirely safe, the fear and uncertainty still gnawing at the edges of my consciousness, I took solace in the fact that I wasn't alone, that I had Glenda and Paul by my side. My conscious mind began losing the battle against the constant ache in my leg, the pain a relentless tide. I found myself drifting, my thoughts becoming hazy and unfocused, my eyelids growing heavy with the weight of exhaustion.

DESCENT INTO DARKNESS

4338.209.2

"Shit!" I hissed through clenched teeth, my heart pounding in my chest as my eyes widened in sudden panic. The half-naked woman stood before us, a sharp arrow held firmly in her hand. Blood dripped slowly along the shaft, leaving a macabre trail.

The scene was surreal, the darkness amplifying the intensity of the encounter. Each breath I took was laced with pain, making it harder to stay composed. The urgency in the woman's voice was palpable, but my wounded leg was growing numb, rendering me helpless.

Refusing to submit to her command, I slurred my response, "Like fuck we will," struggling to find strength in my voice as I moved my injured leg too abruptly.

Glenda, sensing the imminent danger, grabbed hold of Paul's arm and squeezed it tightly, her grip a testament to her fear and determination to protect us. I could feel the tension radiating from her body, a palpable force that seemed to crackle in the air between us. Her fingers dug into Paul's flesh, leaving white marks that stood out starkly against his sun-bronzed skin.

"Stay back!" Glenda yelled, her voice laced with defiance as she positioned herself closer to Paul, her body a shield between us and the unknown threat that lurked in the darkness. Her words hung heavy in the air, a challenge to the woman who stood before us, a declaration of our resolve to fight for our lives if necessary.

The woman, now closer, dropped the arrow and raised her hands in apparent surrender, the gesture a startling contrast to the fierce determination that blazed in her eyes. "Keep your fucking voices down," she warned, her tone urgent. "It's not safe. We have to go. Now." Her words carried a weight of authority, and I felt a shiver run down my spine at the implications of her warning.

The conflicting emotions swirled within me. I grappled with the fear of the unknown, the terrifying possibilities that lurked in the shadows, questioning whether this woman was friend or foe, a saviour or a devil in disguise. But as another growl resonated from the darkness, deeper and more menacing than before, a sound that seemed to shake the very earth beneath our feet, my instincts screamed that staying put was not an option. There was something out there, something far more dangerous than the woman before us, a predator that hungered for our flesh and blood.

Paul hesitated before he spoke, his voice filled with a forced calm that belied the fear that lurked beneath the surface. "Where are we going?" he asked, casting a sideways glance in Glenda and my direction, his eyes seeking reassurance.

"To your camp," the woman said flatly, as though the destination should have been obvious, a fact that we should have grasped without question. Her words carried a hint of impatience, a frustration with our hesitation.

"There's something else out there," hissed Glenda, her voice tight with fear as she shone the phone's light in the direction of Lois' fixed stare, the beam cutting through the darkness like a beacon, illuminating the expanse of sand and rock that stretched out before us. In the distance, I could see the faint outline of something moving, a shape that seemed to flicker and shift in the shadows, a ghost that danced at the edges of my vision.

The realisation dawned upon me then, a sickening twist in the pit of my stomach that left me breathless with terror. The threat was real, a tangible presence that lurked just beyond the reach of the light, waiting to strike with deadly precision. And running, as much as it pained me to admit it, seemed like our only chance of survival, a desperate gamble that could mean the difference between life and death. *But how could I outrun the creature that had already tried to devour my leg?* The question echoed in my mind, a mocking reminder of my own weakness, my own vulnerability in the face of the horrors that surrounded us. My mind spiralled into a catastrophic whirlwind of thoughts, a cascade of nightmares that left me trembling with dread.

As Glenda turned the light back toward us, I gasped, my heart leaping into my throat at the sight that greeted me. The woman had silently moved closer, crouching in front of us, her presence both unnerving and intriguing, a study in contradictions that left me reeling with confusion. Up close, I could see the hardness in her eyes, the steely determination of a warrior's spirit that had been forged in the fires of adversity.

"Shit!" Glenda and Paul exclaimed simultaneously, their voices mingling in a chorus of shock and disbelief, mirroring the jolt of surprise that reverberated through my own body, a physical reaction to the woman's sudden proximity.

The woman introduced herself as Charity, her voice steady and determined. "You can trust me," she assured, her grip firm on Paul's arm. "We must go," she urged.

Another deep growl pierced the darkness, a sound that seemed to come from the very bowels of the earth, a primal roar that sent shivers of terror racing down my spine. Lois bared her teeth in response, a low growl rumbling in her throat, a warning to the unseen threat that lurked just beyond the reach of the light.

"Come on," Paul urged, pulling Glenda to her feet as he stood tall, his voice filled with a newfound resolve, a determination to survive that seemed to radiate from his very being. "If this woman wanted to kill us, she would have done it already." His words carried a ring of truth, a logic that cut through the fog of fear, and I felt a flicker of hope spark to life in my chest, a tiny flame that refused to be extinguished.

"Or feed us to the creature," Glenda whispered, her voice barely audible over the pounding of my own heart.

"For fuck's sake," Charity interjected, her voice sharp with impatience as she gestured for us to follow her, her movements urgent and precise. "Don't waste any more time. We need to move." She turned to Glenda and paused, her gaze intense and unwavering. "Give me your light," she demanded, her hand outstretched.

My throat tightened with unspoken words of caution, a desperate plea for Glenda to hold onto the one thing that seemed to keep the darkness at bay. But all that escaped my lips was a hoarse whimper, a pathetic sound that seemed to hang in the air like a condemnation of my own weakness. Reluctantly, I allowed Paul and Glenda to support me, their arms strong and steady as they helped me to my feet. I acknowledged the harsh reality that being alone in the darkness with that unknown entity would be far more perilous than following Charity's lead, a gamble that could mean the difference between life and death.

"Stay close," Charity directed, her voice cutting through the stillness of the night as she shone the light ahead of us, the beam illuminating a narrow path through the sand. "And keep up," she added, her words a warning and a challenge.

My survival instincts were heightened to a fever pitch, every nerve in my body screaming with the need to run, to flee from the horrors that lurked just beyond the reach of the light. As we ventured further into the abyss, each step a painful reminder of my own mortality, my own fragility in the face of the unknown, I found myself silently pleading for protection, for deliverance from the fate that seemed to loom over us.

With each ragged breath, each stuttering heartbeat, my prayers grew more desperate, more urgent, a silent litany of hope and fear that poured from my very soul. I begged the universe, the gods, anyone who might be listening, to spare me from the creature's wrath, to grant me the strength to endure, to survive this new nightmare.

But the black sky above offered no solace, no comfort in the face of the terrors that surrounded us. It loomed overhead like a vast and indifferent void, a mirror of the emptiness that seemed to yawn at the edges of my consciousness.

❖

Approaching camp, my weary eyes struggled to stay open. The pain and exhaustion had taken their toll, making it a relentless battle to remain lucid, to cling to the fragile threads of consciousness that seemed to slip through my fingers like grains of sand. As we reached the crest of the final dune, the soft sand shifting beneath our feet, my gaze lifted, drawn to the sight of flickering flames dancing their way toward the heavens, the orange glow a beacon of hope amidst the suffocating darkness.

I strained to focus, to decipher the meaning behind the lights, my mind grasping for some sense of clarity amidst the fog of pain and weariness that enveloped me. But my brain pleaded for respite, the throbbing ache behind my eyes a relentless drumbeat that drowned out all other thoughts. My head drooped once more, the weight of it too much to bear, as I leaned heavily against Glenda's and Paul's shoulders, their strength the only thing keeping me upright, the only thing anchoring me to the world of the living.

"Who is the camp leader?" Charity's voice broke through the haze.

"I am," Paul replied without hesitation, his voice steady and sure.

"We need to talk. You and I," Charity asserted, her tone leaving no room for negotiation.

Summoning every ounce of energy, every last shred of willpower that remained within me, I forced my eyes to open, blinking away the blurriness that obscured my vision. The world around me swam in and out of focus, the edges of my sight tinged with a hazy glow that made everything seem surreal, like a waking dream. I squinted into the distance, my parched lips mouthing the words, "Someone's coming," the sound barely audible over the pounding of my own heart, the rush of blood in my ears.

"We need to attend to Kain's wounded leg first," Paul interjected, his voice filled with concern, a reminder of the urgency of my situation, of the precarious state of my own mortality.

Squatting in front of us, Charity lifted the blood-soaked shirt that had been wrapped around my leg, the fabric stiff and crusted with dried blood. A yelp of pain escaped my lips as she examined the injury, my nerves screaming in agony at the slightest touch, the wound a raw and throbbing mass of torn flesh and exposed muscle. "It's barely a scratch. He'll live," she declared, rising to her feet, her words a dismissive wave of the hand that sent a surge of anger coursing through my veins.

Barely a scratch? I seethed inwardly, frustration welling up within me, a hot and bitter taste in the back of my throat. *Bitch!* The word echoed in my mind, a silent curse that I didn't dare give voice to, an impotent rage that burned in my chest like a smouldering ember.

"I'd hardly call that..." Paul began, his voice rising in protest, only to abruptly halt, the words dying on his lips as a shadowy figure emerged from the distance, approaching with swift determination.

"Chris?" I whispered, recognition dawning upon me.

Chris swiftly replaced Paul, taking his position by my side, his strong arms wrapping around me, supporting my weight as we stumbled forward. His inadvertent pressure on my wounded leg elicited a wave of soreness, a fresh surge of agony that tore through me like a bolt of lightning, causing tears to well up in my eyes, blurring my vision once more.

"We need to get him to the medical tent," Glenda asserted, her voice laced with concern, a note of urgency that sent a chill down my spine.

Once again, I felt myself being dragged along, my body moving as if detached from my weary mind, a puppet whose strings were being pulled by some unseen force. The world around me faded in and out of focus, the edges of my vision tinged with a dark haze that threatened to consume me entirely, to drag me down into the waiting arms of oblivion.

"What happened to him?" I heard Chris inquire as we shuffled through the tent flap, finally reaching the refuge of the medical tent where I was carefully laid upon a mattress, the soft fabric a blessed relief against my battered and aching body.

"We don't know," Glenda replied, her voice tinged with worry, a note of uncertainty that sent a fresh wave of fear coursing through my veins, a sickening twist in the pit of my stomach.

"I think..." I attempted to speak, my voice hoarse and raspy, the words sticking in my throat like shards of glass, each syllable a struggle to force past my cracked lips.

Kneeling over me, Chris leaned in closer, his face a mask of concern, his eyes searching mine for some sign of clarity, of understanding. On the other side of the tent, Glenda searched through the medical supplies, her movements quick and efficient.

"I think it was an animal," I managed to say, gritting my teeth against the searing pain that shot through my leg with every breath, every tiny movement.

"A shadow panther," Chris gasped, his eyes widening with astonishment, a flicker of fear dancing in their depths, a recognition of the danger that lurked beyond the flimsy walls of the tent.

"A what?" I asked, confusion marring my face, my brow furrowing with the effort of trying to make sense of his words, to grasp the meaning behind the unfamiliar term.

"Enough talk," Glenda interjected sharply, her voice cutting through the haze of pain and confusion. "I need to concentrate, or Kain might lose his leg." The words fell like a hammer blow, a brutal reminder of the stakes that hung in the balance, of the very real possibility that I might emerge from this ordeal a cripple, a broken shell of my former self.

Any hint of losing consciousness vanished, the fog of exhaustion and pain lifting from my mind like a veil, replaced by a cold and terrifying clarity. My terrified eyes locked with Chris's gaze, a silent plea for reassurance, for some sign that everything would be alright, that I would survive this nightmare intact.

A firm hand squeezed mine, the warmth of the touch a lifeline in the darkness, a beacon of hope amidst the swirling maelstrom of fear and despair. "You're going to be fine," Chris assured me, his voice filled with consolation. "Just fine." The words washed over me like a gentle wave, a promise of safety and security that I clung to like a drowning man to a life raft.

"I'm going to give you a dose of morphine," Glenda announced.

Almost instantaneously, I felt a distinct prick in my upper arm, the needle sliding into my flesh with a sharp sting that was quickly overwhelmed by the rush of warmth that flooded through my veins, the medication taking effect with a swiftness that left me breathless. The pain began to recede, fading into the background like a distant memory, replaced by a blissful numbness that enveloped me like a cocoon.

"Try to relax," Glenda advised, her tone gentle, a soothing whisper that seemed to come from far away, a distant echo that reached me through the haze of the morphine. "You're safe now." The words settled over me like a warm blanket, a promise of protection and security that I wanted desperately to believe, to cling to with every fibre of my being.

My hand was squeezed gently once more, the touch a lifeline in the darkness, a reminder that I wasn't alone, that there were others who cared for me, who would fight for me. "Brianne," I whispered, my voice a barely audible rasp, as I extended my trembling hand to touch her beautifully freckled face, my fingers ghosting over the soft skin, tracing the delicate contours that I knew so well.

In that moment, as the morphine coursed through my veins and the pain receded into the distance, I found solace in her presence, in the warm glow of her love that seemed to emanate from every pore, a balm to my battered and weary soul. She was my anchor, my rock, the one constant in a world that seemed to shift and change with every passing moment, a world that had become a nightmarish landscape of shadows and danger.

And so I clung to her, to the memory of her touch and her smile, to the promise of a future that we had dreamed of together, a future that seemed to slip further away with each passing second. But even as the darkness closed in around me and the unknown horrors of the night gathered at the edges of my vision, I knew that I would fight with every last ounce of strength that remained within me, that I would cling to the hope of seeing her again, of holding her in my arms and telling her how much I loved her.

For in the end, that was all that mattered - the love that we shared, the bond that had brought us together and would see us through the darkest of times. And so I closed my eyes and let the morphine carry me away, let it transport me to a place of peace and tranquility, a place where the pain and the fear couldn't touch me, where I could rest and gather my strength for the battles that lay ahead.

And as I drifted off into the waiting arms of sleep, I whispered her name one last time, a prayer and a promise, a vow to return to her, to find my way back to the life we had planned, no matter the cost.

PLEASURABLE TORMENT

4338.209.3

"Kain," the soft, melodic voice sung to me from the darkness, eliciting a wide smile, its soothing timbre echoing in my ears like a lullaby, a gentle caress that seemed to wrap around me like a warm embrace, a promise of comfort and safety.

"Kain," the voice sounded again, this time lacking its melodic quality, replaced by a sharp, insistent tone that cut through the haze of my drowsy state, accompanied by a sharp poke to my ribs that jolted me back to wakefulness, my body jerking as if struck by a bolt of lightning.

My heavy eyelids fluttered open, the effort of forcing them apart a tiring task that seemed to drain every last ounce of strength. The morning daylight streamed into the tent, casting a warm glow on the surroundings, bathing everything in a soft, golden light that seemed to chase away the shadows of the night, a promise of a new day dawning.

"Good, you're awake," said Glenda, her voice filled with a quiet relief, a note of warmth that seemed to wrap around me like a comforting blanket. Her broad smile was enhanced by the golden strands of her hair pulled back in a ponytail, the sun glinting off the blonde locks like a halo, exuding a sense of calm and reassurance.

As I stretched my tired body, the muscles screaming in protest, a sharp pang of pain shot through my wounded leg, a harsh reminder of the ordeal I had endured, the terror and agony of the previous night rushing back to me in a flood of memories that threatened to overwhelm me. Longing for the oblivion of sleep, for the numbing effects of the morphine that had carried me away from the pain and the fear, I silently pleaded with Glenda to grant me another dose, my eyes beseeching her for the sweet release of unconsciousness, for an escape from the throbbing ache that plagued me.

"Try and hold still," Glenda instructed, her voice firm but gentle, as she tore open an alcohol swab with a practiced efficiency, the sharp scent of the disinfectant filling the air, a bitter tang that cut through the musty smell of the tent. She rubbed the swab onto my arm, the cool touch of the alcohol a shocking contrast to the heat of my skin, preparing to administer another injection, a promise of relief that I clung to with a desperate hope. Caught off guard by the sudden prick of the needle, the sharp sting of the metal piercing my flesh, I let out a soft gasp, the sound escaping my lips before I could stop it, the sensation jolting me back to full consciousness, my mind snapping into focus with a sudden clarity.

Confusion clouded my mind as I realised something was amiss, a nagging sense of wrongness that I couldn't quite place, a feeling of disconnection that sent a shiver of unease down my spine. The injection failed to trigger the expected movement in my leg, the limb lying still and unresponsive, a dead weight that seemed to drag me down, to anchor me to the ground. Panic gripped my chest, my heart pounding like a drum, my breathing quickening as I struggled to form words through the mounting fear that threatened to choke me. "I can't feel my leg," I wheezed, my voice laden with desperation, a cry for help that I couldn't hold back.

Glenda's piercing gaze locked onto me, her eyes filled with concern, a flicker of worry dancing in their depths as she searched my face for some sign of understanding, of explanation. "Are you certain?" she questioned, her voice laced with urgency, a note of disbelief threading through her words, as if she couldn't quite bring herself to accept the truth of my statement.

Tears welled up in my eyes, the hot sting of them blurring my vision, threatening to spill over and run down my cheeks in a flood of emotion that I couldn't control. "Am I going to lose it?" I choked out, my voice trembling, the words feeling like shards of glass in my throat, a painful admission of the fear that gripped me, the terror of the unknown that loomed before me like a gaping maw, ready to swallow me whole.

Taking a deep breath to steady herself, Glenda reached down and pulled back the lower end of the blanket, the rough fabric scratching against my skin, exposing my wounded leg to the cool air of the tent. To my surprise, she swiftly thrust the empty syringe into the arch of my foot, the sharp point of the needle digging into the tender flesh, prompting a sharp pain to surge through my leg, a bolt of agony that tore through me like a lightning strike.

"What the fuck was that for!?" I yelped, my voice rising in a shrill cry of pain and indignation, wincing as the pain radiated through my limb, a throbbing ache that seemed to pulse in time with my racing heart.

A soft smile played on Glenda's lips as she reassured me, her voice filled with a gentle understanding. "Your leg still has feeling," she said simply, the words meant as a promise of hope.

"No!" I cried out, tears streaming down my cheeks, the hot, salty tracks burning my skin as they ran unchecked, a flood of emotion that I couldn't hold back, couldn't control. "I meant the other leg," I sobbed, my voice breaking, the words coming out in a choked gasp that seemed to tear at my throat.

Glenda's expression turned tense, her brows furrowing in confusion, a flicker of uncertainty dancing in her eyes as she tried to make sense of my words, to understand the depth of my fear and desperation. "That doesn't make any sense," she muttered almost to herself, her voice betraying a hint of frustration, a note of bewilderment that seemed to echo my own confused state of mind. Then, with a newfound determination, "Close your eyes," she issued the command, her voice firm and unwavering.

Sniffling, I complied, my eyelids fluttering shut, blocking out the world around me, the warm glow of the sunlight fading into darkness, replaced by a void of uncertainty and fear. I waited anxiously for the next instruction, my mind filled with questions and apprehension.

"Do you not feel anything?" Glenda's voice broke the silence, her words tinged with concern, a note of worry that sent a shiver of unease down my spine, a cold finger of dread that seemed to trace its way along my skin.

"No," I replied, shaking my head, bewildered by her query, my mind grasping for some sense of understanding, some explanation for the strange sensation, or lack thereof, that seemed to grip my leg, to hold it in a vice of numbness and disconnection. "Should I have?" I asked, my voice small and uncertain, the hesitant whisper of a plea for reassurance, for some sign that everything would be alright.

After a momentary pause, a beat of silence that seemed to stretch on for an eternity, Glenda's voice carried a mixture of reassurance and uncertainty, a note of forced optimism that didn't quite ring true, a hollow promise that seemed to echo in the stillness of the tent. "You're going to be just fine," she said, the words feeling like a lie, a false comfort that did little to ease the fear that gripped me, the terror that gnawed at my insides like a ravenous beast.

The rustling of the tent signalled Chris's entrance, the sound of the fabric parting like a whisper in the stillness, drawing my attention, my gaze snapping to the opening, my heart leaping into my throat with the sudden intrusion.

"We need to get Kain to the lagoon, now!" Glenda informed Chris, urgency in her tone even before a proper greeting could be exchanged, the words tumbling out in a rush of desperation and fear.

The mention of the lagoon sent shivers of panic coursing through my body, a cold sweat breaking out on my skin, my heart pounding like a drum in my chest. I whispered, my voice barely audible, a faint, trembling sound that seemed to come from some distant place, some corner of my mind that was still gripped by fear and dread. "Not the lagoon," I said, shaking my head vigorously in protest, the movement sending a wave of dizziness washing over me, the world spinning and tilting around me like a carnival ride gone horribly wrong.

Glenda's gaze bore into me, her eyes searching mine for answers, for some explanation for my reluctance, my fear. "Why not?" she asked, her voice filled with a quiet intensity.

Overwhelmed by the terror that gripped me, the memories of my previous encounter at the lagoon flooding back to me in a rush of images and sensations, I could only shake my head, my mouth unable to form words, to articulate the deep-rooted fear.

"It's okay," Chris interjected, his voice calm and soothing. "The beast has been killed," he said simply, the words a reassurance that did little to ease the fear that gripped me, the terror that seemed to seep into my very bones, to wrap around me like a suffocating blanket of dread.

But it's not the beast I'm worried about, I screamed inwardly, the words echoing in my mind, a silent cry of anguish that tore at my soul, taunted by the haunting memories of my previous encounter at the lagoon, with my uncle present no less, the image forever burned into my mind, a scar that would never heal, a wound that would never close.

Glenda swiftly took charge, her voice resolute. "Help me lift him," she instructed Chris, as he squatted beside her.

Chris slid his arm beneath my shoulders, attempting to lift me, his muscles straining with the effort, but with a wounded leg and the other seemingly paralysed, our efforts only led to stumbling and a helpless collapse back to the ground, my body crumpling like a puppet whose strings had been cut, a broken doll that lay in a heap on the floor of the tent.

Wide-eyed, Glenda made a swift decision, her mind racing with the possibilities. "I'll get Karen," she said, her voice filled with a quiet urgency, a determination to see this through, to get me to the lagoon no matter the fear that gripped me.

"No need," Karen's voice rang out from the tent's entrance, a sudden intrusion that sent a jolt of surprise through me, my heart leaping into my throat at the unexpected sound. "I figured you might need some help," she said, quickly moving to her husband's side. She turned to Glenda, ready to assist, her voice filled with a quiet strength. "What do you need?" she asked simply.

Glenda wasted no time, taking full command of the situation, her voice filled with a steely resolve. "We need to carry Kain to the lagoon," she said, the words sending a fresh wave of dread washing over me, my heart sinking even deeper into despair, the fear that gripped me tightening its hold, squeezing the air from my lungs in a painful gasp.

My heart skipped a beat, a surge of dread coursing through me as I realised that Glenda was determined to take me there, against my desperate wishes, my silent pleas for mercy, for some reprieve from the horror that awaited me.

"He currently has no use of his legs," Glenda added, her words sinking my heart even deeper into despair, a brutal reminder of the helplessness that gripped me, the vulnerability that left me exposed and defenceless, a lamb being led to the slaughter.

"I'll take the bulk of his weight," Chris told his wife, his voice filled with determination. "Can you support his waist and legs?" he asked.

As the reality of my situation settled upon me, the inevitable journey to the lagoon unfolding before my eyes, a fate that I couldn't escape, couldn't avoid, I closed my eyes, a silent prayer falling from my lips, a desperate plea for mercy. I resigned myself to what lay ahead, to the fate that had been chosen for me, the path that I had no choice but to follow.

"Of course," Karen replied with unwavering support, her voice filled with a quiet strength, a determination that matched her husband's.

Grunts and moans filled the air as the couple lifted me from the mattress, their strength and determination carrying me forward, even as uncertainty and fear gripped my soul, making it hard to breathe, hard to think, hard to hope.

❖

Reaching the water's edge, dread consumed me as Karen and Chris carefully lowered me onto the bank of the lagoon, their disregard for my pleas to return to camp and recover like a normal human adding to my frustration. The gentle lapping of the water against the shore seemed to mock me, a cruel reminder of the fate that awaited me, the horrors that lurked beneath the surface of the crystal-clear depths.

My eyes fixated on Glenda as she extended her fingers, cautiously dipping them into the clear lagoon water, the ripples spreading out from her touch like a silent warning, a whisper of the power that lay hidden within. A visible shudder coursed through her body, a physical manifestation of the eerie influence of the lagoon, although she seemed determined to ignore it, to push past the unsettling sensations that gripped her.

Bracing myself, I anticipated the familiar zings of pulsating energy that would accompany the sprinkling of water on my wound, the electric tingles that would race through my body like a current, igniting every nerve ending with a flash of sensation that bordered on pleasurable pain. But instead, to my surprise, Glenda firmly grasped my leg, her fingers digging into the flesh with a determined grip, and swiftly submerged it into the lagoon.

The anticipated zings were replaced by an overwhelming surge of pleasure that engulfed my entire leg, the sensation intensifying with each passing second, racing toward my groin with a speed and intensity that left me breathless. It was like nothing I had ever experienced before, a pleasure so intense that it bordered on agony, a sweet torture that consumed me whole, leaving me helpless and vulnerable in its wake.

Helplessly surrendering to the sensations, I emitted a groan that straddled the line between pleasure and pain, the sound tearing from my throat like a wounded animal, a primal cry that echoed across the still surface of the lagoon. My body twisted and writhed, a marionette whose strings were being pulled by some unseen force, a puppet dancing to the tune of the lagoon's dark magic.

Reacting swiftly, Karen and Chris pulled me out of the water, their hands gripping my arms and legs with a desperate strength, breaking the spell that had momentarily consumed me, the connection that had bound me to the lagoon's power. I gasped for breath, my lungs burning with the effort, my heart pounding in my chest like a drum, the blood roaring in my ears with a deafening intensity.

Gasping for breath, I sought solace in the freshness of the air, the coolness of the breeze that caressed my skin, desperately yearning for any form of relief from the conflicting sensations coursing through my body. The aftershocks of the pleasure still lingered, a ghostly echo that refused to fade, a reminder of the power that the lagoon held over me, the control that it exerted over my very being.

"He's fine," Glenda reassured the couple, her voice calm and steady, seemingly oblivious to the torture she had just subjected me to, the agony that she had inflicted upon me with her actions.

Biting my lower lip and blinking rapidly, fighting against the waves of pain and the relentless surge of sexual energy that demanded release, I pleaded, "I want to be alone for a while," my voice hoarse and strained, hoping to find some respite from the overwhelming intensity of the moment.

"Don't be such an idiot. You can't be alone right now," Karen scoffed, her voice sharp and cutting, dismissing my plea without a second thought, her eyes narrowing with a mixture of contempt and disbelief.

Turning to Glenda, my tear-filled eyes implored her to understand the turmoil I was experiencing, the depth of the pain and confusion that gripped me, but it was clear that my silent plea fell on deaf ears, that she was blind to the suffering that she had caused.

"Karen's right," Glenda affirmed, her voice firm and unyielding, extinguishing any glimmer of hope I had held onto, leaving me feeling exposed and vulnerable, a raw nerve that had been stripped bare for all to see. "It's not safe for you to be alone out here."

"Then take me back..." I started to implore, the words tumbling out in a desperate plea, a last-ditch effort to escape the fate that awaited me.

"I'll stay here with him," Chris interjected, looking down at me with a gaze filled with compassion and understanding, a flicker of empathy that shone through the darkness. "I can clean his wound."

Suppressing the unsavoury thoughts that filled my mind, the dark imaginings that whispered of further torment and degradation, I halted myself from rejecting Chris's offer, realising that having one person present for whatever followed was preferable to the scrutiny of all three of them witnessing my intimate struggles, the shame and humiliation that burned within me like a fire.

Glenda shrugged her shoulders, a gesture of indifference that sent a chill down my spine, addressing Chris with a detached air, "As long as you make sure his leg gets submerged for a reasonable amount of time."

At the mention of another submersion, my leg involuntarily jerked, a reflexive response to the trauma I had already endured, the memory of the overwhelming sensations that had consumed me still fresh in my mind. *I can't bear to go through it again*, I thought, a silent scream that echoed in the depths of my soul, a plea for mercy that went unheard.

"Regardless of how much he groans about it," Glenda emphasised, her voice cold and clinical, tightening her grip on my leg, her fingers digging into the flesh like talons, her words sinking in with a grim finality that left no room for argument.

Chris nodded silently, his expression solemn and resolute, conveying his understanding and commitment.

Finally released from Glenda's grip, she rose to her feet, her figure towering over me like a colossus, a looming shadow that seemed to block out the sun itself.

Karen's uncertain pout revealed her reservations, a flicker of doubt that danced across her features, her eyes darting between Chris and me with a mixture of concern and apprehension. "Are you sure this is a good idea?" she questioned, her voice filled with a hesitant uncertainty.

"We're sure," I interjected, my voice filled with an urgency that bordered on desperation, a frantic need to get the two women on their way, to escape their probing gazes and judgmental stares.

Chris shrugged in response to Glenda's questioning gaze, a noncommittal gesture that spoke volumes.

"You could lose your leg if you don't let the water help you," Glenda admonished me, her voice sharp and cutting, her grip firm as she passed by, extending her hand to Karen and guiding her to her feet, a silent command to follow, to leave me to my fate.

Frustration welled within me, a bitter bile that rose in the back of my throat, threatening to choke me with its acrid taste. *Is Glenda truly oblivious to the lagoon's effects?* I pondered silently, my mind reeling with the implications of her words, the callousness of her actions. *How could she not see the torment that she was inflicting upon me, the depths of the suffering that she was condemning me to?*

I watched the two women ascend the first sand dune, their figures growing smaller in the distance, their forms blurring and wavering in the shimmering heat that rose from the sun-baked earth. A part of me longed to call out to them, to beg them to return, to take me with them. But I knew that it was futile, that my pleas would fall on deaf ears.

"Come on," Chris coaxed, his voice gentle and soothing, crouching beside me, reaching for my leg with a tentative hand, his touch light and hesitant, as if he feared to cause me further pain. "Let's get you cleaned up."

"It's fine, I can do it myself," I retorted, my voice sharp and defensive, pushing Chris's arms away with a stubborn determination, my resistance fuelled by a mixture of defiance and fear, a desperate need to maintain some semblance of control over my own fate.

A cool shiver coursed down my shoulders, the soft voice of Clivilius speaking to my mind, a whisper that seemed to come from everywhere and nowhere at once, a presence that filled the air around me like a tangible thing. *Let the man help you*, it whispered gently, its tone filled with a seductive persuasion, a promise of relief and release. *He can be useful to me.*

I gulped. *I don't want to*, I defiantly retorted within my thoughts, my inner voice filled with a stubborn resolve, daring to challenge the voice that urged compliance, the force that sought to bend me to its will.

Then your leg won't heal, the voice persisted, its tone filled with a cold finality, a reminder of the stakes that hung in the balance, the price that I would pay for my disobedience.

"Fine," I relented sharply, my voice filled with a bitter defeat, a resignation that overshadowed my tone, a surrender to the inevitable that left a sour taste in my mouth. "Have it your way."

"I'm just trying to help you," Chris responded, his voice filled with a gentle reproach, raising his hands defensively, his eyes filled with a hurt that cut me to the core.

Softening my stance, I sighed softly, the sound filled with a weary resignation, realising that my harsh words had been mistakenly directed at him, a misplaced anger that had found an undeserving target. "I know," I reassured him, my voice filled with a genuine gratitude for his intentions, a recognition of the kindness that he had shown me, the selflessness of his actions.

As Chris encouraged me closer to the water, his hand guiding me forward with a gentle insistence, my expectation for the anticipated sexual urges grew, a rising tide of desire, and I nervously held my breath, bracing myself for the onslaught of sensations that I knew would come.

The water didn't disappoint; an instant exhilaration shuddered through my body as Chris pushed my foot into the clear water, igniting every nerve ending with a flash of pleasure. Splashing water over my leg, Chris began to wipe away the crusty blood, his touch gentle and soothing.

Biting my lower lip, I leaned back, resting on my elbows as I mentally battled the sexual urges that pulsated through every vein in my body, a raging inferno that threatened to reduce me to a quivering mess of need and desire. It was a struggle that I knew I couldn't win, a battle that I was destined to lose, but still I fought, clinging to the last shreds of my sanity with a desperate tenacity.

Peering through half-opened eyelids, "Do you not feel it?" I asked Chris softly, my voice barely above a whisper, amazed that he remained completely calm and seemingly unaffected by the lagoon's waters, the power that flowed through them like a current, a force that could not be denied.

"Feel what?" Chris asked, his voice filled with a genuine confusion, urging me toward the water as he submerged me to my knees, the sensation intensifying with each passing second, a rising tide of pleasure that threatened to drown me in its depths.

I gasped loudly, the sound tearing from my throat like a wounded animal.

"Painful?" asked Chris, his voice filled with a gentle concern, a hint of worry that tugged at my heartstrings.

If the water has no sexual impact on Chris, there's no need to reveal my secret now, I concluded, my mind racing with the implications of this revelation, the possibilities that it presented. Quickly stopping my head mid-shake, I swapped it for a vigorous nod, a silent affirmation of the pain that I claimed to feel, a lie that burned on my tongue like acid.

Sinking back into silence, Chris seemed content with the explanation.

Your leg needs him, Kain, Clivilius whispered softly, its voice filled with a seductive persuasion, a promise of relief and release, a temptation that I couldn't resist, a siren's call that drew me ever closer to the edge of oblivion.

My brow furrowed, a silent question forming on my lips, a confusion that clouded my mind like a fog. *I don't understand what you want from me!* I silently screamed, my inner voice filled with a desperate frustration.

Help him feel my presence, the voice commanded, its tone filled with a cold authority, a force that I couldn't resist.

What the fuck!? Another shockwave of energy pulsed up my legs and culminated in my groin, a flash of pleasure so intense that it bordered on agony, a sweet torture that consumed me whole, leaving me helpless and vulnerable in its wake. My arousal was instant, a raging inferno that burned within me like a wildfire, consuming everything in its path.

Eyes shut tight, I gasped again, the sound filled with a desperate need, a primal hunger that demanded to be sated.

"Perhaps that's enough," said Chris, his voice filled with a gentle concern, attempting to drag me back from the water.

Your leg, Kain, the voice whispered, its tone filled with a seductive persuasion, a reminder of the price that I would pay for my disobedience, the consequences of my defiance.

"No!" I cried out, my voice filled with a desperate urgency, causing Chris to stop in his tracks, his eyes widening with surprise and confusion. "Maybe you should get in the lagoon," I suggested, the words tumbling from my lips before I could stop them, a desperate plea for help, for salvation from the torment.

Chris looked at me oddly, his brow furrowing with a mixture of confusion and disbelief, his eyes searching mine for some sign of clarity, of understanding. "You think I should go for a swim? Now?" he asked, his voice filled with a hesitant uncertainty, a hint of the unease that gripped him, the doubt that clouded his mind.

"Not a swim," I said, realising how absurd my outburst must have sounded, how desperate and unhinged I must have appeared in that moment. "Maybe just wade up to your knees or something," I suggested, my voice filled with a forced casualness, a nonchalance that belied the turmoil that raged within me.

Chris shrugged, a silent acquiescence to my request, a willingness to humour me in my moment of need. "I guess I could," he said, his voice filled with a resigned acceptance, rolling up his trousers and stepping into the water, the cool liquid enveloping his skin.

I watched with interest, my eyes fixed on his form as he waded deeper into the lagoon, the water still appearing to take no effect, to have no hold over him, no power to sway his mind or cloud his judgment.

Chris waded out a little further, his movements sending gentle ripples lapping against my still semi-submerged legs, the sensation intensifying with each passing second, tingling sexual urges vibrating up my thighs, a rising tide of desire that threatened to drown me in its depths. *How the hell does Chris feel nothing?* I wondered, my mind reeling with the implications of this revelation, the possibilities that it presented, the questions that it raised.

And as I lay there, my body consumed by the fire that burned within me, my mind lost in a haze of desire and confusion, I couldn't help but feel a flicker of envy for Chris, for his apparent immunity to the lagoon's power.

Unexpectedly, Chris removed his shirt and threw it to shore. The sudden movement sent larger waves against my legs, and a strong vibrating energy travelled up my thighs, pulsating in my groin. My eyes widened as I gazed at Chris's hairy chest. He wasn't the toned type of guy and had a slight tubbiness to him, but his gentle curves drew my attention deeper.

It's just the water fucking with you, I told myself, and forcing my eyes closed I leaned back on my elbows.

A warm, rough finger touched my right calf.

My cock throbbed intensely. *Please stop*, my mind begged.

Don't resist Kain, or I will make your leg mine.

"Shit!" I hissed; a response intended for both Clivilius and the second finger that now slowly travelled up my leg. The two fingers were joined by a third and fourth. Quickly, a hand pressed firmly against my flesh as it moved up my thigh. Travelling up the inside of my shorts, fingertips glided lightly across my balls. *Fuck! Why does that feel so good!?*

The fingers continued their exploration, causing a strength in my shaft that didn't seem humanly possible.

The hand retreated. I wanted to breathe a sigh of relief, to think of Brianne, but I couldn't. A thick fog smothered my brain, the happy neurons firing out of control and waves of pleasure eliminated any thought that attempted to intervene.

A shadow passed over my face. Opening my eyes, Chris's chest hovered above me. I stared into the maze of black and smattering of grey hairs that covered most of his chest and trailed down his abdomen and further below. Unable to control my body, I placed my hands on Chris's hips and slowly slid them behind him, pressing my fingers firmly into his wet flesh.

The unzipping of Chris's trousers sent an uncanny zing of expectant pleasure shuddering down my spine, as though all inhibitions were being stripped away. Chris's firm member poked through his trousers, the lubricated head glistening in the sunlight.

Slowly, Chris leaned toward my face and as unwanted instincts kicked into gear, my mouth opened to receive him. Deep grunts of indescribable pleasure escaped Chris's lips as he moved himself with a calm rhythm inside my mouth. A hand moved unabashedly down my abdomen and slipped beneath my shorts. Fingers wrapped tightly around my engorged cock, massaging it to the same rhythmic movement, as though he were making us as one.

Chris's moaning grew louder and faster, matching his intensified movements. I could sense that he was close. *And so am I!*

A wet thumb slid across the head of my cock, smearing my precious liquid over it. The final stimulant applied, almost instantly I culminated in Chris's palm as it cupped over the tip of my uncontrollable member. Rubbing my own fluids over my still pulsating cock, Chris withdrew from my mouth, and I watched as he squirted copious amounts of ejaculate across the Clivilian sands.

Elated and satisfied, I reflected on the pleasurable torment. *You better heal my fucking leg!* I warned Clivilius, as my elbows finally buckled, and I fell back to the ground.

Collapsing beside me, Chris's breathing was just as heavy as my own, and in silence, we lay beside each other. I didn't dare look at him, and as the warm sun began to dry my skin, my eyes closed.

ECHOES OF LOSS

4338.209.4

"Chris! Kain!" Karen's urgent voice pierced through the air, jolting me from my daze as I turned to face her, my eyes widening with alarm. Dusty sand was already being scattered over the remnants of our previous encounter, an instinctual response to cover our tracks, as Karen hurried toward us, her face etched with worry and determination.

"Chris, your shirt!" I hissed, my voice low and insistent, grabbing the discarded garment from beside us and tossing it to him with a quick, furtive motion.

"Not a word of this... to anyone!" Chris whispered sharply, his tone leaving no room for argument as he hastily pulled the shirt over his head, concealing any evidence of our illicit rendezvous.

"No shit!" I replied, my agreement punctuated with a mix of relief and anxiety, the weight of our shared secret hanging heavy in the air between us.

Karen arrived breathless, her chest heaving with exertion, her face flushed and glistening with a sheen of sweat. Her urgency was evident in the tense set of her shoulders, the flicker of fear that danced in her eyes. "Have either of you seen Joel out here?" she asked, her gaze darting around the surrounding landscape, searching for any sign of the missing boy.

My heart sank as I realised the potential consequences of our hasty actions. I hadn't even considered the possibility of someone else stumbling upon our forbidden encounter, too caught up in the heat of the moment to think beyond my own intoxicating desires.

"No," Chris responded, shaking his head, his voice steady and assured, a mask of innocence that belied the guilt that gnawed at my insides. "It's just been Kain and I since you left us earlier."

I ransacked my memory, desperately trying to recall the last time I had laid eyes on Joel, my mind racing with the implications of his disappearance. "I don't think I've seen him since dinner last night," I replied, my words tinged with a growing sense of fear and concern, a knot of dread tightening in the pit of my stomach. "Is everything okay?" I asked, wincing as the weight of my own question settled in, the absurdity of seeking reassurance in a desolate wasteland haunted by eerie creatures and plagued by a relentless, unsettling voice in my head. Of course, everything was far from okay, but it seemed futile to voice that realisation aloud.

"It appears that Joel is missing," Karen revealed, her voice heavy with worry. She reached out to steady me as I stumbled on my injured leg, the pain shooting through my body like a bolt of lightning.

A furrow formed on my brow, mirroring the mounting unease that churned within me, a sickening twist in the pit of my stomach. *Everything is definitely not okay,* I reminded myself, accepting Karen's support with a grateful nod, even as the uncertainty of our situation loomed large.

"How is your leg doing?" Karen inquired, her concern etched across her face, her eyes filled with a gentle compassion that belied the urgency of our predicament.

"It's still really painful," I replied, my voice strained with the effort of each step, wincing as I attempted to put weight on my wounded limb, the agony shooting through me like a white-hot knife.

"Come on," Karen urged, her gaze darting around nervously, scanning the surrounding landscape for any sign of danger. "Let's get back to camp. Paul's requested that everyone gather at the campfire."

Chris appeared puzzled, his brow furrowed with confusion, questioning the urgency of the situation. "Why the rush?" he asked.

"Just come on," Karen replied, her hand gesturing impatiently for us to start moving. "We need to find Joel."

Despite the pain that surged through my leg with each hobbling step, I pressed forward, gritting my teeth against the agony.

"Help Kain, would you," Karen scolded her husband, her tone sharp with impatience, her eyes flashing with a mixture of annoyance and concern.

Chris cast a nervous glance in my direction, uncertainty flickering in his eyes. I averted my gaze, unable to meet his questioning stare, focusing instead on the pain that radiated from my leg.

As Chris moved beside me, his strong arm wrapping around my waist, I gingerly draped my own arm across his broad shoulders, allowing him to bear the brunt of my weight. "It's fine," I assured Karen, waving her away as she moved to my other side, knowing that her towering height would only complicate matters further. Despite the desire for more support, the yearning for someone else to share the burden of my pain, I resigned myself to the reality of the situation. My slight stature made Chris an ideal support, and I had no choice but to make the best of it, to grit my teeth and push through the agony.

We were still battling the first dune when a loud bark caught our attention, sending a terrifying shiver down my spine, the hairs on the back of my neck standing on end. It was all too familiar, a haunting echo of the horrors we had already faced. Turning back to the lagoon, my heart in my throat, I saw Lois standing at the edge, her fur bristling, her teeth bared in a feral snarl as she growled at the water between barks, a warning and a challenge to some unseen foe.

"I didn't know Lois was here too," Karen remarked, her voice tinged with surprise.

"Me neither," Chris responded, his own confusion echoing mine.

"I wonder what she's found?" Karen pondered aloud, her curiosity getting the better of her, taking a few hesitant steps toward the lagoon, her gaze fixed on the rippling surface of the water, as if she could divine some hidden truth from its depths.

"I think we should keep moving," I interjected, my voice firm and insistent, uninterested in uncovering any further mysteries this godforsaken place held, desperate to put as much distance between myself and the lagoon as possible.

Karen glanced over her shoulder, her eyes meeting mine for a brief moment, considering my words before replying, her tone laced with a quiet determination. "You two keep moving. I'll go and see what the problem is."

Taking another step forward, a jolt of pain shot through my leg, my muscles screaming in protest as Chris hesitated, causing me to wince involuntarily, my vision swimming with the effort of remaining upright.

"Karen, please be careful. We don't need you going missing too," Chris cautioned, his voice laced with concern, his grip tightening around my waist.

An uncomfortable shudder ran through me, my mind consumed by the harrowing possibility of all of us disappearing without a trace, swallowed up by the vast, unforgiving landscape that stretched out before us, our fates sealed by the cruel whims of some unseen force.

"I'm sure it's nothing," Karen reassured us, her tone attempting to mask the unease that flickered in her eyes, the fear that lurked just beneath the surface of her words, before briskly making her way toward the lagoon.

Sighing heavily, Chris redirected his attention to me, his gaze filled with a quiet resolve. "Come on, then," he urged, his voice a low murmur, a gentle encouragement that spurred me forward, even as my body screamed in protest with every agonising step.

"Lois!" Karen's voice rang out from behind us, a sharp, urgent cry that pierced the stillness of the air, sending a fresh wave of fear coursing through my veins.

Neither of us turned back, our gazes fixed firmly ahead, focused solely on moving toward the camp, on reaching the safety and comfort of familiar faces. The further we ventured, with no sign of Lois or Karen's return, my unease intensified, a gnawing dread that settled in the pit of my stomach, a sickening twist that refused to be ignored. I tried to reassure Chris multiple times, my voice filled with a false bravado, assuring him that his wife and Lois would rejoin us shortly, even as my own doubts and fears simmered.

It was as we climbed the final hill, our muscles burning with the effort, our breaths coming in short, ragged gasps, that Lois ran past us, her fur slick with water, her eyes wide with a primal terror that sent a chill down my spine. Quickly coming back, she circled us several times, her movements erratic and frenzied, stopping twice to shake the water from her saturated fur, a desperate attempt to rid herself of some unseen taint.

Karen wasn't far behind, her own face pale and drawn, her eyes haunted by some unspoken horror that lurked just beyond the edges of our understanding. We paused to wait for her to reach us, our own breaths held in anxious anticipation, our hearts pounding in our chests with a sickening rhythm.

"What was the problem?" Chris asked, his voice tight with worry, his brow furrowed with concern as he searched his wife's face for some clue, some hint of the truth that she seemed so desperate to conceal.

"It was nothing," replied Karen, quickly shaking her head, her words ringing hollow in the stillness of the air, a blatant lie that fooled no one.

Taking my eyes away from Lois, I cast a glance at Karen, my gaze searching her face for some hint of the truth, some glimpse of the horrors that she had witnessed. And there, in the depths of her eyes, I caught a fleeting glimpse of something that sent a chill down my spine, a warning glare directed at Chris, a silent plea for him to let the matter drop, to leave well enough alone.

Clearly it was something, I told myself, gulping dryly, my throat constricting with the effort of swallowing down the fear that threatened to choke me. *But Karen and Lois both appeared to be uninjured,* I continued silently, my mind racing with the implications of their apparent wellbeing, even as my heart clenched with a sickening sense of dread.

"Let's keep moving," I told them, my voice strained with the effort of maintaining some semblance of calm.

Resuming our journey, we continued toward the camp, our steps heavy with exhaustion, our bodies aching with the strain of our ordeal. But we pressed on, driven by the desperate need for safety.

The anticipation grew as we neared our destination. Lois bounded into the camp, her tail wagging with a newfound energy, finding solace in Glenda's welcoming embrace, her face buried in the woman's chest as if seeking comfort and reassurance.

Paul and Charity stood nearby, their faces grim and solemn, their presence a reminder of the communal gathering that awaited us.

A broad smile graced my face as I witnessed the reunion of Lois and Glenda, and for a moment, I allowed myself to forget the pain that wracked my body, the fear that gnawed at my insides.

❖

"The feeling has returned in my uninjured leg," I informed Glenda, gratitude evident in my voice, a flicker of hope rekindling within me at this small yet significant milestone in my recovery.

Glenda's face softened as she rose to her feet, her eyes meeting mine with a gentle warmth. "Well, that's a relief," she replied. "And the other leg?" she inquired, concern still etched in the furrow of her brow.

"Seems to be quite the miracle," Karen chimed in, joining our conversation as we gathered near the campfire.

Nodding appreciatively, I acknowledged Glenda's advice. "I'll be sure to give it plenty of rest," I assured her, fully aware of the need for caution and recovery, the long road that still stretched before me.

Chris interjected, his eyes lighting up with an idea, a spark of enthusiasm animating his face. "We can make you some crutches," he suggested, his mind already contemplating the practicality of the solution, the steps needed to bring it to fruition.

Karen scoffed, dismissing the notion with a wave of her hand. "Forget making crutches," she exclaimed, her tone brimming with determination. "Just have Luke bring us some real ones," she instructed Paul, her words carrying an air of practicality and efficiency, a no-nonsense approach to problem-solving.

"That's a much better idea," Glenda agreed, her attention momentarily diverted towards the tents, her gaze drawn by some unseen force.

Intrigued by her sudden shift in focus, I followed her line of sight, my own eyes landing on the figures of Beatrix and Uncle Jamie as they emerged from around the canvas walls, their movements heavy with a palpable sense of grief and sorrow. A sense of foreboding washed over me as they approached, Uncle Jamie cradling a bundle in his arms, the stained sheet concealing a weighty secret, a truth that I feared to confront.

My heart sank, a leaden weight settling in my chest, and unspoken questions echoed within me, a swirling maelstrom of doubt and dread. *What... or who... lay beneath that soiled shroud?* The possibilities tore at my mind, each more devastating than the last. Unable to voice my concerns, I awaited their arrival with a heavy, uneasy silence hanging in the air.

Paul straightened his back, stepping forward with a determined air, a resolute set to his jaw. "Jamie," he began, his voice cracking slightly with emotion, a betrayal to the depth of his own grief. "I know things are painful right now, but we need to know when you last saw Joel."

Uncle Jamie halted abruptly, a heavy silence hanging in the air as he wrestled with his words, his face a mask of anguish and despair. Ignoring the searing pain that shot through my leg, a reminder of my own physical limitations, my gaze swept across the group, desperately seeking answers, some clue to the fate that had befallen Joel.

Recognition dawned on me like a bolt from the blue, a realisation that struck with the force of a physical blow. "Duke," I gasped softly, the pieces falling into place with a sickening clarity. Aside from Joel, the spirited dog was the only other member of the camp who remained unaccounted for, a glaring absence that sent a chill down my spine. My eyes narrowed at the bundled sheet cradled in Jamie's arms, a growing sense of unease gnawing at my insides. *It's the right size*, my mind whispered, a traitorous thought that I couldn't shake. A burning sensation ignited behind my eyes, tears of grief and rage mingling with the ever-present pain that wracked my body.

Uncle Jamie's voice held a weighty burden as he replied, his tone low and sombre, each word seeming to cost him a great effort. "It was just before the attack last night," he confessed, his shoulders sinking under the weight of his own guilt and sorrow. "He was in bed in the tent when I took off after Duke."

Paul pressed on with his questioning, unwilling to let the matter rest, determined to uncover the truth no matter how painful it might be. "And when you returned?" he prodded, his voice taking on a harder edge.

Uncle Jamie's face fell, his silence a painful admission, a confirmation of our worst fears.

Glenda folded her arms nervously across her chest, her anxiety palpable. "Then it's settled," she interjected, her voice tinged with unease, a brittle edge to her words. "Joel is missing."

And what of Duke? The question burned on the tip of my tongue, a desperate need for answers, for some shred of hope to cling to in the face of this unimaginable loss. But the words caught in my throat, trapped by a knot of fear and despair, a suffocating tightness that threatened to choke the very life from me.

Charity broke away from the campfire. "I am certain that Joel has been taken by the Portal Pirate. I will hunt him down and bring Joel back," she declared with unwavering conviction, her words a promise and a challenge all at once.

"What the actual fuck?" I muttered under my breath, the shock and disbelief seeping through in a hushed whisper, my mind reeling with the implications of her words, the sheer audacity of her claim.

"I'm coming with you," Uncle Jamie blurted out, his voice filled with a mix of desperation and resolve, a fierce determination to do whatever it took to find his son, to bring him home safe and sound.

My eyes widened, silently protesting the idea, a surge of panic rising within me at the thought of being left behind, of facing this nightmare alone. *No! You can't leave me here*, I pleaded internally, my mind scrambling for a way to intervene, to make him see reason.

Charity nodded, her agreement unyielding, a steely glint in her eye. "Prepare your things. We leave immediately."

Watching the terror that gripped my uncle's eyes, the raw anguish that twisted his features, my heart felt as though it was being torn in two, ripped asunder by the cruelty of fate and circumstance.

With determined strides, Charity closed the distance between her and Uncle Jamie, her firm hand cradling his chin, urging him to meet her gaze, to face the reality of the situation head-on. "If you want any chance of finding Joel alive, we must leave immediately," she pressed, her voice carrying the weight of urgency, a grim reminder of the stakes at play.

Unable to bear witness to my uncle's torment any longer, I averted my gaze, my eyes landing on a gruesome sight that made my stomach churn with revulsion. A black panther-like creature lay motionless in the dust near the campfire, its lifeless form a brutal reminder of the dangers that lurked beyond the safety of our camp. Dried blood marred its mouth, a grisly testament to the violence that had unfolded, the horrors that had been unleashed upon us.

"I need to say farewell to Duke first," Uncle Jamie pleaded, his voice quivering with a mix of anguish and resolve, a desperate need for closure, for one final moment with his beloved companion.

Charity's response was cold and decisive. "Life is full of decisions and consequences. You need to make a choice, Joel or Duke."

A wave of nausea washed over me, a gag rising in my throat that I stifled with the palm of my hand, fighting back the bile that threatened to spill forth. Feeling a sense of despair closing in, an oppressive weight that seemed to crush the very breath from my lungs, I glanced back at my uncle, his expression etched with agony, a raw and visceral pain that tore at my heart.

"Duke knows you love him, Jamie," Beatrix interjected, her voice soft and gentle, stepping in front of Uncle Jamie and gently prying Duke's lifeless form from his arms, cradling the dog's body against her chest with a tenderness that brought tears to my eyes. "He won't ever forget that."

Leaning in, Uncle Jamie placed a tender kiss on Duke's wrapped head, a final gesture of love and devotion, a silent farewell to his loyal friend. "I'm so sorry, Duke," he whimpered, his voice thick with emotion, a raw and aching grief that seemed to pour from every fibre of his being. Taking a deep, shuddering breath, he straightened his back, standing tall, a flicker of resolve sparking to life in his eyes. "I'll grab my things."

I'm going too! The words echoed in my mind, a desperate plea that refused to find voice, trapped behind the lump that had risen in my throat, the knot of fear and helplessness that threatened to choke me.

But your injured leg, the eerie voice of Clivilius returned, sending a shockwave of terror rippling through my entire body, a cold and insidious reminder of my own limitations, my own vulnerability in the face of the horrors that surrounded us. *You would only be a burden if you go.*

Uncle Jamie suddenly paused, his footsteps halting, his shoulders slumping as if under the weight of some unseen burden. Casting a glance over his shoulder, he spoke with a tremor in his voice, a quiet plea that cut me to the core. "Take good care of Henri for me," he requested, his words heavy with the unspoken knowledge that he might never return, that this might be the last time we ever saw each other.

Paul stepped forward, scooping the plump little dog into his arms, cradling him against his chest with a gentle protectiveness that brought a fresh lump to my throat. "We'll keep him safe, Jamie. You have my word."

Without another word, Uncle Jamie retreated into his tent, Charity trailing close behind, her presence a grim reminder of the dangers that lay ahead, the perils that they would face in their quest to find Joel and bring him home.

I'm not a burden, I seethed silently, a flicker of defiance sparking to life within me, a stubborn refusal to be left behind, to be cast aside like so much dead weight. Distancing myself from Chris and Karen, I took a faltering step forward, a symbol of my renewed independence, my determination to prove myself capable and strong.

"Clivilius!" Glenda's piercing scream shattered the air, her body collapsing to her knees as she pounded her fists into the ground, her face contorted in a mask of anguish and despair. Looking up, she clutched at her chest, her eyes wide with a mixture of agony and revelation, a truth that seemed to consume her very being.

"Glenda?" Paul's voice rang out, a note of concern lacing his words, a flicker of fear dancing in his eyes as he approached cautiously, taking measured steps toward her trembling form. "Are you alright?"

"My father is alive!" Glenda blurted out, her hands shooting up triumphantly as if possessed by a sudden surge of elation, a manic energy that seemed to radiate from every pore. A trance-like state seemed to consume her, rendering her unresponsive to Chris's attempts to rouse her, his hand waving uselessly in front of her face.

Beatrix, too, broke away from the group, her eyes fixed on some distant horizon, a faraway look in her gaze as she cradled Duke's lifeless body in her arms, a silent guardian watching over the fallen.

"Beatrix, where are you going?" Paul called out, his voice tinged with confusion and disbelief, a desperate need for answers in the face of so much uncertainty and chaos.

"Home!" she shouted back, her response curt and resolute, a steely determination in her voice.

Seizing the opportunity, I interjected without hesitation, my own voice ringing out with a fierce resolve. "I'm going with Beatrix," I announced, my words a challenge and a promise all at once, a declaration of my own agency and free will.

"You need to rest," Karen said sternly, reaching for me with a disapproving frown, her fingers grasping at my arm in a futile attempt to hold me back.

"I need crutches," I retorted, pushing Karen away from me as I struggled to my feet, my injured leg screaming in protest with every movement. "If Beatrix brings me some crutches, I can go with my uncle."

"Don't be so foolish," Karen scolded, her voice stern and disapproving, a flicker of genuine concern in her eyes that I couldn't quite bring myself to acknowledge.

Ignoring Karen's pleas, I began to follow in Beatrix's footsteps, my bare feet sinking into the soft dust as I moved forward, each step a painful reminder of the obstacles that I would have to overcome if I ever hoped to see my uncle again.

Even with crutches, how can you be certain your leg will heal? Clivilius's voice echoed in my mind once again, a sinister whisper that sent a fresh wave of fear coursing through my body, a cold and creeping dread that seemed to seep into my very bones. *You will only bring harm upon yourself if you go.*

You promised! I silently argued, my thoughts a desperate plea for reassurance, for some shred of hope to cling to in the face of so much uncertainty and doubt.

Silence.

I've kept my end of the deal, I asserted, frustration and fear intermingling within me as I sought some validation, some acknowledgement of the sacrifices I had made, the price I had paid for Clivilius's aid.

Have you, really? The voice was a mocking whisper, a cruel taunt that sent a chill down my spine, a sickening twist in the pit of my stomach.

The chill of doubt ran down my spine as I retraced my steps, mentally reviewing the events that had unfolded, the choices I had made and the consequences they had wrought. *Did I miss something?* I wracked my brain, convinced that I had fulfilled my end of the bargain, that I had done everything that had been asked of me. *I gave you Chris,* I reminded Clivilius, my voice laced with a mixture of desperation and defiance, a stubborn refusal to be cowed by the entity that had taken up residence in my mind.

Are you absolutely certain? The question hung heavy in the air, a suffocating weight that pressed down on my chest, stealing the breath from my lungs.

Vivid memories of the glowing sperm in the lagoon and the tales of Uncle Jamie flooded my mind, a sickening realisation dawning on me. My eyes widened with a horrifying clarity, a truth that I had been too blind to see, too stubborn to acknowledge. *Chris hadn't ejaculated in the water* - I had failed to uphold my end of the bargain, had failed to fulfil the terms of the deal that I had struck with Clivilius.

I'm not doing that again! I protested vehemently, my thoughts a desperate cry of defiance, a refusal to be a pawn in Clivilius's twisted games any longer.

What will your child think when she discovers that her father lost his leg? The voice was a cruel mockery, a taunting reminder of the price I would pay for my defiance, the consequences of my failure to hold up my end of the bargain.

I gasped, fear pricking every fibre of my being, a cold and creeping dread that seemed to seep into my very soul. *How do you know about the baby?* I demanded, a sense of unease creeping in as I realised that even Brianne and I hadn't learned the gender yet, hadn't shared that precious knowledge with anyone.

I am Clive, the voice proclaimed, a chilling affirmation that sent shivers down my spine. And with those three simple words, my world came crashing down around me, the fragile illusion of control that I had clung to shattering like glass.

UNSEEN PASSAGES

4338.209.5

A suffocating sense of dread washed over me as I approached the massive translucent screen of the Portal, its blankness mocking my desperate search for Beatrix. My heart sank as I realised she had vanished before my eyes, leaving me burdened with guilt and an agonising void. I frantically scanned the screen, my fingers trembling, but it offered no answers, only a haunting emptiness that echoed my own despair.

Karen's concerned face appeared beside me, her voice gentle, yet stern. "Kain, your leg is bleeding," she pointed out, her worry etched on her features, her brow furrowed with a mixture of compassion and apprehension.

I glanced down, the sight of blood seeping through the bandages amplifying my weariness. With a heavy sigh, I limped over to the base of a sandy hill and collapsed, my strength drained, unable to stand any longer, the weight of my own body too much to bear.

"Come on, Kain. We should head back to camp," Karen urged, attempting to pull me up, her hands grasping at my arms with a gentle insistence.

Determined to wait for Beatrix's return, I shook my head stubbornly, refusing to budge, my resolve unwavering even in the face of my own exhaustion and pain. I couldn't leave, not now, not when there was still a chance that Beatrix might come back, that she might hold the key to my salvation.

Karen sighed, her expression reflecting resignation, a quiet acceptance of my stubborn refusal. "Fine, but I'm going to bring Glenda and some supplies back to look after that wound," she said, her voice filled with a quiet determination.

With a final, worried glance in my direction, Karen turned and walked away, leaving me to wait alone at the base of the hill, a solitary figure in a vast and unforgiving landscape, a tiny speck of humanity in the face of an uncaring universe.

Time crawled agonisingly slow as I sat there, trapped in a vortex of my own thoughts, the minutes stretching into what felt like an eternity of waiting and wondering. Adjusting the bandages on my leg, I tried to distract myself from the pain, from the gnawing fear that ate away at my insides, but my mind incessantly circled back to Beatrix and Luke.

Just as despair threatened to consume me, to drag me down into the depths of my own misery, Karen returned.

"Where's Glenda?" I asked, my voice hoarse and strained.

"Kain," she began, concern etched on her face, her eyes filled with a quiet sympathy that cut me to the core. "Glenda, Charity, and Jamie have all left the camp. They've gone portal pirate hunting."

Shock rippled through me, my brow furrowing with confusion, my mind reeling with the implications of her words. "Glenda's gone with them?" I questioned, struggling to comprehend the situation.

"Paul didn't seem like he had much say in the matter," Karen replied with a heavy sigh, her fingers nervously fidgeting with the bandage.

A surge of frustration mingled with worry as I grappled with the absence of our only doctor, the one person who might have been able to help me, to ease the pain that consumed me. "You mean to tell me that I have a gaping hole in my leg and our only doctor has left us?" I voiced my disbelief. "Why would she do that?"

Karen stood silently, her eyes locked on the bandage in her hands, uncertainty shadowing her features, a flicker of doubt dancing in her eyes. "I don't know," she answered softly, her voice barely above a whisper, a confession of her own helplessness.

"But here," Karen said, kneeling beside me, determination in her voice, a flicker of hope sparking to life in her eyes. "I've brought some fresh bandages. Let's get your leg cleaned up."

Reluctantly, I nodded, acknowledging the necessity of the task, the importance of taking care of my physical needs even as my emotional wounds continued to fester and bleed.

Karen quickly and efficiently removed the bloodied bandages, her touch gentle yet firm. But even as she worked, her hands deft and sure, a voice echoed in my mind, Clivilius's unwanted presence unsettling me, a sinister whisper that seemed to come from everywhere and nowhere at once.

There's always a choice, Kain Jeffries, the voice taunted, its words dripping with a cruel mockery. I shuddered involuntarily, trying to push aside the unwelcome thoughts that threatened to unravel my fragile optimism, the tiny shred of hope that I clung to.

"It's not looking great," Karen commented, her touch meticulous as she cleaned the gash, her brow furrowed with concentration, a flicker of worry dancing in her eyes.

Ignoring the tormenting voice, I mustered false confidence, a mask of bravado that I wore like a shield, a desperate attempt to protect myself from the horrors that lurked just beyond the edges of my consciousness. "I'll be fine," I assured Karen, hoping to convince myself as well, to cling to the illusion of control, of agency in the face of overwhelming odds. "Once I get crutches, I'll be able to walk properly."

Deep down, I knew my optimism was a fragile façade, a flimsy defence against the dark thoughts. Fear crept in, fuelled by the thought of Clivilius, or Clive, manipulating me to bring Chris to the lagoon again, to subject him to the same violation of body and soul. The dread churned my stomach, a gnawing reminder of the horrors I desperately sought to escape, the nightmares that haunted my every waking moment.

Sensing my discomfort and anxiety, the tension that radiated from my body like a physical force, Karen finished bandaging my leg with a sense of urgency, her movements quick and efficient. Her eyes held a mixture of sympathy and concern as she looked at me, her unspoken desire to stay and talk a palpable presence that seemed to fill the space with a suffocating intensity.

"I'll be back soon," Karen assured me, patting my shoulder reassuringly, her touch a fleeting moment of comfort. "I have to get some things done back at camp, are you sure you'll be okay here by yourself?"

I nodded, attempting to project strength, to convey a sense of confidence that I didn't truly feel, but inside, a profound sense of loneliness and isolation settled upon me. Watching Karen walk away, leaving me alone with my thoughts and fears, the silence became stifling.

The throbbing pain in my leg served as a constant reminder of the unfortunate events that had brought me to this desolate moment, the choices and consequences that had led me to this place of despair and hopelessness. Sitting there, I felt as if I were trapped at the bottom of a deep hole, devoid of direction or hope, the walls of my own misery closing in around me with each passing moment. The climb out seemed insurmountable, a Herculean task that I had no hope of accomplishing on my own.

Finally, after what felt like an eternity of waiting and wondering, the Portal burst into a kaleidoscope of vibrant colours, a dazzling display that captured my attention and filled me with a sudden, desperate hope.

"Hey, Beatrix!" I called out, a surge of excitement making me attempt to stand, my heart leaping into my throat at the prospect of seeing her again. However, a sharp pang of pain shot through my leg, a brutal reminder of my own limitations, forcing me back onto the ground with a gasp of agony, my body crumpling like a puppet whose strings had been cut.

Undeterred, I waved eagerly at Beatrix, my arm flailing in the air like a drowning man grasping for a lifeline, but she remained at a distance, waving back as though mistaking my waving for a mere hello, a casual greeting in the midst of the pain that gripped me. Disappearing into the swirling hues, Beatrix vanished, leaving me bewildered and longing for help, a sense of frustration and desperation welling up inside me.

Determined to seize the opportunity when Beatrix emerged once more, I mustered the strength to rise to my feet, my body screaming in protest with every movement, my injured leg throbbing with a pain that seemed to radiate through my entire being. Cautiously, I made my way toward the Portal, each moment a battle against the agony that consumed me.

Just as I neared, the Portal burst to life again, a dazzling display of light and colour that seemed to fill the world around me, and Beatrix stepped out, her face a mask of determination and purpose.

"Beatrix!" I exclaimed, reaching out for her arm, only to realise that I was still far from reaching her, my fingers grasping at empty air, a futile gesture of desperation and need. "I need crutches," I blurted, the words tumbling from my lips in a rush, determined to make my request before she could escape once more.

"You'll have to talk to Luke," Beatrix replied, dismissing me with a wave of her hand, her tone filled with a casual indifference that cut me to the core, a reminder of my own insignificance in the grand scheme of things. In her other hand, she dropped a sleeping bag by the Portal.

Ignoring the swirling dust that rose from the bag's landing, the particles stinging my eyes and coating my throat with a dry, choking sensation, I persisted, hobbling closer to Beatrix's side, my voice filled with a desperate urgency that bordered on hysteria. "But my leg," I pleaded.

Clearly unimpressed by the interruption, Beatrix glared at me, her eyes filled with a cold indifference that sent a chill down my spine. "Looks like it's bleeding," she pointed out.

Glancing down, I noticed a trickle of fresh blood staining my leg, the crimson liquid seeping through the bandage like a morbid promise, a reminder of the price I had paid for my own weakness, my own stubbornness to resist the temptations that had been laid before me. "Not again," I mumbled, my body tensing as I tried to ignore the nagging presence in the depths of my mind, the sinister whisper that reminded me of the inevitable choice that lay before me, the bargain that I would inevitable strike with Clive, the entity that claimed to hold the key to my salvation, to the healing of my battered and broken body.

"You should probably go and visit Glenda," Beatrix suggested, her voice filled with concern.

My eyes widened, startled by the mention of Glenda, my heart leaping into my throat at the prospect of seeking her aid. "Glenda's gone," I informed her, my voice filled with a quiet desperation.

A visible shudder ran through Beatrix's shoulders, a flicker of fear dancing in her eyes, a moment of vulnerability that was quickly masked by a hardening of her features. "Gone? Is she..." Beatrix hesitated, her voice trailing off before she finally finished the thought. "Dead?"

"Oh, no," I quickly reassured her, almost chuckling at the idea, a bitter laugh that tasted like ashes on my tongue, a mockery of the very concept of humour in the face of such unrelenting darkness. "She went with Charity and Uncle Jamie to hunt the Portal pirate."

Beatrix shook her head briefly. "You'll still have to ask Luke for crutches," she replied nonchalantly, seemingly unfazed by the news of Glenda's departure, her tone filled with a casual indifference that bordered on cruelty. "Sorry."

"Beatrix," I tried to persuade her, my voice filled with a desperate urgency, a plea for her to listen, to understand the depth of my need, but once again, she vanished before me, disappearing into the swirling vortex of the Portal like a ghost, a fleeting apparition that left me alone.

"Fuck's sake," I grumbled, frustrated by the elusive nature of our interactions, the constant dance of hope and disappointment that seemed to define my existence, a never-ending cycle of futility and despair.

Reluctantly, I waited in silence as Beatrix made multiple trips through the Portal, carrying an assortment of camping supplies, each one a reminder of the comforts and amenities that seemed like a distant memory in the face of the harsh realities that surrounded me. Amidst throwing her occasional puppy-dog eyes in an attempt to sway her, to break through the walls of indifference that seemed to surround her like a shield, I couldn't help but pay attention to the items she brought, my mind racing with possibilities and regrets. "If only we had some of this stuff last night," I muttered, holding up a large camping light, momentarily distracted by thoughts of missed opportunities.

Suddenly, Beatrix halted in her tracks, camping gear in hand, her gaze fixed on something behind me. Following her line of sight, I spotted Paul approaching, his face a mask of determination, his steps purposeful as he made his way towards us.

"You'll have to ask Luke for crutches," Beatrix informed Paul preemptively, not allowing him a chance to speak.

Paul turned his attention to me, his eyes searching my face for some explanation. I shrugged in defeat, feeling exhausted by the repetition, the constant cycle of hope and disappointment. *If I hear Beatrix say that one more time...* The thought trailed off, a silent plea for release from the endless torment.

Returning his gaze to Beatrix, Paul questioned, his voice filled with a quiet urgency. "Have you seen Luke?"

"No," Beatrix replied after a brief pause, her voice filled with a hint of uncertainty, a flicker of doubt that danced in her eyes. "I haven't seen him since he passed us the first time I arrived here."

Paul furrowed his brow, rubbing his chin in contemplation. Finally, he spoke, his words filled with a quiet determination. "Beatrix, I need you to find us a couple of caravans or motorhomes. They will make our living and sleeping arrangements a little more comfortable and also, hopefully, provide us with more safety than the tents currently do."

I was taken aback, Paul's request and decisive manner catching me off guard, the idea seeming to come out of nowhere, a sudden shift in the direction of our efforts. And yet, even as I struggled to wrap my mind around the implications of his words, I couldn't help but consider the advantages of having a caravan instead of a tent, the promise of shelter and security.

"But I don't have enough money for such an expense," Beatrix protested, throwing her hands up in the air, her voice filled with a mixture of frustration and disbelief, a rejection of the very idea that seemed to border on the absurd. "How am I supposed to get them?"

Frowning, I realised she had a point, the practicalities of our situation crashing down around me like a house of cards, the fragile illusion of hope and possibility shattering like glass. Caravans would undoubtedly be a significant expense, a luxury that seemed far beyond our reach. *But if we can't afford caravans, what else can't we afford?* The thought sent a chill down my spine, raising unsettling questions that I didn't want to contemplate, the spectre of our survival looming large in my mind.

Undeterred by Beatrix's concerns, Paul remained unfazed, his eyes sparkling with a hint of mischief, a flicker of excitement that seemed to dance in their depths. "You have a Portal, a place of escape where nobody can reach you," he suggested, a smile playing on his lips, a glimmer of possibility that seemed to light up the darkness. "I'm sure you have the creative abilities to pull the mission off."

Beatrix narrowed her eyes suspiciously, a hint of a smile tugging at her lips, a flicker of intrigue that seemed to dance in her eyes, a silent acknowledgment of the challenge that had been laid before her. "A mission, you say?" she inquired, unable to conceal her interest, the prospect of adventure and excitement seeming an irresistible call.

Please, Beatrix, accept it, I silently pleaded, my heart racing with a desperate hope, a longing for some measure of relief from the constant struggle for survival that consumed our every waking moment. The thought of having a safe and comfortable place to rest, to recover from the attack that I had suffered, filled me with a sense of longing that bordered on desperation, a fierce desire to cling to any shred of normality that we could find in this twisted world.

"Sure, I'll do it," Beatrix agreed, her smile breaking through uncontainably, a flicker of excitement dancing in her eyes, a spark of life that seemed to chase away the shadows.

Yes! I cheered inwardly, a surge of relief washing over me. Dabbing at the blood that dribbled down my leg again, I silently thanked whatever gods or forces might be listening for this small mercy.

Suddenly, Paul's expression darkened, a flicker of concern in his eyes, a shadow passing over his face like a storm cloud, and my heart sank, a leaden weight settling in the pit of my stomach. *What's wrong now?* I wondered anxiously, my mind racing with possibilities and fears, the fragile hope that had blossomed in my chest withering and dying like a flower in the harsh glare of the sun.

"By the way, where's Duke?" Paul asked Beatrix, his voice filled with a quiet urgency.

An unsettling pause hung in the air, a suffocating silence that seemed to stretch on for an eternity, before Beatrix responded resolutely. "What do you want first, Duke or caravans?"

After a few ums and ahs, Paul replied, his voice filled with a forced casualness, a false bravado that did little to mask the uncertainty that lurked just beneath the surface. "Get them in whatever order works best for you. I don't want to be too prescriptive or restrictive."

Beatrix nodded briskly, a gesture of acknowledgment that seemed to carry the weight of a promise. And soon after completing the delivery of camping supplies, she left Clivilius, disappearing into the swirling vortex of the Portal.

"How's the leg?" Paul turned his attention to me, his voice filled with concern.

"Could be worse," I replied, my voice filled with a forced optimism. I was acutely aware that if I were to stand a chance at beating Clive at its own game, at breaking free from the chains of manipulation and control that bound me, I needed to maintain a positive outlook, to cling to the hope that somewhere, somehow, there was a way out of this nightmare.

"If you're going to hang around here for a while and wait for Luke, you might want to ask him to bring us another doctor," Paul suggested, a gentle sigh escaping him, a flicker of sadness reflecting in his eyes.

"You don't think she'll come back?" I stammered, my voice filled with a desperate hope.

Paul shrugged, his eyes filled with uncertainty. "I honestly don't know. She's determined that her father is alive here in Clivilius somewhere. I doubt that she'll stop looking for him now."

"But..." I faltered, struggling to find the right words, my mind racing with possibilities and implications. "But how is that even possible? That her father is here?"

Paul chuckled softly as he responded, the sound a jarring contrast to the gravity of the situation. "Charity, shadow panthers, and Portal pirates... I'm not sure anything is beyond the realm of possibility here."

Puzzled, I furrowed my brow, contemplating Paul's words, my mind racing with questions and doubts, the mysteries of this place seeming to deepen with each passing moment. *Has Paul experienced the silent voice of Clivilius?* The thought flashed through my mind like a bolt of lightning. *Or Clive?* I corrected myself, the name feeling strange and unfamiliar, a reminder of the entity that claimed to hold sway over this place, the force that seemed to pull the strings of our fate like a puppet master. *Are they truly one and the same?* I wondered, my head tilting sideways in a mix of anxiety and curiosity, my mind grasping for some shred of understanding in the face of the impossible. *Or are they separate entities, connected yet distinct, two sides of the same twisted coin?* The mysteries of Clivilius seemed to deepen, a tangled web of secrets and lies that threatened to ensnare us all, to drag us down into the throws of madness.

And as I sat there, lost in thought, I couldn't shake the feeling that we were all mere pawns in some grand cosmic game, our fates intertwined in ways that we could scarcely begin to comprehend.

THE JAWS OF CLIVILIUS

4338.209.6

Gingerly settling on the ground, I propped my injured leg up on a nearby rock, wincing as the movement sent a fresh wave of pain shooting through my body. The constant ache was a cruel taunt that mocked my every attempt to move or explore. As I surveyed the area surrounding the Portal, my eyes took in the scattered camping equipment that littered the ground, a haphazard array of supplies that spoke of hasty departures and desperate arrivals.

The need for crutches had become more pressing with each passing moment, a gnawing urgency that ate away at my thoughts like a cancer. Confined to this spot, unable to venture far without enduring excruciating agony, I felt like a prisoner in my own body, a helpless captive of my own frailty. But even as despair prevailed, I clung to the thin thread of determination that still burned within me, a stubborn refusal to give in to the darkness that lurked at the edges of my mind.

Determined to make the most of my time, to find some sense of purpose, I began sorting through the camping equipment scattered near the Portal, my hands moving with a methodical precision as I carefully divided the items into piles. Those destined for the camp found a place to my left, while those bound for the Drop Zone were relegated to my right.

As I sifted through the assortment of gear, my attention was drawn to several items that caught my interest. Different types of tents stood before me, their shapes and sizes a testament to the ingenuity of their designers.

Some were sturdy dome tents, their sleek lines and waterproof rainfly speaking of easy setup and reliable protection from the elements. Others were spacious cabin tents, their cavernous interiors capable of accommodating a larger group.

Tarps and groundsheets lay nearby, their presence a silent guardian against the unpredictable whims of nature, ready to shield us from any unforeseen downpours that might threaten to wash away our tenuous grip on survival. My eyes fell upon a collection of camping stoves, lanterns, and a portable camp shower, their practicality evident in every curve and line, a promise of warmth and light in the face of the encroaching darkness.

A set of portable camping chairs beckoned to me, their presence a siren song of relaxation and comfort after a long day of exploration and toil. And then there were the sleeping bags and air mattresses, some appearing brand new with self-inflating technology, their pristine surfaces a stark contrast to the grime and dirt that clung to my own skin. They promised a semblance of comfort in this rugged terrain, a small oasis of softness in a world of hard edges and unforgiving surfaces.

Amidst my organising, I noticed Paul making slow trips between the Portal and our camp, his arms laden with supplies, his face etched with a grim determination that spoke of the weight of responsibility that rested on his shoulders. Curiosity getting the better of me, I couldn't help but question his solitary efforts, my voice breaking the silence that had settled over the scene.

"Hey Paul, why aren't Karen and Chris helping you?" I inquired as he approached.

With a smile that didn't quite reach his eyes, Paul reassured me, his voice filled with a forced levity that did little to mask the strain that lurked beneath the surface. "Oh, they're busy with something else. Don't worry, I got this."

Though a pang of curiosity gnawed at me, a desperate need to know what could be more important than the task at hand, I decided not to pry further, to respect the boundaries that Paul had erected around himself like a shield. In truth, keeping my distance from Chris at that moment seemed like the best course of action.

As the sorting neared its end, my mind wandered, contemplating the origins of these provisions. My uncle had regaled me with tales of Beatrix's resourcefulness, and an unsettling feeling crept over me, a nagging sense of unease that I couldn't quite shake. *Some questions were best left unanswered*, I mused, a tinge of unease lingering in the back of my mind like a bad taste.

Lost in my thoughts, I barely registered the sudden commotion that shattered the stillness, the Portal erupting with vibrant hues that danced and swirled in a mesmerising display of light and colour. For a moment, I half-expected Beatrix or Luke to emerge from the shimmering vortex.

But as the seconds ticked by and neither appeared, intrigue gripped me, a burning need to know why the Portal had stirred to life in their absence, what secrets lay hidden within its swirling depths. Cautiously, I inched closer, my heart pounding in my chest as I contemplated the possibility of an opportunity to return home.

My hand hesitated, hovering mere inches from the dazzling colours, a silent war raging within me as I grappled with the temptation to reach out and touch the unknown, to seize the chance that lay before me like a glittering prize.

But before I could act on the impulse, a force collided with me, sending me sprawling backward, my body landing harshly on the dusty ground with a sickening thud. Pain radiated through my injured leg as it connected with a small rock, a white-hot agony that tore through me like a knife, stealing the breath from my lungs and bringing tears to my eyes.

Blinking away the moisture that blurred my vision, I struggled to regain focus, my mind reeling with the suddenness of the impact, the disorientation that clouded my thoughts like a fog. And there, sprawled out before me, was a man, his face a mask of confusion and fear as he slowly regained his bearings, his eyes darting around the unfamiliar landscape with a growing sense of panic.

Gradually, he rose to his feet, his movements stiff and awkward as he dusted off his clothes, his fingers trembling slightly as they brushed against the rough fabric. I couldn't help but wonder how he had arrived here, what twist of fate had led him to this unforgiving place, this wasteland of broken dreams and shattered hopes.

The man's gaze darted around, his eyes registering a mix of daze and confusion, a silent plea for understanding in a world that defied explanation. Unsettled, I realised I knew nothing of this stranger's intentions or identity, no way to gauge the threat he might pose.

"It must be Luke," I muttered under my breath, the words feeling heavy and bitter on my tongue as I recalled my own disorienting arrival in Clivilius, the terror and confusion that had gripped me in those first few moments. *He does enjoy pushing people a little too much,* I added in silent reflection, a flicker of resentment sparking to life within me at the thought of Luke's callous disregard for the lives he toyed with.

On his feet once more, the man spun in a full circle, his eyes wide with disbelief as he took in the barren landscape that stretched out before him, the Portal shimmering like a mirage, a tantalising promise of escape that hovered just out of reach. Curiosity piqued, he reached out as if to touch it, his fingers trembling with a desperate need for answers, for some shred of understanding in the face of the impossible.

"You can't go back," I called out, a warning and a plea all at once. I felt a sense of duty to spare him from Clive's unsettling presence, to protect him from the darkness that lurked just beyond the veil, waiting to ensnare any who dared to tempt its threshold.

Startled, he pivoted on his heels, facing me with a mixture of confusion and desperation, his eyes searching mine for some glimmer of hope, some sign that this was all just a terrible dream from which he might soon awaken. "What do you mean? Where am I?" he pleaded, his voice raw with emotion, a desperate need for answers that cut me to the core.

"Didn't you hear the voice when you came through?" I responded, my own curiosity mingling with concern, a nagging sense of unease that settled in the pit of my stomach.

He paused, his brow furrowing as he seemed to wrestle with his own thoughts, his mind struggling to make sense of the events that had transpired. "I think so," he finally admitted, his words hesitant and unsure, a confession that seemed to cost him dearly.

Extending my arms in a welcoming gesture, I limped toward him, my own pain momentarily forgotten in the face of his distress. "Well, there you go," I said, my voice filled with a forced levity that did little to mask the gravity of the situation. "Welcome to Clivilius."

His disbelief was evident as he turned away, his shoulders slumping with the weight of the realisation that had settled over him. Reaching once again toward the Portal's translucent screen, his fingers trembling with a desperate need to escape, to flee from the nightmare that had now become his reality.

"I told you," I called out again, my voice filled with a quiet urgency, a desperate need to save him from the unpleasantness that Clive held in store for those who dared to defy its will. "You can't go back."

"No!" he shouted, whirling around to face me, his eyes blazing with a fierce determination that bordered on madness. His head shook with vehement denial, a stubborn refusal to accept the truth that lay before him like a gaping wound. "There must be some mistake."

A pang of sympathy tugged at me, a flicker of understanding that danced in the depths of my own eyes as I recognised the struggle that raged within him, the desperate need to cling to some shred of hope. But even as I felt the weight of his pain, the depth of his despair, I knew that the sooner he accepted his fate, the sooner he could move forward.

Mustering a smile that felt like a lie, I extended my hand in greeting, closing the gap between us despite the sharp twinge in my leg, the agony that shot through me with every step. "I'm Kain," I introduced myself, my voice filled with a forced cheer that rang hollow in the stillness of the air.

He stared at my outstretched hand for a moment, his eyes filled with a mixture of suspicion and fear, a silent war raging within him as he grappled with the decision to trust, to accept the lifeline that I offered. But after a brief hesitation, he grasped my hand with an unexpectedly firm grip, his fingers digging into my flesh with a desperation that bordered on pain.

After a brief shake, he released his hold, his eyes scanning the surroundings once more, a flicker of hope sparking to life within their depths as he seemed to search for some sign of salvation, some glimmer of light in the darkness.

"So, where's Luke?" he inquired, his gaze darting around the barren landscape.

"I'm sure he'll be here very soon," I reassured him, my voice filled with a confidence that I didn't quite feel, a false bravado that did little to mask the uncertainty that gnawed at my insides. But even as the words left my lips, the Portal erupted once more, its vibrant colours pulsating with an electrifying energy that seemed to fill the air with a tangible presence.

Grabbing his arm gently, I guided him away from the Portal. "It's best if we don't stand too close," I advised, my voice filled with a quiet urgency, a desperate need to protect him.

"Shit," he muttered under his breath, his eyes widening with disbelief.

In the midst of our conversation, a white ute materialised through the Portal, its sudden appearance sending plumes of dust swirling into the air, a choking cloud that hung heavy in the stillness of the morning. As the haze dissipated, a tall, rugged man emerged from the vehicle.

"Luke!" I exclaimed, relief washing over me at the sight of a familiar face. But even as the name left my lips, a thought occurred to me, a nagging question that demanded an answer. "Why is he here?" I blurted out, my voice filled with a mixture of curiosity and apprehension, a desperate need to understand the machinations that had brought this stranger into our midst.

"Nial owns a fence construction business," Luke replied, his voice filled with a casual indifference that bordered on callousness, a reminder of the cold practicality that governed his every action. He made his way toward us with a purposeful stride, his eyes fixed on the newcomer with a calculating intensity that sent a shiver down my spine.

I nodded in understanding, a flicker of sympathy sparking to life within me as I registered the full weight of Nial's misfortune. Though his presence here was a cruel twist of fate, the necessity for fencing in this treacherous land was not lost on me. Security and protection were paramount, and in that moment, I silently hoped that Nial's expertise would prove invaluable.

"Do these include your office keys?" Luke questioned, drawing my attention to the jingling set of keys that dangled from his hand like a prize.

"Yeah," Nial replied, a perplexed expression crossing his face as he reached for the keys, his fingers trembling slightly as they closed around the cool metal.

"Where's your office?" Luke asked, his tone filled with a quiet sense of purpose.

Nial's confusion deepened, his brow furrowing as he struggled to make sense of the question, to understand the implications of Luke's words. "It's a home office. Why?" he responded.

"Great!" Luke exclaimed, his face breaking into a smile that didn't quite reach his eyes, a mask of false cheer that did little to mask the darkness that lurked just beneath the surface. With a flick of his wrist, he breathed life into the Portal once more, the vibrant colours swirling and pulsating with an otherworldly energy.

"The key is still in the ignition," he gestured toward Nial's ute, his words a command and a dismissal all at once. And with that, he passed through the Portal.

As Nial continued grappling with his unfamiliar surroundings, his eyes wide with disbelief, I noticed Paul approaching, his face etched with a grim determination.

"You've just missed Luke," I informed Paul, my voice laced with a hint of sarcasm, a bitter acknowledgment of the man's elusive nature, his tendency to slip away just when we needed him most.

Coming to a halt, Paul furrowed his brow, his hand rising to his forehead in a gesture of frustration, smearing dust across his skin in the process.

"But this is Nial," I quickly added, seizing the opportunity to introduce the two men, to pass the responsibility of welcoming Nial into our settlement to Paul. Turning my attention to Nial, I hurriedly explained, the words tumbling from my lips in a rush of desperation and need. "Paul is our camp leader. He's the one who keeps us organised and safe," I blurted, surprising myself with how much I really wanted to believe what I was saying, how much I needed to cling to the illusion of order and control.

Paul nodded, his eyes meeting Nial's with a mixture of curiosity and concern. "Nice to meet you, Nial. I'm sorry you got caught up in all of this," Paul offered, his voice filled with a quiet sincerity, as he extended his hand for a shake.

Nial hesitated for a moment, his eyes darting between Paul's outstretched hand and his face, a silent war raging within him as he grappled with the decision to trust. But after a brief pause, he reached out and grasped Paul's hand, his grip firm and sure. "Yeah, me too," he replied, his voice barely above a whisper, a confession of his own fear and uncertainty.

Aware that Nial was still grappling with the impossible situation, his mind reeling with the implications of his sudden arrival in Clivilius, I couldn't help but sympathise, my own memories of those first few moments still fresh in my mind, the terror and confusion that had gripped me like a vice, refusing to let go. After all, I, too, struggled to comprehend the workings of this place, the twisted logic that seemed to govern our every move, the unseen forces that pulled the strings of our fate like puppets on a stage.

Pressing a finger against the trickle of blood that seeped from my leg, I reminded myself of the urgency of the situation, the need to seek proper care before the wound became infected, before the pain became too much to bear.

"Kain, let's load Nial's ute with the remaining camping supplies that need to be taken to camp and the three of us can return to camp," Paul suggested, his voice filled with a quiet authority.

Concerned about not being able to request crutches once we returned to camp, I hesitated for a moment, my mind racing with the possibilities and implications of leaving the Portal behind, of abandoning the one lifeline that seemed to connect us to the world we had left behind. But even as the doubts swirled within me, I knew that Paul was right, that resting my leg and tending to the wound were crucial, that I couldn't afford to let my own stubbornness and pride get in the way of my own well-being.

"Yeah, that's a good idea. My leg is getting too painful to walk," I admitted, my voice filled with a quiet resignation.

"You need to rest your leg," Paul urged, his voice filled with a genuine concern, a flicker of empathy that danced in his eyes. Taking a deep breath, he continued, "And you really should consider going to the river or lagoon to put some water on your wound. I'll return to the Portal because I need to speak with Luke and I promise you that I will ask Luke to get you some crutches."

Reluctantly, I nodded, acknowledging the wisdom in Paul's advice, the practicality of his words, even as a part of me longed to stay. "Thanks, Paul. I appreciate it," I said, my voice filled with a quiet gratitude.

❖

As we neared the small camp, my gaze was immediately drawn to the gruesome display of the Shadow Panther's head, the sight sending a jolt of fear and revulsion through my body. Mounted on a wooden pole, the creature's menacing visage was placed prominently at the entrance, a macabre warning of the horrors that lurked beyond the flimsy boundaries of our makeshift home.

The panther's jet-black fur gleamed dully in the harsh sunlight, its open jaws frozen in a silent snarl that seemed to mock our fragile sense of safety. Razor-sharp teeth, stained with the remnants of past kills, glinted like knives, a chilling reminder of the creature's deadly prowess. The bloodied, pink tongue lolled obscenely from its mouth, a grotesque contrast to the lifeless eyes that stared blankly ahead, devoid of the primal fury that had once blazed within them.

The matted fur around the panther's neck was encrusted with dried blood, a grisly testament to the violence of its demise. It stood as a stark warning that we couldn't afford to let our guard down, that even the strongest among us were vulnerable to the dangers that lurked in the uncharted wilderness of Clivilius. The sight sent a shiver down my spine, a cold finger of dread that traced its way along my skin, leaving goosebumps in its wake.

Glancing at the rearview mirror, I could see the fear and uncertainty etched on Nial's face as he stared at the severed head, his eyes wide with horror and disbelief. The colour had drained from his cheeks, leaving him pale and drawn. I couldn't blame him for his reaction - the sight was enough to unsettle even the most hardened among us, a brutal reminder of the savagery that existed in this twisted realm.

"That's why we need you, Nial," Paul asserted, his voice cutting through the heavy silence that had settled over the vehicle. He pointed towards the ominous trophy, his finger trembling slightly as he traced the outline of the panther's snarling visage. "We need you to help us build security fences around the camp's perimeter to keep us safe from the Shadow Panthers and any other dangers that may lurk in this new world."

Nial rubbed his weary eyes, the gesture speaking volumes of the exhaustion and despair that weighed upon him. His voice trembled as he spoke, a barely audible whisper that hung in the air between us like a confession. "I can't believe this is real," he admitted, the words heavy with a sense of disbelief and denial. "I have a wife and young toddler to get home to. I can't stay here."

As the ute came to a halt, the engine sputtering into silence, Paul unbuckled his seatbelt and turned towards Nial, his face etched with a deep empathy. "I understand how difficult this is for you, Nial," he said, his voice low.

"We've all got loved ones we've left behind," I chimed in, my own voice thick with emotion as I swallowed the lump that had risen in my throat. The ache of separation was a constant companion, a dull throb that pulsed in time with my heartbeat, a reminder of all that I had lost, all that I might never see again.

"But the fact is, we are here now and we need to work together or none of us are going to survive this place," Paul continued, his tone growing more insistent, his hands gesturing towards my injured leg as a poignant reminder of the dangers that we faced, the price that we had already paid for our survival.

Shaking his head, Nial's voice was barely above a whisper, a fragile thread of sound that threatened to break at any moment. "I don't know if I can do this," he confessed, the words heavy with a sense of despair and hopelessness, a surrender to the overwhelming reality of our situation.

"You don't have to do this alone," Paul assured him, his words laced with a quiet strength, a promise of support and solidarity. "We're here for you..."

But even as Paul spoke, I felt a wave of emotion crashing over me, a tidal wave of grief and anger and fear. The weight of it all was too much to bear, the constant struggle for survival, the unrelenting fear that gnawed at my insides like a ravenous beast.

Feeling overwhelmed by my turbulent emotions, I flung open the door and stepped out of the vehicle, my movements jerky and uncoordinated. "I'm going to the lagoon," I declared solemnly, my voice barely recognisable to my own ears as I gingerly shifted myself away from the front seat, each movement sending a fresh wave of agony shooting through my leg.

"Paul can deal with Nial," I muttered to myself, the words bitter on my tongue as I allowed their voices to fade into the distance behind me. With each arduous step, I sent a silent message to my captor.

Clive, we need to talk!

FIRES

4338.209.7

As I trudged through the unforgiving heat, each step a painful reminder of the burden I carried, my exhaustion mingled with frustration at Clive's relentless demands. The journey to the lagoon was a desperate gamble to save my leg, but the price I had to pay felt unbearably steep.

The sand seemed determined to trip me up, and I stumbled, sinking to my knees in the gritty terrain. Dust clung to my sweat-soaked skin, finding its way into my mouth and throat, choking me. Coughing and spitting out the unwelcome grit, I found myself hunched over, feeling defeated. The weight of Clive's expectations pressed down on me, leaving me grasping for alternatives. "There has to be another way," I muttered, my voice filled with desperation. The sacrifice of bringing Chris to the lagoon felt like a surrender of my own strength and agency. I had already lost so much, and now I teetered on the edge of losing myself as well.

"My dignity, my freedom," I whispered bitterly, pushing myself to stand. I couldn't afford to lose my leg now. The image of Brianne, carrying our unborn child, flashed in my mind, igniting a stubborn determination to keep going.

Finally, as I crested the dune, the lagoon stretched before me like a mirage. The sunlight danced on its shimmering surface, promising healing and relief. I hobbled closer, navigating the rocky terrain to keep my balance, but a daunting sense of dread accompanied me. The throbbing in my temples intensified, the pain building into a tempest.

With a mix of reluctance and hope, I lowered myself onto the rocky edge of the lagoon, sliding my legs into the cool water. Relief washed over me as the soothing embrace of the lagoon enveloped my wounded leg. But the pleasure was short-lived, as a surge of pain pulsed through my chest, constricting my breath. I gasped, struggling to intake enough air, while a sharp zing of enticing pleasure shot up my injured limb. I understood the lagoon's healing power, but the whispered voice in my mind reminded me of the steep price I had yet to pay.

Fighting against the sexual pulses of energy that now remained constant, I studied my leg eagerly for any sign of improvement. My brow furrowed, a thin trail of fresh blood seeped from the top of the gash and dribbled into the lagoon, turning the water a cloudy shade of red.

I see you, Kain Jeffries, Clive's voice echoed in my mind, sending a chill down my spine.

Anger surged through my veins, threatening to engulf me. "I see you!" I shouted, saliva flying from my mouth. "What the fuck does that mean?"

Kain, the voice softly murmured. *You must bring Chris to the lagoon.*

My hard cock ached from the relentless onslaught, the weight of the demands crashing upon me. "Fuck you, Clive!" I yelled, yanking my leg from the water. With determination, I prepared to leave the cursed lagoon behind.

"Who's Clive?" a familiar voice called out from behind me.

My heels, softened by the water, ground against the hard rock as I quickly pivoted to face the short man. Chris reached out and placed a firm hand on my shoulder, steadying me as my legs wobbled. *It's too convenient,* I told myself silently, as my salty eyes couldn't unlock their fix on Chris. As a fierce determination burned within me, like a raging bushfire ready to consume everything in its wake, I grabbed hold of Chris's arm and pulled him towards me as I attempted a side manoeuvre. Chris's body twisted awkwardly as it moved in the lagoon's direction and taking the prime opportunity, I gave his chest a firm push.

Chris gave out a squark as he fell backwards and as his hand found mine and gripped it tightly, my eyes widened in terror. My aching leg caved under pressure and, unable to stop the momentum, I followed Chris into the water with a thundering splash. It was deeper than I expected and I swallowed several mouthfuls of water as my head sank below the surface and I coughed up several more when I finally breached.

"What the hell is wrong with you!?" Chris scolded, shoving my shoulder as he retreated to the safety of the shore.

Knowing I couldn't waste this chance to heal my leg, I reached out for Chris once more, but my grip faltered, and I found myself splashing clumsily into the water. "Shit," I muttered, pushing forward, determined to make it right.

As Chris pressed his hands against the rock and hoisted himself upwards, my hands finally made contact with him. Unable to take hold, my hands slid down his round torso, causing the man a failed attempt at escape. My fingers somehow managed to find the tip of Chris's trousers and sinking my fingers beneath the fabric, I gripped tightly and yanked hard at the precise moment that Chris made a second attempt to pull himself from the water.

Chris's trousers came loose as he lifted his body, his bare arse passing barely an inch from my face. A loud moan escaped Chris's lips and, with trousers now at his ankles, his knees slammed down into the solid rock.

You're so close, my mind pleaded with me not to lose hope.

Chris swore loudly and his back arched as his hands pressed into the rocks.

The lagoon will heal his knees, I justified to myself, as I hoped to bring Chris back into the water. Gripping his calves as they hung over the edge of the rock, I yanked the solid man toward me. But it didn't go as expected. Chris moved barely a few inches before his elbows buckled beneath his weight. My eyes widened in terror as Chris's forehead connected with the smooth rick with a sickening thud.

"Chris!" I called out, panic surging through me as I scrambled out of the water. Rushing to his side, I rolled him onto his back, my heart pounding. A stream of crimson flowed from the gash above his brow, staining the rock beneath him.

"Chris!" I shouted again, shaking his unmoving body, desperate to bring him back. "Shit!" I cursed myself for the reckless choices I had made.

A familiar soft voice spoke eerily into my mind. *Bring him to me, Kain,* Clive prodded.

My eyes moved slowly down Chris's torso, quickly passing his exposed crotch to where his feet still hung in the water. Moving to the edge of the rock, I took hold of Chris's legs and carefully dragged him closer to the water until his bum sat as close to the edge as I dared without him falling in completely. A sudden movement caught the corner of my eye, and instinctively glancing toward it, I caught the unfortunate sight of Chris's dick as it began to harden. I wanted to look away, but a stronger part of me begged me to keep watch. *You've come this far,* I told myself determinedly. *It would be foolish to inflict so much pain and not ensure the deal was actually completed.*

Yes, the voice whispered, affirming my resolve. *Finish what has been started.*

Staring at the task that I was being forced to fulfil, I gulped dryly. Staring at the blood that continued to drizzle across Chris's forehead and down his cheek, I knew that I couldn't withdraw now. Kneeling beside Chris, I swallowed a dry gulp as my hand inched closer. Closing my eyes, I winced as the tips of my fingers touched the firm flesh. A hot anger began to circulate through my veins as my hand wrapped around Chris's dick and I slowly began to jerk him off. As the anger intensified, I found my grip tightening, and my pace quickening.

Suddenly, Chris's eyes flew open and as he sat up almost instantaneously, my hand withdrew and I quickly retreated backwards. With a loud gasp, Chris reached for his pulsating cock and in a final moment of what could only be described as torturous pleasure, he released the pressure, sending spurts of precious cargo into the clear lagoon waters.

It is finished, Clive whispered calmly in my head.

Uncertain of Chris's awareness, I knew I couldn't stay to find out. As he struggled to catch his breath, I made my hasty escape, leaving behind the lagoon and the consequences of my choices.

❖

As I approached the camp, I could feel the newfound vitality in my leg, granting me a glimmer of hope amidst the troubles that plagued my mind. But the flickering of multiple small fires around the perimeter immediately caught my eye, their dancing flames casting an ominous glow that unsettled me to the core. The sight filled me with a sense of unease, and I couldn't shake the feeling that this new development held dire implications.

Suddenly, Karen's voice pierced through the air, startling me out of my thoughts. "Where's Chris?" she called out. Her unexpected presence made my heart race and my face tense with nervous energy. I couldn't bring myself to meet her penetrating gaze.

Mustering what little composure I had left, I replied with feigned nonchalance, "He decided to stay at the lagoon a little longer." But even to my own ears, my voice sounded strained and unconvincing.

Karen's eyes narrowed. "I'll go and fetch him," she declared, her tone laced with determination as she turned on her heel and strode away.

As I watched her retreating figure, my mind spun with a whirlwind of possibilities. *What would transpire when she found Chris? Would he divulge the truth about what had happened between us? Had his own wounds miraculously healed like mine?* A sickening thought struck me then, causing me to gasp involuntarily - *would Clive make the same demands of Chris that he had of me?* The very notion filled my mouth with the acrid taste of metal, nearly making me gag on the spot.

Desperate for any distraction from the suffocating guilt and apprehension that threatened to overwhelm me, I turned to Paul and Nial, who huddled together near the main bonfire. "What's with all the extra fires?" I asked, trying to keep my voice steady.

Paul's face was etched with worry as he replied, "We had to set them up. We need to increase our visibility and security after what happened. We can't risk another attack."

I nodded slowly, comprehending the necessity of the measures even as a sinking feeling settled in my gut. The thought of burning through our precious wood supplies at such an alarming rate made my stomach churn with unease.

"It's going to consume a lot of wood," I noted aloud, giving voice to the concern that nagged at me.

"I know," Paul acknowledged, his shoulders slumping with resignation. "But we don't have much of a choice. Not until we can get more security in place."

Turning to Nial, who had remained conspicuously silent throughout the exchange, I sought to appeal to his expertise. "This is why we need your help," I said gently, holding his gaze. "We need to get those fences built as soon as possible."

Nial met my eyes, his expression a conflicted mix of reluctance and grim understanding. "I get it," he said at last, his voice heavy with weariness. "But it's all so overwhelming. I have a wife and a toddler back home. I can't even begin to process all of this."

"I know it's hard," Paul interjected, reaching out to place a comforting hand on Nial's shoulder. "But we're all in this together. And we need your skills and expertise to help us survive in this new world."

Despite the optimism in Paul's tone, his words only served to intensify the churning in my gut. I watched as Nial nodded slowly, his eyes fixed on the mesmerising dance of the flames before us. It was painfully clear that he was still struggling to come to terms with the harsh reality he now faced, and I couldn't blame him in the slightest. Yet I also knew that if we were to survive another night and avoid further demands from the malevolent presence that lurked in our minds, rapid adaptation was crucial.

Out of the corner of my eye, I noticed Karen leaving the campsite, heading in the direction of Chris's approaching figure. A heady mix of anticipation and dread swirled within me at the realisation that the truth might soon come to light.

Suddenly desperate to make myself scarce before Chris's return, I announced abruptly, "It's been a long day. I'm going to turn in."

Paul's brows furrowed in surprise. "You're not going to eat with us?" he asked, a hint of confusion colouring his tone.

I shook my head brusquely, already backing away. "I'm not really hungry."

Paul shot me a sideways glance, his eyes searching my face for answers I wasn't ready to give. "Okay," he said at last, though his tone made it clear that he sensed something was amiss.

With a final nod of acknowledgment to Nial, I made a hasty retreat to my tent, seeking solace in the confines of the thin fabric walls. Collapsing onto my sleeping bag, I stared up at the empty expanse above me, feeling the weight of my actions pressing down on me.

As I lay there, the boisterous chatter from around the campfire filtered through the walls of my tent, impossible to ignore. Straining my ears, I caught a snippet of Karen's voice rising above the rest: "The clumsy bugger slipped on the rocks." Those words, brief as they were, were enough to make the knot in my stomach tighten painfully. As regret crashed over me in unrelenting waves, a single thought echoed in my mind, tormenting me with its implications: *What the hell have I done?*

4338.210

(29 July 2018)

REFRESH

4338.210.1

As I finally managed to rouse myself from a fitful slumber, having made three futile attempts to fall back into the blissful oblivion of sleep, I groggily rubbed at the crusty remnants that had gathered in the corners of my eyes. My leg, though not an overwhelming source of pain during the night, had still caused enough discomfort to keep me awake longer than I would have liked. The sound of Paul and Nial's voices drifting in from outside sent a jolt of panic through my stomach, my heart pounding against my rib cage like a caged bird desperate for freedom. But as I strained my ears to listen more closely, I realised that their tone held more excitement than worry.

Stifling a yawn, I stretched my arms above my head, trying to shake off the lingering tendrils of sleep that clung to me like cobwebs. Despite the late hour, an eerie silence enveloped the tent, a bitter reminder of the absence of Glenda and Uncle Jamie, who had ventured out to hunt down a Portal pirate.

"Three members," I corrected myself, my voice tinged with a mournful note. From his bed, Henri snorted disapprovingly, fixing me with a baleful stare. I had moved his bed into my tent the previous night, driven by a mixture of pity and a desire to keep him close. Lois, on the other hand, seemed to have taken it upon herself to remain glued to Paul's side in Glenda's absence.

Reluctant to leave the cocoon of warmth my sleeping bag provided, I took my time emerging and changing into fresh clothes before slowly stepping out of the tent. The delectable aroma of food cooking over the campfire immediately assailed my nostrils, tantalising my grumbling stomach. Yet, even as the scent teased my hunger, a deep frown creased my brow, overshadowing any pleasure the promise of a meal might bring. My gaze was inexorably drawn to Chris, the man I had so grievously wronged, and I found myself unable to look away. Quickly, I shook my head, cutting off the dark thoughts that entered my mind. I didn't need the reminder of my misdeeds; the weight of guilt was already a leaden ball in the pit of my stomach. As the balding head turned away from the fire to face me, breaking the spell, I had barely taken a few steps before the familiar voice called out, halting me in my tracks.

"Kain," Chris said simply, his tone firm yet devoid of any discernible emotion.

Biting the inside of my cheek, I slowly pivoted to face him, my movements as reluctant as a man facing the gallows. A heavy silence stretched between us, broken only by the crackling of the fire. My eyes kept darting to the noticeable cut on the side of Chris's head, a visual reminder of my actions. Shifting uncomfortably, I felt my heels sink into the soft earth beneath me. *What the heck am I supposed to say to him?* I thought, my mind a whirlwind of guilt and self-recrimination. There was no excuse for what I had done.

The awkward silence hung in the air like a miasma, leaving a sickening, acidic taste in my mouth. Wiping away the beads of sweat that had begun to trickle down my left temple with a clammy hand, I swallowed hard, pivoting on my heel and sending a small cloud of fine dust particles into my shoe, deepening my already weary frown.

"Do you want some food before you run away?" Chris asked, his words laced with a pointed emphasis on the final phrase.

For a moment, I considered refusing, my shame warring with my hunger. But a painful growl from my stomach reminded me that I hadn't eaten since early the previous day, and I hesitated, torn between the desire to flee and the gnawing emptiness in my gut. Swallowing against the dryness in my throat, I turned back to Chris, realising with a pang of embarrassment that I was now salivating uncontrollably at the tantalising aroma wafting from the pot.

"Where is everyone?" I asked, cautiously approaching Chris and swiping at the saliva gathering at the corners of my mouth, not wanting to give the impression of a drooling dog.

"Paul and Nial have gone to the Portal," Chris replied, ladling several spoonfuls of the gooey slop into a bowl. "Apparently, they have some wild theory they want to test."

"Really? A theory about what?" I asked, surprise and cautious optimism warring within me at the hope that they might have stumbled upon a way to return home.

"I'm not exactly sure, but it had something to do with Nial's laptop."

I furrowed my brow, trying to come up with a plausible explanation, but my mind drew a blank. "I assume Lois is with them?" I asked instead.

Chris chuckled, a sound that seemed almost foreign in the sombre atmosphere of the camp. "Of course."

"And Karen?" My gaze darted around the deserted camp, searching for any sign of her presence.

As if on cue, Karen emerged from her tent, her arms laden with a pile of clothing.

I eyed her suspiciously, her appearance seeming too timely to be mere coincidence. It was as if she had been observing our interaction, waiting for the right moment to make her presence known.

"Kain," she called out, striding purposefully in my direction. "Get me your dirty clothes, and I'll wash them with ours."

I stared at the lanky woman, my eyes wide with surprise. *Is she just being helpful?* I wondered, my mind racing with possibilities. *Or is this an attempt to get me alone with her, so she can confront me about what happened to Chris?* The thought sent a cold shiver down my sweat-soaked spine, my muscles tensing with apprehension.

"The camp is starting to stink," Karen continued, her determined gaze fixed on me like a laser beam. "I think everything around here could do with a good scrub."

"Of course," I agreed, succumbing to the stifling tension that threatened to give me a pounding headache. "I'll go and get my clothes."

I heaved a heavy sigh as I ducked back into the tent, greeted by Henri's disgruntled grunt. He seemed determined to stay in his bed, his eyes following me accusingly as I moved about the small space. "Karen's right, it is beginning to stink in here," I muttered, more to myself than to the dog, as I bent over to gather a collection of unsorted clothes. In my haste, I grabbed everything I could find, regardless of their state of cleanliness. It seemed like a good idea to take it all, especially since my clothes were getting mixed with Uncle Jamie's and Joel's garments anyway. I piled as much as I could carry into my arms, the mound of fabric threatening to topple over as I stumbled out of the tent, nearly losing my balance under the weight.

"You're going to have to accompany me," Karen sighed, eyeing the mountain of clothes in my arms. "I didn't realise you had so much washing already."

Struggling to see over the precariously balanced pile, I poked my head out, my voice muffled by the fabric. "It's not all mine," I managed to say, my fingers clutching at a rogue sock that threatened to make a break for freedom.

"Probably just as well," Karen said, taking a few steps toward me before quickly retreating, her nose wrinkling at the pungent odour emanating from the clothes.

"To the river?" I asked, my arms beginning to tremble under the weight of my burden.

"No," Karen replied, shaking her head. "I thought I'd go to the lagoon. There are more rocks there to lay clothes on to dry, seeing as we don't exactly have anything to hang them on here."

I gulped, my gaze darting to Chris, who intentionally avoided eye contact, his attention focused on the bubbling pot before him. The temptation to change my mind and hide in the tent was strong, but I didn't want to risk Karen probing further into my reluctance to go to the lagoon. *As long as I didn't touch the water, everything should be fine*, I reassured myself, taking a deep breath as I prepared to follow Karen. She was already walking away, her long strides eating up the distance, eager to get the task done. My anxious stomach grumbled loudly, reminding me of my hunger.

"I'll eat when I get back," I called out to Chris as I passed by, disappointed that I would have to endure the growing hunger pains. Yet, a small part of me was relieved to be spared the uncomfortable ordeal of staying in Chris's presence.

Chris shrugged, silently acknowledging my words, and turned his attention back to his cooking, the spoon scraping against the bottom of the pot.

"Oh, and feed Henri for me, please?" I added, my heart sinking a little deeper with each word. The constant reminders of the dangers of this strange place left me with an uncomfortable feeling that I might never get the chance to meet my child, a thought that twisted like a knife in my gut.

"Sure," Chris replied, his brow furrowing. "I'll make sure he eats something."

Swallowing the acidic bile that burned the back of my throat, I pushed the thoughts of Brianne and the uncertain future to the recesses of my mind. With a renewed determination, I hobbled after Karen, ignoring the aching in my leg that grew more pronounced with each step. As we walked, I struggled to keep pace with the lanky woman, who took long strides, battling the constantly shifting sands beneath our feet. The closer we got to the lagoon, the more my anxiety intensified, a cold sweat breaking out on my brow.

Reaching the peak of the final hill, I stared down at the shimmering water of the lagoon, a wave of discomfort washing over me, twisting my gut like a gnarled tree. I desperately hoped I wouldn't have to touch the water, especially with Karen present, the fear of what might happen if I did a leaden weight in my chest.

Karen led us to the edge of the lagoon, choosing the rockiest area to set up for washing. With a sinking feeling, I realised that this was the same spot where Chris had injured himself. I tormented myself silently, wondering if that was the reason Karen had chosen this particular location. *Does she know what happened?* The contentious thoughts chased each other in endless circles through my mind. *Even if she doesn't know, would Clivilius still reveal the truth to her?*

"Your leg is bleeding again," Karen said, her hand coming to rest on my shoulder as she steadied me. In my distraction, I had fumbled with the clothes, dropping several items onto the rocky ground.

I sighed heavily, frustrated by the recurrence of my leg wound. *Not this shit again*, I whined inwardly, not wanting to deal with Clivilius's ultimatums or the complications they brought. "It's starting to throb now," I told Karen, releasing the clothes and dropping them onto a large, flat rock beside her smaller pile.

Karen furrowed her brow, lost in thought for a moment. "Look," she said finally, her voice tinged with concern. "Why don't you go and get your leg cleaned up and put some more river water on it? I can take care of the washing."

My eyes widened in surprise, the offer catching me off guard. I meant to politely confirm her suggestion, but my surprise had other intentions, and I ended up blurting out, "Not the lagoon water?"

"I can't very well be washing clothes in water that you're polluting with your blood, can I?" Karen's pointed response almost made me chuckle, the absurdity of the situation momentarily overriding my anxiety.

Managing to maintain a serious composure, I replied, "That is very true."

"It's fine, I've got this," Karen assured me, nodding with determination. "But if you could come back later and help me bring the washing back to camp, that'd be really helpful."

"Of course," I agreed, grateful for the temporary reprieve from both the washing and Karen's presence.

"Thanks, Kain," Karen said, immediately turning her attention to the large pile of clothes, her hands already sorting through the garments.

As I walked away, a deep sense of relief washed over me, the release of pressure finding its escape in an embarrassingly loud way. I didn't dare look back to see if Karen had heard, my cheeks burning with a mixture of embarrassment and amusement. A long-hidden smile crossed my lips as I chuckled softly, grateful for the temporary respite from the tension that had been my constant companion since arriving in this strange and dangerous place.

❖

As I walked along the riverbank, putting as much distance between myself and the lagoon, the camp, and Karen, the sound of rushing water provided a soothing backdrop to my troubled thoughts. Despite the gnawing hunger in my stomach, I couldn't bear the thought of being alone at camp with Chris, the weight of my guilt and the awkwardness of our interactions too much to bear.

I decided to follow the river back towards the camp, my steps heavy with exhaustion and the burden of my thoughts. The cool breeze carried the scent of the water, refreshing my senses and providing a momentary respite from the oppressive heat of the day. As I walked, I found myself lost in contemplation, my mind replaying the events of the past few days like a broken record.

The betrayal of Chris's trust, the demands of Clivilius, and the constant fear of discovery all weighed heavily on my mind, threatening to crush me under their combined weight. I couldn't help but wonder what the others would think of me if they knew the truth, if they discovered the depths to which I had sunk in my desperation to heal my leg.

As I continued along the riverbank, I scanned the area for a suitable spot to tend to my wound. The rushing water called to me, promising relief and cleansing, and I found myself drawn to its edge. When I found a relatively secluded area, I crouched down, gingerly immersing my leg in the cool, refreshing water.

The moment the water enveloped my limb, a sense of relief washed over me, the throbbing pain in my leg dulling to a more manageable level. There was a familiar zing of pleasure, a ghostly echo of the overwhelming sensations I had experienced at the lagoon, but it paled in comparison to the intensity of those feelings. Still, it gave me a glimmer of hope that I might be able to give myself a proper wash without the distracting and potentially dangerous effects of the mysterious water.

As I sat there, letting the river work its magic on my tired and aching body, I took a moment to examine my leg more closely. To my surprise and relief, the bleeding that had caught Karen's attention earlier seemed to have stopped, and the wound looked cleaner than it had before. The stitches that Glenda had given me the night of the attack now seemed to be taking solid hold, keeping the flesh together as they should. I had no recollection of Glenda's actions, but there was no doubting her heroic efforts to save my leg. The first signs of healthy tissue were now forming around the edges of the wound, and I grew more confident that, given time and proper care, my leg would heal properly, even without Glenda's expert aid.

It was a slow process, but the wound seemed to be closing, and I knew that as long as I continued to refresh it regularly with clean water, I had a good chance of avoiding infection and making a full recovery. The thought brought a small smile to my face, a rare moment of positivity.

As I sat there, lost in my thoughts and the soothing sensation of the water, I allowed myself a moment of peace, a brief respite from the constant stress and fear that had become my constant companions. The river seemed to wash away some of my worries, carrying them downstream and away from me, even if only for a little while.

❖

Making my way back to the camp, my mind still reeling from the events of the past few days, I couldn't help but notice Nial sitting by the crackling campfire. He was tending to a small wound on his hand, and the sight of it caused a knot to form in the pit of my stomach. It seemed like we couldn't go a single day in this godforsaken place without someone getting injured.

Concern evident in my voice, I approached Nial, my curiosity piqued by his presence. "What happened?" I asked, my eyes drawn to the wound on his hand, which looked relatively minor compared to some of the injuries we had seen in recent days.

Nial recounted the tale of his and Paul's experiment with the internet, explaining how they had managed to establish a connection to Earth. My interest was immediately piqued by the mention of communication with our loved ones, overshadowing the unfortunate encounter with a falling picture frame that had led to Nial's injury. The prospect of being able to reach out to those we had left behind stirred a new sense of hope within me, even as I acknowledged the relatively trivial nature of Nial's wound. Compared to a shadow panther attack, it was nothing more than a scratch.

"What sparked the idea to try?" I asked, genuinely curious about their endeavour. The thought of being able to connect with the outside world, even in a limited capacity, was both exciting and daunting, and I found myself eager to learn more about their efforts.

Nial explained that Paul had suggested using the internet to order supplies for the camp through Nial's fencing business, a plan that I had to admit was rather impressive. The idea of being able to acquire much-needed resources from Earth was a tantalising one, and I couldn't help but feel a glimmer of admiration for Paul's ingenuity.

"And did you manage to make an order?" I inquired, my heart racing with anticipation as I awaited Nial's response. The possibility of actually receiving supplies from home seemed almost too good to be true, but I clung to the hope that their attempt had been successful.

Nial nodded, a hint of uncertainty in his voice. "I think so," he replied, his gaze shifting to the gruesome trophy of the shadow panther's head that sat nearby, a sickly reminder of the dangers we faced.

A surge of hope filled my chest at his words, and I found myself leaning forward, my voice eager as I asked the question that had been burning in my mind since he first mentioned the internet connection. "Does this mean we can communicate with our loved ones?"

The possibility of contacting Brianne, of hearing her voice and knowing that she was safe, ignited a fire within me, and I felt a renewed sense of determination to find a way back to her and our unborn child.

"I guess it does," Nial replied, his tone somewhat uncertain as he gestured towards the head of the shadow panther. "But given the lack of security around here and..." He paused, his gaze shifting to the gruesome trophy, "I'm not convinced that we should be telling anybody about this place."

My heart sank at his words, and I felt a twinge of disappointment as the reality of our situation came crashing down around me once more. As much as I longed to reach out to Brianne, to tell her that I was alive and fighting to get back to her, I had to admit that Nial had a valid point. *Even if I could somehow get a message to her, what could I possibly say?* She would never believe that I had passed through a Portal and was now trapped in a strange new world, fighting for survival against creatures that defied explanation.

"But still, it's worth a try, isn't it?" I found myself saying, the words escaping my dry lips before I could stop them. Despite the rational part of my brain telling me that it was a futile endeavour, I couldn't help but cling to the hope that somehow, someway, I could find a way to connect with Brianne and let her know that I was coming back to her.

Nial raised an eyebrow, his gaze fixed on me with an intensity that made me shift uncomfortably. "Your fiancée is pregnant, isn't she?" His statement sounded more like an affirmation than a question.

I nodded, my heart tightening at the thought of her facing the challenges of pregnancy and impending motherhood alone. "Yes," I replied, my voice barely above a whisper.

"And how do you expect the baby to be delivered with no doctor?" Nial asked, his wounded arm serving as a sobering reminder of the harsh realities we faced.

A furrow formed on my brow as I considered his question, my mind racing with the implications of Brianne giving birth without proper medical care. "Glenda's only going to be gone a few days," I replied, trying to sound more confident than I felt. "As soon as they've found Joel, they'll all be back."

"For all of our sakes, I hope you're right," Nial responded, his voice tinged with concern and a hint of skepticism.

I took a deep breath, attempting to steady my racing thoughts as I grappled with the possibility that Glenda and the others might not return as quickly as I hoped.

Glenda is coming back, isn't she? I asked myself silently, desperately seeking reassurance in the face of the mounting uncertainty.

With a fresh bowl of slop in hand, I excused myself from the conversation, telling Nial that I needed to check on Henri. As I made my way to the tent, my mind continued to churn with thoughts of Brianne and the baby, and the more I pondered the possibility of connecting with them, the stronger my determination grew.

Entering the tent, I sat down on the edge of the mattress, the spoon clinking against the sides of the bowl as I absentmindedly stirred the unappetising contents. The idea of speaking with Brianne, of hearing her voice and knowing that she was okay, had taken root in my mind, becoming a

...mer of hope in this desolate world that I clung to with ...ry fibre of my being.

I glanced across at Henri, nestled in his little bed, and felt a surge of resolve course through my veins. "I won't abandon their future," I declared, my voice echoing resolutely in the confines of the tent.

A SAFE HOME

4338.210.2

Lois came bounding into the tent, her sudden entrance signalling the return of Paul to the camp. I had been laying down, trying to rest my aching leg despite the improvement in its appearance. I wouldn't have been surprised if the soreness lingered for a few more weeks, but I was feeling more confident that the worst was behind me and that the healing process was well underway.

As Lois sniffed around Henri, who did his best to feign disinterest in her presence, I couldn't help but notice the poor fella's sulking demeanour. He had been in his bed all day, clearly missing his brother's companionship.

"Kain," Paul called out to me as he entered the tent, his voice carrying a high tone of excitement that immediately piqued my curiosity.

I sat upright, wincing slightly as the movement caused a twinge of discomfort in my leg.

"You have a caravan," Paul announced, his words catching me completely off guard.

"Huh?" I asked, my confusion evident in my tone and expression.

"Beatrix has delivered the first caravan, and given your injured leg—" Paul paused, nodding towards my legs hidden beneath the sleeping bag fabric, "I'm assuming that is why you are in here resting?"

"Yeah," I agreed with a nod, not wanting to confess that my self-imposed isolation was also a means of avoiding Chris. The camp's limited space made it difficult to find solitude.

n that case, it makes sense that you take the first avan. If anything else attacks us in the middle of the night, doubt you'll be running anywhere," said Paul, his words causing a small knot to form in my gut.

I was taken aback by Paul's remarks, unsure if he was being entirely serious. The thought that we could experience another night attack so soon was unsettling, to say the least.

Paul continued, "I've parked it outside for you."

Despite the lingering threat of the unknown dangers that lurked beyond the camp's borders, the idea of moving out of the tent and into a more secure shelter sent a surge of energy coursing through my veins. I scrambled out of the sleeping bag, collecting Henri from his bed, and followed Paul outside.

The sight that greeted me left me gobsmacked. Just as Paul had said, a caravan sat fifty yards from the campfire, situated within the perimeter marked by the fire sticks.

"I have to unhitch it from your ute again, though," said Paul as we approached the caravan. "I'm expecting Beatrix to bring us a few more."

My heart thumped loudly in my chest as I walked alongside Paul towards the new vehicle. The prospect of not having to spend another night in a tent was more than a little exciting. "How is Beatrix paying for them all?" I asked, my curiosity getting the better of me as Paul handed me the keys and I opened the caravan's door with a loud creak.

Paul chuckled softly. "I didn't dare ask her."

I scoffed silently to myself, acknowledging that Paul's decision not to pry was probably wise. As I stepped inside, I let Henri down, allowing him to explore our new surroundings. "It's nice," I commented, taking in the plush furnishings that adorned the interior. The cozy kitchen, complete with a small refrigerator, stove, and sink, would be a welcome upgrade from our current living arrangements.

The sleeping area looked comfortable, and the seating area was reasonably sized.

Henri meticulously sniffed every nook and cranny of the caravan before finally settling beside the double bed at the far end. After several attempts, he managed to jump onto the bed, circling a few times before plopping down with a satisfied snort.

"Looks like there's no complaints from Henri," said Paul, a light chuckle escaping his lips as his face beamed with the pride of a father who had successfully provided his children with the perfect Christmas gifts.

"Is this really all mine?" I asked, my excitement growing with each drawer and cupboard I opened and closed. While I didn't expect to find anything inside, the emptiness meant that I would no longer have to live out of a backpack, a prospect that filled me with a sense of relief and anticipation.

"It is indeed," Paul confirmed. "I know it's practically empty now, but between Luke and Beatrix, I'm sure it won't be more than a few days before you'll have yourself a fully stocked and self-sufficient little home here."

I nodded in silent agreement, my mind already racing with the possibilities of personalising the space and making it truly my own.

"You can move your belongings in as soon as you like," said Paul. "I'll head back to the Drop Zone to wait for Beatrix, but there's really not much more that can be done there right now."

"And what will become of the tents?" I asked, curious to learn if Paul had already formulated plans for their future use.

Without hesitation, Paul responded, "Until we get the first sheds operational, we'll use the tents for more storage. I think it's safest if we can avoid sleeping in them as much as possible."

"Can't really argue with that," I said, nodding in agreement. The memory of the shadow panther attack was still fresh in my mind, and the thought of having a more secure shelter brought a sense of comfort and relief.

As Paul headed for the door, he stopped abruptly on the first step, turning back to face me. "Henri seems to be comfortable with you. Are you happy to look after him in Jamie's absence?" he asked.

At the mention of his name, Henri raised his head momentarily before resting it back on the bare mattress, seemingly content in his new surroundings.

A warm, understanding smile passed my lips. "Of course," I answered without hesitation. The bond I had formed with Henri was one of the few bright spots in this strange and often frightening new world, and I was more than happy to provide him with the care and companionship he needed.

After confirming that I was satisfied with the caravan's location, I helped Paul unhitch it from the ute. As Lois jumped into the front cab, the pair headed back to the Portal, leaving plumes of dust billowing in their wake.

Stepping back inside the caravan, I inhaled deeply, the strong scent of detergent filling my nostrils and indicating that the vehicle had undergone a thorough cleaning recently. The freshness of the air and the pristine condition of the interior added to the sense of a new beginning, a small glimmer of hope in the midst of the challenges we faced.

As I sat beside Henri on the squeaky mattress, I couldn't help but feel a sense of gratitude and relief. "It does feel nice to have our very own space, doesn't it," I said softly, giving him a gentle scratch behind the ear. "We'll be safer in here."

As I set about the task of transferring my meagre belongings to the comforting confines of the caravan, I began with Henri's bed and toys, meticulously arranging them to recreate a semblance of familiarity in our new abode.

As I worked, my gaze fell upon Duke's empty bed, and a deep pang of sorrow resonated within me. The sight of the vacant bed served as a stark reminder of the companionship we had lost, the bond between the two dogs that had been so cruelly severed. I found myself grappling with the decision of whether to bring Duke's bed into the caravan, uncertain if its presence would provide solace to Henri or only intensify his grief.

After a moment of contemplation, I made the bittersweet choice to place Duke's bed in a corner of the tent, a silent farewell to the memories it held. The vacant bed stood as a solemn testament to the dangers that lurked in this unforgiving realm, a constant reminder of the fragility of life and the ever-present threat of loss.

Yet, even as I bid farewell to Duke's memory, a resolute determination tugged at my consciousness. The thought of bringing Brianne here, to this haven amidst chaos, filled me with a sense of purpose and hope. Despite the dangers and uncertainties that surrounded us, I clung to the belief that we could create a life together in this new world, that our love could overcome even the most daunting of obstacles.

As I continued my task, lost in my own thoughts and emotions, Paul returned to the camp, the arrival of a second caravan infusing a glimmer of hope into our otherwise desolate existence. He quickly engaged in conversation with Nial, their voices blending into the backdrop of activity as I carried out my relocation in serene silence.

The camp gradually surrendered to an eerie hush, its occupants lost in their individual pursuits and contemplations. The weight of the day's events and the constant stress of survival seemed to hang heavy in the air, a palpable presence that permeated every corner of our makeshift settlement.

As I moved about the caravan, arranging my few possessions and attempting to create a sense of personal space, I couldn't help but notice the dull ache that throbbed in my leg. It was a constant reminder of the healing process, both physical and emotional, that lay ahead of me. With each twinge of pain, I was forced to confront the reality of my situation, the fact that I was no longer the same person I had been before passing through the Portal.

Yet, even as the pain persisted, I found myself drawing strength from the small comforts that surrounded me. The soft glow of the caravan's interior lights, the gentle hum of the refrigerator, and the warmth of Henri's presence all served as reminders that even in the darkest of times, there were still moments of peace and solace to be found.

As the exhaustion of the day began to take its toll, I eased myself onto the plush mattress next to Henri, my body sinking into the welcoming embrace of the soft bedding. The weariness that enveloped me grew insurmountable, and I found myself surrendering to the pull of sleep, my eyelids growing heavy as the world around me began to fade away.

◆

A sharp, resounding knock on the caravan door shattered the veil of my unsettling daydream, jolting me back to the present. Henri's symphony of barks filled the air, a cacophony of sound that pierced through the lingering haze of my troubled thoughts. With weary eyes still heavy from the clutches of fatigue, I roused myself from the depths of my reverie, rubbing away the remnants of the disturbing images that had plagued my mind.

Cautiously, I swung open the door, the hinges creaking in protest as the bright sunlight flooded the interior of the caravan. There, standing before me, was Paul, his face etched with a mixture of determination and exhaustion. With a hefty grunt, he set down a weighty object at his feet.

I furrowed my brows, my gaze fixed upon the unfamiliar contraption that now occupied the space before me. It was a jumble of wires, metal, and strange components, a puzzle waiting to be unravelled.

"It's a power generator for the caravan," Paul announced, his voice strained as he stretched his tired muscles, the exertion of carrying the heavy device evident in his movements. "The latest gift from Beatrix. She's managed to bring us ten of them."

Curiosity ignited within me, my eyes widening in astonishment at the sheer magnitude of Beatrix's acquisition. "We've got ten caravans now?" I exclaimed, genuine surprise colouring my tone. The thought of our camp expanding so rapidly was almost too surreal to comprehend. Perhaps I had dozed for longer than I had realised, the passage of time blurring.

Paul shook his head, a slight chuckle escaping his lips as he clarified the situation. "We've just received our third caravan, but it's good for us to try and get ahead where we can."

I nodded in agreement, the logic of his words resonating with me. Yet, even as I acknowledged the wisdom of his approach, a lingering skepticism tugged at the corners of my mind. *Could we truly find a semblance of stability in this tumultuous realm?*

As Paul turned to depart, a sudden sense of urgency gripped me, propelling me to call out to him. "You're not going to help set it up?" I asked, my words laced with a hint of desperation.

Pausing abruptly, Paul pivoted back towards me, his eyebrows raised in a mixture of surprise and apology. "I've got no idea how these things work," he confessed, a nonchalant shrug accompanying his words.

A sigh escaped my lips, louder than I had intended.

Sensing my distress, Paul quickly continued, his voice filled with reassurance. "But Chris knows what he is doing with them."

At the mention of Chris's name, a wave of conflicting emotions surged through me, a turbulent mix of unease and gratitude. Paul seemed oblivious to the inner turmoil that coursed through my veins, forging ahead with unwavering enthusiasm.

"He and Karen have plenty of experience with these sorts of things from all the camping and outdoor expeditions they go on regularly. If you talk to Chris, I'm sure he'll be happy to help you get power to your new home," Paul assured me, a satisfied smile gracing his face.

"Thanks," I murmured, the word feeling hollow on my tongue. Gratitude mingled with a lingering unease that gnawed at my conscience, overshadowing the relief that should have permeated my being.

Paul took a few steps forward before halting once more, turning back towards me with an air of excitement. "I've allocated Karen and Chris the second caravan and Nial the third. Beatrix has promised we'll receive more over the next few days," he divulged, providing a glimpse into the evolving dynamics of our ever-changing camp.

With a final nod and a wave, Paul bid me farewell, his figure retreating into the dusty landscape, leaving me alone with my thoughts and the daunting task that lay before me.

Emerging from the confines of the caravan, I stepped out into the harsh glare of the sun, my senses assaulted by the arid breeze that whipped across the barren expanse. The other two caravans now stood in close proximity, their presence a testament to Paul's wisdom in maintaining a delicate balance between closeness and privacy.

As I surveyed the scene before me, a flicker of determination ignited within my chest. I refused to succumb to the vulnerability of seeking Chris's aid, the weight of our recent altercation still heavy on my mind. "Connecting a generator can't be that difficult," I muttered to myself, my hands planted firmly on my hips as I fixed my gaze upon the incomprehensible device that lay at my feet.

❖

Time seemed to slip away, the minutes bleeding into hours as I grappled with the intricate task of connecting the generator. Frustration tinged my voice, expletives escaping my lips as I fumbled with the wires and components, my scowl etched deeply upon my face.

"Do you need some help?" The familiar voice shattered the air, causing me to startle, my heart plunging into the depths of my churning stomach. Slowly, I turned to face Chris, my face flushing with a mix of embarrassment and trepidation.

"I'm assuming it was because of the voice?" Chris said, his words laced with a gentle shrug as he cautiously stepped closer, hinting at the incident that had driven a wedge between us.

My eyes narrowed, piercing through him with a fierce intensity, a surge of curiosity mixed with unease enveloping my being. *So, he does hear the voice too?* The revelation sent a shiver down my spine, the implications of our shared experience weighing heavily upon me.

"If it's alright with you," Chris continued, extending his hand towards the generator, his voice steady and assured, "the incident never happened."

His proposition resonated with me, an unspoken understanding passing between us, easing the tension that had permeated the air. "Sure," I acquiesced, my voice slightly hoarse, the desert dryness clinging to my throat. I yearned to suppress the thoughts of the voice and its insidious influence, to grasp onto a sliver of normality in our strained interactions. Yet, uncertainty still lingered, leaving me at a loss for what more I should say.

"Come on," Chris beckoned, gesturing towards the power generator, his demeanour calm and collected. "I'll teach you how to get this thing hooked up."

As I regarded Chris, a glimmer of hope flickered within me, a newfound appreciation for his ability to maintain composure and a sense of control. With a sigh of relief, I followed him, allowing a fraction of trust to seep back into my wary heart.

"Where should we start?" I asked, my voice tinged with uncertainty as I surveyed the jumble of wires and components.

"First things first, we need to connect the power cable from the generator to the caravan's electrical input," Chris explained, flashing a reassuring smile that put me at ease. "Don't worry, it may seem daunting, but it's actually pretty straightforward. We just need to match the colours of the wires. Red goes with red, black with black, and so on."

As he spoke, Chris deftly sorted through the wires, his experienced hands separating them into neat bundles with practiced precision. He moved with a fluid grace, effortlessly untangling the web of cables that had seemed so impenetrable to me.

"See these connectors here?" Chris pointed to a row of terminals, his voice steady and measured. "They're designed to secure the wires in place. We'll strip the ends of the wires and insert them into the appropriate terminals."

I watched intently as Chris demonstrated the process, carefully stripping the insulation off the wire ends and inserting them into the terminals with a confident ease. His movements were deliberate and precise, a demonstration of his expertise in this field.

"Now, it's important to ensure a solid connection," Chris explained, his tone patient and instructive. "We'll tighten these screws to hold the wires securely. Just tight enough to prevent any loose connections, but not too tight that we damage the wires."

Under his guidance, I mirrored Chris's actions, my hands moving with a newfound sense of purpose. Together, we meticulously connected each wire, the click of the screws echoing through the air as the connections grew stronger, a tangible symbol of our collaboration.

"Great job, Kain," Chris praised, his smile widening with genuine appreciation. "Now that the power cable is connected, let's move on to the control panel inside the caravan."

With renewed confidence, I followed Chris into the caravan, the anticipation of bringing this humble abode to life filling the air. We stood before the control panel, a myriad of buttons and switches beckoning to be activated, their promise of power and functionality nearly palpable.

"Here's where the magic happens," Chris said, his tone laced with excitement and a hint of reverence. "This control panel allows you to monitor and control the electrical systems in the caravan. We'll start by flipping the main switch to 'On'."

As I reached for the switch, a surge of anticipation coursed through my veins, the weight of the moment pressing upon me. With a flick of my finger, the switch shifted into position, and suddenly, the control panel illuminated, vibrant symbols and indicators springing to life before my eyes.

"Now, let's test the lights," Chris suggested, a playful glimmer in his eyes as he gestured towards a nearby button. "Press that button there."

I pressed the button, holding my breath as the room was instantly bathed in a warm, inviting glow. It was a moment of pure delight, the tangible result of our efforts manifesting before us in a display of light and comfort.

A grin broke across my face as I turned to Chris, our eyes meeting in a moment of shared satisfaction and accomplishment. "It worked!" I exclaimed, unable to contain the excitement that bubbled up within me.

Chris chuckled, his laughter echoing through the caravan, a sound that seemed to chase away the lingering shadows of our past. "Of course it did. You did a great job, Kain. Connecting the power generator is just the first step to unlocking the full potential of this caravan."

As we continued to explore the control panel, toggling switches and activating various systems, a newfound sense of empowerment washed over me. It was as if we were reclaiming a piece of the world we had left behind, rekindling the spark of ingenuity and adaptability that defined us as humans.

Soon, the caravan hummed with newfound life, a reassuring veil of security descending upon us. As I flicked another switch, illuminating the kitchen with a warm glow, an unabashed grin spread across my face, the worries of the past momentarily forgotten.

In this simple act of bringing power to the caravan, I found a glimpse of the world I once knew, a reminder of the significance and vitality that electricity bestowed upon our lives. This generator, fuelled by the solar energy harnessed from the relentless sun that beat down upon this barren landscape, became a beacon of hope, a promise that even in this desolate realm, remnants of the life I had left behind could be reclaimed.

As I stood there, basking in the glow of the lights and the hum of the appliances, I silently vowed to never take for granted the luxuries and comforts that power afforded us. In that moment, I realised that the generator represented more than just a source of electricity; it was a symbol of resilience, of our ability to adapt and thrive.

TWISTED INTRIGUES

4338.210.3

Not long ago, from the safety of my new caravan home, I had heard the commotion of the arrival of another two settlers. Unable to deal with the tumultuous event, I had kept my distance, choosing to remain secluded within the confines of my humble abode. The raised voices had carried through the thin walls, a cacophony of emotions that I couldn't quite decipher. But as the tantalising aromas of freshly cooked chilli and warm bread wafted through the small open window, my stomach began to turn on itself, reminding me that I had yet to eat something substantial today. The gnawing hunger had reached a point of desperation, and I realised that if I continued to stubbornly avoid engaging with the other settlers, I would fade into nothingness by morning.

"I guess you're hungry too?" I said to Henri, ruffling his furry head affectionately. His small, eager eyes met mine, and he wagged his tail in response, a silent plea for sustenance. "Come on then, let's feed you."

Henri jumped off the bed with a newfound energy, his excitement evident in every bounce of his paws. I reached into the bottom cupboard and retrieved a tin of dog food, the metal cool against my fingertips. As I pulled the lid open, the rich aroma of chunky meat and vegetables smothered in gravy filled the air, a tempting scent that made my own mouth water. "Even this smells appetising," I chuckled, scooping generous spoonfuls of the hearty meal into Henri's food bowl. "I must be starving," I muttered, catching myself before I instinctively licked the small dollop of gravy that sat precariously at the end of my pinky.

Within minutes, Henri devoured his small feast, his tail wagging happily as he savoured every morsel. I knew he didn't enjoy socialising with groups of people or other dogs, his introverted nature mirroring my own in many ways. But I was determined that it was time for him to get used to it, to adapt to the new community we found ourselves in. Every time Uncle Jamie brought Duke and Henri over to the Manor when he visited Mum, Duke was always excited to play with Hudson, their barks and yips filling the air with joy. Henri, on the other hand, would content himself with stealing scraps from the kitchen before finding a secluded spot to hide until the visit was over, his solitude a comforting blanket.

"I know you don't like it," I said, carrying Henri as we left the caravan, the fresh air hitting my face like a gentle caress. "But you can't stay in your bed all day anymore."

Setting Henri down on the dusty ground, I approached the campfire cautiously, hoping that the tension from the arrival of the new people had dissipated. Paul, his face alight with energy and optimism, was quick to greet me, shoving a bowlful of chilli con carne into my hands before I could even utter a word. The hearty aroma filled my nostrils, and my mouth watered at the sight of the steaming meal, the vibrant colours of the beans and meat a stark contrast to the dull hues of the world around us.

"Thanks, Paul," I said, mustering a smile that felt foreign on my face. "Looks delicious."

He beamed, his enthusiasm infectious. "It's my specialty. Enjoy!"

As I savoured the warm and comforting flavours, the spices dancing on my tongue, Paul introduced me to the newcomers, Grant Ironbach and his sister, Sarah. Grant, the Director of the Bonorong Wildlife Sanctuary in Hobart, and

Sarah, who also worked at the sanctuary, had an air of warmth and genuine kindness about them, their smiles sincere and their eyes filled with a depth of understanding. Instantly, I found myself liking them, drawn to their gentle demeanour and the passion that radiated from their very being.

Paul wandered off as the conversation continued, and I couldn't help but be intrigued by Grant and Sarah's unique personalities, woven seamlessly with their shared love for wildlife. Grant exuded an aura of determination and adventure, his eyes sparkling with the excitement of exploring untamed wilderness, as if the very essence of nature flowed through his veins.

"I've heard about your work at the sanctuary," I said, my curiosity getting the better of me, the words tumbling out before I could stop them. "It must be incredible to work with such fascinating creatures."

Grant's face lit up with a genuine smile, his eyes crinkling at the corners. "It truly is a dream come true," he replied, his voice filled with a reverence that spoke volumes about his passion. "From the majestic Tasmanian devils to the endangered quolls and unique bird species, every day brings new wonders. But it's not just about the animals; it's about creating a balance between conservation and education, so future generations can appreciate and protect these beautiful creatures."

Sarah, with her infectious enthusiasm, chimed in, her voice melodic and filled with warmth. "And the rewards are immeasurable. Like the time we rehabilitated a Tasmanian devil with a broken jaw. It took a lot of patience and teamwork, but seeing her released back into the wild was incredibly fulfilling."

Their dedication and unwavering commitment to the animals shone through their words, painting a vivid picture of the love and care they poured into their work. It was evident that their roles at the sanctuary extended far beyond the confines of a job; it was a calling, a purpose that filled their hearts with joy and meaning. Grant's love for adventure and outdoor exploration mirrored the untamed spirit of Clivilius itself, while Sarah's artistic nature and her songwriting showcased her deep connection with the rhythms and melodies of the natural world.

"I have to admit," I confessed, a twinge of envy colouring my words, "I envy your passion and the impact you're making. It's inspiring."

Grant's eyes sparkled with a mix of gratitude and determination, his voice filled with conviction. "We believe that everyone can contribute to the well-being of our planet in their own way. It's not just about grand gestures but also the small steps we take each day."

Sarah nodded in agreement, her long hair swaying gently in the evening breeze. "Absolutely. Whether it's raising awareness or making sustainable choices, we all have a role to play. And it's incredible to witness the positive changes that can come from collective efforts."

Their words resonated within me, planting a seed of inspiration that began to take root in my mind. The idea that even small actions could make a difference, that we all had the power to effect change, was a comforting thought.

However, as the relatively normal conversation continued, a knot began to form in the pit of my stomach, a nagging sense of unease that I couldn't quite shake. Something was definitely off, a discordant note in the otherwise harmonious exchange. The pieces of the puzzle didn't quite fit together, and I found myself grasping at straws, trying to make sense of the subtle shifts in the atmosphere.

The tension in the campfire's glow lingered, an unspoken unease that contradicted the cheerful façade presented by the settlers. I glanced around, observing the expressions on the faces of my fellow survivors, searching for clues that might shed light on the underlying current of disquiet. Some wore forced smiles, their eyes betraying the strain of maintaining a semblance of normality, while others exchanged quick glances, their gazes filled with unspoken worry and apprehension.

As the fire crackled and sparks danced into the night sky, my mind raced with questions, a maelstrom of thoughts that refused to be silenced. *Why were Grant and Sarah so optimistic despite the dangers and hardships we faced? What had they experienced that gave them such unwavering hope, a resilience that seemed to defy the very nature of our predicament?* The answers eluded me, slipping through my grasp like wisps of smoke, but deep down, I knew that there was more to their arrival than met the eye.

I made a silent vow to keep my guard up, to listen closely to the secrets whispered between the lines, the unspoken truths that lurked beneath the surface of their words. Clivilius was a place of mystery and danger, a realm where nothing was quite as it seemed, and it was becoming increasingly clear that the arrival of Grant and Sarah was about to unravel another layer of its intricate tapestry.

◆

As the sun began its descent, casting an ethereal orange glow over the camp, I noticed Henri lying alone, his small form curled up away from the lively campfire and the company of other dogs. He seemed content in his solitude, finding solace in the quiet corners of the camp. The air was thick with an undercurrent of mystery and unease, whispering secrets that danced just beyond my reach, teasing me with their elusive nature.

"Looks like you've had enough of the commotion too, huh?" I murmured to Henri, my voice soft and understanding as I gathered him in my arms. He nestled against my chest, his small body warm and comforting. In that moment, I felt a deep connection with Henri, a shared longing for the familiar and the safe, a desire to escape the relentless weight of the unknown.

Together, Henri and I sought refuge in the sanctuary of my caravan, our footsteps echoing against the metal floor as we crossed the threshold. The worn and tired ache in my leg throbbed with each step. But as I closed the door behind us, the caravan became a haven amidst the uncertainty, a momentary respite from the swirling thoughts and unanswered questions that plagued my mind.

A pang of guilt tinged my thoughts as I settled into the relative comfort of the caravan, knowing that some of our fellow settlers would remain sleeping in tents tonight, their vulnerability exposed to the elements and the unseen dangers that lurked in the shadows. But Paul's insistence on maintaining a semblance of normality, his unwavering belief in the power of routine and structure, compelled me to find solace in the comfort that this small space provided. It was a reminder that even in the midst of danger, we could cling to the familiar, to the things that grounded us and gave us a sense of purpose.

Beatrix's promise of additional caravans in the days to come echoed in my mind, a glimmer of hope amidst the tangled webs we found ourselves entwined in. I reassured myself, reminding my weary spirit that others had found their own sanctuary within these metal walls. Karen, Chris, and Nial had already claimed their own refuge, their presence a comforting thought in the vastness of Clivilius. Yet, the absence of Glenda, Joel, and Uncle Jamie weighed heavily upon me, their whereabouts a mystery that gnawed at the edges of my consciousness. Only Paul and the new arrivals, Grant and Sarah, remained without the shelter of a caravan, their optimism a mysterious contrast to the unease that permeated the camp.

In the dim light of the caravan's interior, I prepared to settle in for the night, the weariness of the day seeping into my bones. The soft glow of the lamp above the bed illuminated the space, casting a warm ambiance upon the worn fabric and aged wood. I stood, my hand poised to switch off the light, ready to surrender to the embrace of sleep, when a sudden, unexpected knock shattered the fragile calm.

Curiosity ignited within me as I opened the door, the cool night air rushing in to greet me. There, standing before me, was Paul, his face etched with weariness and a hint of concern. The weight of his presence hung in the air, a palpable force that demanded attention.

"Kain, I need to talk to you," Paul's voice carried a gravity that belied his usually calm demeanour, laden with a concern that set my nerves on edge.

I motioned for him to enter, stepping aside to allow him passage into the sanctuary of my caravan. He stepped inside, shutting the door behind him with a soft click that seemed to echo in the confined space. The air grew thick with tension as his eyes darted around, ensuring that we were shielded from prying ears and curious gazes.

"What's going on, Paul?" I asked, my curiosity interlaced with a growing unease, as though the very air crackled with hidden truths waiting to be revealed.

Paul's breath caught in his throat, his shoulders sagging under the weight of the words he was about to speak. When he finally spoke, his voice was lowered to a hushed tone, a conspiratorial whisper that sent a chill down my spine. "Kain, there's something you need to know about Grant and Sarah."

My heart skipped a beat, a foreboding chill coursing through my veins as I leaned in closer, desperate to hear the truth that had been hidden. "What about them?"

Paul exhaled heavily, a mixture of anger and empathy colouring his words as he revealed the shocking truth. "They've been deceived, just like the rest of us. Luke tricked them into coming here, making them believe that they were only here to assess the possibility of establishing a wildlife sanctuary in Clivilius. They have no idea that once they stepped through the Portal, they would be cut off from Earth forever."

Shock reverberated through me, the weight of the revelation crashing upon my shoulders like a tidal wave. Grant and Sarah, the beacons of hope and untarnished optimism, were now ensnared in Luke's web of deceit, their dreams and aspirations shattered by Luke's callous actions. They had unwittingly embarked on a one-way journey to Clivilius, severed from the life they once knew, trapped within the enigmatic embrace of this mysterious realm.

"But why would Luke do that? Why would he trick them?" I asked, the questions tumbling out in a torrent of confusion and despair. The memory of my own forced arrival, Luke's violent shove through the Portal, resurfaced with a vengeance, sending tremors through my core, threatening to unravel the fragile composure I had fought so hard to maintain.

Paul sighed, his eyes reflecting a sombre blend of sorrow and determination as he grappled with the weight of the truth. "I don't have all the answers, Kain. But I suspect Luke has his own motives, his own plans for Clivilius. And Grant and Sarah, along with the rest of us, are caught in the middle of it, pawns in a game we don't fully understand."

Conflicting emotions surged within me, a tempest of empathy for Grant and Sarah's unwitting entrapment mingling with the weight of a heightened sense of peril. Even those who radiated trust and goodwill could harbour hidden agendas, their true intentions masked beneath layers of deception and manipulation.

As Paul concluded his revelation, a kaleidoscope of thoughts whirled within me, each one more unsettling than the last. Grant and Sarah, with their infectious optimism and unwavering hope, held the potential to be a beacon of salvation, a key to unlocking the path that would reunite Brianne with us in Clivilius. But caution gripped my heart, urging me to remain vigilant, to peel back the layers of their optimism and uncover the truths that lay beneath.

Paul's words echoed in the recesses of my mind, a constant reminder of the delicate equilibrium we teetered upon in this intricate realm of shadows and secrets. I glanced at the outside light, the symbol of our shared vigilance, and a newfound determination coursed through me, steeling my resolve. "I'll keep the light on, Paul," I declared, my voice resolute and unwavering. "We need all the light we can get, both metaphorically and literally. We must navigate the shadows that encroach upon our path, protecting what matters most, even as we seek the truth that eludes us."

Paul nodded, a flicker of hope illuminating his weary eyes, a glimmer of the strength that had carried us this far. "We will, Kain. We'll find a way. Together."

With those words, we parted ways, each retreating into the solitude of our own thoughts, the darkness of the night descending upon us like a shroud. Within the confines of Clivilius, where the mysteries whispered and shadows danced, a journey of revelation and trepidation unfolded before us, bound by the unyielding resolve to unravel the enigma that threatened our very existence.

As I lay in my bed, the weight of Paul's words pressing down upon me, I couldn't help but feel a deep sense of unease, a gnawing fear that we were all caught in a web of lies and deceit that ran deeper than we could possibly imagine. The flickering light of the lamp cast eerie shadows on the walls of the caravan, a reminder of the darkness that lurked just beyond our reach, waiting.

4338.211

(30 July 2018)

GLIMMERS IN THE MIRAGE

4338.211.1

As Nial and I embarked on our journey toward the Drop Zone, a palpable unease hung in the air, growing thicker with each step, like a suffocating fog that clung to our skin. The landscape stretched out before us, a vast expanse of scattered supplies strewn haphazardly across the barren ground, like fragments of a broken puzzle that refused to fit together.

Lost in the labyrinth of my own thoughts, I reached the crest of the final hill, my heart heavy with the weight of the unknown. I surveyed the desolate expanse that lay before us. The air crackled with an electric anticipation, a tangible force that seemed to whisper secrets just beyond my grasp, urging me to seek solace in the clarity of the present moment, to anchor myself in the here and now.

"Everything okay?" Nial's voice pierced through the veil of my introspection, jolting me back to the harsh reality that surrounded us.

I drew in a deep, shuddering breath, attempting to steady the racing thoughts that threatened to overtake me. "Yeah," I replied softly, my voice barely a whisper against the oppressive silence. But even as the word left my lips, I knew it was a hollow reassurance, a feeble attempt to mask the turmoil that raged within.

As my gaze swept across the desolate landscape once more, my attention was suddenly captured by a commotion near the Portal, a flurry of activity that stood out in stark contrast to the eerie stillness that permeated the air. Beatrix stood by a motorhome, her eyes fixed on Paul, who towered over an unfamiliar man sprawled on his back directly in front of the vehicle. I gasped softly, my brain scrambling to connect the disjointed dots of the scene, to make sense of the unexpected tableau that unfolded before me.

"Shit! Adrian. What the hell are you doing here?" Nial's exclamation snapped my attention back to our immediate surroundings, his voice laced with a mixture of shock and disbelief. Without hesitation, he rushed ahead, crouching in front of the prone figure, delivering a few sharp slaps to his drowsy face in an attempt to rouse him from his stupor.

My brow furrowed in confusion as I observed the scene, a myriad of questions swirling in my mind. *Who was this Adrian, and what twist of fate had brought him to the unforgiving realm of Clivilius? And perhaps more intriguingly, how did Nial know him?* The threads of curiosity intertwined with a tinge of unease, a nagging sensation that whispered of hidden secrets and untold stories.

"Not surprising," Luke chimed in, his voice laced with a casual indifference that set my teeth on edge. "Hobart's a small place." His words hung in the air, a reminder of the tangled web of connections that seemed to follow us.

Paul turned towards us, his eyes reflecting a blend of concern and urgency, a silent plea for assistance. "Can you two take him back to camp?" he requested, motioning towards Adrian, who remained in a groggy state, his limbs sprawled awkwardly on the dusty ground.

Nial's grip tightened on Adrian's shoulders, his voice a mixture of concern and frustration as he attempted to guide him to his feet. "Let's get you to camp," he assured him, his words carrying a delicate balance of reassurance and urgency.

"We'll come back," I interjected, extending a helping hand to Nial as we grappled with Adrian's uncooperative form. The pungent scent of a freshly smoked joint drifted toward us, causing me to sneeze uncontrollably, my eyes watering from the acrid smoke that hung in the air.

Despite his acknowledgment of Nial's presence, Adrian appeared far from cooperative, his movements sluggish and uncoordinated as he steadied himself on his feet. With a determined stride, he veered toward the vehicle he must have arrived in, brushing off Nial's pleas to leave the ute and join us on our journey back to the relative safety of the camp.

"I'm just getting the rest of my gear," Adrian insisted, his words slurred but laced with a stubborn determination that seemed to fuel his pursuit of the vehicle. He stumbled forward, his hands grasping at the door handle, a desperate attempt to cling to the remnants of his former life.

Frustration welled up within me as I observed Adrian's actions, a simmering anger that threatened to boil over at any moment. The scorching sun beat down upon my sweat-soaked face, intensifying the exasperation that coursed through my veins. Our trek to secure the fencing supplies had led us to the Drop Zone, yet the desired materials remained elusive, leaving us entangled in yet another unexpected encounter with someone thrust into the unforgiving realm of Clivilius against their will. Lingering doubts cast shadows over our path, remnants of Luke's deceptive methods in establishing our fragile settlement, a constant reminder of the treacherous ground upon which we stood.

Amidst the ongoing squabble between Nial and Adrian, their voices rising in a crescendo of anger and confusion, the driver's door slammed shut with a resounding thud, the sound echoing across the desolate landscape. The engine roared to life, a mechanical beast awakening from its slumber, ready to carry its passengers to an unknown destination. Nial stood resolute at the front of the vehicle, his hands resting on the bonnet, a silent plea for resolution.

A cloud of dust billowed into the air as the motorhome surged forward, propelled by a newfound vitality, its wheels kicking up a storm of sand and debris in its wake. Through the haze, I watched as Beatrix, who must have returned to Earth through the Portal, vanished from sight, her form swallowed up by the swirling vortex of energy that pulsed with an otherworldly power.

Amidst the clamour of angry voices and the roar of the engine, Nial managed to wrangle himself into the ute alongside Adrian, his face a mask of grim determination as he struggled to maintain control of the situation. Through the chaos, Nial called out to me, his voice barely audible above the din, urging me to join them in their impromptu journey.

But I had reached my threshold for commotion for the morning, my mind and body craving a moment of respite from the relentless onslaught of unexpected events. "I'm all good. I'll stay here and wait for the fencing supplies to arrive," I called out. With a wave of my hand, I bid them farewell, a final gesture of declining the offer to join them in the ute.

As the vehicle sped away, kicking up a trail of dust in its wake, I found myself alone once more, surrounded by the scattered supplies and the weight of uncertainty that hung heavy in the air.

❖

As I wandered through the dusty expanse of the Drop Zone, awaiting the return of a Guardian with the much-needed fencing supplies, my mind drifted to thoughts of Brianne and our unborn child. The harsh landscape stretched out before me, the scorching sun beating down upon the desolate land, and yet, within the depths of my imagination, I caught a glimmer of something more—a vision that transcended the bleak reality that surrounded me.

In the shimmering heat of the day, a mirage seemed to materialise in the distance, teasing my weary eyes with illusions of greenery and life. The heatwaves danced and twisted, conjuring visions of lush fields and vibrant forests, a stark contrast to the arid wasteland that stretched out before me. In that fleeting moment, I caught a glimpse of a different Clivilius—a transformed land where my family could find solace and sanctuary, a place where we could build a life together, far from the dangers and uncertainties that plagued us.

I closed my eyes, surrendering to the whims of my imagination, allowing myself to be swept away by the tantalising promises of the mirage. In my mind's eye, I envisioned a humble home nestled amidst the natural beauty of this strange and wondrous world, crafted with our own hands and imbued with love and resilience. I could almost see Brianne's radiant smile, her freckled cheeks catching the early morning rays of the sun as she tended to a small garden, her belly round with the promise of new life. The laughter of our child echoed in my ears, their tiny feet dancing across the untamed earth, embracing the wonders of this wild world with the innocence and curiosity of youth.

In that reverie, the challenges and dangers that loomed around me faded into the background, momentarily forgotten in the face of the idyllic scene that unfolded before me. The desolation of Clivilius transformed into a canvas of endless possibilities, where love and resilience could carve out a place of solace and belonging, a haven amidst the chaos and uncertainty that had become my constant companions.

But as quickly as it had appeared, the mirage vanished, dissipating like a wisp of smoke carried away by the scorching winds of reality. I was left with the stark realisation of our current circumstances, the weight of the challenges that lay ahead pressing down upon my shoulders once more. And yet, the vision had been more than a fleeting glimpse of hope—it was a reminder of what we were fighting for, a tangible representation of the future we yearned to create for ourselves and our loved ones.

With renewed determination, I opened my eyes, refocusing on the Drop Zone. The mirage may have been ephemeral, but the vision it had kindled within me remained steadfast, a flickering flame of hope that refused to be extinguished by the harsh realities of this world. It served as a reminder of the purpose that propelled us forward, the dream of creating a better life for ourselves and our community, no matter how arduous the path ahead might be.

As I stood amidst the arid landscape, contemplating the significance of the mirage and the promises it held, a whisper slithered into my thoughts, an insidious presence that I had come to know all too well. The familiar voice, the Voice of Clive, intruded upon my consciousness, its presence evoking a mixture of anticipation and unease, a duality that had become a constant in my interactions with this enigmatic entity.

Ah, Kain, dreaming of a paradise amidst this desolation, are we? the voice taunted, its tone dripping with perverse delight, as though it took pleasure in the inner turmoil it stirred within me. *How enchanting it must be to envision such beauty, such serenity, in a world so rife with danger and uncertainty. But tell me, dear Kain, what would you be willing to offer in return for this paradise you so desperately crave?*

I clenched my fists, my resolve hardening as the voice's words echoed in my mind. The Voice of Clive had played its twisted game before, demanding sacrifices in return for the healing I so desperately needed. I glanced down at my wounded leg, the memory of the pain and the slow, agonising process of recovery still fresh in my mind. The healing was far from perfect, but I had to admit that, given the lack of meaningful medical attention and the harsh conditions of Clivilius, its current status was rather remarkable. And yet, I had learned the hard way the price that came with accepting the offerings of this manipulative entity, and this time, I was determined to stand firm, to resist its temptations and the allure of easy solutions.

But even as I steeled myself against the voice's machinations, my curiosity couldn't resist the urge to learn more, to delve deeper into the twisted web of promises and deception that Clive wove with such skill. "What do you want now, Clive?" I retorted, my voice laced with defiance, a bravado that belied the uncertainty that lurked beneath the surface. "I've given enough, sacrificed too much already. I won't be a pawn in your manipulation again."

The voice chuckled, a sinister sound that reverberated through my thoughts, sending shivers down my spine. *Oh, Kain, your resistance is admirable, truly it is. But I can see the longing in your heart, the yearning for a better life for your family, for the chance to create something beautiful amidst the isolation and despair. I could grant you that mirage, you know —that idyllic paradise you saw in your mind's eye. All you need to do is bring Brianne and the baby to Clivilius—a simple trade, really, for such a grand reward.*

My blood ran cold as Clive's proposition hung in the air, the weight of its implications crashing down upon me. The mirage, the promise of a haven for my loved ones, seemed tantalisingly close, within reach if only I were willing to make the necessary sacrifices. And yet, the thought of betraying my determination to find a way back home, of willingly subjecting Brianne and our unborn child to the dangers and uncertainties of Clivilius, sent a wave of conflict crashing over me, threatening to drown me in its depths.

No! my mind replied firmly, my silent voice unwavering even as my heart raced with the temptation of Clive's offer. *I won't bring Brianne here, won't sacrifice our chance to find a way back to Earth, to the life we once knew. I won't condemn our child to a future in this harsh and unforgiving world, no matter how alluring the promise of paradise may be.*

The voice hissed its rebuke, its disappointment palpable, a tangible presence that seemed to press down upon me from all sides. *Very well, Kain. You deny yourself the pleasures I could bestow, the chance to create a life of beauty and meaning amidst the desolation. But remember, every choice has consequences, and there will come a time when you'll have to face them, when the weight of your decisions will come crashing down upon you like a house of cards.*

With those final words, the voice faded, leaving behind a lingering sense of unease, a nagging doubt that tugged at the corners of my mind. I took a deep, shuddering breath, my mind still reeling from the encounter, from the temptation and the conflict that Clive's words had stirred within me. I centred myself in the reality of the present, reminding myself of the path I had chosen, however difficult and uncertain it may be. The mirage, once so tempting, now held a bittersweet taste—a reminder of the sacrifices and challenges that lay ahead, of the strength and resilience that would be required.

Despite my best attempts to persuade myself that I had made the right decision, that rejecting Clive's offer was the only path forward, a tight knot formed in the pit of my stomach, a noose that seemed to tighten with each passing moment. I couldn't shake the inevitable thought that if there really was no way back home, if the Portal remained an impassable barrier between Clivilius and Earth, I would be doomed to remain alone all my days in this strange and unforgiving world, forever separated from the woman I loved and the child we had dreamed of raising together.

As I stood at the Drop Zone, burdened by the weight of my emotions and the conflict that raged within me, my attention was suddenly drawn to Luke, who had returned through the Portal with a delivery of the temporary fencing components we so desperately needed. With each piece he brought through, a renewed sense of purpose and determination filled me.

I eagerly grabbed the materials, feeling their weight in my hands, a tangible reminder of the security and protection we were working to create for our small camp. The fencing represented a step forward, a means of fortifying our position and carving out a space of our own within the vast and untamed wilderness of Clivilius.

As Luke and I worked together to unload the supplies, the sun beating down upon us with relentless intensity, we engaged in intermittent conversation, our words punctuated by the sounds of exertion and the clanging of metal against metal. My curiosity got the better of me, and I couldn't help but inquire about the origins of the fencing, eager to learn more about the mysterious circumstances that had brought these much-needed resources to our doorstep.

I turned to Luke, my voice filled with intrigue, a hint of hope glimmering in my eyes. "Is this the order that Paul and Nial placed the other day? The one they were so excited about?"

Luke nodded, a momentary flicker of reservation crossing his features, as though he were weighing the consequences of revealing too much. There was more to this story, I could sense it, hidden beneath the surface of his casual demeanour. Determined to maintain that spark of hope, to glean any information that might provide clues to a way back home, I probed further, my voice gentle but insistent.

"Yeah, it is," Luke finally confirmed, his voice tinged with a hint of caution, a reluctance to divulge the full extent of the truth. "But there's more to it, mate. More than I can really say."

My brow furrowed, the gears in my mind turning as I considered the implications of his words. *What was Luke not telling me? What secrets lay hidden behind his guarded expression and cryptic statements?* Before I could voice my curiosity, however, Luke abruptly cut himself off, a flicker of unease crossing his features, as though he had suddenly become aware of the precariousness of our situation.

"What's the matter?" I questioned, my concern etched across my face.

Luke hesitated for a moment, his gaze fixated on a distant point beyond the Drop Zone, as though he were searching for the right words. Then, with a heavy sigh, he began to share a story—one that left me equal parts impressed and wary, a tale of audacity and cunning that spoke to the lengths we were willing to go to ensure our survival in this new world.

Luke's voice took on a low and measured tone as he began, his words carefully chosen, as though he were revealing a secret of great import. "Beatrix and I came up with this ingenious plan, see? I activated my Portal Key inside the delivery truck, without the driver even knowing it was happening. Now the Portal location is registered, locked in, so we can access the truck whenever we need to, whenever supplies are running low."

My eyes widened in astonishment at the audacity of their scheme, the sheer boldness of their actions. Despite Luke's often chaotic and unpredictable nature, the resourcefulness and cunning he and Beatrix had displayed never ceased to amaze me. And yet, even as I marvelled at their ingenuity, a wave of caution washed over me, a nagging sense that there were risks involved, consequences that couldn't be ignored.

"And what about the driver?" I asked, my voice laced with concern, a hint of trepidation creeping into my tone. "Won't he notice that the truck is being emptied out? Won't he suspect something is amiss?"

Luke's expression darkened, a shadow of regret passing over his features, as though he were grappling with the moral implications of their actions. "Don't worry," he assured me, slapping my shoulder lightly in a gesture of camaraderie. "We've been careful, made sure to cover our tracks. By the time the truck returns to the warehouse, I'll have emptied it of all the fencing equipment, leaving no trace behind. The driver won't suspect a thing, won't even know we were there."

As Luke continued with his task, his focus shifting back to the unloading of the supplies, I made the decision to return to camp, eager to share the news of the fencing's arrival with Nial and the others. It was time to rally our fellow settlers, to begin the process of fortifying our position and building the protections we so desperately needed, however long our stay in Clivilius might last.

IN THE SHADOW'S EMBRACE

4338.211.2

Luke's right eye raised as he cast a curious glance in Beatrix's direction, a silent question hanging in the air between them. Ignoring his unvoiced curiosity, Paul's attention remained fixed on Luke as he spoke, his words carrying a sense of urgency and purpose. "You may as well bring anything from the house that looks useful."

"Include furniture with that," I interjected, my mind immediately latching onto the idea. I hobbled over with my new crutches, seizing the opportunity to make my needs known. Startling the three of them with my sudden appearance, I added, "I could really do with a good couch to rest my leg."

Luke's brow furrowed as he turned his gaze towards me, his eyes filled with a mixture of concern and curiosity. "Has it still not healed fully yet?" he asked, his voice tinged with a hint of surprise.

I couldn't help but feel a pang of frustration in my voice as I replied, the words spilling out before I could temper them. "No. I don't seem to be as privileged as Joel." The bitterness in my tone was palpable, a reflection of the pain and uncertainty that plagued me.

Luke pressed for more information, his curiosity evident in the way he leaned forward slightly. "Any news on that front?" he inquired, his eyes searching mine for answers.

I shook my head, my concern etched on my face, visible even in the fading daylight that cast long shadows across the camp. The absence of Joel, Jamie, and Glenda weighed heavily on my mind, a constant source of worry that gnawed at my thoughts.

Paul chimed in, his contribution doing little to ease the tension that hung in the air. "We've not seen anything of Joel, Jamie, or Glenda." His words were matter-of-fact, but the undercurrent of unease was unmistakable.

Luke's response wavered, uncertainty creeping into his voice as he attempted to reassure us. "Give them a couple more days." But even as he spoke, I could sense the doubt that lingered beneath the surface, the unspoken fear that something had gone terribly wrong.

"And then what?" Beatrix's impatience seeped into her question, her tone tinged with frustration. She stood with her arms crossed, her gaze fixed on Luke, demanding answers that he seemed unable to provide.

Luke shrugged, his shoulders rising and falling in a gesture of helplessness, seemingly lacking a definitive answer.

Paul let out a sigh, sensing the escalating tension that threatened to boil over. Realising that the situation was getting out of hand, I couldn't hold back my frustration any longer. The words burst forth from my lips, a torrent of pent-up anger and desperation. "You've really got no idea what you're doing, do you, Luke?" My accusation hung in the air, sharp and cutting.

"It's not that easy," Beatrix snapped back, her voice rising to match my own. She stepped forward, her eyes blazing with a fierce protectiveness as she defended Luke.

"You don't have to tell me that," I retorted, leaning heavily on my crutches, my weight abruptly shifting as I struggled to maintain my balance. The pain in my leg flared, a reminder of the physical and emotional wounds that I carried, the scars that Clivilius had left upon my soul.

Before the tension could escalate further, Paul intervened loudly, his voice cutting through the growing animosity.

"Enough!" he shouted, his words echoing across the camp, demanding attention and compliance.

Sensing the shifting mood, I let out a sigh, realising that the argument was getting us nowhere. I conceded inwardly that I needed to trust their judgment more, to have faith in the decisions they were making, even if I couldn't fully understand them. My frustrations had clouded my judgment, and I knew that I needed to find a way to rein them in.

"And while I think of it, my car is still parked at the Adelaide airport car park. Can you collect it for me and bring it here?" Paul's request redirected the conversation.

Beatrix gave me a final one-eyed glare, her gaze lingering on me for a moment before she reluctantly turned her attention back to Paul. With a muttered and hesitant response, she acquiesced to his request. "Sure." The word was clipped, a begrudging acceptance of the task that had been laid before her.

Luke's countenance suddenly lit up, his eyes widening with excitement as a new idea struck him, chasing away the shadows of uncertainty that had lingered in his expression. "I am flying from Hobart to Adelaide first thing in the morning. I won't have time to collect Paul's car, but I can register a Portal location to make it easier for you, Beatrix." His words tumbled out in a rush, a flurry of enthusiasm that was almost infectious.

"Thanks, but there's no need to fly, I've already registered several locations in Adelaide," Beatrix replied, her voice steady and confident, a contrast to the frustration that had coloured her words just moments before.

"Oh," responded Luke, his face drooping in thoughtful concentration, as if he were trying to make sense of this new information, to reconcile it with the plans he had already set in motion.

Luke's head rose as he finally spoke, his voice filled with a renewed sense of purpose. "I've already got my flight booked. I may as well use it. Besides, I might find something useful at the airport. In any event, it'll give you a much closer point of entry for collecting Paul's car." His words were measured, a careful consideration of the variables at play, a testament to the strategic mind that lurked beneath his often chaotic exterior.

"All right," Beatrix agreed with a gentle shrug, realising there was no point in arguing further. She seemed to sense the determination in Luke's voice, the unwavering resolve that drove him forward.

"What are you actually going to Adelaide for, Luke?" Paul asked his brother, a hint of concern creeping into his voice. It was a question that had been lingering in the back of my mind as well.

Luke hesitated for a moment, his eyes darting between Paul and Beatrix, as if weighing the consequences of his answer. When he finally spoke, his voice was confident, brimming with determination. "I'm thinking I might bring our parents and siblings to Clivilius," he declared, his words hanging in the air, a bold proclamation that sent ripples of surprise through the group.

Beatrix gasped audibly, her eyes widening with a mixture of shock and concern. "Is that a good idea?" she asked, her voice tinged with uncertainty.

Paul, speaking on Luke's behalf, surprised everyone with his response. His voice was steady, filled with a quiet conviction. "It'll be a lot more mouths to feed, but I think you're right. I think they could really help us here."

Beatrix's curiosity got the better of her, and she couldn't help but ask, her eyes narrowing slightly as she regarded the two brothers. "How many?"

Paul turned to Luke, seeking clarification, his brow furrowed in concentration. "Only Adelaide?" he asked.

Luke clarified his position, providing more details, his words measured and precise. "I think so, for now. Eli is still visiting Lisa in the United States." The names were unfamiliar to me.

The complexity of Luke's family dynamics fascinated me, and thankfully, Beatrix also. "Girlfriend?" she inquired, her voice rising slightly at the end, a hint of curiosity colouring her words.

"Sister," Luke and Paul responded simultaneously, their voices blending together in perfect harmony, a testament to the deep bond they shared as brothers.

"Oh, you've got a big family," Beatrix remarked, her eyes widening slightly in understanding. I could see the gears turning in her mind, trying to piece together the intricate web of relationships that bound the Smith clan together.

Luke and Paul exchanged knowing glances, a silent communication passing between them. "Yep," they agreed in unison, their voices tinged with a mixture of pride and weariness.

Paul redirected the conversation, shifting the focus back to Luke's plan of action. His voice was firm, filled with a sense of urgency that demanded attention. "Are you going to bring them to Bixbus tomorrow?" he asked, his gaze fixed intently on his brother, searching for answers in the depths of Luke's eyes.

Luke's response was casual, his uncertainty evident in the way he shifted his weight from one foot to the other. "I'm not sure yet. I still haven't worked out the best way to approach them. Any ideas?" he asked, seeking input from Paul, a silent plea for guidance in navigating the treacherous waters of family dynamics.

Paul shrugged, initially unsure, his brow furrowed in thought. But then, a sudden realisation sparked in his eyes, a glimmer of understanding that chased away the shadows of doubt. "I suspect that all you need to do is find a way to convince Dad, and the rest will easily follow." His words carried a weight, a sense of certainty that seemed to bolster Luke's resolve.

Luke mused, rubbing his chin thoughtfully, considering Paul's words with a quiet intensity. "Hmm, I think you're onto something there," he murmured, his voice trailing off as he lost himself in the labyrinth of his own thoughts.

As the conversation continued, my mind began to wander again, drifting away from the present moment and into the depths of my own memories. I reflected on the complexities of my own family dynamics, the intricate web of relationships that had shaped my life. The Jeffries were a large family, with eight of us living at Jeffries Manor. Each member was unique in their own way, yet fiercely loyal to each other, bound together by the unbreakable ties of blood and love.

Thoughts of Brianne and our unborn child crossed my mind, a bittersweet reminder of the life I had left behind. The longing in my heart was a constant ache, a dull throb that pulsed in time with the beating of my heart. I couldn't help but feel a mix of emotions — a desperate yearning to be reunited with the woman I loved, and a fierce determination to find a way back to her.

"Come on, Beatrix," Luke interrupted my thoughts, pulling me back to the present with a sudden jolt. "Let's get you these keys." His voice was filled with a sense of purpose.

As Luke and Beatrix departed the campfire and made their way towards the Portal, a wave of emotions washed over me, threatening to drag me under. The contrast between Luke and Paul's large, tightly-knit family and their developing plans to bring them all to Clivilius weighed heavily on my heart, a bitter reminder of all that I had lost.

Jeffries Manor, the place I had once called home, was a distant memory now, a fading echo of a life that seemed to slip further away with each passing moment. The laughter that had once filled its halls, the constant bickering of siblings who loved each other fiercely beneath the surface — it all felt like a cruel mirage, a tantalising glimpse of a world that I could no longer touch.

Brianne, the woman who held my heart in her hands, and our unborn child — they were the embodiment of my hopes and dreams, the very reason for my existence. But now, they were also the source of my deepest agony, a constant reminder of the void that had been carved into my soul. The pain of losing them, of being ripped away from the life we had planned together, was a torment that gnawed at my very being.

As I stood there, my leg throbbing with an incessant pain that pulsed through my very being, I felt the physical ache become a mere echo of the turmoil that raged within me. The wounds of Clivilius, both visible and hidden, had left an indelible mark upon my spirit, scarring me in ways that I feared would never truly heal. In the span of just a few short days, the battles I had fought in the suffocating darkness had shattered me, reducing me to a mere shell of the man I had once been, a hollow husk drifting through an unforgiving landscape.

I longed for the comfort of Brianne's embrace, for the soothing balm of her love to heal the festering wounds that ate away at my soul. She was my anchor, my rock in the storm, the one constant in a world that seemed to shift and change with every passing moment. Without her, I felt adrift, lost in a sea of despair that threatened to drag me under, to consume me whole and leave nothing but a fading memory in its wake.

In that moment, a profound realisation washed over me, a bitter truth that cut through the haze of my emotions like a knife through tender flesh. Family, as I had once known it, was becoming a distant memory, a shattered illusion that slipped through my fingers like grains of sand in an hourglass. The bonds that had once held us together, the ties that had defined our very existence, were crumbling before my eyes, leaving behind a gaping void that nothing could fill, a hollowness that echoed through the chambers of my heart.

The settlers here, the ragtag group of survivors who had been thrown together by the cruel whims of fate and Luke's whims, were becoming my unchosen family, a surrogate for the loved ones I had lost, the pieces of my heart that had been ripped away. But even their presence, the camaraderie and shared struggle that bound us together, couldn't heal the wounds that ran so deep, couldn't quell the raging storm that tore through my very being, consuming me from the inside out.

A surge of conflicting emotions pulsed through me, a dizzying whirlwind of despair and defiance that left me reeling, struggling to find my footing in a world that seemed to shift and change with every passing heartbeat. The weight of family, of the power it held over our lives, felt suffocating, almost oppressive. It was a reminder of the darkness that permeated Clivilius, the malevolent force that had brought me here, that taunted me with whispered promises and demanded my very soul as sacrifice.

And in the midst of this torment, the voice of Clive echoed in my mind, a haunting whisper that refused to be silenced, a siren's call that tugged at the very fabric of my being. Clive's words, once demanding and manipulative, now held a strange allure, a twisted promise of salvation that I couldn't quite bring myself to trust, even as it beckoned to me with honeyed words and tantalising visions of a future that seemed just out of reach.

Light the fire. Share the light. The words lingered in my thoughts, dripping with both hope and despair, a dichotomy that tore at my very soul. I questioned their meaning, their true intent, wondering if this was a genuine path to redemption, a way to claw my way out of the darkness that threatened to consume me, or just another twist in the web of lies that Clive had woven around me, a trap waiting to snap shut and leave me broken beyond repair.

Yet, despite my doubts, the mirage persisted, a vivid vision of a thriving settlement where Brianne and our unborn child were safe and happy, a sanctuary in the deserts of Clivilius, a haven amidst the danger and despair that seemed to permeate every corner of this unforgiving land. It tugged at my heartstrings, pulling me towards the allure of a future that seemed so close, yet forever out of reach, a dream that danced just beyond my fingertips, taunting me with its promise of hope and happiness.

The voice of Clive resonated within me, pulling me deeper into the conflicting currents of my emotions, a maelstrom of fear and longing that threatened to tear me apart. Clivilius, with its horrors and revelations, had become a twisted crucible, testing the limits of my courage and resilience, pushing me to the very brink of madness and beyond. The darkness that threatened to consume me held a strange allure, a sick fascination that made the struggle between light and dark all the more harrowing, a battle for the very essence of my soul.

My gaze leaving Paul, I cast my eyes around the group of settlers at the campfire, the faces of my chosen family, and a mixture of hope and doubt swirled within me, a tempest of conflicting emotions that left me reeling. Could we truly find solace in each other's arms, a reprieve from the darkness that threatened to engulf us all, or were we mere pawns in Clive's twisted game, destined to suffer the consequences of unforgivable choices, to bear the weight of our sins for all eternity?

I felt as though the weight of destiny itself rested upon my shoulders, a burden that threatened to crush me beneath its unrelenting pressure, to grind me into dust and scatter me to the unforgiving winds of Clivilius. With a hesitant resolve, I whispered, "Let's do this," my voice tinged with a vulnerability that I couldn't quite hide, a raw and aching wound that laid bare the depths of my pain.

The path ahead was shrouded in uncertainty, a winding road that disappeared into the darkness, and the shadows within me mirrored the shadows that surrounded us, a reflection of the horrors that lurked just beyond the edges of perception. The crutches creaked beneath my weight, a constant reminder of the physical toll this journey had taken on my body, and each step I took was a painful reminder of the terror I had endured, the sacrifices I had made, and the torment that lingered within my soul.

I couldn't shake the feeling of being trapped in a web of conflicting emotions, caught between the seductive whispers of Clive's voice and the desperate yearning for a future that seemed forever out of reach, a tantalising mirage that danced just beyond the horizon. The voice had whispered in the recesses of my mind, its words both alluring and treacherous, a siren's call that promised everything and nothing all at once. It was a call that stirred both hope and fear within me, a glimmer of possibility in a world steeped in darkness, a chance at salvation that felt like a double-edged sword, ready to cut me to the very core.

The mirage of the thriving settlement, where my loved ones were safe and content, burned brightly in my mind. It offered solace in the midst of the storm, a promise of a better tomorrow, a future where the wounds of the past could finally begin to heal. But I knew the cost, the terrible price that Clive demanded for such a dream to become reality, a pound of flesh that would strip away everything I held dear.

If I bring Brianne here, to this unforgiving land of shadows and secrets, I would be tearing her away from everything and everyone she has ever known, ripping her from the comfort and safety of the life we had built together. It was a choice that weighed heavily upon my soul, a decision that threatened to break me in ways I couldn't even begin to fathom.

Surely, it is worth the price, the soft voice spoke to my mind, a whisper that seemed to come from the very depths of my being, a temptation that tugged at the strings of my heart.

With a newfound determination, I turned to look back at Paul, the fire of defiance burning in my eyes, a fierce and unquenchable flame that refused to be extinguished.

"Light the fire. Share the light," I said, my voice filled with a raw determination that seemed to rise from the very depths of my soul, a battle cry against the forces that sought to break us, to shatter our resolve and leave us broken and bleeding in the dust.

offered solace in the midst of the storm, a promise of a better tomorrow, a future where the wounds of war that could finally begin to heal. Yet, I knew the cost, the terrible price that Circe demanded for such a dream to become reality, a pound of flesh that would strip me of everything I held dear. Cheating Circe of her life, to this unforgiving land of shadows and secrets. I would be risking her mercy, risking everything and everyone she has ever known, risking her from the comfort and safety of the life we had built together. It was a choice that weighed heavily upon my soul, a decision that threatened to break me in ways I couldn't even begin to fathom.

"Surely, it is worth the risk," the soft voice spoke to my mind, a whisper that seemed to come from the very depths of my being, a sound that tugged at the strings of my heart. With a nod and determination, I turned to look back at Circe, the fire of determination burning in her eyes, a fierce and unquenchable flame that refused to be extinguished.

"In the fire, She's the light," I said, my voice filled with a new determination that seemed to rise from the very depths of my soul, a battle cry against the forces that sought to break us, in tremendous resolve and leaving Circe limping and bleeding in the dust.

TO BE CONTINUED…

Printed and bound by CPI Group (UK) Ltd, Croydon, CR0 4YY
29/04/2024
01005952-0001